100 Heroes:
People in Sports Who Make This a Better World

Other books by Richard E. Lapchick

New Game Plan for College Sport

Smashing Barriers: Race and Sport in the New Millennium

Never Before, Never Again: The Stirring Autobiography of Eddie Robinson, the Winningest Coach in the History of College Football

Sport in Society: Equal Opportunity or Business as Usual?

Five Minutes to Midnight: Race and Sport in the 1990s

Rules of the Game: Ethics in College Sport

On the Mark: Putting the Student Back in Student-athlete

Fractured Focus: Sport as a Reflection of Society

Broken Promises: Racism in American Sports

Oppression and Resistance: The Struggle of Women in Southern Africa

Politics of Race and International Sport: The Case of South Africa

100 Heroes:

People in Sports Who Make This a Better World

Richard E. Lapchick

with Jessica Bartter, Jennifer Brenden,
Stacy Martin, Drew Tyler and Brian Wright

NCAS Publishing
Orlando, FL

100 Heroes:
People in Sports Who Make
This a Better World

Library of Congress Control Number:
ISBN

Printed in Canada
First Edition 2005

Published by
NCAS Publishing
Orlando, FL

Produced by
PPC Books
Redington Shores, FL

I dedicate this book to the 100 heroes whose stories are told here. Each and every one inspires me to stay off the sidelines and continue to work to make sport a positive force for a healthier, safer, more loving and more inclusive world.

I have to mention two of the heroes.

Jodi Norton, the former diver who has spent her adult life helping others challenged by lupus.

and

Darryl J. Williams, who was gunned down by three hateful white teenagers and has used his adult life, which has been confined to a wheelchair as a quadriplegic, to teach others the transforming power of love.

— RICHARD LAPCHICK

Table of Contents

Acknowledgements

I picked five individuals because of their love and respect for sport to help me compile the stories of these 100 heroes who make this a better world through sport. It is with great appreciation that I acknowledge their commitment to making sport live up to its ideals and using sport to affect the lives of others. I salute the team captain, Jessica Bartter and our teammates, Jennifer Brenden, Stacy Martin, Drew Tyler and Brian Wright for their initiative and hustle in bringing this project to fruition.

I also tip my hat to Philomena Pirolo and Maria Molina whose faith in and support for what we are trying to accomplish keeps us all going.

I would also like to thank Richard Astro who served as chief editor and wrote the Foreword.

Most importantly, I would like to thank my family which fills me with strength and courage each day. My wife Ann, our children Joe, Emily, Chamy and her husband Michael and grandchildren Taylor and Emma form my rainbow of love and happiness. Their support and understanding in trying times and full schedules continues to feed my ever-growing passion for and commitment to them.

Additionally, I must thank everyone associated with the National Consortium for Academics and Sports for the past 20 years because together we have made so many fond memories, cultivated friendships and touched lives. At the top of that list is Keith Lee, the COO of the NCAS, Tom Miller, the Chair of the NCAS Board, and Robert Weathers, the Associate Director for Outreach. Keith, Robert, Richard Astro and I have been together all these 20 years. It has been so good that I wish for 20 more.

FOREWORD

This volume contains portraits of 100 sports heroes who have been honored by the National Consortium for Academics and Sports during the past twenty years. Many are household names; others are less widely recognized, and some may only be known to those whose lives they directly touched. But all share one thing in common: they are gifted women and men who used the power and appeal of sport to enhance educational achievement and to affect meaningful social change; and they did so with dignity, with courage, and with integrity. By so doing, each helped to fulfill the mission of NCAS.

Sports heroes seem to be in short supply these days. We read about coaches who compromise their own integrity by gambling, abusing alcohol, or misusing funds. We read about athletes who cheat by taking performance enhancing drugs, who abuse their spouses, or who attack the very fans who come to see them play. But for every sordid story, there are coaches, athletic directors, general managers and players who give far more to sport and to the world than sport gives to them. And so we have written this tribute to our 100 heroes who restore our belief in sport not only as games that entertain but also teach the virtues of discipline, teamwork, and an understanding and appreciation of diversity. These heroes used sport as a vehicle to reach out to people in need of help and so work to create a better and more just world.

It was our belief that sport has the power to create positive social change that led to the establishment of the National Consortium for Academics and Sports 20 years ago in Boston. One year earlier, Richard Lapchick and I had founded an organization we called the Center for the

Study of Sport in Society at Northeastern University to deal with problems in intercollegiate sport at a time when student-athletes were routinely exploited by the very coaches who recruited them to their campuses. I was the Dean of Arts and Sciences at the University, and I appropriated a small portion of my College's budget to support the Center. Richard gave up an important post at the United Nations for some modest secretarial assistance, an even more modest salary, and a small, windowless office. For him it was a labor of love; for me it was a very large gamble since if the Center failed, we would have been out of work. Happily, we were successful, so much so in fact, that we were able to hire Tom "Satch" Sanders as our Associate Director and to expand the modest educational programs. We began with the New England Patriots, the Boston Bruins and the Boston Red Sox whose participating players worked to help at-risk student-athletes in area middle and high schools. We expanded into new initiatives that you will read about elsewhere in this volume and that exist unto the current day. When those programs attracted the interest of professors, coaches and student-athletes in other colleges and universities, both in and beyond the Boston area, the idea of establishing a consortium was born.

Organizing the NCAS was no easy task. We were swimming upstream against a very strong current. Officials at some schools we contacted about becoming NCAS members said no politely; others weren't even polite. Anecdotally, I remember one conversation Richard, Satch and I had with the athletic director of a large Midwestern university who smiled and nodded throughout our session. We left convinced his school would join. The next day we learned that he was nearly deaf and without his hearing aid, and that he simply wanted to be cordial. And when he incorrectly concluded that our goal was to reform his athletic department, he wouldn't even acknowledge us anymore. But thankfully, a handful who saw value in the activist programs we were promoting signed on, and in 1985, the National Consortium for Academics and Sports (NCAS) was born. Richard became its Executive Director, and I returned to my deanery.

Running any kind of consortium is a tricky business, since on the one hand it is necessary to give participating consortium members enough latitude to "do their own thing," while at the same time maintaining program coherence and consistency from one consortium member to another. Working with university personnel poses an even greater challenge given the institutional autonomy that characterizes American higher education and which, depending upon the needs of the moment, is either a blessing or a curse. And when one is dealing with schools as diverse as UC-Berkeley,

Temple and William Patterson, who were three NCAS charter members, the challenge is even greater.

While we were gradually able to add staff, largely through the largesse of private foundations and federal agencies that provided support for our programs, the plain fact is that were it not for Richard Lapchick, NCAS would have died a quick and little-noticed death. Richard spent the better part of five years traveling the country, meeting with coaches, with faculty, with athletic directors, and with provosts and presidents selling the message of the Consortium. And through sheer force of personality, he got the job done.

Over time, Richard has become the social conscience of sport. While in those early years, his was a voice in the wilderness, he pressed his case that sport can and ought to help us overcome injustice, racism, poverty and disease. And while he has been critical of those who use their position in sport only to aggrandize their own ends, his has not been the shrill voice of anger or the lament of despair. Rather, he has always shined an affirming light, celebrating excellence and criticizing only for the purpose of improvement.

Many of the problems that Richard and I identified when we formed the Center and NCAS have been solved, their negative consequences muted. It is no longer acceptable for college coaches and athletic directors to exploit student-athletes. It still happens, of course, but when it does there are penalties and there is justice. The scourge of apartheid is no more. The doors to management positions in collegiate and professional sport are finally, if slowly, opening to women and men of color. And the governing bodies of sport who once shunned the NCAS now embrace us and the principles for which we stand.

Good timing? Perhaps. But it's been more than that. Richard would be the last to argue that he alone has been responsible for the important and dramatic social changes that have occurred in sports world during the past twenty years. But it is or ought to be clear to anyone who cares that Richard has been in the vanguard of the effort to reform sport, and that no one has been more effective in ensuring that sport lifts up, encourages and inspires, that it helps us affirm the principles of justice and equality which are the foundations of our Republic.

Richard Lapchick has never won Olympic Gold. He has neither a Super Bowl nor a World Series ring. But his contribution to the world of sport is every bit as important as those of even the most celebrated athletes whom we honor in this volume. In his own time and with his own voice, he has made a real and enduring difference. In essence then, this book of vignettes about 100 heroes is really a book about 101. And the last is truly first.

Richard Astro
December, 2005

INTRODUCTION

Because of the work that we do in the National Consortium for Academics and Sports and the DeVos Sport Business Management Program we become all too aware of the problems that exist in sport. Each day we seem to read about a rule being violated, an athlete getting in trouble with drugs or arrested for sexual assault, steroid use in baseball, the NFL, or track and field, the threat that gambling poses to college sports and agents recruiting young athletes with illegal monetary inducements. The list goes on and on. That is why it was so joyous for me when Dr. Taylor Ellis, the Dean of Undergraduate Education in the College of Business Administration at the University of Central Florida, came to my office February of 2005.

I had just finished writing a book I called *New Game Plans for College Sport* and was frankly tired of writing. I vowed that I would not take up another book project for several years. Taylor changed all of that on the morning after the 2005 Consortium banquet. He came in, sat down, and said, "When I was a boy, I wasn't involved in school. I had no sense of direction or sense of purpose." He said, "then someone gave me this book" and he handed me the book. Taylor placed the well-worn Barlow Meyers' *Real Life Stories: Champions All the Way,* published 45 years earlier, on my desk. He said, "About that time in my life somebody gave me this book about seven athletes and the obstacles they overcame to do great things in life. This book transformed my life and gave me a sense of direction and hope." Taylor said, "Every year you honor five or six such athletes at the Consortium's award banquet. You have to write a book about them." The seed for *100 Heroes* had been planted.

It was a no-brainer to think about undertaking the project in spite of my vow to the contrary. This book could be, I thought, a real celebration of sport. It could portray the power of sport to transform not only individuals, but their impact on society more generally. I ran through my head the names of all the award winners I could recall and knew that their stories would inspire people collectively who could not be in the presence of these people in the halls when we honored them.

With the 20th anniversary of the Consortium exactly a year away, I knew that we would have to work hard to get this project done. I enlisted the support of Jessica Bartter, who is the Communications and Marketing Coordinator of the National Consortium. We began to draw all of the names and addresses together and contact the previous award winners who were still alive. Their support for the project was overwhelmingly positive. We began to collect the biographical materials and stories that were the basis for the awards. We also asked Drew Tyler, Stacy Martin, Jennifer Brenden, Brian Wright, all graduate students in the DeVos Sport Business Management Program, to help write the individual stories.

Before discussing the sections of *100 Heroes: People in Sport Who Make This a Better World*, I must stress that there are obviously extraordinary leaders in sport who are not included here. This only includes people honored with Giant Steps Awards and who were inducted into the Hall of Fame of the NCAS. Thus such giants as Arthur Ashe, Wilma Rudolph, Rafer Johnson and so many others are not in this book.

Our *Barrier Breakers* section includes well-known heroes. Three people named Robinson, one of whom was a legendary coach for 56 years at Grambling State. Jackie and Rachel not only broke down baseball's segregation but also did great deeds over the next six decades. Rachel carried on Jackie's legacy. Coaches Boone and Yoast were the real titans who integrated high school football in northern Virginia. Nancy Lieberman paved the way for other generations of athletes in college and professional women's basketball. Lee Elder was the first African-American to play in the Masters. Phillip Castillo, Pam White-Hanson and Ryneldi Becenti were Native American athletes in a time when Native Americans rarely competed in sport. Donna Lopiano was a legendary player and women's athletic director in Texas and life-time advocate for the opportunities of women in sport. Ernestine Bayer and Anita DeFrantz were pioneering rowers, one considered the mother of the sport and the second the first African-American medalist in the Olympics, a woman who stood up against an American president for his decision to boycott the Moscow Olympics and ultimately became the most powerful woman in sport as the Vice President of the International Olympic Committee. Annie Boucher, a grandmother who rocked the college sports world as a student-athlete in her 50's. And finally, the greatest of all, Muhammad Ali who stood tall for justice and human rights from the time he won an Olympic gold medal in 1960 through the writing of this book which was concluded just as the Muhammad Ali Center was opened in Louisville, KY in the fall of 2005.

Then there are a series of coaches described in the section *Coaching to Win in Life*, some known nationally, some known primarily to the people they touched directly. They helped the young people under their charge to grow socially, athletically and academically. Sometimes they did things in games to emphasize sportsmanship in participation rather than the pursuit of victory. They come from urban areas and rural areas, from north and south, from California to Mississippi to Miami to St. Louis to Boston. They made their athletes winners in life.

Playing to Win in Life is about six athletes whose star quality as athletes gave them a platform to work towards contributing to a better society.

Transcending Sport to Help Society presents the stories of 14 athletes of such magnitude that a special section was devoted to them. They included the dominant softball player of her time, Dot Richardson; Kareem Abdul-Jabbar, perhaps the greatest big man in the history of the NBA; "Tiny" Archibald, one of the best little men in the history of the NBA; Dave Bing, former NBA star who has become one of the most successful African-American entrepreneurs in America; Alan Page, the great Minnesota Viking football player who became a Supreme Court judge; Dean Smith, the winningest coach in the history of men's basketball; Pat Summit, his equivalent in women's basketball; Joe Paterno, who at the time of this writing was still coaching at Penn State and leading his team towards a great season; former Senator Bill Bradley, a great New York Knicks player and Rhodes Scholar who eventually ran for president; Tom Osborne, the dynamic coach at Nebraska who became a U.S. Congressman and was running for Governor at the time of this writing; "Dr. J" Julius Erving, who transformed the game of basketball with his style; Jackie Joyner-Kersee, who perhaps was the greatest athlete of her generation; Lawrence Burton, former NFL player who helped build the legends of Boys Town; and Geno Auriemma, one of the most successful coaches of all-time at the University of Connecticut.

Another section, *Hurdlers Overcoming Obstacles*, tells the story of ten athletes who overcame great physical, emotional and addictive barriers to demonstrate to all around them what the human spirit was capable of doing when it was determined to win in life.

The lives of 13 athletes are portrayed in the section *Creating a Better World.* These athletes devoted an important part of their lives to having an impact on changing the social circumstances in which they found themselves to make it a better world for everybody. Most of the 13 are not household names but their acts affected so many outside of their own households.

The *Fighting Racism* section discusses five athletes whose individual acts stood tall against racism. Dionte Hall, barely a teenager, Darryl Williams, a sophomore in high school in Boston, Michael Watson, just graduating from college, and David Lazerson and Richard Green, an Hasidic Jew and an African-American in Crown Heights, took on the forces of hate swirling around them.

The *New Game Plan for College Sport* section is on eight individuals who devoted a large part of their lives to making college sport live up to its ideals. They include a president, three athletics directors, an academic advisor and three men who worked from outside of college sport to make it better inside.

The section on *Creating the Environment* discusses the 11 leaders who, through their own example, began to change how different sports organizations and entities could work towards making sport live up to its ideals. At the high school level, Dr. Clinton Albury in his own Florida school and H. Ross Perot in his state of Texas, led a movement for "No Pass, No Play" raising the academic standards of high school athletes. At the pro level, Rich DeVos, the owner of the Orlando Magic, saw the power an individual franchise could have to infect a community with spirit and to do positive things through an enormously expansive philanthropic body of work. Lewis Katz and Raymond Chambers, owners of the New Jersey Nets, worked hard to earn money and have worked even harder to put it back into the community. Mike Ilitch, owner of the NHL's Red Wings and Little Caesar's Pizza, uses his power in sports to positively impact his community. After a 13-year professional playing career, "Satch" Sanders spent 18 years working with other pros easing their transition in and out of the NBA. At the Olympic level, Billy Payne, shared his Olympic dreams with his community by orchestrating the 1996 Summer Games in Atlanta. This section includes David Stern and Paul Tagliabue, two league commissioners and Gene Upshaw, a players association chief who showed that players and management could work together to better their game.

One of the most moving sections is *Coming to America* about the lives of four people who chose to leave their war-torn societies and move to America where they became fine student-athletes as well as story tellers about what drove them out of their countries and why Americans gave them hope. They came from Burundi, Sudan, Afghanistan and Bosnia. They all came with courage.

100 Heroes concludes with stories about the legends that live on after their passing. Some were coaches, some were athletes, one an entrepreneur, philanthropist and team owner, all made sport and society better than where they found it. Their spirit underlines the meaning of heroes.

Just as Taylor Ellis' book inspired him to go on to lead a meaningful and wonderful life, it is our hope at the National Consortium for Academics and Sports that those we have honored over the past 20 years will inspire all of the readers to understand what they can do to make this a better world and to help others believe in what they cannot see.

CHAPTER 1

BARRIER BREAKERS

The term "*Barrier Breaker*" describes that rare individual who took down walls that previously had inhibited or barred a group of people from the equal opportunity that American society holds as the hallmark of democracy.

No name resonates more with this description than that of Jackie Robinson who broke baseball's color barrier in 1947. By his side at the time, his wife Rachel helped keep his strength intact. After his early death, Rachel continued his legacy and created her own by helping hundreds of young African-American students attend college and succeed in a world where they were preordained to fail.

Herman Boone and Bill Yoast combined forces to lead the Titans of Alexandria, Virginia to a state football championship in their first year of coaching together. But their story is even more about the successful integration of their team in the 1960's in spite of tremendous opposition. Boone and Yoast became household names after the release of "Remember the Titans" which chronicles their remarkable story.

Ryneldi Becenti, Phillip Castillo and Pamela White-Hanson are three Native American athletes who broke barriers in their own sports and then went back to help younger Native Americans use sport to fight high drop out rates and alcoholism on Native American reservations. Becenti became the first Native American woman to play in the WNBA.

Two female rowers who not only created opportunities for women in rowing, but inspired generations of women who followed them are Ernestine Bayer, considered the "mother of modern rowing," and Anita DeFrantz, the first African-American female to win a medal in the Olympics in her sport. DeFrantz subsequently led the protest against President

Carter's boycott of the 1980 Olympics. She became a Vice President for the Los Angeles Organizing Committee in 1984. As a senior member of the IOC today, she is considered sport's most powerful woman.

Donna Lopiano, a great softball player, became a pioneering athletic director for the women's program at the University of Texas. For more than a decade, she has led the Women's Sports Foundation in its barrier-breaking role for women and girls in sports.

Nancy Lieberman elevated the game of women's basketball in the 1970's at Old Dominion University and then throughout a distinguished professional career inhibited only by the lack of opportunities for women in basketball when she was at the height of her game.

Annie Boucher, already a grandmother, used the sport of tennis to help her achieve her high school and college degrees.

Lee Elder became the first African-American to play in the Master's golf tournament and paved the way for Tiger Woods and other people of color.

Eddie Robinson, who led Grambling State University for 56 years, was the winningest coach in the history of the sport upon his retirement and had sent more players to the National Football League than any other coach in the history of college football.

Finally, Muhammad Ali has led a life that is unparalleled in the world of sport. Almost simultaneously with the publication of *100 Heroes*, the Muhammad Ali Center in Louisville was opened. It is a living tribute to a man who by his work in and outside the ring gave hope to millions.

In their own time and in their own way, each of these distinguished women and men changed the face of sport and the societies in which they lived. Their work to make a better world should serve as a stimulus to inspire us to do more ourselves.

Rachel Robinson

by Jessica Bartter

Perhaps best known as the wife of Jackie Robinson, Rachel Robinson is a woman of countless achievements and accolades, both in her own right and those achieved jointly with her husband. She has earned the titles of civil rights leader, humanitarian, activist, author, teacher, nurse and leader, though none of them came without opposition. And that was just in her free time as her life mainly consisted of being a wife and a mother. Strong, compassionate, loving, determined, elegant and stylish are just a few of the words used to describe Mrs. Robinson.

Born in 1922, Rachel Isum was raised in Northern California before moving to Southern California to attend the University of California, Los Angeles in 1940. A shy, nursing student, she was soon introduced to the big man on campus, Jackie Robinson. Jackie was the first student to letter in four varsity sports at UCLA and did not go unnoticed by his fellow students. But Rachel was surprised to learn he, too, was shy. She also noted he was a serious man, proud to be a black man, with a warm smile, a pigeon-toed walk and extremely handsome looks. Needless to say, they felt an immediate connection and the courtship blossomed.

After two years at UCLA, Rachel transferred to the UC San Francisco School of Nursing to become a registered nurse. Her days were filled with a full course load and eight-hour hospital shifts. After three years of this arduous schedule, Rachel graduated in June of 1945 with the Florence Nightingale award for clinical excellence. Two months later, her fiancé, Jackie Robinson, signed with the Brooklyn Dodgers, joining forces with the Dodgers president and general manager, Branch Rickey in a fight to change the world.

It has often been said, "Behind every strong man, there is a strong woman." Rickey took this to heart knowing the task he presented to Jackie of integrating Major League Baseball was going to be faced with much adversity, confrontation and perhaps failure. Rickey chose Jackie for his character and skill and made him promise that he could silently endure the racially motivated physical and mental abuse that was sure to follow but not before he asked Jackie if he had a girl. Though Rickey knew Jackie would need the support of a woman by his side to dilute the pain of deep rooted racial segregation, even Rickey could not have predicted Jackie would become "the target of racial epithets and flying cleats, of hate letters and death threats, of pitchers throwing at this head and legs, and catchers spitting on his shoes"[1] as *Sports Illustrated* described two years later in 1947 when Jackie Robinson officially broke the color barrier in Major League Baseball. With Rachel's support and encouragement, Jackie responded to the provocation of racial insults and inequities that often included violence with his play on the field, earning the respect of his teammates and in time, the opposition. Jackie even earned the National League Rookie of the Year title with 12 home runs, a league-leading 29 stolen bases and a .297 batting average along with the greatest achievement of all: social change.

Several teammates of Jackie's credited Rachel for being his "co-pioneer" and "anchor" and acknowledged her beauty and intellect that "replenished his strength and courage" for the 10 years he competed in the big leagues. Jackie, himself, later wrote of Rachel as "Strong, loving, gentle and brave, never afraid to either criticize or comfort. When they try to destroy me, it's Rachel who keeps me sane."[2]

After Jackie's successful career as a professional athlete, his mission in life to help others and commit to a changed and more equitable America was only strengthened. Together, Rachel and Jackie thought their work could best be utilized in politics and in the civil rights movement. Most notably, the Robinsons supported Dr. Martin Luther King and even organized an outdoor jazz concert on their property to raise funds to be used as bail money for civil rights activists who had been jailed for their involvement in the movement. To date, the same concert is still held the last Sunday every June, previously held in Connecticut but has now been moved to New York City.

After years of homemaking and raising their three children, Rachel returned to school to get her masters degree at New York University and later worked as a researcher and clinician at the Albert Einstein College of Medicine's Department of Social and Community Psychiatry. Five years later, Rachel became the Director of Nursing for the Connecticut Mental

Health Center and as Assistant Professor of Nursing at Yale University. Her independence and self-sustaining capabilities proved vital to her existence at the untimely death of her husband in 1972. Looking back, Rachel said, "I am one of the fortunate ones granted a mission at the age of twenty-three, a great partner, and the spirit to prevail."[3]

Within weeks of the loss of Jackie, Rachel was faced with the challenge of taking over his business that was originally intended to be a construction company. Though new to the business world, Rachel decided the company lacked the resources to be the construction company Jackie envisioned but rather, was capable of being a real estate development company. Thus the Jackie Robinson Development Company was born. By 1980, 1,300 housing units were built for families of low to moderate incomes in Jackie's honor.

Rachel was so proud of her husband and what he had accomplished that she wanted to continue to improve society through Jackie's name. Although Jackie Robinson will always be remembered for being the first man to integrate baseball, she wanted to do something else that would carry on Jackie's legacy and continue to make a difference in society. Thus, the Jackie Robinson Foundation was created in 1973. The Jackie Robinson Foundation is a not-for-profit organization that provides leadership and education opportunities to academically gifted students of color with financial need. During its first 30 years, the Jackie Robinson Foundation distributed $1.2 million in scholarships to 956 students enabling them to attend the college of their choice. The students chosen to carry on Jackie Robinson's legacy have sustained an impressive 92 percent graduation rate.

In 1997, Major League Baseball celebrated the 50th anniversary of the integration of baseball. According to *The New York Times*, Rachel reflected, "This anniversary has given us an opportunity as a nation to celebrate together the triumphs of the past and the social progress that has occurred. It has also given us an opportunity to reassess the challenges of the present. It is my passionate hope that we can take this reawakened feeling of unity and use it as a driving force so that each of us can recommit to equality of opportunity for all Americans."[4] While she is very proud to have helped so many over the years, it is important to her to see the process of change continue. Rachel Robinson's commitment to helping those in need, to the fight for racial equity and to bettering society in general, deserves a prominent and enduring place in our social history.

[1] Schwartz, Larry. "Jackie changed the face of sports." ESPN.com. [October 21, 2000; December 9, 2005] http://sports.espn.go.com/espn/classic/news/story?page=moment001024robinsondies

[2] "The Robinsons." The History Channel. [2005; December 9, 2005] http://www.historychannel.com/exhibits/valentine/index.jsp?page=robinsons

[3] Robinson, Rachel. Jackie Robinson: An Intimate Portrait. New York: Harry N. Abrams, Inc., 1996.

[4] Chass, Murray. "Standing by Her Man, Always With Elegance" *The New York Times*, April 16, 1997.

Jackie Robinson

by Jessica Bartter

If his life was measured by his own words that "A life is not important, except in the impact it has on other lives," Jackie Robinson's life was one of the most important of the 20th century. However, by account of all who knew him, that would be an understatement.

Robinson, who was an athlete, entrepreneur, a civil rights activist, actor, author, father and husband, is remembered by many as a spectacular ball player, but it was the mere fact that he stepped onto the field in a Brooklyn Dodger uniform that had such an everlasting impact on the United States. In 1947, Robinson became the first African-American to play for any Major League Baseball team in the modern era. By donning the Dodger uniform, Robinson integrated professional athletics and broke the color barrier that existed in Major League Baseball for decades. But Robinson couldn't do it alone. It took the foresight of Branch Rickey, president and general manager of the Brooklyn Dodgers, to recognize that Robinson was an individual with the requisite determination and willpower to affect such social change. Rickey knew the task any player of color would face would be detrimental to one's spirit and play in the form of abuse and threats, but chose Robinson because he believed Jackie had sufficient strength and staying power to get the job done. Rickey challenged Robinson to endure the abuse in silence and fight back with his brilliant play on the field instead. And brilliant he was. In his debut season, Robinson had 12 home runs, a league-leading 29 stolen bases and a .297 batting average that earned him National League Rookie of the Year as his team was crowned National League Champions and that nearly beat their archrivals, the New York Yankees, in one of the most exciting World Series ever played.

Robinson's accomplishments did not come about easily. He was forced to tolerate racial insults from the stands and on the field, was the target of many wild pitches and spiked cleats, and was haunted by hate letters and death threats to himself and his family. In upholding his promise to Rickey, Robinson fought back on the field and used his unselfish team play and magnificent skills to earn the respect of his teammates and eventually the nation. In particular, he was befriended by shortstop Pee Wee Reese, himself a Southerner whose friendship help mute the worst of the abuse. In just his third season, Robinson was named the National League's Most Valuable Player. Robinson led the league in 1947 and 1949 in stolen bases. In 1949, he won the batting title with a .342 average. From 1949 to 1952, Robinson led second basemen in double plays and was named to the National League All-Star team every year from 1949 to 1954.

Stardom as an athlete was nothing new for Robinson who lettered in baseball, track and field, football and basketball in high school and college. He was the first to do so at the University of California, Los Angeles, but before UCLA, he attended Pasadena Junior College to be near his mother. Since track and field and baseball had the same season, Robinson managed to break his older brother's broad jump record of 25' ½" and star in a baseball game in the same day. Robinson was named Most Valuable Player of the junior colleges in Southern California after leading his team to the state championships in baseball. After transferring to UCLA, Robinson earned All-American accolades for his accomplishments on the gridiron.

Unfortunately for UCLA athletics, Robinson was forced to leave college because of financial challenges. Robinson enjoyed a short stint with the Honolulu Bears playing semipro football but left Pearl Harbor just two days before the Japanese attack in 1942. Shortly thereafter, he received a draft notice and joined the armed forces to put his patriotism into action. But segregation was still commonplace in the military and Robinson felt he was fighting a war at home, rather than overseas. Robinson spoke out against racial injustices he witnessed in the military and stood up for his rights. An intelligent man, Robinson was well aware when army regulations changed to outlaw racial discrimination on any vehicle operating on any army base. In 1944, when Robinson was ordered to the back of the bus by the driver, he refused, causing him to be court-martialed and eventually leading to his honorable discharge blamed on the bone chips in his ankle from football.

Upon leaving the military, without a college degree and with little experience in the working world, Robinson began his professional baseball career with the Kansas City Monarchs of the Negro Leagues. Rickey first discovered Robinson as a Monarch and called him to New York. Robinson's wife Rachel recalls that it was here, in 1945, that in a role-playing session "Rickey subjected Jack to every form of racial attack he could imagine to test his strengths and prepare him for the ordeals sure to come." Robinson believed Rickey was sincere and determined to rid baseball of its social inequalities and "promised that regardless of the provocation he would not retaliate in any way." After suffering through an excruciatingly painful spring training in Central Florida, Robinson spent the next year with the Dodgers' AAA team, the Montreal Royals, while he and Rickey continued to expand their relationship. Robinson scored the winning run in the 7th game of the Little World Series in 1946, leading to his debut in 1947 with the Brooklyn Dodgers on April 15, 1947, therefore changing the face of baseball forever.

In 1949, Robinson decided to end his silence and become true to himself. After a decade of success with the Brooklyn Dodgers in which they went to six World Series and finally beat the Yankees in 1955, Robinson announced his retirement. His impact on our society in general and professional sports specifically had been etched in stone and Robinson had paved the way for many to follow to continue the journey to social equality that he initiated. Robinson recognized the magnitude of being the first, but knew that if he was not followed by more players of color in the big leagues, his accomplishment would be insignificant. As a sign of success for "the great experiment," many other African-Americans were signed including teammates Don Newcombe, Joe Black and Roy Campanella. The New York Giants quickly followed suit, signing Monte Irvin and Willie Mays, and the Cleveland Indians integrated the American League when they signed Larry Doby and then Luke Easter.

Robinson remained active after he finished playing. He opened a men's apparel shop in Harlem, served a radio station as the director of community activities and was vice president of Chock Full O'Nuts. Robinson balanced his business endeavors with his civic engagements. While still a ballplayer, Robinson marched with Dr. Martin Luther King and his involvement in the civil rights movement only increased after retirement. Jackie and his wife Rachel organized an outdoor jazz concert on their property to raise funds to be used as bail money for civil rights activists who had been jailed for their involvement in the movement. To date, the same concert is still held the last Sunday every June, first in Connecticut but has now been moved to New York City. Robinson served on the board of directors of the NAACP for eight years and was one of their leaders in fundraising. Robinson traveled the country making appearances and demonstrating his support for numerous causes, proving one person can make a difference. In one of Robinson's last efforts to do good work for others, he established the Jackie Robinson Construction Company. The Construction Company's mission was to build homes for families with low and moderate incomes.

In 1972, Jackie Robinson's jersey, number 42, was retired along side those of Roy Campanella and Sandy Koufax at Dodger Stadium in Los Angeles. Years later, number 42 was permanently retired throughout Major League Baseball. Indeed, after Mariano Rivera retires from the Yankees, no baseball player in MLB will ever wear his number again.

Sadly, Jackie Robinson lost his life to diabetes and heart disease on October 23, 1972. Though his life was tragically short, his impact on others will last forever. Today, Rachel Robinson recognizes that despite the progress that was made by her husband and so many others in so many hard fought battles, challenges and threats still remain. Yet, she hopes that we can look back on Jack's triumphant struggle and see "that a fighting spirit and hard work can overcome great obstacles."[1]

[1] Robinson, Rachel. Jackie Robinson: An Intimate Portrait. New York: Harry N. Abrams, Inc., 1996.

Herman Boone and William Yoast

by Jessica Bartter

A follower of Dr. Martin Luther King, Herman Boone practiced King's civil rights beliefs in his everyday life as a high school teacher and football coach. So when the Supreme Court handed down a ruling that ended all state-imposed public school segregation in 1971 it is no surprise that Boone became a part of what some considered at the time to be a radical movement.

The Rocky Mountain, North Carolina native was one of 12 children in his family who grew a passion for sports early in life. After a successful career as an athlete, he accepted his first job at I.H. Foster High School in Virginia where he taught and coached basketball, baseball and football. He returned to North Carolina in 1961 to coach football at E.J. Hayes High School. In his nine years as head coach, Boone led his team to a record of 99-8. His 1966 squad was named "The Number One Football Team in America" by *Scholastic Coach's Magazine*. Despite the unmistakable success Boone enjoyed as a head coach, he was asked to sit as an assistant coach at Williamston High School in 1969. The chairman of the local school board was hoping Boone would accept the position to help assist Martin County integrate their schools, academically and athletically. Boone valued his experience and skill too highly to serve Williamston High as its "token black coach." His wife was carrying their third daughter at the time so Boone quickly looked elsewhere for another opportunity to support his family. The opportunity arose in Alexandria, Virginia where Boone accepted the assistant coaching job at the all-Black T.C. Williams High School.

A year later, Virginia, too, began integrating its public schools by combining T.C. Williams High School with one white school and another black school. Boone heard through the grapevine that the T.C. Williams athletics director was looking for an African-American head coach to take over the consolidated football team and that he was hoping for Boone. As a man of values, Boone was not about to accept a job on the basis of his skin color after turning one down for the same reason just one year prior. After talking with the athletic director and confirming that he would be hired for his character and reputation as a coach, Boone was still reluctant. A man named William Yoast, head coach of the all-white Hammond High School was a 20 year coaching veteran, a local favorite and obvious next-in-line to be offered the position. Boone was apprehensive about taking a job where he would most likely feel unwelcome. After initially declining the offer, Boone was approached by members of the black community in Alexandria expressing their desire to have him prove to the rest of the community that a black man was perfectly capable of leading an integrated high school football team to success. Boone realized he was up for the challenge.

Yoast was left feeling snubbed as a victim of politics. He decided to leave rather than spend the next year coaching under a man he viewed not as deserving as himself. On his way out, ten returning players from Yoast's team signed a petition refusing to play without Yoast at the reigns of the team. All of them were willing to miss their senior season and potentially lose their chance at a college degree. Yoast was in the coaching field for his love of football and for its ability to impact the lives of so many kids. Remembering the roots of his passion, Yoast quickly convinced his players to come back with him and promised they would make it through the season together. After Boone offered Yoast the defensive coordinator title, Yoast was back on board. As a coach, all Yoast ever wanted to do was help as many kids as possible. For him, skin color was irrelevant.

Boone and Yoast accepted the challenge together, determined to win football games. Yet they did not fully anticipate all the controversy that would arise, both on and off the field. Football players that were formerly cross-town rivals were suddenly teammates, both unaware of how and some not interested in trying to get along. Boone faced criticism from his assistant coaches, many of whom were formerly Yoast's assistant coaches, as well as community members, school boosters, parents and even players. Even before the start of the season, neighbors made sure Boone and his family knew they were not welcome. In addition to signing a petition calling for the black family to leave the white neighborhood, neighbors just watched and laughed as a toilet bowl full of feces was thrust through the window of their house. Though he worried for the safety of his family,

Boone knew the potential impact of sports and remained steadfast to win games in hopes the tone of the community would change.

Change in attitude on the 1971 T.C. Williams High School football team came from the top, and trickled down. The mixed-race coaching staff put aside their differences and unified in attempt at a winning season. Players eventually followed their lead and learned to get along on the field, while many even got along off the field and became friends. The sight of this and the increase in wins turned the community around as well. Boone's offense and Yoast's defense went on to have an undefeated season and a state championship, proving that color does not matter in the huddle. In the process, both coaches took the opportunity to teach the kids about more than just football. Boone and Yoast cared about each of their players as if they were their own sons and were genuinely concerned with their actions off the field. Boone earned the respect of many young white teenagers while Yoast did the same with his black players, something entirely new to Alexandria, Virginia. Likewise, their players and the community learned to respect one another.

Boone and Yoast's football team had such an impact on the city of Alexandria that the story of the Titans of T.C. Williams High was still being told decades later. A screenwriter named Gregory Allen Howard overheard the inspiring tale in a barber shop one day and believed it would make a great movie. Walt Disney Pictures produced the inspiring tale that cast Academy Award winner Denzel Washington as Coach Herman Boone and William Patton as Coach Bill Yoast. The real Boone and Yoast served producer Jerry Bruckheimer as consultants advising on the set, allowing for much of the movie to be true to real life. Released in 2000, *Remember the Titans* grossed over $115,000,000 domestically.

Shortly after the movie was released, the players, coaches and cheerleaders of the championship team formed the 71 Original Titans Foundation. The Titans Foundation is a nonprofit organization dedicated to helping high school students pursue post-secondary education. The original Titans wanted to give something back to their community in Alexandria and decided to raise scholarship money for T.C. Williams High School students by selling Titan memorabilia and giving talks and granting interviews about how their team members triumphed despite all their differences.

After their controversial inaugural season together, Coach Boone remained head coach of the Titans for five more seasons before retiring in Alexandria. Coach Yoast served as his assistant for four more then coached elsewhere for 15 more years. The release of the film inspired by their lives made them celebrities overnight, thus disrupting their retirements. Since the Hollywood fame, both have traveled the country giving countless speeches and presentations, both remaining as humble as ever. The movie has given Boone and Yoast the platform to better spread their message of justice, equality and respect. They are proud to still have the honor of impacting the lives of children, the work to which they dedicated their lives more than 30 years ago.

Ryneldi Becenti
by Jessica Bartter

Native American athletes are hard role models to come by. The National Collegiate Athletic Association (NCAA) estimates that only 0.4 percent of student-athletes during the 2003-2004 academic year were American Native/Alaskan Native. The percentage of Native American college student-athletes is less than half of the percentage of Native American college students and general populations of Native Americans according to the 2000 Census. Can we attribute this discrepancy to the lack of visibility and support, the alcohol issue, gaming opportunities or strong family obligations on the reservation? Some say all of the above, and while many Native Americans struggle off the reservation, a passion for basketball catapulted Ryneldi Becenti into successful collegiate and professional basketball careers outside the Navajo Reservation's boundaries.

Basketball's popularity on the Navajo Reservation breeds talent and enthusiasm for the sport. Yet, opportunities beyond high school are minimal. While college scouts can travel to several schools in one city in one day's time, they may have to travel several days to one school to visit one student-athlete on a reservation. Native Americans seldom leave their reservations to go to college. The lack of encouragement from the outside fuels the fire. The rare opportunities that arise are often turned down or forfeited because of the culture shock felt by young Native Americans while on a college campus. Professional athletic careers are even more rare and were nonexistent in the Women's National Basketball Association (WNBA) until Ryneldi Becenti broke that barrier in 1993.

Becenti's career flourished with her courage to leave the reservation. She told *The Denver Post* that she knew to be "the best you have to play the best, and that means leaving to play African-Americans, Anglos and others."[1] The sacrifice of leaving home was balanced by the opportunities she received elsewhere. After two successful seasons at Scottsdale Community College, where she became the team's first player to score 2,000 career points, Becenti joined the Sun Devils at Arizona State University. In just two seasons, Becenti recorded the second most assists in an ASU career with 396. She became the school record holder with 17 assists in one game, and the Pac-10 Conference record holder for her average of 7.1 assists per game.

In 1992 and 1993, Becenti accumulated several accolades including All-American honorable mention honors, All-Conference first team selections and four-time Pac-10 Player of the week recognition. Becenti was honored to represent the United States, specifically the Navajo Reservation, by playing on the U.S. squad in the 1993 World Games. While each was a tremendous accomplishment, selection to the Phoenix Mercury of the WNBA was the most gratifying since it was a first for any Native American.

Becenti attributes her renowned basketball skills to her parents who traveled to play in tournaments on the reservation nearly every weekend. Her mother even played competitively through the first six months of her pregnancy with her only daughter, perhaps implanting the repetitive sound of a leather ball hitting wood in her destiny. Sadly, Becenti's mother passed away before her sophomore year in high school. Today, basketball keeps them "connected" as she always feels her mother's presence and can talk to her on any basketball court.

Throughout college though, Becenti was never short of support as her father missed only two home games in all four years. The two he missed were because of blizzards which made even local travel virtually impossible. For every game, he and hundreds of other reservation residents traveled the five and one half of an hour drive to Arizona State University to witness the magic of one of their own. Another several hundred Navajos who lived in the Phoenix area also filled the arena. In total, Becenti's followers made up half the attendance, doubling the women's basketball attendance record at ASU. Becenti believes she would have not succeeded off the reservation if she didn't receive such support. In seeing her followers in the stands, a little bit of home was brought to her, helping Becenti fight the homesickness and isolation that could not be denied off the Reservation. It was the maroon and gold painted faces of her little brothers, the sight of her oldest brother in uniform straight off the Navy base in San Diego, the sound of her grandmother's hands clapping together and the cheers of her fellow Native Americans that drove her to be her best.

After Becenti chased her dreams as far as they would go in the WNBA, she returned to the Window Rock on the Navajo Reservation where she coaches girls' basketball. Ryneldi Becenti recognizes that for most young people, it is easier and more influential to look up to someone of their own race. She gladly accepts the responsibility as a role model and embraces the ability to show and educate other Native Americans to the opportunities available to them through basketball.

[1] Draper, Electa. "Trying to turn the game into more than a dead end" *The Denver Post*, May 17, 2005.

Phillip Castillo

by Jessica Bartter

Sixty miles west of Albuquerque, New Mexico, 110 miles east of the Arizona border, surrounded by the reservations of the Laguna, Isleta, Canoncito, Navajo, Zuni and Zia Indians, sits a small community of less than 3,000 Native Americans called Acoma Pueblo. Also known as "Sky City," Acoma Pueblo is a Native American community that was built atop a 367 foot sandstone mesa on 70 acres. It is believed to be the oldest community in the United States that has been continuously inhabited, perhaps since the 10th century.

It is on this plateau and surrounding villages that Phillip Castillo found his love for running. At the young age of six, Castillo entered his first competitive race. He enjoyed it so much that he continued to compete in "fun runs" in the surrounding communities until high school. Some of his best practice was done on the 30 minute journey from his house to the home of his grandmother.

As a freshman in high school, Castillo recognized that he had the skill and interest in running to truly excel if he committed himself to the cross country team. And excel he did. In just his sophomore season, Castillo placed second in the New Mexico High School State Championships. His high school was in the midst of discussions that involved cutting the track program due to funding, but his success in the state championships quickly changed their minds. After saving the program, Castillo enjoyed more success and in his senior year earned a spot at the National High School Championships. Castillo's speed and patience with long distances helped him pace right into an 8th place finish.

It was no surprise that collegiate athletic departments across the country began calling on Castillo after he finished 8th in the nation. Although Castillo was offered several fully paid recruiting trips, he was unfamiliar with the recruiting process and so turned them all down. Castillo and his family were not aware that accepting such trips did not imply commitment to that school. Nonetheless, Castillo found the perfect school for him, Adams State College, where he enrolled in 1990. Adams State, in Alamosa, Colorado, had a strong NCAA Division II track and field program and was only a four hour drive from Castillo's home.

In 1992, Adams State's men's cross country team had a perfect score at the NCAA Championships when the top five finishes were won by five of their runners only four seconds apart. Castillo and his teammates Peter DeLaCerda, David Brooks, Paul Stoneham and Jason Mohr were the first to accomplish such a feat for Adams State.

Castillo also became the first Native American to win a NCAA Division II cross country title. Castillo wanted to ensure that he would not be the last. He began volunteering with an organization called Wings of America to share the joy he found in running with other Native American youth. Wings of America, an American Indian youth development program of the Earth Circle Foundation, Inc., was established in 1988 to reach Native American youth, one of the most at-risk populations in the United States. The founders, as well as Castillo, recognize running for its fundamental place in the spiritual and ceremonial traditions of Native Americans thus a running-based program was built as a way to reach Native American youth. Castillo coached the annual American Indian Running Clinic. With the help of NIKE, Wings of America was able to bring prominent coaches, sports physicians, running club directors, Olympians and collegiate athletes, like Castillo, to the Native American youth while presenting a camp experience that was informative and affordable. Castillo used running as a unique way to help teach Native American youth traditional Indian games, nutritional information, mental and physical training and other useful skills.

If Castillo had not already earned the role model title in his community, his future success secured it. He went on to graduate after earning the All-American title an impressive nine times. After graduating, Castillo stayed at Adams State to earn his masters degree in health. He also continued to train. Castillo worked as a movie manager, waiter and physical education teacher at an elementary school to make ends meet while he passionately continued to run. After earning his masters degree, Castillo learned of the opportunities that the United States Army offered someone like him. Castillo was attracted to the army's running program that allowed soldiers to train full-time while being paid and the fact that they would pay off his student loans that totaled more than $30,000. So in 1998, Castillo enlisted and after 17 vigorous weeks of training, he proudly graduated and became an infantry soldier.

In 1996, the State of Colorado asked for Castillo's assistance in carrying the Olympic torch across the state on its way to Atlanta. Castillo's focus was on the 2000 Olympics instead because his hard work was starting to pay off as he qualified for the 2000 Olympic Trials in the marathon event. He was ranked 45th in the nation but finished 54th in the trials. While he didn't make it to the Olympics, Castillo is rightfully proud of his effort. Had he not dedicated himself for so many years, through countless arduous training sessions, Castillo would not have received the opportunities he did. He encourages youth to not be selfish with their talents and share them with their communities, much like he did.

For a few years, Castillo continued to train, eventually running in 20 marathons. His personal best was 2:19:19, which is an average of 5:19 for 26 miles. After his retirement from competitive racing in 2003, Castillo's role in life took on a new importance. As a second lieutenant in the U.S. Army, Castillo controls the lives of the 40 men that make up his platoon. He admits that, at times, his running routine of 140 miles a week was easier than some of the stresses of being a leader in army. Yet, he wakes up each day committed to make the lives of his men better as well as the lives of his wife and three daughters. Castillo is proud to be a father, a Native American and a soldier ready to fight for the freedom for his family and fellow Americans. Phillip Castillo's life journey has showed him that taking risks is sometimes the only way we can achieve our dreams. He knows that leaving his reservation, as scary as it may have been, was necessary to follow his dreams and he encourages today's Native American youth to never stop pursuing their passions, no matter where they may lead.

Pam White-Hanson

by Jessica Bartter

On the 27,000 square miles of beautiful desert plains, consisting of breathtaking canyons, refreshing lakes and rivers, and luscious valleys that make up the Navajo Reservation and cross the borders of Arizona, New Mexico, and Utah, a young girl spread her wings and grew a passion for running long distances. Born and raised on the Navajo Reservation, Pam White-Hanson joined the elite class of Native American athletes that leave their home and people in exploration of new experiences and greater opportunities.

White-Hanson's journey began at Adams State College, a NCAA Division II school and member of the Rocky Mountain Athletic Conference, located in Alamosa, Colorado. There she joined fellow Native American and cross country runner, Phillip Castillo, also named a Courageous Student-Athlete by the National Consortium for Academics and Sports. Castillo, a junior runner when White-Hanson began her career at Adams State, was a member of the Acoma Pueblo tribe and in 1992 was the first Native American to win a NCAA Division II cross country championship. White-Hanson hoped to follow in his footsteps and add her name to the list of national champions.

A severe case of plantar fasciitis almost prevented White-Hanson from fulfilling her dream, but this courageous student-athlete was determined. Plantar fasciitis is an overuse injury affecting the sole of the foot. A diagnosis of plantar fasciitis meant her fibrous band of tissue connecting her heel bone to the base of her toes was inflamed causing intense pain in the heel of her foot. Typically, plantar fasciitis patients are prescribed rest, ice after activities, shoe inserts, and for the pain, anti-inflammatory drugs such as aspirin and ibuprofen. None of these standard treatments worked for White-Hanson's pain and her last option in order to continue training was surgery. The surgery involved a release of part of the plantar fascia, the long, flat ligament extending from her heel to her toes that previously had stretched irregularly, causing damage and inflammation through small tears in the ligament. The reconstructive surgery to eliminate White-Hanson's painful condition took two full years of recovery. Neither the pain, surgery nor recovery time prevented White-Hanson from becoming a six-time All-American cross county runner. Also, as a member of the Adams State cross country team, she led her team to three NCAA Division II National Championships. Despite it all, White-Hanson managed to complete her undergraduate degree in just four years.

White-Hanson wanted to share her success with as many Native Americans as possible, and in particular hoped to show the youth of the Navajo Nation all that was possible outside its borders and that the Native American traditions need not be sacrificed in order to expand one's horizon. She began working for Wings of America, an American Indian youth development program of the Earth Circle Foundation, Inc. Wings of America was established in 1988 to reach Native American youth, one of the most at-risk populations in the United States. The founders recognized running for its integral place in the spiritual and ceremonial traditions of Native American people and believed a program built on running would be the most beneficial way to reach Native American youth. The mission of Wings of America is "to enhance the quality of life of American Indian youth. In partnership with Native communities, Wings uses running as a catalyst to empower American Indian and Alaskan Native youth to take pride in themselves and their cultural identity, leading to increased self-esteem, health and wellness, leadership and hope, balance and harmony." White-Hanson's involvement began as a coach for the annual American Indian Running Clinic. With the help of NIKE, Wings of America was able to bring prominent coaches, sports physicians, running club directors, Olympians and collegiate athletes together to present a camp that was informative and affordable. White-Hanson and other camp coaches taught traditional Indian games, a run-walk fitness program, nutritional education for a healthy lifestyle, mental and physical preparedness, and led a non-competitive 5K fun run to conclude the camp's activities while allowing the youth to put their new skills to work.

As a successful student-athlete, both in the classroom and on the field, White-Hanson was easy to admire. Her magnetic personality and welcoming smile encourages Native American youth to work hard and to succeed. Because of her incredible accomplishments as a student and an athlete, White-Hanson served as a role-model to youth who before had never even dreamed of leaving the Navajo Nation to pursue a college education. White-Hanson continued her work with Wings of America while she returned to Adams State College to obtain her master's degree in bilingual education of the Navajo language. Though many have tried, her success is hard to emulate, thus leaving Pam White-Hanson and Phillip Castillo in an elite class of Native American runners spreading their wings beyond the reservation and into the hearts of so many young Native Americans.

Anita DeFrantz

by Jessica Bartter

Anita DeFrantz has lived a life defying the odds. She did not play sports as a child despite the fact that she grew up in Hoosier basketball territory in Indiana. She rowed in college despite the fact that she was on an academic scholarship. She won an Olympic medal in rowing despite the fact that she had been introduced to the sport just three years prior. She defied President Jimmy Carter's 1980 Moscow Olympic boycott despite the fact that the U.S. Olympic Committee had not previously contradicted any president's orders and sent Olympians into competition. She was elected vice president of the International Olympic Committee despite the fact that no female before her held that position. And that was just during the first 50 years of her life.

DeFrantz grew up in Indianapolis where she learned a great deal of compassion and strength from her parents. Both her mother, who was a teacher, and her father, who ran an organization called Community Action Against Poverty, displayed commitments to youth, community and education, and encouraged DeFrantz to do the same. In 1970, DeFrantz enrolled at Connecticut College on an academic scholarship with no athletic intentions but as a sophomore discovered the sport of rowing. While walking on campus one day DeFrantz stopped to ask a man what the long, thin object he was carrying was used for. The man, Bart Gulong, turned out to be the rowing coach and was carrying a rowing shell. DeFrantz's interest and 5 foot 11 build caused him to encourage her to participate in the new sport at Connecticut College. Though DeFrantz had never tried it before, she knew most of the girls that went out for the team would also be beginners; so she gave it a shot. Gulong had been right in predicting DeFrantz's athleticism and shortly after she began he suggested she consider training for the Olympics. At the time, DeFrantz was not even aware that it was an Olympic sport for women but that was because it had just been included in the next Olympics.

DeFrantz graduated in 1974 with her bachelor's degree with honors after competing collegiately for three years. She excelled so well that she earned a spot on the national team every year from 1975 until 1980. Coach Gulong's suggestion came to fruition as DeFrantz traveled to Montreal for the 1976 Olympic Games. Just three years after learning the sport, DeFrantz and the rest of the American team came in third place behind the East Germans and Soviet Union in the Olympic debut of women's rowing. In the midst of Olympic training, DeFrantz applied and enrolled in law school at the University of Pennsylvania. After graduating in 1977 and passing the bar exam, DeFrantz began practicing law.

In October 1977, DeFrantz participated in her first of many changes involving the Olympic Committee. She and three other Olympians were summoned to testify regarding the rights of athletes. Their testimony helped produce the Amateur Sports Act of 1978 which restructured the way Olympic sports are governed in the United States.

While a bronze medal in the Olympics is nothing short of an amazing accomplishment, DeFrantz hoped to return to the 1980 Olympics and capture the gold. Her participation with the national team kept her in tiptop shape while fulfilling her professional career as a lawyer. DeFrantz worked for a public interest law firm in Philadelphia that protected children before taking a year off in 1979 to focus on what would be her last Olympic opportunity. To DeFrantz's dismay, then President Jimmy Carter announced in January 1980 that the United States planned to boycott the 1980 Olympics in Moscow because of the Soviet invasion of Afghanistan.

As a lawyer, DeFrantz immediately knew she and her teammates had rights as athletes. She did not want to stand by and watch as President Carter stripped so many of them of their Olympic dreams. DeFrantz believed the Olympics were pure of political confrontations between countries and that a boycott represented the exact opposite of what the Olympics are all about. DeFrantz was a member of the U.S. Olympic Committee's Athletes Advisory Council since her Olympic debut in 1976. She and other members pleaded with the United States Olympic Committee (USOC) to defy President Carter's order and eventually filed suit to allow them the opportunity to compete. DeFrantz knew the USOC could enter a team regardless of President Carter's suggestions. Yet, the Carter Administration's threat to ruin the USOC's funding was taken seriously enough that DeFrantz, her teammates and every other 1980 Olympic hopeful would have to wait four more years.

Until the boycott decision was official in April of 1980, DeFrantz continued to train, hoping for the best. She had become the face and name connected with the opposition to Carter's position and the associated unpatriotic accusations left her very unpopular and made her the recipient of hate mail. Though the suit was lost, DeFrantz's fight for athlete's rights was just beginning.

While the opposition DeFrantz presented made her disliked by many, she certainly attracted notice. In 1981, Peter Ueberroth hired her on the management team of the 1984 Summer Olympic Games scheduled to take place in Los Angeles. Ueberroth asked her to serve the Los Angeles Olympic Organizing Committee as liaison with the African nations and as chief administrator of the Olympic Village. DeFrantz is credited with helping to save the 1984 Summer Games by preventing African nations from boycotting because South African runner Zola Budd was allowed to run for Great Britain.

DeFrantz was named vice president for the newly created Amateur Athletic Foundation (AAF) of Los Angeles which was established from $93 million of the $230 million profit the Games produced. In 1987, she became president of the AAF. Just the year before, the International Olympic Committee (IOC) was looking to fill a vacancy and found DeFrantz. DeFrantz was only 34 years old and the appointment was a lifetime position. Her appointment means she is a voting member of the IOC until the age of 75 when the position becomes honorary. DeFrantz is one of two Americans to represent the United States. She was the first woman and the first African-American to do so. DeFrantz finally gained the platform necessary to make her case for athlete's rights.

In 1988, DeFrantz spoke out against the injustice she witnessed at the Olympic Games. Canadian Ben Johnson tested positive for performance enhancing drugs after running the 100 meter dash in 9.79 seconds. DeFrantz refused to shy away from the controversy and spoke out publicly to fight for pure, drug-free Olympic competitions. Eight years and two Olympics later, DeFrantz continued to fight for clean sports by preventing the Atlanta Committee for the Olympic Games from using less expensive and not as concise drug testing methods for the 1996 Atlanta Games.

As a member of the IOC, DeFrantz made an impact fighting for athletes' rights and the purity of the Games. Yet, her commitment and intelligence made her worthy of a position with the IOC that exhibits more power. From 1992 until 2001, DeFrantz sat on the Executive Board and in 1997 she accomplished a feat no female has successfully done in the past. DeFrantz was named one of the four vice presidents of the IOC serving a four year term. In the history of the IOC which dates back to 1894, a woman has never held such a prestigious position.

DeFrantz, whose high school did not offer team sports for girls, has worked tirelessly to provide opportunities for underprivileged youth, ensuring opportunities exist for girls. The Amateur Athletic Foundation is committed to the eight counties of Southern California but focuses on Los Angeles. And while no child is turned away, special emphasis is placed on girls, ethnic minorities, the physically challenged and developmentally disabled and other underserved communities. DeFrantz knows sports can change one's life and bring so much opportunity to a child, socially and physically. Nonetheless, she is realistic with the children, informing them of their slim chances in becoming professional athletes and encouraging them to focus on their educations as well. DeFrantz believes this message should also be carried by the coaches and has committed the AAF to a special coaching education program since 1985. In its first 20 years of existence, DeFrantz has led the AAF in its endeavors that have provided nearly $50 million in grants to youth programs and has trained over 50,000 coaches.

DeFrantz is active in several youth, sport and legal organizations including Kids in Sports, the NCAA Advisory Board, the Juvenile Law Center, the Knight Foundation Commission on Intercollegiate Athletics, Children Now and FISA, the international rowing federation. DeFrantz also sits on several different Olympic committees utilizing her historic position well.

In 2004, the First Lady of California, Maria Shriver, created The Minerva Awards in an effort to honor women for their humanity and commitment to service. Shriver chose four special women whose stories she believed would inspire others in the community, state and nation. Fittingly, DeFrantz was a 2005 recipient of The Minerva Awards. Shriver named the Awards after the Roman Goddess portrayed on the California State Seal who represents both a warrior and a peacemaker.

Anita DeFrantz, the descendant of slaves and great-great granddaughter of a Louisiana plantation owner and one of his slaves, has proven herself to be a true leader. She has achieved many firsts, both for her family and for our nation. This internationally known figure has put so many before her selflessly and persistently. She truly is a warrior and a peacemaker.

Ernestine Bayer

by Jessica Bartter

Competitive sport opportunities for women in the 1920's and 30's were scarce and participation in recreational sports was generally discouraged. In 1928, the Olympics sponsored only three sports for women: track and field, swimming and gymnastics. In 1931, Major League Baseball Commissioner Judge Kenesaw Mountain Landis banned women from professional baseball. In 1933, softball was as much of a man's sport as it was a woman's. Female involvement in sport was limited to sitting in the stands. Women were expected to remain on the sidelines and cheer for their men. Fortunately, the 1930's was also a time for pioneers; a handful of brave women entered uncharted territory to play the games that until then they could only watch.

Ernestine Bayer met the love of her life in 1927 when she was 18 years old. His name was Ernest, and coincidentally, they were both often called Ernie. Ernest and Ernestine eloped in 1928 and kept their marriage a secret for almost nine months. Ernest was an oarsman and was training for the 1928 Olympic Games. Rowing in the 1928 Olympics was limited to men only. The sport even condemned marriage, suggesting that men lost their strength and devotion to rowing after getting married. Thus, Ernest and Ernestine kept their marriage a secret to avoid anything that might have hurt Ernest's Olympic chances.

Ernestine watched her husband train on the Schuylkill River in Philadelphia. Ernest trained as hard as ever and earned his spot on the coxless-four seated American team. Ernest traveled to Amsterdam aboard the SS Roosevelt to represent his country. After defeating Italy in the semi-finals, the American team lost to Great Britain. When he returned home, silver medal in hand, the Bayers announced their marriage.

After watching her husband train day after day for years, Ernestine noticed a woman take out a boat and row on her own. This was highly frowned upon, particularly among many male rowers, but it inspired Ernestine. She wondered why more women did not row. Ernestine did not wonder long before she decided to take action. Ernestine then founded the Philadelphia Girl's Rowing Club in 1938, the first women's rowing organization in the country. Just two years prior, Sally Sterns became the first woman coxswain of a male rowing team at Rollins College. Now Sterns and thousands of other women would have new opportunities for women's teams thanks to Ernestine Bayer. Ernestine is often referred to as the mother of women's rowing.

Ernestine organized races at the Philadelphia Girl's Rowing Club and in 1939 won the Independence Day race on the Schuylkill River in a coxless-two seater. Ernestine went on to organize and win countless races well into her 80's. In the 1940's and 50's, she competed in every event she was allowed to enter. As she grew older, Ernestine continued to compete in masters rowing tournaments. In 1992 at the age of 83, Bayer won the Head of Charles of the women's veteran singles. At the age of 86, Ernestine set a world indoor rowing record for women ages 80-89 with a time of 11:14.0. With her handicap, she finished well ahead of all but two of her competitors in the 60 and over age group. While many of her competitors were young enough to be her children, her real daughter, Tina Bayer, sat cheering in the stands pushing her mother through the last grueling moments. It is no surprise that Ernest and Ernestine's daughter Tina shared their love for rowing. Together, they traveled the world watching and competing in the sport they loved.

Women's rowing was finally debuted in the 1976 Montreal Olympic Games. Ernestine was asked to sit on the first U.S. Women's Olympic Committee. While she was already a legend to many, Ernestine's place in sporting history was secured after the establishment of Olympic rowing. She was inducted into the Hall of Fame in 1984. Ernestine says the thrill of her life was being asked to fill the #2 seat of the 1984 Olympic Gold Medal Women's Eight.

In 1997, Ernestine lost the love of her life and partner in her journey to establish rowing. Ernestine spread Ernest's ashes on the Schuylkill where they had enjoyed so many peaceful days on the water. Yet, Ernestine's passion for rowing remained and she was crowned World Masters Champion in 2000.

U.S. Rowing renamed their Woman of the Year Award as the

Ernestine Bayer Award because of her outstanding contributions to rowing. Each year, the Award is given to another woman who demonstrates Ernestine Bayer's dedication, determination and love for rowing.

Donna Lopiano

by Jessica Bartter

There are many important benefits for young girls who participate in sports, yet there are counter pressures in our society that discourage young girls from being strong and active. Donna Lopiano ignored such pressures as a child. While many young girls growing up in the 1950's and 1960's viewed sports as men's games and preferred to watch, Lopiano could always be found playing with the boys. In fact, she did not even notice the difference between her and her neighborhood playmates until her gender denied her a spot on a Little League team that had recruited her. When she was just 11 years old, lined up at the field to get her uniform, another little leaguer's father pulled out the rule book and demanded Lopiano be taken off the team because the rules stated that no girls were allowed. That very team went on to win the Little League World Series without her. For the previous six years, she had spent hours after school perfecting her baseball pitches against the side of her family's house. She idolized Mickey Mantle, Whitey Ford and Don Drysdale and dreamt of pitching for the New York Yankees.

Lopiano was hurt by being excluded and her pain drove her harder toward success. She did not appreciate being told she could not pursue her dream and has worked tirelessly over the last four decades to prevent the same from happening to more young impressionable girls. Until she was old enough to stand up for the injustices in women's sports, Lopiano was forced to conform to the standard that males play baseball and females play softball. Lopiano learned to execute her powerful pitches with an underhand release and quickly excelled in softball. In 1963, Lopiano was discovered by the Raybestos Brakettes, an amateur softball team for whom she played until 1972. During her ten seasons Lopiano earned All-American honors nine times and was named MVP three times. She had a .910 winning percentage, winning 183 games and losing just 18. In 817 innings she struck out 1,633 opponents. A force at the plate herself, Lopiano twice led her team in batting averages with .316 and .367. In addition to sharpening her softball skills, her career with the Brakettes provided her with the opportunity to travel and explore other parts of the world. By the time she was 18, she had already toured France, Hong Kong, India and Australia playing the game she loved.

One of the most amazing parts of Lopiano's amateur softball career is the fact that it spanned over her high school, collegiate and post-graduate education. In between long practices, intense training, international travel and national championships, Lopiano managed to graduate from Stamford High School, Southern Connecticut State University with a bachelor's degree in physical education and the University of Southern California where she earned her master's and doctoral degrees. Lopiano's career as a Raybestos Brakette did not interfere with her success on the field hockey, volleyball and basketball teams either. Including her amateur career, she played in 26 national championships in the four sports. The success she earned as an athlete led her to coaching positions for collegiate men's and women's volleyball, women's basketball and softball teams.

At just 28 years old, Lopiano was hired by the University of Texas, Austin as Director of Intercollegiate Athletics for Women. Her energetic attitude and high standards appealed to the selection committee. Lopiano put the pressure on the coaches both on and off the field. In her first ten years, she went through 16 coaches in eight different sports. She made it clear to her staff that winning was a priority as well as education. Lopiano warned coaches that their jobs depended on whether or not their teams were top ten programs. Lopiano also stressed that their jobs were equally dependent on the success their student-athletes achieved in the classroom. Within just one year after she began holding her coaches accountable for academic performances, the department's mean SAT score increased by 100 points. During her 17 years at the University of Texas, the Longhorns graduated 95 percent of their women athletes who completed their athletic eligibility. Athletically, Lopiano's Longhorns were equally successful. Eighteen National Championships (AIAW and NCAA), 62 Southwest Conference Championships, more than 300 All-Americans and over a dozen Olympians made Lopiano's women's program a dominant one in collegiate athletics. Her program's success was a direct result of her philosophy that money and coaches were the two key ingredients for a collegiate program. Lopiano believed that if her programs were adequately funded, she could attract the best coaches who would accept her demands, athletically and academically. By attracting the best coaches, Lopiano predicted the best athletes would follow. Lopiano grew her department's budget from $57,000 in 1975 to almost $3 million in 1987.

While the short-term numbers prove Lopiano's success, she made great strides for women's sports in the long run as well. A pioneer for her time, Lopiano has served females everywhere with her advocacy for Title IX. Title IX of the Education Amendments of 1972 is a federal law that prohibits discrimination on the basis of sex in all education programs and activities receiving federal funds. Title IX is commonly referred to for its impact on sports but also pertains to drama, band and other extracurricular student activities. Title IX is credited with increasing female involvement in sport more than tenfold. In 1970, only one in every 27 high school girls played varsity sports compared to one in every 2.5 girls 30 years later. Title IX has led to increased funding and support for women's sports, bringing the ratio of girls playing much closer to the ratio of boys in sports which is equal to one in every two. Lopiano was very effective in advocating female participation in sports, and many women have her to thank for encouraging them to become involved.

Lopiano moved to the Women's Sports Foundation (WSF) in April of 1992 to continue her advocacy for female athletes' rights. The Women's Sports Foundation is a 501(c)(3) nonprofit organization that was founded in 1974 by tennis legend Billie Jean King to advance the lives of girls and women through sports and physical activity. The Foundation's programs, services and initiatives are dedicated to participation, education, advocacy, research and leadership for women's sports. In the past 13 years as Executive Director, Lopiano has secured funding for girls' and women's sport programs and has educated the public and corporations about the importance of women's health and gender equality in sport. Lopiano believes the 1996 Summer Olympics was a celebration of Title IX showing the first generation of success stories in gymnast Kerri Strug, sprinter Gail Devers, softball player Dot Richardson, swimmer Amy Van Dyken and basketball player Lisa Leslie who all took home gold medals. Young girls everywhere suddenly had role models in the sports world who were female despite the lack of professional athletic opportunities for females in the United States. Individuals and parents under the age of 40 are also of the Title IX generation and have been a major influence on children, according to Lopiano, by encouraging participation in sports to both sons and daughters.

The Sporting News named Lopiano one of "The 100 Most Influential People in Sports," *College Sports* magazine ranks her among "The 50 Most Influential People in College Sports," *Ladies Home Journal* named her one of "America's 100 Most Important Women," and she was named as one of the century's greatest sportswomen by *Sports Illustrated Women*. She is an inductee of the National Sports Hall of Fame, the National Softball Hall of Fame and the Texas Women's Hall of Fame. In honor of her many contributions to women in athletics at the University of Texas, the crew team christened the Varsity Eight shell "Donna A. Lopiano" in April 2005. Lopiano sat on the United States Olympic Committee's Executive Board for years and was awarded the 2005 International Olympic Committee Women and Sport Trophy. Annually since 2000, the IOC Women and Sport Trophy has been awarded to a person or organization in recognition of their outstanding contributions to developing, encouraging and strengthening the participation of women and girls in physical and sports activities, in coaching, administrative, journalism and media positions.

A champion athlete in her own right, Donna Lopiano is also considered a champion of equal opportunity for women in sports. Her educational advocacy for gender equality in sports made Lopiano a pioneer whose boldness, intelligence and drive have made a monumental and lasting impact on the face of American sports.

Nancy Lieberman

by Brian Wright

At the tender young age of seven, Nancy Lieberman knew that she would make athletic history. Born in the basketball-crazed city of Brooklyn, New York, Lieberman too developed a deep love and passion for the game. Her talents on the court were discovered at an early age but due to the negative stereotypes about women's sports Lieberman was often discouraged from participating. Women and girls alike were discouraged from playing competitive sports, and those who decided to play sports were perceived as a "tomboys." As a child, Lieberman's mother had gone as far as to puncture one of her basketballs in attempt to discourage Lieberman from pursuing her basketball aspirations. Though these stereotypes challenged Lieberman's goals of becoming a professional basketball player, they never discouraged her as she was confident that she would make history in sports.

Lieberman disregarded all the negative feedback she received about playing sports and continued to develop her skills. She took her game to the outdoor courts and gyms of Harlem and competed with some of the best young players in the city. Lieberman did not only compete with the boys, she dominated them. She developed a knack for the game along with a rugged and tough style of play which differentiated her from other players in the city. Playing hard and playing tough became second nature for Lieberman. Standing at 5 foot 10 Lieberman was able to tower over her smaller opponents and use her physical style of play to outmatch and overpower them. In her sophomore year of high school Lieberman earned a reputation around New York City as one of the best basketball players in the city and was invited to the ABAUSA's National Team Trials. This trial invitation was unprecedented in women's basketball due to her young age but her amazing talent was too attractive to pass up for the team. As a 15 year old high school student Lieberman earned one of the prestigious 12 team member spots and was named to the USA National Team. Lieberman would continue her basketball success in the years to come helping the USA National Team win gold and silver medals in the World Championships and Pan American Games of 1975 and 1979, respectively. On the first ever Women's Olympic basketball team Lieberman contributed a great deal to her team's silver medal performance and she was the youngest basketball player in Olympic history to ever win a medal. Lieberman had competed at the highest levels of international basketball competition at age 18, even before she ever set foot on a college campus.

Lieberman chose Old Dominion University. Lieberman, or "Lady Magic" as she was often called for her flashy passes and brilliant scoring drives, continued to amaze spectators while performing in college. At Old Dominion, Lieberman helped grow the women's basketball program into a national powerhouse. She led them to a National Women's Invitational Tournament Championship in 1977 as well as back-to-back AIAW National Championships in 1978 and 1979. In her final two seasons at Old Dominion, Lieberman and company achieved a 72-2 record. She was a two-time winner of the Wade Trophy which honors the nation's best women's basketball performer for their academic, community service and on court performances along with the Broderick Award which awards the nation's best collegiate female athlete. Lieberman was honored with both of these awards in consecutive years, which is a feat still unmatched today in women's collegiate athletics. Upon graduating from college, Lieberman was regarded not only as one of the best female athletes to ever play college basketball, but also one of the best collegiate basketball players ever on a men's or women's team.

Lieberman hoped to play on the U.S. women's team in the 1980 Olympics in Moscow, but a boycott by President Jimmy Carter and the USA Olympic teams would deny her this opportunity. Though disappointed about the missed opportunity, Lieberman agreed with the decision to withdraw from the Games because of the Soviet Union's invasion into Afghanistan. In 1980, Lieberman entered the Women's Basketball League (WBL) draft and was selected by the Dallas Diamonds. In her first season with the Diamonds, Lieberman lead them to their first and only Championship series appearance. Though the Diamonds would eventually lose the five-game series Lieberman had made her mark on the league and franchise.

In an effort to help another female activist for the advancement of women's sports, Lieberman took a leave of absence from the Diamonds to train tennis great Martina Navratilova. She returned to the Diamonds in the 1984 season as a member of the newly formed Women's American Basketball Association (WABA). In the 1984-1985 WABA season Lieberman led the team to the Championship while earning Most Valuable Player honors averaging 27 points per game. Lieberman was again leading by example in excellence on the court for women playing at the highest levels of sport. Lieberman deeply desired to show women, young and old, that they could make a good living in sports. In 1986, Lieberman made history once again by becoming the first woman to join a men's professional basketball team. She joined the Springfield Fame of the United States Basketball League (USBL) and played an entire season with them before leaving to play for the Long Island Knights the following season. In 1988, Lieberman made her final move as she joined the Washington Generals on a World Tour with the storied Harlem Globetrotters. Such sports career decisions were unprecedented thus far, and played a very significant role in promoting the visibility of women playing professional sports in the United States.

In 1988, Lieberman became the color commentator for NBC during the Olympic Games in Seoul, Korea. Lieberman covered the Women's Olympic basketball team on their way to winning a second Olympic gold medal. Lieberman would later go on to write two books, one on her life story as an athlete, and the other on the evolution of women's basketball with Robin Roberts of ESPN and ABC. As a player Lieberman was a pioneer for women's sports. As an analyst at the Olympics Games Lieberman promoted women's sports and in 1993 she was rewarded by becoming the first woman inducted into the New York City Basketball Hall of Fame. Not long after, Lieberman was inducted into the Naismith Basketball Hall of Fame for her great accomplishments on the court. In 1997, with the conception of the Women's National Basketball Association (WNBA), Lieberman felt that this was the league that she had dreamt of as a child and wanted to be a part of the inaugural season. At age 38, Lieberman decided to return to the court and take part in the historical opening season of the WNBA. Lieberman trained and was the 15th overall selection in the WNBA draft by the Phoenix Mercury. Lieberman entered the season as the oldest player in the League, but her experience and leadership on and off the court paid dividends for the Mercury as she helped lead them to the regular season Western Conference Championship and the semi-finals of the WNBA playoffs. The home fan attendance of the Mercury also was evidence of Lieberman's ability to attract fans to women's sports just as she had done her entire life. The Mercury achieved a league high average of 13,000 fans per game. In 1998, Lieberman decided to move on into a front office executive position of General Manager and Head Coach of the expansion WNBA Detroit Shock franchise. Lieberman was very successful in this endeavor as well leading the Shock to a winning record in its first season as well as a coveted trip to the WNBA playoffs. Throughout her illustrious career as an athlete, analyst, coach and executive, Lieberman has been very successful not only for herself but for the advancement of women's sports as a whole. The growth of women's sports, particularly basketball, can be directly linked to her courage and desire to achieve more for women within the world of sports.

Nancy Lieberman is currently the Head Coach of the Dallas Fury of the National Women's Basketball League. She has continued her role as a broadcaster for ESPN during WNBA and NCAA women's collegiate games. Lieberman also hosts basketball camps and clinics for young girls trying to improve their athletic abilities and teach them they can make a career of playing the sports they love. Through her lifetime of success on the court, as well as her commitment to women's sports off the court, Lieberman has fulfilled her early age promise of making history in sports.

Annie Boucher

by Jessica Bartter

A student-athlete with seven years of competitive playing experience in their sport may be considered a seasoned veteran, ready for the challenges of the college elite. And if the student-athlete was a self-taught, 44 year old mother and grandmother, who did not begin playing until the age of 37, those seven years of experience would certainly come in handy.

Annie Boucher, a Jamaican native, moved to New York City in her early twenties with her daughter Sandra. Day in and day out, Boucher worked hard, nine to five as a keypunch operator for Paine Webber, and 24 hours a day as a single parent raising her daughter. One summer day in 1978, a fit, good-looking woman dressed in tennis gear caught Boucher's eye. Boucher, attracted to the healthy persona portrayed by the stranger, stopped the woman to ask where she was headed. The stranger's answer compelled Boucher to run upstairs to her apartment, rummage through her closet for a tennis racket and follow the woman to the neighborhood courts. The tennis racket, which she had purchased years ago for $5, finally got its first use out on the court.

It only took six months of self-motivated practice for Boucher to make the finals of the neighborhood tennis tournament. There she met the "best female player in the neighborhood," Camille Bodden. Boucher took her opponent point by point and did not pay attention to the score; mainly because she did not know how to keep score in tennis. Her concentration was only broken when the score keeper, Camille Bodden's father, yelled at her to say, "You've won the match already; you don't have to serve anymore."[1] Boucher achieved the first of many goals tennis had now presented to her.

Boucher continued her hard work and practice after work and on weekends for several years. Encouraged by her daughter's marriage and the support of other tennis companions, Boucher earned her GED in 1986 through an adult education center in Queens. Boucher had previously dropped out of high school in her homeland of Jamaica before going to England to attend nursing school. But before she was certified, Boucher became pregnant and after four years on her own, relocated to New York City.

Realizing a new avenue in life, Boucher continued to pursue her education and enrolled in Queensborough Community College. Ready to take her academics seriously once and for all, Boucher was reluctant to participate in extracurricular activities including her new passion, tennis. Yet, the classes proved to be easy for Boucher to handle and she joined the tennis team that fall. In fact, Boucher also joined the basketball team in the winter and the softball team in the spring. Boucher enjoyed early success at Queensborough. She was quickly named captain of the tennis team and went undefeated at the No. 1 singles and doubles position with a 9-0 record.

In academe, Boucher found her calling to be psychology. Facing a challenging academic load, she decided to put her athletics on hold for a year. Like every student-athlete must inevitably learn, Boucher realized she could once again balance the academics with athletics and joined the tennis team in her third year at Queensborough. As if she had never left, she repeated her undefeated run at No. 1 singles and doubles until the final match of the season. As she chased down her opponents shot, while up 5-0, 40-0, her ankle broke. The pins and screws needed to repair her ankle ended her athletic career at Queensborough. But they did not prevent her from winning Team MVP honors and the Queensborough's Outstanding Female Athlete award. And like a true student-athlete, Boucher was most pleased with her 3.2 GPA.

Inspired by her new found love for psychology, Boucher enrolled in a four-year university to continue her studies and complete her degree. At Alfred University, Boucher was also able to continue her athletic excellence. In her first year of competition since the ankle injury, Boucher went 3-4, helping the team to a 3-4 record. The next year, Boucher earned an impressive 9-1 record, assisting the Saxons with an undefeated season, a first for Alfred University tennis. To keep her skills sharp, she often practiced with the men's tennis team during the off-season.

After graduating from Alfred University in 1992 with a bachelor's degree in psychology, Boucher moved to Jamaica, New York where she resides with her husband, Chet Turnquest. The couple have a grandson, Haki Nkrumah. Haki followed his grandmother to Alfred University where he played tennis as well.

Boucher jumped over many hurdles to achieve such great accomplishments, but the most remarkable impact has been on her opponents and fellow student-athletes who were nothing but inspired when meeting her despite the fact that she most likely beat them. Her story reinforces the saying "better late than never" and proves that with desire and commitment, age is irrelevant to success.

[1] Scheer, Stephanie. "Grandma's on the varsity" *Sports Illustrated*, December 16, 1991.

Lee Elder

by Jessica Bartter

In 1975, it had been 29 years since Kenny Washington integrated the National Football League, 28 years since Jackie Robinson integrated Major League Baseball and 25 years since Nat "Sweetwater" Clifton integrated the National Basketball Association. In each case, their historic achievements could not have been possible without help from others. Dan Reeves signed Washington, Branch Rickey signed Robinson and Joe Lapchick signed Clifton. But nobody with enough power had spoken out enough against the injustices of country club practices and the game of golf remained segregated. In 1962, Charlie Shifford became the first African-American to play on the Professional Golfers' Association (PGA) of America Tour. But golf remained a game of tradition and invitation only events and the most prestigious tournament, The Masters, excluded whomever they wished, especially African-Americans. The Masters has been held at the Augusta National Golf Course in Georgia since 1934 and kept all white for over 40 years until a man named Lee Elder stepped up to the tee box for the first time, leading the way for change.

Elder was introduced to golf as a nine year old when he began caddying to earn money for food. His love for golf grew as a teenager when he got a job as a caddy for Alvin C. Thompson. While Thompson had the skills to succeed on the PGA Tour, the possible earnings were not nearly as high as the money Thompson earned challenging golfers on courses across the country. As a black man, Elder was not permitted in many of the country clubs where he caddied so he negotiated competitions for Thompson with other caddies out in the caddyshack. Often, Thompson even bet that he and his caddy could beat any two golfers at a club and they usually did. Elder picked up many pointers from Thompson and could drive the ball a long way. He even snuck onto the back holes of a segregated course in Dallas, Texas where he caddied most often to practice with clubs he borrowed from a course manager. Despite Elder's ability to drive long distances he believed he could make more money as a caddy than as a golfer with the United Golf Association, the all-black golf tour.

Elder later joined the army where he earned acclaim for his golf skills. In 1961, in his late 20's, Elder finally joined the United Golf Association and dominated the tour, making a name for himself. Six years later, Elder joined the PGA to compete on the tour. Pete Brown and Charlie Shifford had won on the tour, yet neither were invited or voted by past Champions to play in the most prestigious golf event, The Masters. Presumably, the lack of opportunities was upholding the long-standing tradition of whites only at Augusta National. Finally in 1972, The Masters Tournament began automatically inviting all PGA Tour winners, opening the door for a new face in the game of golf.

Sadly, in a country built on apartheid, Elder was able to integrate golf in South Africa before doing so in the United States. In 1971, Elder was invited to play at the South African PGA Tournament, the first integrated tournament in South Africa. Though Elder wanted to make history, he wanted to make sure that it meant more than just a golf game. Elder agreed to play in South Africa only after being assured that the gallery would be integrated and that he and his wife would be permitted to stay and go wherever they chose. Elder was not content with the social change he instigated in South Africa and was intent on seeing the same in the United States. And change he saw on April 21, 1974 when he sank an 18-foot putt on the fourth hole of a sudden death playoff to win the Monsanto Open in Pensacola, Florida, qualifying him for the Masters, the first African-American to do so. Elder was 40 years old in his first Masters Tournament when he shot a 74 and 78 on opening day, missing the cut by five shots. Yet, Elder won with the significance of the event. Elder made history by walking on the course in 1975. He returned to the Masters Tournament again in 1977 and every year until 1983. During that time, he made the cut twice. Though he never walked off the course with the prized green jacket, Elder carved a path for others to follow. At the time, Augusta National Golf Club had no members of color and did not for more than a decade following Elder's inaugural competition. Elder also became the first African-American to golf with the American team in the Ryder Cup in 1984. The Ryder Cup matches up the best American golfers with those of Europe, a competition that has been played every year since 1927.

Elder left the PGA Tour and in 1984 joined the Senior Tour where he dominated for years. Elder won the Suntree Senior Classic and the Hilton Head Seniors International in 1984, the Denver Post Championship, the Merrill Lynch/Golf Digest Commemorative, the Digital Seniors Classic and the Citizens Union Senior Golf Classic in 1985, the Merrill Lynch/Golf Digest Commemorative in 1986 and the Gus Machado Classic in 1988.

Elder has been witness to too many injustices in his lifetime and does his best to take a stand whenever possible. He has spoken out against the lack of opportunities for women and minorities in golf. The Lee Elder National Junior Golf Program was started to promote the game to minority youth. The junior program teaches basic instructions and golf etiquette to youth who most likely would not otherwise have the opportunity to play golf. Elder remains troubled by the lack of people of color playing golf. Indeed, a lack of awareness and opportunity in golf for inner-city children keeps the percentage of those young people involved disturbingly low. Elder's program was developed to help lead the way and to increase the number of African-Americans teeing up on courses across the country. Lee Elder fought tirelessly to earn his spot in golf's history. The path he paved was long overdue but this pioneer's best reward is to see it followed over and over.

Eddie Robinson
by Richard Lapchick

Eddie Robinson's coaching career at Grambling in deep, rural Louisiana lasted through 11 presidents and three wars. Grambling has been home to Coach and his wife, Doris, for 58 years. They have been married that long and he coached for 56 years—all at the same institution! When he retired in November 1997, many people in America stood up and took note for the first time of the winningest coach in the history of college football. In the African-American community, he was very likely the best known coach in America and was surely the most beloved. However, institutionalized racial barriers kept Robinson a secret from most of white America outside of the world of sports.

Initially a coach in a segregated society, Eddie Robinson helped football transcend race in the America he loves and treasurers. I co-authored his autobiography in the hope that it would help Americans of every color and in every corner of our country discover the full meaning of the life of this great son of America. At a time when so many coaches and players seem ready to extol their own virtues, Robinson was always reluctant to discuss any of his victories or records. I had to drag game stories out of him because he wanted to talk about his players and fellow coaches as men. He wanted to talk about life and philosophy, which was a pure pleasure for me to listen to. Nonetheless, getting him to talk about himself was very difficult.

In his autobiography, *Never Before, Never Again*, Coach Robinson wrote, "They said I would never be able to reach my third grade dream of coaching football. I saw a coach then, he looked so good and his boys seemed to worship him. The fact that he was their hero was written all over their faces. That was the life I wanted. Seventy years later I ended a 56 year ride as a college head coach!"

He knew that life had changed dramatically in America. "I know life isn't easy for young people now. They face all these challenges that my generation didn't have. When I was growing up in Jackson and Baton Rouge, children weren't killing each other; crack didn't exist; I never heard of steroids; most families had a mother and father. Many of today's student-athletes were raised in poverty and despair. They know that some white people will decide who they are just because of what they look like. Yes, indeed, life is hard today."

After achieving one of sports' most incredible records with his 400th win in 1995, Coach Eddie Robinson said, "I wish I could cut up all of these victories into 400 pieces and give them to all the players and assistant coaches I have had. They are the ones who truly deserve the credit." Now that I know him I see that these words were coming straight from his heart.

The stories about his retirement brought new exposure for Coach in communities where his messages of tradition, loyalty, family and racial understanding are desperately needed. Eddie Robinson began to become a household name after every major newspaper and TV stations featured him on multiple occasions throughout the 1997 season. Viewers and readers caught glimpses of his wisdom and his wit, finally revealing the genius of this great American leader who happened to be a coach and happened to be African-American.

Never a public crusader for civil rights, Coach courageously challenged racism in his own way by proving that a black man could be a great football coach and, simultaneously, have the tenacity and determination of those in his charge as he led adolescents into manhood. Thirty years later, many of today's civil rights leaders hail Eddie Robinson's life in the same breath as that of Jackie Robinson's. Rev. Jesse Jackson said, "Eddie Robinson has always been a hero in my eyes. Without question, he is an ambassador for our people, not only African-Americans, but all of the Americans. That's why I have such respect for Coach Robinson."

In 1941, he assumed the role of mentor, role model, father, and counselor to his student-athletes both on and off the field. Grambling and college coaching were never the same. Nor have the thousands of young men who played for Coach Robinson. He guided the once obscure Grambling State Tigers to national and international acclaim while helping to produce championship teams and players. But it was never about just training athletes. Robinson believed that as a coach he has many more responsibilities than just teaching the mechanics of football. The career-related accomplishment of which Coach is proudest of is that 80 percent of his players graduated in a sport where the national average during his tenure had been less than 45 percent. At a time when most head coaches today delegate caring for student-athletes to assistants, Coach Robinson spent 56 years personally going into the athletic dorm with his now famous cow bell at 6:30 a.m. each weekday to be sure his men were awake and ready to go to class. Coach has proven the power of an individual to make a huge difference in the lives of young people. Some have gone on to become lawyers and doctors. Joseph B. Johnson became Grambling's president. Raymond Jetson became a Louisiana State Representative.

Coach Robinson helped motivate men at Grambling to succeed on and off the field. Under Robinson's leadership, Grambling became one of the most productive training camps for professional football; more than 300 of his players went to pro camps. More than 200 have made the active rosters in the NFL. Three have been inducted in the NFL Hall of Fame. Many of his former players have become coaches themselves. Several players were, like their coach, pioneers for African-American athletes: Tank Younger was the first player drafted from an historically black college; Buck Buchanan was the first African-American to be selected as the NFL's number one draft choice; James Harris was the first African-American starting quarterback; and Doug Williams was the first African-American quarterback to start and win a Super Bowl.

Of all of his accomplishments, he maintains that his greatest achievements are that he has had only one wife and one job for over 56 years. Robinson came to Grambling in 1941 just months after marrying Doris, his sweetheart since he was 14! The marriage is still going strong.

They still hold hands 65 years after they first met. I've seen it and it is moving. I have been told on many occasions, "Listen, Rich, I have to go now to have lunch with Doris," or, "It's time for dinner with Doris." At first I thought he might just be tired from hours of talking to me. But then we would always pick it up at 10:00 p.m. and go until 1:00 a.m. For years I believed I didn't know any man who loved his wife as much as I did. I may have met him that first night with Coach.

In spite of the racial barriers that surrounded his life, Coach somehow maintains a positive attitude about opportunity in America for people of all colors. Coach believes: "We are in a position to do a lot of good and that's the real importance of this work. America offers more opportunity to young people than any other country in the world."

Looking back at the issue of race, Coach wrote, "We made

extraordinary statements to break stereotypes: Buchanan was the first Grambling player picked in the first round of the NFL draft in 1963. Grambling won 17 SWAC championships and nine National Black Championships. The Howard Cosell documentary on Grambling in 1968 had black and white sports fans calling me a "great football coach." As we traveled across the South, we tried to use Grambling green (dollars) to quietly integrate hotels and restaurants. None of my players or coaches were seen at demonstrations in the 1960's. We made our own. The civil rights movement was helping to change the laws. Our goal was to help to change attitudes."

Legendary Penn State Coach Joe Paterno talked of Robinson's historic contributions to the game of college football, "Nobody has ever done or will do what Eddie Robinson has done for this game. Our profession will never be able to repay Eddie Robinson for what he has done for the country and the profession of football."

Muhammad Ali said, "They call me the greatest. I know that the greatest football coach who ever stepped foot on the field is Coach Robinson. I have admired what he has done in turning boys into men. He is a credit to sport and to humanity."

Muhammad Ali

by Richard Lapchick

Considered brash and bold when he was young, Muhammad Ali became a messenger of peace for the United Nations. He was considered to be the athlete who most divided the races after he proclaimed allegiance to the Black Muslims and proclaimed that he would not go to Vietnam to fight. Ali has undoubtedly become the public figure who helps unite people across racial groups and makes people feel comfortable when they are in the presence of people who do not look like themselves.

Ali is a person of such personal magnitude that a 96,000 square foot Muhammad Ali Center was opened in the fall of 2005 to commemorate the life of this giant. Ali captured the public's attention with his great athletic skills. By the time he was 18, he had won six Kentucky Golden Gloves Championships, two National Golden Gloves Championships and two National AAU titles. Barely 18, he won the gold medal in the 1960 Rome Olympics. In coming home, Ali faced the ugly reality of racism in America. After a public parade welcomed him back to Louisville, the site of the new Ali Center, Ali went into a restaurant and was refused service.

With that as the backdrop, Ali trained hard to try to win the world heavy weight Championship. Facing a menacing Sonny Liston as a 7 to 1 underdog, Cassius Clay upset the champion and took the title in 1964. Within 24 hours he announced that he had become a member of the Nation of Islam and was changing his name from Cassius Clay to Cassius X. His polarization from the media and white America began. He soon took the name of Muhammad Ali.

Ali refused induction into the United States Army. He said he refused to fight, because, "I ain't got no quarrel with them Vietcong." That action seemed to erect concrete barriers. He soon lost his boxing licenses all across America. Stripped of his championship, Ali was unable to fight for nearly three years. Ali became a spokesperson on college campuses against the war in Vietnam as it became more and more unpopular.

Ali won his case in the Supreme Court and in 1970 beat Jerry Quarry, followed the next year by the fight with Joe Frazier which Frazier won. In the meantime the most heralded match of Ali's career, "The Rumble in the Jungle," was being prepared in Zaire against George Foreman who came in as a 3 to 1 favorite. It was in this fight that Ali invented his famous "rope-a-dope" strategy that tired Foreman out and allowed Ali to beat Foreman and reclaim the championship. After winning the "Thrilla in Manila" in the third fight with Frazier, Ali, dancing on top of the world, was upset in a stunning match by Olympic champion Leon Spinks. Ali won the rematch becoming the only heavy-weight to win the championship three times. Ali closed his long career which started at age 12 and ended at 39 with only five defeats and 56 victories.

In retirement, Ali tirelessly traveled the world, winning friends and working for peace, serving as an ambassador for presidents to release hostages. Muhammad Ali has won the admiration of generations of people, even those who never saw him box. During this period, he met his fourth wife, Lonnie, who had lived nearby Ali when she was a child in Louisville. She has been his angel.

I have to relate some personal experience with Ali whom I first met in the 1960's.

Ali was in Boston in 1997 when the verdict in the civil case of O.J. Simpson was rendered. Now America's odyssey with and against O.J. Simpson may finally fade from view. But then it was red hot and ugly. Almost simultaneously, the continued resurgent star of Muhammad Ali, which began with the opening ceremonies of the Olympics, seemed very much on the sports horizon. It is ironic that we have dealt in such personal depth in such different ways with two of our nation's greatest African-American athletes.

The publication of *Healing*, Ali's book with Thomas Hauser and the release of "*When We Were Kings*," then a new documentary about Ali's historic Rumble in the Jungle in Zaire, brought Ali to city after city to talk about racial healing. In most cases, Lonnie Ali talked to the students assembled at each school. Gyms were packed with young people from elementary school through high school. They had all been prepared so they could understand what Ali had done to make their principals and teachers so excited that Ali could actually be coming to their school.

I was informed that students were drilled about his artistic boxing career, his stand against the Vietnam War and his work for civil rights of African-Americans. All were true and provided great perspective.

Whenever Muhammad Ali was sighted entering a gym, pandemonium broke out. Even children who didn't know the history were simply swept away by the stature and charisma of this man who has been slowed by Parkinson's syndrome but whose mind was as sharp as ever.

Moments built on one another to create a momentum of enthusiasm that few students or their teachers had ever experienced. The first school was the Hennigan Elementary School. They had gifts for Ali and one fifth grader had written a poem that he was "the greatest and not Ali." Ali called him forth and did an Ali Shuffle that not many believed he had in him. He has so many things inside which he mostly expresses without words.

My then seven year old, Emily first met Ali when she was a very shy five year old. She was standing with my wife, Ann, when Ali caught her eye from the other side of a table. This girl, who takes 15 to 20 minutes to warm up to friends she hadn't seen for a week, flew across the room and jumped into his open arms. That was 1995.

We went to dinner with the Ali family on the second night of his stay in Boston. It was Muhammad, Lonnie, their son Assad, Ann, Emily, noted photographer Howard Bingham and Henry Louis Gates of Harvard's Afro-American Studies Department. We were the guests of the LoConte family at the great Italian eatery in Boston's North End, known simply as LoConte's.

It was early in the evening, which happened to be the night of President Clinton's State of the Union Address. The evening was so special to be with the Ali's that no one thought of trying to hear the President. Then a waiter came to our table to say that the jury was coming back with O.J. Simpson's civil case verdict. Professor Gates asked if there was a TV to watch the verdict. An old black and white set was promptly brought out.

I watched Ali as he watched intently but without expression as to what he hoped for in a verdict. Everything went against O.J. this time. We turned the TV off and resumed the conversations around the table.

Ali drew a picture for Emily. She made him a valentine. Emily and Assad sent notes to each other. It was one of those nights that I know I will always remember.

I listened to the news on the way home. Commentators speculated that this new verdict would further divide the races in America as they said it had in the criminal case. I wondered how commentators were still blind to how huge the racial divide has been, with or without the O.J. Simpson case.

I thought long and hard that night about these two African-American men. Both had incredible athletic careers. Both became beloved by the public and crossed over racial lines. Simpson seemed to spend his life trying to prove that there was no divide between the races. Ali's legacy included standing up as a proud black man, emphasizing boldly that race does matter as no other athlete has done so forcefully before or since.

It seems ironic that one now roams free but lives in disgrace in the eyes of the majority of Americans, accused of dividing the races. The other, who once was accused of dividing the races because he stood so tall as a black American, now brings people of all racial groups together by preaching "healing" and appealing to everyone, irrespective of race, religion or age.

As a young boxer, Muhammad Ali called himself "The Greatest." Now the world calls him "The Greatest" nearly five decades after he won his gold medal. Yes, Muhammad Ali is still "The Greatest."

CHAPTER 2

COACHING TO WIN IN LIFE

Coaching is among the most rewarding careers a man or woman can undertake. A coach leads, trying to teach teams skills and the concept of teamwork which will bring them together to pursue a common goal. For many coaches, the only goal is to win and they do so consistently and brilliantly. For others, the goals are more expansive, more permanent. These coaches teach sportsmanship, teamwork, the ability to win and lose with equal grace, the concern for a teammate, leadership, and the many health benefits of sport, all of which are as or more important than won-lost records. This is a section about 17 coaches who have done just that and whom we honor in *Coaching to Win in Life.*

Derrick DeWitt and Dave Frantz changed the course of a community's vision of itself by giving an opportunity to Jake Porter, a mentally challenged player on Frantz's team, to score a touchdown on the game's final play.

Willie Davis, unable to finish his own education, was asked to step beyond his janitorial role in Louisiana to lead junior high school teams that had no coaches. He won titles and taught the children under his charge about the value of education by example.

James Ellis took a group of mostly African-American swimmers in an urban environment into pools and competitions that had traditionally been reserved for white youngsters. He built champions of color in a sport where there were few before.

Jack Aker, a seasoned Major League Baseball player, took his skills in the off-season to Native American reservations to teach the game to young people who would otherwise never have had the opportunity to play baseball. Aker, a Native American himself, was one of the few Native American players in the history of Major League Baseball.

Dorothy Gaters took a group of girls in Chicago and together they performed miracles. Many of her players, most from Chicago's most poverty stricken area, have gone on to play professionally in Europe and in the United States.

Bert Jenkins survived the brutality of the Nazi régime as an heroic American soldier who came home an amputee. Rising to new challenges, he became the winningest high school basketball coach in the history of the sport in Mississippi.

Until her own health concerns forced her to the sidelines, Marian Washington led Kansas University for three decades on the basketball court, producing a group of outstanding female scholar-athletes and championship teams.

Vivian Stringer led three different teams to the Final Four over the course of her extraordinary career. Like Washington, there are legions of women across America who value what Stringer did for them as individual human beings more than the games they won on the court under her leadership.

Carolyn Peck showed that age does not matter as the youthful basketball coach led Purdue to a National Championship. After guiding the Orlando Miracle to success in the WNBA, she rebuilt the University of Florida's women's team.

Mike Sheppard created a legacy as baseball coach at Seton Hall University for nearly three decades where he led his team to countless wins on the field and produced a group of men who still look back to their coach as teaching them the most valuable of life's lessons.

Rob Hamilton converted a group of under-achieving Boston youth and emphasized the importance of their being scholar-athletes and not just city athletes.

Bob Shannon led his East St. Louis high school team to championships in one of the most violent and poverty-stricken communities in the country. In the process he saved the lives of his players and as well as producing winning teams.

Ken Carter was made famous by the movie "Coach Carter" because he forced his basketball players to produce in the classroom before he allowed them back on the court. His fame with his players preceded the national recognition afforded him after the release of the movie.

Beverly Kearney, a highly decorated track and field athlete and coach, sent a powerful message to her athletes as she coached from a hospital bed, then with a walker, leading her women to the 2005 National Championship.

Jennifer Rizzotti, one of the best college basketball players from the University of Connecticut went on to play professionally and coach in college simultaneously.

Willie Stewart led the Anacostia High School football team against opponents on the field and in the streets. With Stewart's guidance, players learned of opportunities beyond the poverty, drugs and the violence of Washington, D.C.

Derek DeWitt, Dave Frantz and Jake Porter

by Drew Tyler and Brian Wright

The Boston Celtics captured the hearts and imagination of the public by winning 13 straight National Basketball Association World Championships. UCLA did it with their 88 game winning streak under head basketball coach John Wooden. Most recently, the great teams of Michael Jordan and company in Chicago won 72 of 82 regular season games, and the New England Patriots won 21 straight games during the 2003 and 2004 seasons. These athletic teams have one thing in common: they were beloved for winning. Yet the story of coaches Dave Frantz and Derek DeWitt who enabled Jake Porter to score a touchdown in the waning seconds of a game for Northwestern High in McDermott, Ohio inspires those who hear it as much as even the most diehard fans of the Celtics, Bruins, Bulls or Patriots.

At an early age, Jake Porter was diagnosed with Chromosomal Fragile-X, also known as Fragile-X syndrome. Fragile-X syndrome is a genetic condition that is identified by a weakness or break in the structure of X chromosomes. The result can be mental retardation or autism. It is the second leading cause of mental retardation and Down syndrome, and is responsible for one out of every 10 cases of autism. Fragile-X syndrome is found in 1 in 3,000 men and 1 in 4,000 women. One in 250 women carries the gene without knowing she is doing so.

Porter moved to McDermott, Ohio at the age of 13. McDermott is in Scioto County which is one of the few counties in which the school system integrates mentally challenged children beginning in elementary school. Porter was immediately accepted by his peers in school, and was a popular student and active participant in extra curricular activities. Porter was involved with the boy's football, basketball and track teams. While he didn't play in actual games, Porter never missed a football practice. Athletics, teamwork and the opportunity to socialize with his fellow classmates made it all worthwhile for him.

In the final game of his senior season, Porter's head football coach at Northwestern High, Dave Frantz, called the opposing coach from Waverly High to discuss letting Porter play in the game. Frantz and Waverly High's Coach Derek DeWitt agreed that if the game resulted in a lopsided score that Porter would get a chance to play. Heading into the game Northwestern High was a tremendous underdog and was felt by many to have little or no chance to beat Waverly.

True to form, Northwestern High trailed 42-0 with just five seconds remaining in the game. At this time Frantz decided it was time for Porter to play. Porter ran onto the field and entered the huddle for the instructions on the next play. The play called was "84-iso." It was designed for Porter to get the ball and run to the left side of the offensive line. The line set, the receivers set and the ball was snapped. The quarterback turned and handed the ball to Porter in the backfield and he took a couple of unsure steps. As he stopped and looked towards his team for direction he saw that the teammates and opposing players were pointing downfield towards the end zone. Porter began to run and didn't look back until reaching the end zone 50 yards away.

The reaction was overwhelming. People shouted and cheered while others could not help but shed a tear for this child's amazing delight and joy. Porter celebrated with his teammates in the end zone as if they had won the game. Had they? Well that depends on where you look. The score may not reflect a win for Northwestern but ask anyone in the stadium who was there that night and they will tell you that there was no loser.

Coach Dave Frantz gave a young athlete an opportunity to compete in a sport where most would not accept him. Coach Derek DeWitt gave up a shutout to honor the dedication of an opposing player and the humanity of an opposing coach. With his courageous and positive spirit, Jake Porter showed us all that sports can have an impact beyond wins and losses. Porter made it clear that through courage, positive attitudes and passion, anything is possible. Without ever making the game winning shot, or scoring the final touchdown to win the game, Porter has shown us all what it really means to be a winner.

Willie Davis

by Drew Tyler

The story of Willie Davis' life and work is remarkable. For years, Davis was employed at Arthur F. Smith Junior High School in Alexandria, Louisiana where he worked as a custodian. He was also a coach. Every day Davis mopped the halls, washed the windows, mowed the lawn and cleaned the toilets. And when his work was done, he grabbed his whistle and coached. Davis gave all he had to his work as a custodian and a coach, but more importantly he used the lessons he learned in life to inspire thousands of students.

Several years ago when there was a shortage of coaches at the school, the head girls' basketball coach asked Davis if he would help with the team. Davis was thrilled by the idea, but since he did not have a college degree and could not be certified to work as a coach, the school was unable to compensate Davis for his work. A couple of years later, Davis would be rewarded for his efforts by being named head coach of the boys' 7th and 8th grade basketball team and the head football coach. For his work as coach of the boys' teams, the school paid Davis an additional $900 a year. The money, however, did not matter to Davis. He just loved the game and working with youth.

On the court, Davis, or "Coach D" as his student-athletes preferred to call him, led Arthur F. Smith to three District titles in six years. Coach D even guided the team to a 34-game winning streak on his way to a 101-21 career record. More importantly, off the court Davis made sure his students got the education he never had the opportunity to complete. In his high school days, Davis' father passed away forcing Davis to drop his basketball career in order to work and support his family. Davis was able to graduate from high school, but decided to stay in Alexandria to continue supporting his family. He worked tirelessly in a variety of cleaning jobs before settling down at Arthur F. Smith Junior High School.

There are several reasons why Davis has been so successful. The first in Davis' mind is his love for his three children. He says that it is his understanding of them that has helped him to become a father figure to many of his athletes.

Davis' model for success is really quite simple: a belief in God first, books second and basketball third. Davis' starters were known for their straight A report cards. By using lessons from his own life and constantly setting a positive example for his student-athletes, Davis transformed his life from custodian to educator. Davis taught his student-athletes values and discipline, preached the importance of education, and in the end translated all the positive messages into a winning basketball program for Arthur. F. Smith Junior High School.

Davis became a celebrity around Alexandria. He has been featured in *Sports Illustrated* and on HBO's Real Sports with Bryant Gumbel. Hollywood has a movie in development based on Davis' life that will star John Cusack and Halle Berry. Actor-rapper Ice Cube will play the role of "Coach D."

The national exposure Davis received for his impact at Arthur F. Smith caught the attention of a philanthropist who was inspired to anonymously donate funds for much-needed athletic equipment for the school. The donor also offered to pay for Davis to attend college. In his first online course at Northwestern State University where he is studying education, Davis earned a B. Davis is determined to earn his degree so that he can become a certified teacher and coach.

In 2002, Davis left Arthur F. Smith for a position with the Alexandria Recreational Department. Coaching remains his passion. Students miss the man they say that everyone wanted to be around because he was an inspiration. Davis believes by going to college and reaching for his dream, he can still serve his students. Most of all, Davis was known for the interest he took in each student and the time he spent getting to know everyone. Davis made sure he got to know everyone at Arthur F. Smith Junior High School by standing in front of the school and welcoming the students and teachers every morning. Willie Davis' journey has been nothing short of remarkable. And perhaps the most remarkable thing about it is that for him it has really just begun.

James Ellis

by Drew Tyler

Swimming has traditionally been a sport in upper-class communities, learned in pools that are costly to build and accessible only in private clubs that are expensive to join. Introducing swimming to minorities has been a great challenge to the swimming world, but it is a challenge to which James Ellis has responded. For more than two decades, Ellis has been on a mission to prove that African-American swimmers can not only make it to the top of the swimming world, but that premier swimming talent can be discovered and developed from an inner-city program such as the one he has worked diligently to grow.

In an effort to promote swimming to African-American children, Ellis has been running an inner-city swim program for over 30 years in Philadelphia. An African-American swimmer from Pittsburgh, Ellis began teaching swimming to young athletes while attending college just outside of Philadelphia. As a young coach, Ellis' main goal was to teach discipline to young African-American males. After being put in charge of a new indoor swim facility built by the city, Ellis worked to train young swimmers so that they could compete against the best competition in the country.

Throughout his years of coaching at the Philadelphia Department of Recreation (PDR) swimming facility, Ellis has produced countless school champions. He has seen his swimmers earn national and international rankings and win at major meets such as the Junior Olympics and Junior Nationals. His swimmers have set national age group records, Junior National records, earned National Team selections and participated in the Olympic Trials.

Ellis has made a great contribution to Philadelphia. Over the years, a community of families has formed that crosses social, economic and cultural boundaries. Ellis' athletes cross race, gender and economic lines, forming one of the most diverse teams in all of youth sport. Furthermore, Ellis has played a vital role in the development of a new Minority Outreach Swim Camp held annually at the Olympic Training Center in Colorado Springs. He helped many young swimmers earn college scholarships and has also served as a math teacher in the Philadelphia School District.

In his quest to teach African-American children to swim competitively, Ellis has faced an uphill battle. USA Swimming membership statistics demonstrate that swimming is currently a predominately white sport. Asians make up approximately four percent of those participating in competitive swimming, while African-Americans, Hispanics and Native Americans each account for less than two percent of our nation's swimmers. Recognizing these statistics, Ellis made it his life's mission to change the numbers.

One of the most famous alumni of Ellis' swimming program has been Olympic hopeful Michael Norment. A graduate of the University of Georgia, Norment is a product of the PDR swimming program and in 2000 nearly became the first African-American to represent the United States in Olympic Swimming. Norment's path to stardom began at the age of 12 when his father, a college professor, took a job at Temple University and moved to Philadelphia. Not long after, Norment's father took him to the PDR swim club to take swim lessons from Ellis. Under Ellis' guidance, Norment quickly developed into a swimming champion. Just one year after his first lesson with Ellis, Norment competed in the Black History Swim Meet against swimmers from across the nation. Norment impressed everyone by capturing first place in two events.

In his second year of swimming with the PDR swim club, Norment helped the Club to a highly improbable record-setting performance at the Junior Nationals. After Norment captured the 200-yard breaststroke title, the PDR medley relay team took first place and Jason Webb, another African-American on the PDR club, won the 200-yard backstroke. Impressively, all three victories came in record-setting times. Ellis had done something that no one in the swimming community considered possible. An African-American coach had taken African-American swimmers from the inner-city and won junior national titles.

After his early success, Norment was hooked. He would soon go on to swim at Central High School in Philadelphia and earn a swimming scholarship to the University of Georgia where he would become one of the nation's elite collegiate swimmers. Among his many swimming accomplishments, Norment became just the second African-American to represent the United States in the Pan Pacific Swim Meet, was a member of the National "A" team, took second place in the NCAA Division I 100 yard breaststroke and was named to the All-American Academic team.

Over his 30 years of coaching swimmers in the inner-city, Ellis has seen his program grow in ways he never expected. After his success at the Junior Nationals, the PDR swim club began to garner national recognition. As a result, Ellis noticed that the PDR swim program was no longer just a swim club for African-American kids. Rather, the notoriety of the program had begun to attract swimmers of all races and economic backgrounds. A majority of his swimmers were still African-American, but over time the program had grown to be very diverse. Despite being an inner-city club in north Philadelphia, Ellis' reputation began to attract swimmers from other neighborhoods. Ellis not only found a way to introduce swimming to inner-city minority children, but he uncovered a unique opportunity for young swimmers from different social and economic backgrounds to interact and learn from one another. James Ellis' model has not only developed elite swimming talent, but has gone great lengths to increase diversity in the competitive swimming community. It will only be a matter of time before Ellis shocks the world once again and develops his first United States swim team Olympian.

Jack Aker

by Drew Tyler

For former major leaguer Jack Aker, no spring is complete without a two week excursion to the most desolate reaches of Arizona and New Mexico. Aker's annual trip takes him to Native American reservations in such places as Shiprock, New Mexico and Tuba City, Arizona. It seems that such barren lands would be an odd place for a man like Aker to spend vacation time. After all, Aker was twice named League Manager of the Year for minor league affiliates of the Mets and Indians and in the 1960's and 70's was recognized as one of Major League Baseball's top relief pitchers. Many former ballplayers would most likely prefer a vacation to a tropical paradise, but Aker's commitment to coaching the game of baseball never ceases to bring him back to the desert.

In his 11 years of playing major league baseball, Aker compiled 123 saves and a 3.28 lifetime ERA with the A's, Pilots, Cubs, Yankees, Mets and Braves. During Aker's most dominant major league season, he went 8-4, with a 1.99 ERA and had 32 saves for the Kansas City Athletics. Aker had become a force at the end of the bullpen and was recognized as the American League's "Fireman of the Year."

As a manager for minor league affiliates of the Mets and Indians, Aker was recognized for his excellence as a hitting, pitching and fielding instructor. Throughout his career Aker developed hundreds of professional ballplayers and earned a reputation as one of the most respected mentors in the game.

Aker no longer plays or coaches in professional baseball, but he continues to share his vast baseball knowledge with aspiring young ballplayers around the nation. Founder of Jack Aker Baseball, Inc.,

Aker has created camps, clinics and private instruction opportunities for individuals, teams and leagues throughout the United States. Aker's clinics take place all over the country and can run from two hours to an entire week in length. Clinics are offered to players of all ages and can specialize in hitting, pitching or even coaching.

Ever since his retirement from baseball, Aker has found a great deal of success running clinics. For over 10 years, however, Aker has set aside time that he commits to teaching the game of baseball to Native American children on remote reservations of the Southwest. Since 1994, Aker, who is of Native American descent, has used a grant from the National Indian Youth Leadership Project to spend two weeks each spring working with Native American children who reside on Navajo, Hopi and Zuni Reservations. He visits remote areas that have little or no organized athletics, an absence of male role models and few adults willing to coach sports. Known for high amounts of drug and alcohol abuse and for having teen suicide rates three times greater than the national average, Aker has used baseball to help change the lives of hundreds of Native American children. Not only has Aker taken on the challenge of teaching baseball to Native American children by holding free baseball clinics, he also talks with them about the importance of staying in school and avoiding drugs and alcohol. Aker's baseball clinics offer an alternative to drugs and alcohol, and give the children goals and reasons to stay in school.

During Aker's two weeks in New Mexico and Arizona, he typically works with approximately 400 Native American boys and girls of all ages. Most of the children do not own a glove or have any baseball equipment. In fact, many of the children lack a basic set of baseball skills, but Aker continues to be amazed by the toughness the children demonstrate on the field. On many of the reservations, the children play on practice fields covered with rocks and clay, there are no umpires and the children do not wear uniforms. It is never an easy task for Aker, but despite the lack of amenities, the children and Aker play on. At the end of each camp, Aker gives each participating child a baseball in hopes that they will continue to play after he is gone.

On and off the baseball field, Jack Aker is a skilled and accomplished teacher, and by teaching young Native Americans, so many of whom come from lives without hope or promise, Aker's contribution is not just noteworthy, it is tremendously important.

Dorothy Gaters

by Drew Tyler

In 1974, Dorothy Gaters assumed the precarious position as head coach of John Marshall Metropolitan High School's girl's basketball program. Located in one of the most poverty stricken areas on Chicago's west side, Gaters was chosen to lead the Marshall program because nobody else would take the job. Despite having no prior coaching experience, Gaters became consumed by the project of developing a strong basketball program at Marshall and in time would become a legendary coach throughout the state.

Since Gaters had never coached the game of basketball, she gathered coaching tips by picking the minds of local coaches, such as the late John McLendon, who became the first African-American coach elected to the Basketball Hall of Fame, by listening to television commentators, and watching as many games as possible in person and on television. In time, the tips would pay-off and Gaters would achieve levels of success far beyond anyone's expectations.

After completing her 30th season as Marshall's head coach in 2004, Gaters had compiled an all-time record of 793-89. Furthermore, Gaters had guided Marshall to seven state championships in 10 title games, 16 final four runs and 22 quarterfinal appearances. Gaters' incredible statistics rank her as the winningest coach in Illinois high school girl's basketball history and among the best nationwide.

For Gaters, coaching and teaching at Marshall has become a life-long commitment. Having graduated from Marshall in the 1960's, Gaters remembers a time when the West Side neighborhood thrived with banks, stores and homes. During the late 1960's, however, the area was devastated by riots following Martin Luther King Jr.'s assassination and has never recovered.

Coaching in a poverty-stricken area has provided many challenges for Gaters. Faced with the task of proving that an inner-city program could compete with the best in the state, Gaters has had to deal with losing players to teenage pregnancy and because so many lack the requisite family infrastructure that provides stability or order. Gaters has learned to use basketball as a tool to foster academic achievement. Impressively, Gaters has graduated 90 percent of her players from a high school in which 20 percent of the regular student body drops out.

In the mid-1990's, college programs which had previously overlooked Gaters finally started to pursue her coaching expertise. Many coaches would have jumped at the opportunity to leave the West Side, but not Gaters. Gaters' commitment to Marshall Metropolitan High School and her family was more important to her than the opportunity to coach at the collegiate level.

In the 1994-95 season, Gaters' team went 18-10. There was not a season before and has not been a season since that the Marshall girl's basketball team has done worse. In fact, they have not lost more than six games in any other season. But to Gaters, the numbers, stats and records don't matter. It is the effort she gets from her girls on and off the court. Gaters stresses the importance of her players' effort in the classroom, in the community, in practice and in games. While Gaters is thrilled with the program she has built and all that she has learned in the process, it is most important to her that the program builds healthy, well-rounded girls who contribute positively to their community and hold high regard for their educations.

After coaching her team to a 31-1 record and a state championship in 1999, Gaters was nationally recognized as Coach of the Year by the Women's Basketball Coaches Association. In 2000, Gaters was rewarded for her accomplishments and dedication to the game of basketball when she was elected to the Women's Basketball Hall of Fame. Dorothy Gaters is not a great basketball coach through her love for the sport alone, but also for her genuine care and concern for her players.

Bert Jenkins

by Drew Tyler

After experiencing a debilitating and life-altering injury, Bert Jenkins could have given up on his life-long aspirations. Jenkins, however, refused to let any setbacks prevent him from pursuing his dreams. Jenkins' story is one of heroism, a refusal to give up and hard work to overcome the obstacles he faced. His inspirational experiences serve as a reminder to all that with hard-work, grit and determination, there is no obstacle that is too large to be conquered.

Jenkins' journey began as a young American soldier fighting in World War II. Drafted at the age of 19 while a student at Mississippi State University, Jenkins was immediately shipped out for training in England and soon found himself on the Utah Beach of Normandy only days following the famous "D-Day" attacks. Jenkins' outfit, the 313th infantry regiment of the 79th division, would immediately move inland and dig foxholes to prepare for an air attack by the Germans. It was only Jenkins' first night on shore, but he would quickly be thrust into the center of battle and learn the true meaning of courage as his outfit was barraged by German bombs and shrapnel falling from the sky.

Over the next 136 days, the 313th infantry regiment fought without rest. The continuing battles which seemed to go on forever earned every soldier in Jenkins' outfit a promotion. Jenkins was promoted from buck private to private first class. Jenkins recalls the valor of his fellow soldiers and the lessons he learned from his time on the front line. Unfortunately, Jenkins' service in the United States Army would soon come to a tragic end at the infamous Battle of the Bulge.

Fighting alongside his comrades, Jenkins would fall at the Battle of the Bulge after taking an enemy bullet in the leg. Jenkins did not know that the bullet would change his life forever. After dragging himself into a ditch to gain cover from enemy gunfire, Jenkins passed out from pain and blood loss. The next day, a weak and tired Jenkins was captured by German troops and was taken to a prisoner of war camp. Upon his arrival at the POW camp, Jenkins was taken into surgery, where despite his protests, a German doctor performed a crude amputation of his injured leg.

At the time of the amputation, a young Jenkins feared that having only one leg would prevent him from ever being able to realize his dream of becoming a successful basketball coach. Over time, however, it has appeared that the handicap has been anything but a disability. Jenkins has lived a completely normal life and has used the small setback as further motivation to drive him toward his dreams. Many men in Jenkins' situation would have suffered a broken spirit, but Jenkins refused to let the injury get the best of him and went on to live an exceptional life.

After returning from World War II, Jenkins began to develop a reputation as an elite high school basketball coach throughout the state of Mississippi. Despite having only one leg, Jenkins manned the sidelines of Gulfport High School's boy's basketball team for over three decades and led them to unprecedented success. Over his career at Gulfport, Jenkins guided his teams to seven state championships, 14 conference titles and an overall record of 876 victories to just 180 defeats. The 876 victories made Jenkins the all-time winningest high school basketball coach in the state of Mississippi. In 1989, he was recognized as the National High School Coach of the Year by the NCAA. Ten years later, Jenkins was honored once again when he was inducted into the Mississippi Sports Hall of Fame.

Throughout his legendary career on the basketball court, Jenkins worked hard to lead his players to championships, but also prided himself in his ability to guide young boys toward manhood. Jenkins was a true leader of the young men of Gulfport High School. Playing for Jenkins was not easy, but in the end the boys learned lessons that would stick with them throughout the rest of their lives. In addition to motivating hundreds of young men on the basketball court, Jenkins also helped to educate hundreds of Gulfport students in the classroom as an English and Physical Education teacher. Jenkins took on responsibilities that are often shared by several men, and he did it all on just one leg.

One of the most famous Gulfport High School basketball products was former Louisiana State University and NBA star, Chris Jackson. At Gulfport, Jenkins helped to develop Jackson into one of the greatest high school basketball players in the nation. Jackson was twice named

Mississippi Player of the Year and during one amazing stretch converted a record-setting 283 consecutive free throws. Coach Jenkins had a practice policy which required all his players to shoot free throws until they missed, but with Jackson on the team the policy was forced to be revised since he didn't want his players staying in the gym all night.

Following his Gulfport career, Jackson went on to become a collegiate star as a freshman at LSU. In just his third collegiate game, Jackson scored 48 points against Louisiana Tech and in his fifth game he set an NCAA freshman record with 53 points against the University of Florida. Former Georgia coach Hugh Durham compared Jackson's impact on collegiate basketball to the impact Herschel Walker made on football as a freshman. Jackson was a brilliant athlete, but without the guidance and coaching excellence of Jenkins he may have never experienced the amount of early success that he did at LSU.

Throughout his life, Bert Jenkins experienced some of the greatest setbacks imaginable, but there was nothing that could prevent him from following his dreams and becoming a top basketball coach. As a war hero and respected educator, Jenkins served as a leader and role model to thousands of Gulfport High School students. He proudly worked the sidelines of the basketball court for over three decades and will forever be remembered as a legend in Mississippi sports history.

Marian Washington

by Drew Tyler

In January 2004, health concerns forced Marian Washington to retire as head coach of the University of Kansas Lady Jayhawks women's basketball program after 31 seasons. The retirement came as a shock to the Kansas basketball community. For 31 years, Washington had devoted herself to the University of Kansas and become a legend in a tradition-rich Kansas basketball history.

Coach Washington's legendary status stems from her considerable contributions on and off the basketball court. On the court, Washington's playing career began at West Chester State University in Pennsylvania. During her career at West Chester, Washington was a two-time AAU All-American and helped guide her team to a women's basketball national title. The Golden Rams national title was the first ever in West Chester State women's basketball.

Just four years after her playing career ended, Washington was named head women's basketball coach at Kansas in 1974. As a coach, Washington guided the Lady Jayhawks to a 560-363 record over 31 seasons. During the stretch, the Lady Jayhawks reached 20 wins 17 times, recorded seven Big 12 titles and six conference tournament championships. Washington also achieved postseason success with 11 NCAA tournament appearances, including two trips to the Sweet Sixteen. Her accomplishments led to three conference Coach of the Year awards.

As a coach, Washington also had an incredible grasp of her position and served as a role model to her student-athletes. According to Washington, her life's mission has been to make a difference. Specifically, Washington strives to make a difference in the lives of youth. Using athletics as an arena to develop strong character and athletic talent, Washington has worked diligently to achieve her goals.

Along the way, Washington served in a variety of roles while at the University of Kansas. She served on the national officiating committee, the Kodak All-American selection committee and the Women's basketball Coaches Association board of directors. Additionally, she has achieved many career distinctions. Most notably, Washington served as the first and only Director of Women's Athletics at the University of Kansas from 1974-1979. During her stint in the position, Washington helped grow Kansas' athletic program to new heights. Furthermore, she was the first African-American to ever serve on the coaching staff for an Olympic women's basketball team and was the first African-American woman to coach the U.S. team in international competition.

Throughout her career, Washington fearlessly worked to improve women's athletics and has been credited for creating many groundbreaking opportunities for female athletes. Breaking barriers has led to many lifetime achievement awards for Washington. On two separate occasions, the Black Coaches Association (BCA) named Washington Coach of the Year and in 2003 honored Washington with a Lifetime Achievement Award. She was the first female to serve as president of the BCA and the first person to be elected a second term. After her retirement in 2004, Marian Washington received her much deserved national recognition when she was elected into the Women's Basketball Hall of Fame.

C. Vivian Stringer

by Drew Tyler

C. Vivian Stringer made history when she became the first coach in men's or women's college basketball to lead three different universities to the NCAA Final Four. Known as the "master builder" of collegiate basketball programs, Stringer guided Cheyney University in 1982, the University of Iowa in 1993, and Rutgers University in 2000 to women's basketball highest point of national prominence. During her magnificent run, Stringer has been a highly touted leader and role model to her players, as well as a respected innovator and teacher of the game.

2005-2006 is Stringers 34th season as a head coach in women's collegiate basketball. Through the 2004-05 season, Stringer compiled an overall record of 723-246 (.746). In 2004, after a 68-48 victory over Princeton, Stringer became just the fourth women's coach to reach 700 career Division I victories. Along with her three Final Four appearances, Stringer has also led teams to 18 NCAA Tournament appearances, including seven regional finals.

Stringer's career began at Cheyney University, a small, historically-black school located outside of Philadelphia. In 1982, when the NCAA sponsored the first-ever women's basketball national championship game, Stringer put the Cheyney Wolves in the national spotlight by leading them on a "Cinderella" run to the national title game. Despite a loss to Louisiana Tech in the championship, Cheyney gained immense popularity, playing in front of packed houses every night.

After 11 seasons at Cheyney, Stringer made a move up to the Big 10 Conference when she accepted the head coaching position at the University of Iowa where she immediately turned the program into one of national prominence. The Hawkeyes were able to gain an unprecedented amount of popularity and became the first women's basketball team to ever record an advanced sellout. After leading Iowa to the Final Four, Stringer became the first coach to ever lead two different schools to the national semifinals.

Prior to the 2005-06 season, she had spent ten seasons transforming Rutgers into a national powerhouse. Under Stringer, Rutgers' success resulted from her aggressive and intense defensive strategy. In 2000, when Stringer guided the Scarlet Knights to the Final Four, opponents averaged just 54.5 points per game, the fourth-best average in the nation. In 2004-05, Stringer's tenacious defense allowed just 51.3 ppg, the second-best mark nationwide.

In addition to her coaching, Stringer has played an active role in the community wherever she has coached. Stringer believes in creating a program with a family feel and has actively sought to create this atmosphere by providing basketball camps for kids, player visits to local hospitals and educational programs for area youth. Stringer teaches her players to become quality citizens and role models as well as talented student-athletes

In 2003, *Sports Illustrated* named Stringer one of the "101 Most Influential Minorities in Sports." Also a recipient of the Black Coaches Association's Lifetime Achievement Award in 2004, Stringer has served as an assistant coach for the USA Olympic women's basketball team in addition to her duties as a collegiate head coach. Throughout her distinguished career, Stringer has received numerous awards and recognitions for her contributions to women's basketball. Stringer has been named National Coach of the Year three times and in 2001 was selected into the Women's Basketball Hall of Fame. When looking back on her Hall of Fame career, Stringer's success can be summed up by the number three. She coached three programs, led them to three Final Fours, earned three Coach of the Year awards, and spent three decades as one of the leading voices for equality and change in women's collegiate basketball.[1]

[1] C.Vivian Stringer Bio. Scarlet Knights Women's Basketball. [January 2005; December 14, 2005] http://scarletknights.com/basketball-women/coaches/stringer.htm

Carolyn Peck

by Drew Tyler

In her young coaching career, Carolyn Peck has achieved a lifetime of success. Having served as head coach for the Purdue Boilermakers, Florida Gators and Orlando Miracle of the WNBA, Peck's outstanding resume serves as a testament to her incredible coaching ability and winning attitude.

Peck's unique attitude on the court has led to her success. Preaching the importance of having fun on the court, Peck insists that her players remain enthusiastic about the game and love every minute they spend playing basketball as much as she enjoys coaching basketball.

Peck's basketball career began with her high school playing days in Jefferson City, Tennessee where she was named Tennessee's Miss Basketball and a two-time all American at Jefferson County High School. Following high school, Peck went on to play at Vanderbilt University from 1985-1988 where she earned a B.A. in communications. At Vanderbilt, Peck averaged 10.6 points and 5.8 rebounds with 180 career blocked shots. Peck was named team captain her junior and senior years and went on to play a brief professional career for the Nippondenso Corporation in Japan from 1991 to 1993.

Following her successful playing career, Peck became an assistant coach at three of the most highly respected programs in women's collegiate basketball. Peck began her coaching career at the University of Tennessee where she served as an assistant for legendary women's basketball coach Pat Summitt. Following two seasons at Tennessee, Peck spent one season at the University of Kentucky before moving on to Purdue University. As an assistant in 1996-97, Peck helped guide the boilermakers to a share of the Big Ten Championship and a run to the second round of the NCAA tournament.

After the season, Peck would be named the new Purdue head coach after former coach Nell Fortner decided to leave the team to become head coach of the USA National Team that competed in the 2000 Olympics. Peck spent just two seasons as Purdue's head coach, but during her time she achieved remarkable success. In her first season, Peck led the Boilermakers to a 23-10 record and a NCAA Tournament "Elite Eight" appearance. The season marked just the second 20-win season in Purdue history, and the "Elite Eight" appearance was just the third ever by a first-year head coach. As an encore to her remarkable first season, Peck achieved the unimaginable by guiding Purdue to a 34-1 record and the 1999 NCAA Women's Basketball National Championship. The amazing run led to National Coach of the Year honors by the Associated Press and the Women's Basketball Coaches Association as well as Big Ten Coach of the Year recognition. Over her two seasons as head coach at Purdue, her cumulative record was 57-11 (.838 winning percentage) with a 9-1 NCAA Tournament record.

Her instrumental role in several winning collegiate programs quickly caught the attention of the WNBA. Following Purdue's National Championship run, Peck left to become General Manager and Head Coach of the Orlando Miracle in 1999. At the youthful age of 32 and with only two seasons of coaching experience, the hire came as a surprise to many. Peck, however, immediately proved to her critics that she was the right person for the job. In the Orlando Miracle's inaugural season, Peck guided the team to a second place tie in the Eastern Conference.

After a successful run in the WNBA, Peck headed back to collegiate basketball when she accepted the head coaching position at the University of Florida in 2002. Peck's career at Florida got off to a rocky start when the Gators posted a 9-19 record in her first season. In her second year, however, Peck led the Gators to the greatest single season turnaround in school history when the team posted a 19-11 record and earned a bid into the NCAA Tournament. During her three years at Florida, Peck not only turned around the basketball program, but helped to mold her players into model student-athletes. Her players have achieved 20 Southeastern Conference Academic Honor Roll accolades, the greatest three-year total in school history.

Already recognized as one of the greatest coaches in women's collegiate basketball, the future of the Florida Gator program is filled with promise for many years to come. In an age where many coaches gain immediate success by bending the rules, Peck has developed a program of great integrity and has shown that with a positive attitude and a love for the game, anything is possible. Peck's athletes are famous for achieving great success on the basketball court and are highly respected for their achievements in the classroom. Peck will take the Gators to new heights because she is not just a gifted coach, but an inspiring leader and outstanding role model for young student-athletes.

Mike Sheppard

by Drew Tyler

Mike Sheppard's journey has taken him down many winding roads, but Seton Hall baseball has always been in his blood. From his strict Catholic school upbringing to his time spent serving in the Marine Corps, Sheppard developed a commitment to hard work that would one day help him to achieve a remarkable amount of success in coaching. As a child, Sheppard grew up just a few blocks away from Seton Hall where he would sneak into Seton Hall baseball games as a kid. Developing into a fine young ballplayer himself, Sheppard played at Seton Hall Prep in high school before moving on to Seton Hall University under coach Owen T. Carroll, the man who Sheppard would one day succeed as coach.

Sheppard's journey took him all the way from a talented young player, to an up-and-coming assistant coach, to one of the most well-respected coaches in all of collegiate baseball. Sheppard's run at Seton Hall was a lifelong journey which would culminate in his recognition as the greatest baseball coach in Seton Hall history. After notching 998 career victories, which ranked 29th all-time among Division I coaches at the time of his retirement, recording 28 winning seasons, guiding Seton Hall to two College World Series appearances, producing 20 future major leaguers, and earning three Big East Coach of the Year awards, Sheppard's name will always be synonymous with Seton Hall baseball.

Sheppard's story, however, is more than just a baseball tale. It is a story of love and courage, and most importantly, a story of dedication to putting one's heart into one's work and doing a job the way it is supposed to be done. At the age of 62, Sheppard suffered a debilitating stroke which many feared would end his illustrious career at Seton Hall. Leaving

Sheppard with a separated left shoulder, a paralyzed left side and slurred speech, returning to the Seton Hall bench seemed highly improbable. But because of his unwavering dedication to his players, Sheppard fought his way back to the Seton Hall dugout.

Sheppard wore two hats throughout his career: one as head coach of the Seton Hall baseball team and another as an associate professor of education. At times it was difficult for Sheppard, but his refusal to turn his back on the Seton Hall program helped to pull him through his hard times. Sheppard had been declared completely recovered by his doctors, but he continues to go to rehab to increase strength on his left side while serving as baseball coach and teaching a full course-load.

For the first time in his career, Sheppard had gained a new perspective on his life and in his role as Seton Hall's baseball coach. When asked by *The Record* about his return "I can remember the first time I really enjoyed it again, it was our first series at Connecticut," said Sheppard. "It was a beautiful weekend, the sky was blue, the grass green. We were losing by three. I turned to the umpire and said 'Isn't this great? He said 'You're losing.' And I said, 'I'm not losing, I'm just happy to be here.'"[1]

Known for his demanding personality, Sheppard's new perspective on life came as quite the surprise to many umpires. As a young manager Sheppard wasn't afraid to put on a show for the fans by getting into an umpire's face. After the stroke, however, Sheppard changed his approach to the game. He continued to coach first base, but would tire towards the end of games. He could no longer swing the fungo bat because of his left shoulder, and he was unable to jog onto the field with the team without losing his balance. The fire still burned in Sheppard's eyes, but for the most part he made it a point to remain reserved while on the bench. Sheppard may not have felt completely like himself, but he was back in baseball and more importantly back into coaching the game he loved.

As a coach, Sheppard masterfully taught his players the art of hitting and pitching, but more importantly, he taught them discipline. Among the hundreds of young men Sheppard coached throughout his career were several future big league stars including Craig Biggio, Matt Morris and Mo Vaughn. "I went in a boy and came out a man because of Shep," says Biggio, now second baseman of the Houston Astros. "When I was there (1985-87), I didn't understand him like I understand him now. When you're 18 years old and go away from home, you think you know everything. You know nothing. In college you need somebody to step on your toes once in a while. Otherwise, you'll get away with murder."[2]

One of the most famous Seton Hall players under Sheppard was former Boston Red Sox All-Star first baseman, Mo Vaughn. Today, Vaughn still looks up to his old coach and credits Sheppard for teaching him the correct way to play the game of baseball. In his early playing days at Seton Hall, however, even Vaughn felt Sheppard's wrath. As a youngster on the team, Sheppard once forced Vaughn to take a taxi to a game at Villanova after arriving late for the team bus. Sheppard prided himself in teaching his players discipline. As hotheaded young athletes, many of Sheppard's players failed to understand him while at the University, but they learned lessons that proved valuable long after their Seton Hall careers were over.

To this day, Vaughn has never forgotten the impact Sheppard had on his life. While at Seton Hall, Sheppard made Vaughn promise that if he ever made it to the big leagues that he would wear No. 42, the number made famous by Jackie Robinson. As fate would have it, Vaughn would make it to the majors and he wouldn't forget his promise. "I tell people that I'm a blessed man," Sheppard says. "I love to come to work every day and teach and coach. I'm happy being a success, but I've been blessed with good ballplayers."[3]

Sheppard also stressed the value of education to his players. Although NCAA rules required student-athletes to obtain a 2.0 GPA by their senior year, Sheppard instituted a standard 2.5 GPA to be maintained throughout his players' careers. Sheppard worked off the court to help his student-athletes meet his demands. He made a two hour study hall mandatory every night to his freshmen, sophomores and any student under a 2.5 GPA. Sheppard also established a "Monitoring System of Athletes" through which Seton Hall faculty members issued monthly reports on the baseball team's performance in the classroom, attendance and grades. Sheppard's Monitoring System became a model for all sports programs at the University.

After Mike Sheppard's retirement following the 2003 season, Seton Hall decided to keep the baseball program under the Sheppard command by promoting Mike's son to head coach. Having spent seven seasons as a Seton Hall assistant coach and two as associate head coach, Rob Sheppard was the perfect successor to his legendary father. Previously, Rob had limited head coaching experience, but he did serve as interim head coach while his father was recovering from triple bypass heart surgery during the 2001 season. The 2001 season got off to a slow start under the younger Sheppard, but after rallying the Pirates to a 14-4-1 record in April, the season ended with the first Seton Hall conference championship since 1987. The accomplishment earned him recognition from the New Jersey Collegiate Baseball Association as Division I Coach of the Year and made it clear that the Seton Hall program would remain in the hands of the Sheppard family.

[1] Sullivan, Tara. "Seton Hall's Good Sheppard" *The Record*, May 10, 1998.
[2] ibid, pp.
[3] Schutta, Gregory. "Hall's Sheppard hits milestone" *The Record*, March 26, 1997.

Robert Hamilton

by Stacy Martin

Robert Hamilton's experience on the basketball court as a student-athlete inspired him to return to the game, this time on the sideline. He initiated a call to action for parents, teachers, coaches and students to get involved in an athlete's life. His hope is for those athletes to develop into scholars largely due to the personal interest that someone takes in them. In the inner-city of Boston, too many children do not feel that anyone cares about them. It was a struggle to survive, let alone succeed, at least until Rob Hamilton came to town. He issued a challenge to those groups so vitally important to a young person's success with the Coaches Academic Leadership League, also known as CALL.

The Leadership League was organized around what Hamilton called the Academic Guardian program, which named a teacher at the school to be responsible for the student-athlete's academic welfare. This component is essential to classroom achievement because it eliminated the blame game that teachers and coaches often play over the responsibility of a player's grades. The academic guardian was in charge of monitoring all of the athlete's class work through frequent progress reports. The accountability and ownership that each instructor felt about his or her student-athlete created a bond that existed on and off the court. Academic guardians soon became fixtures in the bleachers at home games. The student-athletes finally received the attention and caring devotion that some of them had been lacking. CALL prompted parents to become more involved in their children's lives as well, and, of course, the coach was calling plays on and off the court to show his commitment to his team. The League was a way to round out the responsibility of teachers to the development of a young mind.

Hamilton was an assistant basketball coach at Brandeis University shortly after graduating from Middlebury College, but then he moved to the frontlines of tomorrow, the high school arena. He began teaching and coaching at Umana Technical High School, now Umana Middle School, in the inner city of East Boston. He followed that with a coaching stint at Charlestown High School where he also implemented CALL. It involved all of the same elements of guardians, involvement and academic progress reports. Charlestown was laying a foundation then for the basketball powerhouse that they are today. Often in high schools limited resources cause bickering among athletic teams, especially between the boys and girls basketball teams over court time. At Charlestown, there was harmony. Hamilton let the girls' team practice first, while his boys' team went to the library for study hall. In this way he could guarantee completed course work, because he was watching. The team was successful and in pursuit of the State Championship.

Hamilton is a reserved and unassuming man, but his voice carries far beyond gymnasiums. He answered his call to leadership as the president of the Boston High School Basketball Coaches Association. Hamilton utilized the resources he had available to establish Project LEAD, which was an outgrowth of CALL that focused on the key principle of class attendance. The first hurdle is usually getting young adults to actually be present in class, before they can begin to learn. He negotiated a deal with Converse to provide a pair of sneakers for each student-athlete in the city of Boston who met the 90 percent class attendance requirement. Project LEAD opened doors for children without many other opportunities by simply asking them to enter a classroom.

Hamilton knew that he could reach children through basketball, but an official school season was much too short. He created and directed an AAU basketball league called Boston Prep. It wasn't the typical AAU league concerned with skill, talent, and, of course, winning. Boston Prep had a coach as well as an MIT student who worked with the student-athletes. Hamilton negotiated an agreement with a Kaplan Learning Center for an MIT student to teach SAT prep courses to his team. Boston Prep had skill, talent and they were winners in the classroom and on the court.

Hamilton received the Giant Steps Award as a coach in 1988, just seven years after his college graduation. According to him, it changed his life. The recognition that came from the award broadened his horizons as he realized how much more he could accomplish in the world. The personal recognition of goals set Hamilton on a new path in sports, one that moved him further from the game and into the boardroom. His creative thinking and intimate knowledge of the sport landed him a job as the Marketing Director of Reebok Basketball. His dedication and hard work quickly produced dividends for him. He became solely responsible for a young Shaquille O'Neal from Louisiana State University, escorting the present NBA superpower around the globe on world tours and beginning to cultivate Shaquille's brand and image. His executive status sent him on business trips to factories in the Pacific as well. While traveling the world, Hamilton learned a great deal about the world. The breadth of knowledge that he held now was invaluable, but he missed not being in direct contact with the children anymore.

He quenched the thirst for direct connection to the student-athletes by accepting the coaching position at Massachusetts College of Liberal Arts, a small Division III school. At some point in everyone's life they seem to return to where they started. When they get there they can judge where they have been and where they are going. Hamilton was born in the Berkshires near North Adams, where MCLA is located, so for him it was a homecoming. Hamilton instituted the CALL program there, too. He mandated study halls and academic progress from his student-athletes and implemented aggressive tracking systems to keep them on course for graduation. During this time a number of the NCAA's member institutions had violated its rules. MCLA, however, was certainly not on its list. In fact, it was setting a positive example for other schools. Athletes deserve ethical treatment in regard to their personal welfare. They should not be abused by the system as a means to a win. Hamilton and his Trailblazers had a 100 percent graduation rate and they were blazing a trail through academics.

Hamilton believes that the true reflection of a man's success is in his home. His son, Onaje is a reflection of his father's triumphs in the greatest possible way. Hamilton executed the CALL and LEAD programs to get his student-athletes scholarships to college, and his son lived those programs at home and at school. Onaje attended Yale and by his sophomore season was listed as a 2nd team All-Conference performer. Onaje embraced his father's beliefs in education and helping those people around him. Hamilton's reflection seems as clear as a mirror image.

Recently, Hamilton relocated to Miami to join the Miami Heat organization as a senior account manager where he was reunited with Shaq. His involvement in sports has certainly encompassed all of the arenas from high school to college to professional. Rob Hamilton has challenged athletes over the years to be scholars. As a coach he is content with winning seasons, but as a person he celebrates high GPAs and SAT scores. When he tells his story the milestones he recounts about his players are where they attended college and what their test scores were, not their scoring averages. Hamilton has blended academics and athletics into a success story for dozens, indeed, hundreds of young people. He is hoping to dust off the CALL program soon and employ its methodology in the State of Florida. This coach cares so much that he cannot stay out of the game for long.

Bob Shannon

by Drew Tyler

Coach Bob Shannon searched for leaders to play on his East St. Louis High School football team. Despite facing seemingly insurmountable odds, Shannon took young men straight from the streets of the East St. Louis' inner-city and turned them into leaders who succeeded in football and in their educations. Shannon tried to change the expectations of his athletes from simply being star football players to becoming successful in the classroom. Shannon's accomplishments have garnered national attention, but even he admits that he could not get through to everyone.

Developing leadership skills is the basis of Shannon's coaching philosophy. A general lack of leadership among his team's members often troubled Shannon, but he understood the inner-city environment in which they had been raised. In East St. Louis many of his players lacked a supportive family and the temptation of gangs and drugs was often overwhelming, making it difficult to teach positive leadership skills. Shannon believed that because a lot of his students were looking for attention, they did negative things to get it. Shannon worked tirelessly to make his students realize the positive feedback they could receive through football.

Outside the main entrance to the East St. Louis High School football stadium was a sign that read, "No Drugs, Alcohol or Guns Allowed." To many, the sign was a reminder of the city's continuing deterioration and the abject poverty in which so many of its residents lived. The message was simple, but it spoke volumes about the school, the surrounding neighborhood and the students who attended East St. Louis High School games.

In a city filled with problems (educational theorist Jonathan Kozol identified it as among the worst in America), Shannon's football program provided a bright spot for the community. Shannon guided the Flyers' program to hundreds of victories, six state championships and national championships in 1985 and 1989. The accomplishments on the football field brought positive national attention to the city for the first time in years. While Shannon's coaching ability separates him from many other coaches, it's not his coaching skills alone that have earned him such widespread national praise. Rather, it's the discipline, hard work and leadership he demanded from his players both on and off the football field.

In an age where most high school coaches believe in winning at all costs without stressing academics or fun, Shannon understands that winning is not everything. Rather, Shannon believes strongly in the value of education. Certainly Shannon is not the only football coach to recognize the importance of getting an education, but the surroundings in which he preached his philosophy and the young men he taught sets him apart. Shannon's actions are truly distinctive in that they are rarely found in poverty stricken areas such as the inner-city of East St. Louis. In an area where drugs and gangs rule the streets it was extremely challenging to motivate kids to do well. Shannon stands out not only for motivating kids to do well, but for succeeding in his work.

When it came to his players, Shannon demanded leaders who strive to be different. Any player involved with drugs or gangs was immediately thrown off the team. Shannon believes that drugs and gangs posed a potential threat to the health and safety of his players. Shannon wanted athletes who take pride in doing what is right and who by example lead others in the same direction.

Surprisingly, with as much success that he brought East St. Louis High School football on the field and with the overall positive impact he made in the lives of hundreds of troubled youth, Shannon is still far from being universally loved. Known for speaking his mind and not shying away from being outspoken about things that are important to him, Shannon felt that a majority of the school board disliked him and he was forced to resign in 1995. Nonetheless, many people see Shannon as a heroic man.

One of Shannon's greatest admirers is former President of the United States, Bill Clinton. While campaigning for the presidency, Clinton met Shannon at a speaking engagement at East St. Louis High School's gymnasium. Not long after, President Clinton named Shannon one of his "53 Faces of Hope" for inspiring success in his team under difficult circumstances. According to Shannon, the experience reinforced what he had been telling his players about working hard no matter what because anyone could be watching. Shannon's story was told on the *Today Show* among others. The biography, *The Right Kind of Heroes: Coach Bob Shannon and the East St. Louis Flyers* by Kevin Horrigan is an inspiring record of his life and work.

Not surprisingly, Shannon's success as the Flyers' head coach led to many coaching opportunities for him outside of East St. Louis. To Shannon, however, it was not just the challenge of coaching that drove him. Rather, Shannon was motivated by the challenge of developing troubled boys into successful men. Shannon taught character development and created leaders in a place that lacked true role models. For many, working in a tough environment such as the East St Louis inner-city would be undesirable, but for Shannon it was home.

Ken Carter

by Drew Tyler

Ken Carter, who was once named one of the "Ten Most Influential African-Americans in the Bay Area" by *CityFlight Newsmagazine*, has been recognized with many honors and awards for his dedication to improving and maintaining youth academics, athletics and citizenship. Throughout the Richmond, California community, and now across the country, Carter is recognized as an advocate for Richmond's youth. Carter has worked diligently to provide opportunities for youth to build relationships with their peers and he built a sound basketball program at Richmond High School where he taught the importance of academics and citizenship to young athletes.

In 1998, Carter voluntarily took the boy's basketball head coaching position at Richmond High School despite the fact that it was unpaid. He continued to work at his local sports supply store and barbershop. Carter soon made the news when he benched his entire undefeated basketball team for their poor academic performance. The decision sparked controversy and put Carter in the national spotlight.

It was January 4, 1999, when Carter first made headlines as the Richmond High School head basketball coach. After several players failed to uphold the academic standards they had agreed upon, Carter made the controversial decision to lockout all of the players, including the undefeated varsity team. As players arrived to the gym that day, they found the doors chained and padlocked with a message reading, "NO PRACTICE TODAY – All basketball players are to report to the library."

At the time, 15 of the 45 Richmond Oiler players were failing to achieve the terms and conditions they had agreed to meet in a contract they signed at the beginning of the season. Carter recognized that his players had the skill to continue playing basketball, but also understood that education would ultimately prove to be more valuable for most of the young athletes. Carter's contract required all players to participate in class discussions, sit in the front of the room, complete homework on time and maintain a 2.0 grade point average.

Every two weeks Carter would get updated progress reports for his players and after being informed of the academic issues, Carter immediately made the decision that his players would spend practice and game time studying, rather than playing basketball. Among the players locked out was Carter's own son, Damien, who maintained a 3.7 GPA and would go on to receive a scholarship to the West Point Military Academy. Clearly, Carter viewed success on the court as secondary to quality performance in the classroom. Oiler players would win together on the court, but only if they succeeded in the classroom.

During the lockout, Carter forfeited two games and was willing to cancel the entire season if the academic performance of his players failed to improve. Carter took a great deal of heat from basketball boosters and school officials who felt he had overstepped his bounds by canceling games without consulting the school board. Eventually the students responded, their classwork improved and Carter removed the chains from the gym and allowed the Richmond High School season to resume. In the end, the Oilers finished 19-5, losing in the second round of the district playoffs. Their season was certainly one to be proud of, but Carter was most proud of his players that graduated and went to college.

The following October, Carter took on the daunting task of trying to help reform public education in what he regarded as deteriorating schools. For three days, Carter traveled from Richmond High School to the State Capitol in Sacramento using only a kick scooter in hopes of attracting awareness of his mission. In the end, his determination proved worthwhile as it resulted in enhancements made to school buildings and the purchase of school computers.

Later that year, Carter invited 11 student-athletes from Australia to Richmond High School to promote peace and to learn what it takes to be an American high school basketball player. Students had the opportunity to meet each other and learn about each other's cultures and communities. Using basketball as the common bond, Carter found a way to bring something positive to the lives of Richmond High School's students, a place where positive role models are hard to find.

Throughout his career, Carter has been the recipient of numerous awards. Among them are the Harvard Club's Distinguished Secondary Educator Award, NAACP's Impact Citizen of the Year Award, California State Lottery/Governor Gray Davis' Heroes in Education Award, Willie Brown's Leadership Award, California's Unsung Heroes Award and the A.N.G. California Boy's Coach of the Year Award.

Coach Carter left Richmond High in 2002 but coaching has not left him. Most recently, Carter is coaching The Rumble, the champion team of the newly formed Slam Ball league. In addition, Carter is the owner and operator of Prime Time Publications. He is an author, public speaker and the founder and chairman of the Coach Ken Carter Foundation, a non-profit organization, which develops, promotes and provides education, training and mentoring programs for minority youths. In 2002, Carter was selected and honored to carry the torch for the Olympic Games in Salt Lake City.

In 2005, Paramount Pictures released a film starring Samuel L. Jackson called "Coach Carter" which depicted the real-life events of the 1999 Richmond High School basketball season and lockout. Carter's passion, intensity and commitment are as evident on the screen as they were at Richmond High. Despite the Hollywood fame and public attention, Ken Carter still dedicates his time to spread his message encouraging youth to work hard and commit to their goals with accountability and leadership, both academically and athletically.

Beverly Kearney

by Brian Wright

As five-time NCAA National Team Champion, four-time NCAA Coach of the Year winner, nine-time District Coach of the Year, and 16 league titles in the Big 12 and Southwest Conferences since 1993, Beverly Kearney is the epitome of success. Kearney is one of the most successful coaches in the history of collegiate track and field.

Her success in coaching stems partially from her amateur days as a high school and collegiate athlete, as well as from her courageous and competitive spirit. As an amateur athlete Kearney found her speed, quickness and agility to be some of her greatest assets. She excelled in basketball and track and field in high school, and was regarded as an exceptional athlete by those who saw her compete.

Kearney, who became well known for overcoming the time trials and hurdles of track and field, soon endured the emotional trials and hurdles of life for which there could be no practice or preparation. As a senior in high school, Kearney was faced with an unforeseen tragedy when her mother unexpectedly passed away. This loss affected her deeply and had a negative effect on her performance at school.

When describing Kearney as a high school student, her athletic director said she was, "kind of a quiet girl. When she performed in the games you noticed her, but other than that she had a real tough time."[1] Though disheartened at the loss of her mother, Kearney graduated from high school and continued to compete at Hillsborough Community College where she became a Junior College All-American.

As Kearney's collegiate athletic career came to a close, she prepared for a career in social work. At the same time, Joan Falsone, a friend and former assistant athletic director for county schools, recognized that Kearney had what it took to succeed as a coach in track and field and encouraged her to pursue that career path as well. Kearney took Falsone's recommendation and began her coaching career at Indiana State University in 1981. Fifteen years later, Kearney would become the first woman as well as first African-American to hold the position of President of the Men's and Women's Track and Field Coaches Association. In 1992, Kearney decided to take over the University of Texas Longhorn's track and field head coaching position. Over time, Kearney would lead the Longhorn's program to unprecedented success.

In December 2002, Kearney faced another tragedy. While driving down Interstate 10 Kearney was involved in a serious car accident that took the lives of two of the five passengers in the vehicle. Kearney suffered serious physical injuries including spinal chord and back damage. She had three different surgeries in a month's time to try to repair some of the damage done by the accident. The doctors initially believed Kearney's injuries would leave her paralyzed from the waist down. The legs that had guided Kearney to such personal success had been damaged, but her mental strength and will to overcome these injuries was not.

Though doctors predicted otherwise, Kearney can now walk. Her courage and loyalty to her university and athletes led her to coach from her hospital bed and from a wheel chair during the season. Kearney went through strenuous rehabilitation daily and still found the strength to lead the Longhorn's track team in practices and meets. Now, Kearney is back on her feet and it is as if she never missed a beat. Beverly Kearney is the personification of strength, courage and loyalty not only in sports, but in life.

[1] Lee, Rozel A. "Kearney's Feet Have Carried Her on Long Journey" *The Tampa Tribune*, December 30, 2002.

Jennifer Rizzotti

by Jessica Bartter

To say that Jennifer Rizzotti led a double life is a true but somehow contradictory statement. Rizzotti juggled her professional playing career with her college coaching career in basketball, the sport that she loves. While this balancing act was difficult, Rizzotti could not see choosing between the game she loves to play and the game she loves to coach.

In 1996 and starring at the University of Connecticut, Rizzotti was recognized by the Associated Press as the National Player of the Year, was a two-time Kodak All-American first team selection, received the Wade Trophy for college basketball's outstanding senior player and was named Big East Player of the Year. A true student-athlete, she was a GTE/CoSIDA Women's Basketball Academic All-American and the Big East Women's Basketball Scholar-Athlete of the Year. As a Husky, Rizzotti started every game, 135 straight, during her four-year career. Her career was highlighted by UConn's two Final Four appearances and 1995-1996's 35-0 undefeated and National Championship season. The University of Connecticut was the first team to complete a perfect season since Texas went 34-0 in 1985-1986. Upon graduation, Rizzotti left the Huskies as the season and career record holder in assists and steals, averaging 11.4 points per game, and totaling 637 assists and 349 steals.

Rizzotti has continued to surpass expectations and astonish audiences. Rizzotti began her professional career with the American Basketball League's (ABL) New England Blizzard, where for two of her three seasons, she earned All-Star appearances. In her ABL debut, Rizzotti took an elbow just above the eye drawing blood before the clock counted down the first two minutes of the game. As Rizzotti headed to the locker room for a band-aid, she knew she would be back. In the second quarter, Rizzotti returned with seven stitches, entered the game and led a 25-2 New England scoring run enroute to a 100-73 victory. Despite missing most of the first quarter, Rizzotti finished the game with eight points and five assists, and she inspired her teammates through her intensity, hustle and dedication.

After the ABL folded, Rizzotti was drafted by the Women's National Basketball Association's Houston Comets in the fourth round, where she and her teammates earned the 1999 WNBA Championship. Rizzotti later joined the Cleveland Rockers where she spent three years and went on to win another WNBA Championship.

In the midst of her success as a professional athlete, Rizzotti was offered the women's basketball head coaching position at the University of Hartford, just 12 days after her first WNBA Championship. Still only 25, she was the youngest Division I women's basketball coach in the country. Rizzotti was as successful as a coach as she was as a player. In just her third year as the Hawks' leader, Rizzotti coached the team to their first-ever America East Championship and NCAA Tournament appearance. With Rizzotti at the helm, the team has gained national prominence. In her fifth season in 2003-2004 Hartford won a school record 18 games.

Rizzotti has begun a new journey with her husband: building a family. As she coached the 2004-2005 season through her pregnancy, Rizzotti focused on saving her energy for the games and practices. While she predicted her patience would increase after becoming a mother, her intensity did not lessen. Hartford broke its school record and won 22 games and earned their second America East title in 2004-2005. The Hawks also broke records for conference victories with 13 and the best home record in school history with an almost perfect 15-1 record.

One common observation of sport is that it offers participants leadership opportunities by learning about themselves and their teammates. While some athletes make great players, and others make great coaches, Rizzotti has accomplished both, and most amazingly, she did it at the same time. Of course, her athletic prowess contributed to her success, but it was as much her intelligence, leadership skills, dedication, self-discipline, motivation and genuine care for the players with whom she plays and those she coaches that accounts for her distinctive career.

Willie Stewart

by Jessica Bartter and Richard Lapchick

Coach Willie Stewart leads Anacostia High School in Washington, D.C., where life on the streets is more menacing than any opposing athletic team. Stewart first coached at Eastern High School in D.C. before transferring to Anacostia where he has been since 1981. He has won 15 East Division Football Championships and seven District of Columbia Interscholastic Athletic Association Championships in his 30 years of coaching football. Despite his success, many wonder what keeps him at Anacostia which is located in one of the worst neighborhoods in the United States just blocks from Capitol Hill but stricken with poverty, drugs and violence. Stewart and his assistants work for low pay. For years his players wore uniforms and shoes he received from the University of the District of Columbia and until 2004, they never played home games in a real stadium.

Stewart drives his players to school in the morning and home from practice at night. He makes sure they study to overcome the long odds society has laid down for Anacostia students to graduate and go to college. Stewart, who has regularly turned down more lucrative college offers, recognizes the dearth of African-American male role models for inner-city youth.

Stewart has an uncommon concern for the welfare of his players and their communities. Stewart works tirelessly to save young lives. In 2003, Stewart said "During my 25 some years of coaching, I have lost close to 20 athletes to gun violence."[1] In each somber incident, Stewart brings the entire Anacostia football team to the funeral hoping to make them realize it could have been them lying in that coffin and it may soon be if they do not change their behavior. In 1994 alone, four of his players were shot, one of them fatally. Stewart's familiarity with gun violence and his dedication to prevention led him to the Alliance for Justice in 2003. Stewart was the first coach to jump on board with a public education campaign known as Coaches Against Gun Violence. He and seven other Washington, D.C. coaches who followed Stewart's lead agreed to dedicate one of their football games to victims of gun violence. Each of the eight games included a special ceremony where city officials, students, athletes, faculty, community members and others who educated fans about gun violence prevention.

One of Stewart's many success stories involves Lovell Pinkney. In 1989, Pinkney was in the 10th grade when Stewart took notice of his continuing absences from class and football practice. Suspecting the worst, Stewart searched for and found Pinkney hanging on street corners dealing drugs. Stewart tried over and over to make Pinkney realize he had a future in football and that he didn't need to sell drugs to get by. Deep down inside, Stewart knew that path Pinkney had chosen would most likely lead to jail or death. After all, in Stewart's first 12 years of coaching, he had already lost eight players to drug-related killings. Yet, like many teenagers, Pinkney didn't believe it could happen to him, until he narrowly survived a drive-by shooting that convinced him to stop selling crack once and for all. Once Stewart had his full attention, he coached Pinkney into the Player of the Year for Washington, D.C. as a senior. Pinkney's play earned him a spot as a University of Texas Longhorn. In 1995, Pinkney was the 4th round pick in the NFL chosen by the St. Louis Rams. Today, Pinkney realizes he would not be where he is without Coach Stewart's guidance. Because just one person cared about him, he escaped a dead-end future and possible premature death. Pinkney learned the power one individual can have and hopes to do for other athletes what Stewart did for him.

"These are the kids who need the guidance, not the college kids," Stewart told Richard Lapchick. "You can't save everybody, but I still try." The young men at Anacostia High learn more than just football from Stewart. They learn the importance of academics and responsibility from their mentor.

In April 2005, Stewart was asked to testify for the House Reform Committee regarding the use of steroids. Willie Stewart provided testimony alongside Paul Tagliabue, NFL Commissioner, Gene Upshaw, Executive Director of the NFLPA, and Steve Courson, former NFL player as well as doctors, professors and other coaches. Stewart explained to the Committee that many young student-athletes admire professional athletes and believe that performance enhancing drugs are the quickest way to emulate them despite the accompanying risks. Stewart disclosed that he had suspected steroid use in two of his players over the years and that his suspicions proved true in one case. Just two weeks prior to his testimony, one of Stewart's former student-athletes died of kidney failure at age 28. Based upon that experience, Stewart has made it a point to encourage other coaches to become familiar with steroid abuse and to warn their athletes about its dangers.

Stewart's impact on the community of Anacostia has been vital. His genuine interest in his student-athletes has accounted for the saving of countless human lives. Stewart uses football to show troubled teens a way out of poverty, drugs and violence and into a better life. His lessons extend beyond the big plays, throwing tips and tackling techniques; they also deal with life beyond the field emphasizing education, compassion, discipline and feelings of self-worth.

Coach Willie Stewart was honored by the Center for the Study of Sport and Society alongside Coach Tom Osborne and Muhammad Ali in 1994. As Ali watched, awaiting his turn to be inducted into Sport and Society's Hall of Fame he turned to Richard Lapchick to reflect on Osborne and Stewart: "That's what coaching should be all about." Ali said it best and coming from "The Greatest" is perhaps the highest accolade of all.

[1] Feit, Maria. Anacostia Football Coach Joins "Coaches Against Gun Violence." Alliance for Justice. [October 10, 2003; August 30, 2005] http://www.afj.org/news_and_press/press_release_collection/collection/press_anacostiacoach.html

CHAPTER 3

PLAYING TO WIN IN LIFE

There are athletes who, by their example, show others what is possible. They take people without hope and help them find it, they seek out people without promise and work with them to achieve it. In *Playing to Win in Life*, we talk about the stories of six athletes who did just that.

Derrick Brooks, the great Tampa Bay linebacker, worked with young people and helped to fund their educations. In one instance, he took a group of 20 high school students to South Africa.

Justin Allen was a basketball player at Arizona State University who hoped to play in the NBA. That dream was dashed when he was diagnosed with Hodgkin's disease. After extensive hospitalization and therapy, he made it back to the court where he inspired his teammates and fellow students.

Felipe Lopez was the top high school basketball player in the country. Everyone predicted a distinguished NBA career. Recruited by every major program, Felipe was also perhaps the greatest Latino basketball player in the United States. He chose to stay at home and attend St. John's University in order to be near the Dominican community which idolized him. He said that he stayed to give them hope.

Warrick Dunn, one of the NFL's superstars for the last decade, used his own resources to acquire new homes for single mothers and their families. He made down payments and purchased furniture for these homes in the Tampa Bay area.

Priest Holmes, the Kansas City All-Pro player, not only led his team on the field but also created examples for them by his extensive involvement in the Kansas City and Baltimore communities. He helped with programs for low income neighborhood children to prepare to go to college, to be able to escape poverty and the violence of the cities. This was only the beginning of a life-long career in support of children in his community.

Amber Burgess was a student at Columbine High School when 12 fellow students and her beloved coach, Dave Sanders were gunned down on that terrible day. This superstar softball player and gifted student was chosen to be the spokesperson for all students at the national ceremony commemorating the lives of those lost in the shooting. Amber became a great softball player at the University of Nebraska before becoming a professional softball player. However, it was her courage and spirit at Columbine that inspired many other young people to keep their hopes alive.

These six heroes used their game to give other people hope in the battle for life and happiness.

Derrick Brooks

by Jennifer Brenden

Professional athletes are role models, whether they choose to be or not. This is not necessarily something they elect to become but is rather occasioned by the popularity of the professional sports industry and the media outlets that take advantage of that popularity. Professional athletes are in the limelight all the time and people of all ages look up to and admire them. Fans, especially kids with very impressionable minds, want to play like Mike, dress like Kobe, and rap like Shaq.

These days, with the smothering media coverage that exists, all aspects of an athlete's life are public. There are so many athletes in professional sports who are good, upstanding citizens, with big hearts, good values and morals, and who choose to make a positive difference in society with the power that they hold through being an athlete. The problem is that these aren't the athletes and the instances who get media exposure. In general, people yearn for conflict and drama in the news and in the world of sports. That is what catches a fan's attention and is often what draws people to the wide world of sports. Yes, the philanthropic activities of professional athletes are reported, but not to the extent that the rebellious, trash-talking, fight-starting, name-calling, money-seeking activities are. Lawsuits, drug abuse, spousal abuse and physical violence are just a few of the typical topics that are covered in sports news. If all of the benefits, foundations, charities and programs that professional athletes are involved in were talked about and reported as much as all the negative activities, maybe professional athletes would be seen in a little better and more realistic light.

Derrick Brooks, of the Tampa Bay Buccaneers, is a professional athlete who more kids should emulate. His performances, both on and off the field, are very commendable. He is arguably one of the best defensive players in the game and he has also been named as No. 1 on *The Sporting News'* list of 99 Good Guys in pro sports.

Brooks grew up in Pensacola, Florida, not having much in his childhood, but he was happy. He was a very smart kid, but he didn't always take education as seriously as he does today. It took learning a tough lesson from his stepfather in elementary school for him to see the importance and seriousness of education. From then on, being a good student was a top priority for him. He graduated from high school with a 3.94 GPA and he received both undergraduate and graduate degrees from Florida State. The importance of education is what he preaches to all of the kids that he works and talks with.

The All-Pro linebacker has been considered the best in the NFL. He was drafted by the Bucs in the 1995 draft, along with Warren Sapp; and Brooks has been worth every penny that the team paid for him, and then some. He is an excellent open-field tackler and an amazing playmaker. He earned a club record with his eighth appearance at the Pro Bowl and he was the NFL's Defensive Player of the year in 2002, the same year he helped lead the Bucs to their first Super Bowl Championship. He is respected by not only his teammates, but also by players he competes against. This, along with his commitment, dedication, drive and love for the game, make him a very good captain, a leader among his teammates, and a very easy person to follow. Prior to the 2005 season, Brooks had played in 160 consecutive games and started in 144 of them which demonstrates his durability as well as his skill. He has become the franchise's most prolific tackler and ranks among the best in the league.

In 1996, shortly after Brooks was drafted by the Bucs, he created a charity called the "Brooks Bunch," which is an organization that works with Boys and Girls Club members, mostly in the economically disadvantaged areas of Tampa. The goals of the program are to provide the kids with a role model and a mentor, to emphasize the importance of education and to give them opportunities to see the world that they would not otherwise be exposed to.

Giving money to a charity or organization to help kids is a very noble thing to do, but money does not fix all problems. That's why Brooks chooses to be much more hands-on with the kids he works with. He sits down and really gets to know the kids, the parents and their situations, and he makes a personal effort to make some kind of positive difference in their lives. The program is designed not only to help kids in their present situation, but to help prepare them for the future. This means instilling values, beliefs, morals and certain behaviors that will make the kids better people over the course of their lives. Taking on these goals takes time and energy, both of which Brooks is willing to give, a rarity for such a superstar athlete. Brooks tells the kids to be respectful, get good grades and get involved.

A major part of his program includes out-of-town educational field trips that have included tours to Washington D.C., the Western United States (which involved a stop at the Grand Canyon), a trip to colleges and universities in New York, Chicago, Atlanta and Tallahassee, and two trips to Africa. Prior to the trips, the kids have classes to learn about the place or places they will be visiting. There was a special selection process for the trip to Africa, because only 20 kids could go. After attending sessions to learn about the culture and history of Africa, the kids had to write essays explaining what they learned and why they should get to go on the trip. A 2.5 GPA was also a prerequisite.

This trip was the experience of a lifetime for these kids. The following is a list of just a few of the activities that the tour included: eating crocodile and ostrich around a campfire at a safari base camp, watching a mother elephant charge at their car, taking a gondola to the top of Table Mountain, meeting with local high school students, traveling to Soweto to see where Nelson Mandela lived and then traveling to Robben Island to see where he was imprisoned for 26 years, and watching tribal African dances performed by the natives. Each year the trips seem to be getting harder to top. It's going to be hard to go above and beyond a two-week tour in Africa, but knowing Derrick Brooks, he'll find someway to outdo himself. Both professionally and personally, he just keeps getting better and better.

The Derrick Brooks Celebrity Golf Classic is the biggest fundraiser for Derrick Brooks Charities Inc., which was started about three years ago to support all of the programs, events and opportunities that Brooks promotes. Some of the other activities include the game-day ticket program, and teaming up with the Bucs to raise money for hurricane Ivan relief efforts, specifically for his hometown of Pensacola. The Golf Classic always includes several pro football players showcasing their golf skills and has been a huge success.

The work of Derrick Brooks does not go unnoticed. His giving nature and devotion to helping kids is very well-known and talked about amongst the NFL franchises. He was recognized in 2000 when he received the highest charitable award annually presented by the NFL, the prestigious Walter Payton Man of the Year Award. Brooks has been a spokesman for

United Way in several different capacities. Also, in 2002, Brooks was named to the NFLPA Diversity Committee to work with NFLPA executive director Gene Upshaw on the issue of diversity in the NFL.

Brooks is a man who remembers where he came from and who helped him get to where he is today. He was an All-American at Florida State University while earning two degrees. In March of 2003, Florida Governor, Jeb Bush, appointed Brooks to FSU's board of trustees. As demonstrated in all other aspects of Brooks' life, he is a doer, not a talker. He wants to be a part of making big decisions for the University and a part of making things better.

When Brooks isn't out making a difference in the lives of other kids and families, he is spending time with his three children, and his wife, Carol. Derrick Brooks is a very special athlete and a very special person. Society would be a much better place if kids had more role models like Brooks to admire and to emulate.

Justin Allen

by Brian Wright

He was Malta High School's leading scorer with 2,143 points, with senior season averages of 26.7 points, 15.0 rebounds and 4.7 blocks. With statistics like these Justin Allen stepped onto the campus of Arizona State University with hopes of taking his talents to the NBA. At ASU, Allen was revered by his teammates, coaches and faculty. He was famous for his easy going and lovable spirit. His sense of humor was apparent when describing his most memorable moment in his freshman season. "That's the game," he says, "when Eddie House and I combined for 64 points."[1] Allen scored only three points that game.

To Allen, the basketball team at Arizona State was his family and the gym was his home away from home. Heading into his sophomore season, Allen was given a statistic that impacted his life more than any free throw, field goal percentage, or any other basketball percentage he could have ever imagined. On September 14, 2000 he was diagnosed with Stage II Hodgkin's disease and given an 80 percent chance to live.

Allen's diagnosis of Hodgkin's was as big a surprise to him as it was to everyone around him. He actually could feel the tumor but thought it was just a pulled abdominal muscle. Allen, the athletic program and the entire University were in shock. Allen began treatment immediately to stop the spread of the cancer to other organs and lymph nodes in his body. He underwent six months of treatments including radiation and chemotherapy to kill cancer cells and shrink the tumors. Allen was forced to red-shirt the 2000-01 season while undergoing treatments that left him sick and bedridden for 11 to 12 hours a day. He dropped 25 pounds, from 215 to 190.

Despite the extensive treatments, Allen remained dedicated to school and his teammates. Allen was frequently visited by coaches and players while in the hospital. As a sign of unity and compassion the entire basketball team decided to shave their heads when Allen's therapy caused him to lose his hair. Allen's courage through his recovery motivated everyone around him. When members of the Arizona State basketball team would begin to slack off, all it would take was for one person to remind everyone how much Allen wanted to be out there with them and the practice environment would change dramatically. Though exhausted from the therapy, Allen managed to earn a 3.23 grade point average, and graduated with an overall grade point average of 3.46. While balancing school and therapy, Allen attended most Arizona State basketball practices and found relief in shooting on the sidelines while encouraging his teammates. Allen was back on the court in May of 2001. He wanted no pity or special treatment from any of his teammates. He challenged them not to go lightly on him because he would be playing as hard as he could with them. Allen is competitive and courageous. At a time when many people would feel burdened and discouraged Allen thought of his sickness as just another obstacle that he had to overcome. Allen knew that obstacles appear in life, and that they are just obstacles, not barriers barring you from continuing on with your life. Allen remained positive that he would overcome his health challenges and continue living his life to the fullest. This is exactly what Allen is doing. Entering college Justin Allen imagined a season where Arizona State would win the Pac-10 Conference title and the National Championship. Looking back he understands he won a much more important challenge in the game of life.

[1] "Justin Allen's battle against cancer helps another student." Official site of the Arizona State Sun Devils. [March 25, 2002; September 29, 2005] http://thesundevils.collegesports.com/sports/m-baskbl/spec-rel/032502aaa.html

Felipe Lopez

by Brian Wright

New York City basketball is a legend in its own right with storied heroes and folklore that have been passed down from generation to generation. There is something special about the basketball played there and the players and fans who take part in it. Throughout the celebrated lifetime of New York City basketball there have been many legends, but few have lived the life of Felipe Lopez. Lopez is one of the greatest basketball players in New York City high school basketball history. His name is frequently mentioned alongside such New York City basketball greats as Bob Cousy, Kareem Abdul-Jabbar, Pearl Washington, Chris Mullin, Kenny Anderson and Stephon Marbury. A tremendous talent with an enormous heart, Lopez set a new standard for what a basketball legend in NYC would have to accomplish and how one could impact the community through one's status as a basketball celebrity. Through his performance on and off the court, Lopez became a role model for the Hispanic community and a trailblazer in encouraging their participation in the game of basketball.

Lopez was born in Santo Domingo of the Dominican Republic. As a young child he grew up playing baseball, the most popular sport in his native land. Though he enjoyed baseball, it never really captivated him the way that basketball did. As a young child playing in a pick-up baseball game Lopez was hit in the face by a ball and decided that day that basketball was the right sport for him. Though choosing between baseball and basketball was an important issue he faced at the time, Lopez was also confronted with an unfavorable economic situation for himself and his family which was much more important. Due to this economic status of Lopez's family in the Dominican, they were forced to leave the country in search of better opportunities for their family. Lopez stayed behind but would return to his family during the summer of his eighth grade year of school. At age 13, Lopez's arrival in the South Bronx borough of New York City was definitely a change of environment and change of pace for him. He was faced with many cultural challenges including a language barrier, since at the time, Lopez spoke very little English. Lopez adapted very quickly and began to use basketball to learn the culture of inner-city New York. While playing at a local basketball court with some friends Lopez learned exactly what he didn't want to become involved in. Lopez saw a drug transaction transpiring that must have gone wrong because the two drug dealers began to fire gunshots at each other. This scared Lopez and sent him to the gym to work on developing his basketball skills.

Lopez found a famous gym where many other great New York City players have practiced and made it his home away from home. This was the famed Gauchos gym in the South Bronx. This was a safe haven for Lopez and countless other teammates and friends while growing up in South Bronx. Lopez's budding talent and potential could be spotted at first glance when entering the Gauchos gym. Gym owner Lou d'Almeida found himself buzzing and raving about Lopez's talent as well. From the time spent with Lopez in the gym, d'Almeida knew that Lopez was a special kid and a phenomenal athlete. By this time Lopez had grown to over 6 foot 5 and his status around the city was growing larger. Lopez attended Rice High School, a local private school and he began to flourish there as well. Lopez's athleticism and raw talent on the court left college coaches and the media on the edge of their seat while filling high school gyms and stadiums to capacity. Lopez never seemed to disappoint the crowds who were eager to see him get out on a fast break and slam down a monstrous dunk. Lopez played three successful seasons at Rice High School and then the hype began about what college he would attend or whether he would go straight to the NBA.

As a young teenager Lopez understood but didn't know the nationwide and eventual international effect that he was having not only on high school basketball, but within the context of his Latino heritage as well. Lopez was a trailblazer who opened the doors for many Hispanics in the city of New York as well as around the country to compete and become regarded as among the best basketball players in the United States. Though he didn't know the full extent of his celebrity at the time, Lopez had become a role model athlete in the Hispanic community.

In his senior year of high school, Lopez was frequently compared to NBA greats such as Michael Jordan and Charles Barkley, and graced the cover of *Sports Illustrated*, a feat few high school athletes have the privilege of doing. Throughout all of the media attention and hoopla, Lopez never lost sight of his humble background or his commitment to using his newfound celebrity status in basketball to improve his community. Lopez had lived in poor and underserved environments. When asked about this, Lopez told *Sports Illustrated*, "I have so many good ideas in my head, I want to change the unhappy world around me. So I must use creativity in the classroom and on the court to bring hope."[1] This was a profound statement for such a young person who carried the weight of people's mammoth athletic aspirations for him on his shoulders, as well as carrying the torch for the Hispanic community. It showed his understanding of the bigger picture in society, and how he could use sport to impact society in a positive way.

Lopez would go on to set records as a senior in New York City high school basketball as well as leading his team at Rice High to the City Championship. He was named the National High School Basketball Player of the Year. While excelling on the court, Lopez was able to achieve equivalent success in the classroom, graduating from Rice High School with a 3.5 grade point average. With his vast success came options as his senior year concluded. Lopez was offered a $500,000 contract to forgo his collegiate eligibility and play professional basketball in Spain. Lopez also had scholarship offers to almost every college and university with a basketball team in the United States.

After much contemplation and counsel with his family, Lopez chose to remain in New York and attend St. John's University. He made this decision based not only on the academic and athletic standards of the University, but for cultural reasons as well. Lopez wanted to stay in New York because of his respect for his Hispanic heritage and the huge Hispanic population there. He stated one of his largest contributing factors in deciding on an institution was the size of the Hispanic community surrounding the institution. He wanted to be in a large Hispanic community so the youth and other members of the community had the chance to see him play and so that he could be a positive role model for those community members. Lopez also wanted to remain close to his family members. Attending St. John's University was the best decision for him to accomplish all these things.

Lopez achieved a great deal of success as a collegiate athlete at St. John's and left the University with a career average of 17.6 points, 6 rebounds and 2.5 assists per game. Athletically the hype and media attention that surrounded Lopez while in high school were tough expectations to fulfill, and in some people's perceptions, he never had the career his talent initially promised. Lopez was drafted 24th in the first round of the 1998 NBA Draft. He was traded on draft night and played his rookie season with the Vancouver Grizzlies. During his rookie campaign Lopez showed flashes of brilliance and ended the season averaging 9.3 points and 3.3 rebounds. Injuries would ultimately limit Lopez's development and slow down a career that most people who saw him play felt would be a great one. For the next several years Lopez would bounce around the NBA landing briefly with several NBA teams. Though Lopez's basketball career took a different path than many people expected, he is still one of the biggest legends in New York City basketball history, especially in the Hispanic community. In the later years of his career in the NBA, Lopez served as a community relations ambassador for the NBA and brought basketball and other life lessons and training to the various Hispanic countries around the world. He conducted basketball camps and clinics and promoted education, leadership, character building, healthy living and HIV/AIDS awareness and prevention.

Felipe Lopez's family instilled morals and values in him when he was a child so that he developed a commitment to improving the lives of his family and others in the community. He has been an ambassador and pioneer for Hispanics on and off the court. He is a role model citizen and uses his status as a basketball celebrity in a positive way to help others achieve a better life. Felipe Lopez is a legend not only on the basketball court, but also as a social activist in the community.

[1] Crothers, Tim. "Felipe Lopez" *Sports Illustrated*, December 20, 1993.

Warrick Dunn

by Jennifer Brenden

Warrick Dunn had a very busy and a very successful year in 1997. He graduated from Florida State University with a degree in information studies and he was chosen in the first round (12th pick overall) of the NFL draft by the Tampa Bay Buccaneers. In his rookie season, he started in 10 of 16 games, and he led the Bucs in both receptions and rushing. Thanks to his stellar performance, he was given Pro Bowl honors and was also named NFL Rookie of the Year by *Football News*, *Pro Football Weekly* and *Sports Illustrated.* He was also honored by being selected as Offensive Rookie of the Year by the Associated Press, *Football Digest*, and *College and Pro Football Newsweekly*.

As if his football commitments didn't keep him busy enough in his first year of being a professional athlete, he also found the time to create a program called "Homes for the Holidays." Seeking out philanthropic causes are usually not on the top of the priority list for rookie pro athletes, but Dunn has proven that he is not like most of his peers. He wasted no time in figuring out how he could use the power that he holds as an athlete in the professional world of sports to give back to his community and help those that are less fortunate than him.

The program is very special to Dunn because he can relate to the people he is helping. The purpose of the program is to assist single mothers in owning their first home by providing the down payment on a house and then furnishing the house with everything that a first-time homeowner would need, such as furniture, food, linens, lawn mower, gardening supplies, washer, dryer, dishes, pots and pans, and more. It is a very stabilizing factor to be a homeowner, but it is also very hard to become a first time homeowner, especially for a single mother. It is very disheartening for women who work day and night to provide for their kids, yet never feeling like they are getting anywhere. Dunn's program gives women that little extra boost needed to get them in to their first home and it rewards them for working so hard to take care of their families.

This opportunity really is a reward. "Homes for the Holidays" works with other non-profit organizations that run first-time homeownership programs, such as Habitat for Humanity, United Way's IDA program and Community Redevelopment programs. Once a year these non-profit organizations nominate single mothers as recipients of the program. The women must have completed the mandatory course work and be properly prepared to be homeowners.

The reason that Dunn can relate to this situation is because his mom was a single parent and the sole provider of his family. Dunn grew up in Baton Rouge, Louisiana and was the oldest of the six children. Dunn's mother, Betty Smothers, did everything she could to make ends meet, which meant finding extra jobs to earn extra cash wherever and whenever she could outside of her police officer duties. Warrick will admit that he didn't have many material things growing up but, more importantly, he had the love of his friends, family and coaches. Ms. Smothers also taught her son how to give himself and to be generous to those in need. She obviously taught him well, because he is doing just that with the establishment of the "Homes for the Holidays" Program, and eventually, the creation of the Warrick Dunn Foundation.

A horrible tragedy occurred in 1993 when Ms. Smothers was shot and killed in the line of duty. Dunn was just a senior in high school. He became the glue that held the family together. Ms. Smothers was never able to achieve the dream of owning her own home before she died, so Dunn's program enables other single, working women to achieve that dream. Dunn wants to help women out who are working hard to provide for their families. Ms. Smothers is surely looking down on her son and boasting with pride at the wonderful man he has become.

The "Homes for the Holidays" campaign has been so successful and so inspirational that there have been other NFL players who have tried to duplicate the program in their own respective cities. Kurt Warner, the quarterback for the St. Louis Rams, and his wife Brenda, established the program in 2002 when they provided two single mothers with new homes of their own. Warner also extended the program to his hometown of Des Moines, Iowa in 2004. A fellow Rams teammate, Cornerback Jason Sehorn, helped place six single mothers and their families into their first homes from 2000 to 2002, when he played for the New York Giants. There has been a handbook of the program created so that it is easy for other NFL players to implement this program. There are single mothers struggling all over the country that could benefit from this program immensely. The idea is to make it easy for athletes to adapt this program to their own communities.

Since the program has been established, it has helped a total of 52 single mothers and 135 children find permanent homes of their own. And those numbers are going to continue to grow, not only in the three cities in which Dunn operates his program, but in other locations where the program has been instituted by other athletes. Dunn created the Warrick Dunn Foundation in 2002 when he was traded to Atlanta and he expanded the program in his new team's city. With that expansion the program then helped women in Baton Rouge, Louisiana, Tampa, Florida and Atlanta, Georgia.

Dunn has received some very prestigious awards. He was honored with an "Oprah's Angel" by Oprah herself in the spring of 2002. He has received several other special honors for his philanthropic ventures. He was the Atlanta Falcons Man of the Year in 2003, was named to *The Sporting News* "75 Good Guys in Sports" in 1999, 2000, 2003 and 2004, and he was on the list of *Sports Illustrated's* 101 Most Influential Minorities in Sports in 2003. Along with being named NFL Rookie of the Year in 1997 and being given Pro Bowl honors in that same year, Dunn was also a Pro Bowler in 2000 and he was inducted in to the Florida State University Hall of Fame in 2002. During Dunn's tenure at Florida State, he became the first FSU running back to record three 1,000-yard rushing seasons and he ended his career as the Seminole's career leader in rushing yards with a total of 3,959 yards.

Recently, Dunn has been showing his support for the United States. In March of 2005, he traveled to Kuwait, Afghanistan and Iraq with linebacker Larry Izzo of the New England Patriots. They went on a week-long United Service Organizations (USO) Tour helping to dedicate a new USO building called the Pat Tillman Center, at Bagram Airbase near Kabal, Afghanistan. Just a year earlier, he traveled with teammate Keith Brooking, Baltimore tight end Todd Heap and NFL Commissioner Paul Tagliabue on a trip to Germany to visit members of the United States Armed Forces.

All of Warrick Dunn's experiences show the extent he will go to help out those who are in need. He is truly a special man, both on the playing field and off. He hopes that in the future, we will see variations of the "Homes for the Holidays" program all over the country.

Priest Holmes

by Brian Wright

With an amazing stat line of over 7,500 rushing yards and over 80 touchdowns as a professional football player, Priest Holmes has had an extraordinary professional career on the football field. He has been one of the most successful running backs of the past decade as a member of the Baltimore Ravens and Kansas City Chiefs. His success on the field can be largely attributed to his tremendously intensive work-ethic and his desire to perform to the best of his ability every time he steps onto the football field. Along with being a great football player Holmes has also been a dedicated and committed citizen participating in numerous charitable events and community service projects in the Kansas City and San Antonio areas. Growing up as a child in Fort Smith, Arkansas and later in San Antonio, Holmes was raised to always think about improving the community in which he lived as well as focusing on success in academics and sports. It was from this initial guidance instilled in him as a young child that has made him a man of high moral and social values and standards. This led to Holmes' deep passion and commitment to make a difference within the community and help others growing up in situations less fortunate than himself.

As a youth, Holmes was a standout athlete on the field as well as in the classroom. Holmes participated in numerous social clubs and teams outside of football and was a star member of the Marshall High School chess club in San Antonio, Texas. Priest was always an analytical and serious thinker and even used his chess strategies to help him on the football field. This idea paid off and, due to his stellar production as a high school student-athlete, Holmes earned the Offensive Player of the Year award from the *San Antonio Light* newspaper, as well as being awarded a full scholarship to attend the prestigious University of Texas. As a highly-touted recruit, Holmes lived up to the expectations of many who surrounded the University of Texas football team and received "fabulous freshman" honorable mention team honors in 1992 from *USA Today*. Holmes continued his success on the field throughout his collegiate career, ultimately preparing for the National Football League draft at the end of his senior year.

Despite his lightning quick speed and proven ability to have an impact on the football field, Holmes was overlooked by NFL scouts and went un-drafted in 1996. Holmes was unwavering in his desire to play in the NFL and tried out for the Baltimore Ravens during training camp of the 1996 season. Holmes played well and impressed the coaching staff enough to be on the opening day roster. Holmes' commitment to hard work and excellence quickly made him a star on the field. In just his second season in the NFL, Holmes rushed for over 1,000 yards and scored seven rushing touchdowns. This initial success launched Holmes' All-Pro career. He helped the Baltimore Ravens earn an NFL Championship trophy and achieved many personal accolades along the way. Holmes was the NFL's leading rusher in 2001 playing for the Kansas City Chiefs, and was a Pro Bowl selection honoring the season's best offensive and defensive performers. Performing at the All-Pro level in the NFL takes hard work and dedication to train on the field as well as the time spent off the field learning plays and studying film. Though Holmes was committed to performing at the All-Pro level and spending time developing his athletic skills and physique, he always made time to work in the community to make society a better place for young children growing up.

As a player growing up in Baltimore, Holmes wanted to make an impact in the community as quickly as possible. He frequently heard reports of numerous acts of violence and crime that had plagued the youth and families within this region. According to data released by the FBI, the city of Baltimore reported over 18,630 violent crimes within city boundaries. Alarmed by such statistics, Holmes knew that with his celebrity status as an athlete, his positive influence could impact the minds of the at-risk youth in the area and help reduce the city's crime rate.

Holmes decided that one of his first projects would be the Maryland Department of Education's Program GEAR UP which is an acronym for Gaining Early Awareness and Readiness for Undergraduate Programs. This program was designed by the Maryland Department of Education to prepare students from low-income neighborhoods for college.

This was an extremely important program to Holmes due to his firm belief in the importance of education.

While in Baltimore, Holmes also partnered with others striving to make improvements and contributions to the community. Holmes signed on as an official sponsor and contributor to the scholarship fund of Dr. Ben Carson, the Head of Pediatric Neurosurgery at John's Hopkins Children's Hospital. As a sponsor and contributor, Holmes attended local area schools and gave motivational speeches to young people about the importance of staying in school and aspiring to attend college. Following his mission to increase the awareness of the importance of education in the Baltimore Community, Holmes became a sponsor and eventual keynote speaker for the Ronald McDonald Corporation Ray Kroc Youth Achievement Awards. The recipients of the Ray Kroc Achievement awards were given scholarships to attend college from the Ronald McDonald Corporation.

Holmes' commitment to the community in which he lived and worked continued in Kansas City after he decided to continue his football career with the Kansas City Chiefs. Holmes spends countless hours and dollars in the inner-city of Kansas City helping young student-athletes realize their potential on the field and in the classroom. Addressing a lack of funds for athletics in the inner-city of Kansas City, Holmes created the Sports Dental Safety for Kids Project. Through his charitable foundation TeamPriest in collaboration with Chili's Restaurants and the Samuel U. Rodger's Health Center's dental staff, Holmes provided top-of-the-line custom made mouth guards for each student-athlete playing a sport that required a mouthpiece for protection in the Kansas City area. Holmes discovered through research done by the Sports Dental Safety for Kids Project that these mouth guards were very useful in preventing serious injuries including major dental problems and concussions. This project is ongoing for Holmes and his TeamPriest organization, and each year every student-athlete who participates in the various sports requiring mouthpieces in Kansas City receives a custom mouth guard.

TeamPriest's programs are not just geared to student-athletes in the community of Kansas City. Stemming from Holmes's passion for chess as a teenager he started a chess club within the youth community in the inner-city of Kansas City.

Holmes contributions to Baltimore and Kansas City are varied and widespread, but the ultimate goal of each has always and will always remain the same: to positively help young people. His efforts always focus on teaching the importance of education and helping youth strive to reach their full potential on the athletic field as well as in the classroom.

Throughout his amateur and professional careers, Holmes has been a role model as an athlete and as a citizen. He lives his life with the passion and commitment to better society. When asked why he does so much work in the community, Holmes responded "For me it is just a way to give back, I think it's part of being a professional; and it's about taking advantage of your opportunity. As a professional athlete you're definitely going to touch lives, and most likely it's going to be a child's life and you really want to touch that life in a special way."[1] This is the winning spirit that sport is all about. It is not the numbers of wins and losses one attains as a player or coach, or the statistics that one compiles during the game. It is the way one can change society for the better. This is Priest Holmes' message.

Holmes has received numerous community leader and civic awards over the span of his professional career, but the title of one award he has received stands out as a perfect description of what he has meant to the communities with which he has been involved. That award is the Glen S. Pop Warner Award given to the individual who the Award committee thinks has most effectively inspired the youth of today to become great achievers of tomorrow. This is what Holmes has done, not through scoring 20 touchdowns in one season or leading the NFL in rushing, but by touching the lives of America's youth. Priest Holmes is truly a hero for the ages.

[1] "Priest Holmes #31- Interview on community involvement." NFLPlayers.com. [2005; December 12, 2005] http://www.nflplayers.com/players/player.aspx?id=25151§ion=media

Amber Burgess

by Jessica Bartter

It started like any other day of school for most students in Littleton, Colorado; rushing to class, frantically searching for the homework assignment that is due first period, asking mom for lunch money, envisioning the impending summer break and saying hi to friends in the hall before class. Yet, this sunny spring day of April 20, 1999 at Columbine High School ended in tragedy when two students turned on their own, murdering 13 and wounding 21 more in the most devastating school shooting in U.S. history.

Investigations later suggested the targets of the deadly shootings were driven by hate for athletes and minority group members. A likely target during the shootings at Columbine, Amber Burgess, a softball player, happened to be out of town at her grandmother's funeral during the tragic shootings that took the lives of her coach and mentor, Dave Sanders, and her classmates.

A top scholar-athlete and leader at the school, Burgess was asked to address the 70,000 people attending the Columbine High School Memorial Service alongside then-Vice President Al Gore. Since the tragedy, Burgess has dedicated her life toward making a difference in the lives of others and honoring the lives of her fallen coach and fellow students.

While most high school seniors were dreaming about graduation and contemplating college life, Burgess' senior year was stained with tragedy. Though that pain can never be forgotten, Burgess learned to harness it into her community outreach and uses it to benefit others.

A top athlete in the state of Colorado, Burgess was a member of the USA Junior World Softball team. With the Junior National team, she traveled to Taipei, Taiwan to compete. During her senior year, Burgess earned a spot on the U.S. National Blue Team. Burgess was a finalist for the Fred Steinmark Athlete of the Year Award for excellence in athletics and academics given by the Denver Rocky Mountain News.

Burgess' statewide and nationally known talent earned her a softball scholarship to the University of Nebraska where she started college the fall of 1999. Burgess was a leader on and off the field and was truly committed to community service. She was chosen as captain of the team after only one season, a sign of the high regard in which she was held by her teammates. She lives every day to the fullest, and despite being directly affected by the tragedy at Columbine, she was described as one of the most positive and enthusiastic student-athletes among the 700 who were part of Nebraska's program during her collegiate career. As a freshman, Burgess immediately became involved in the Husker Outreach Program. She was an active member of the Student-Athlete Advisory Committee, a monthly volunteer for Meals on Wheels, a weekly volunteer for the Team Spirit hospital visitation program and was nominated for the NCAA Foundation Leadership Conference. Burgess strives to make an impact on the national level with programming ideas and concerns and has been a keynote speaker at a "Stop the Violence" conference.

Burgess' freshman year at Nebraska started with impressive statistics on the field and her senior year ended in the same fashion. She was selected to the Academic All-Big 12 Team three times. The senior catcher and communication studies major was named to the 2003 Verizon Academic All-District VII team selected by the College Sports Information Directors of America. The three-time co-captain was considered one of the top defensive catchers in Nebraska history. She graduated with three of the top ten single-season putout marks in school history. During her senior year, Nebraska opponents stole just 19 bases on her as she caught opposing runners attempting to steal 18 times. Burgess played in over 250 games at the University of Nebraska, which ranked fourth on the all-time list at the time.

After graduating, Burgess was offered the opportunity to continue her softball career. Professional softball had failed in the United States before, and unless she was training for the Olympics, opportunities were scarce. Then, in 2004, the National Pro Fastpitch league was developed. The Denver-based league consisted of six teams which played 60 games each during the June through August season. Though it is a professional sports league, it is different than many would imagine. There are no million dollar contracts and billion dollar stadiums, no arrogant attitudes representing what sport is not, and no steroids or dress code violations.

The National Pro Fastpitch league was hoping for less than half a million dollars to sustain itself in its first year and was not planning to profit. Burgess was ecstatic to be making just over $5,000 for the 60 game season and to showcase softball to the hundreds of thousands of youth and high school softball players across the country. Burgess plays for the love of the game, the true spirit of sport, and it shows on the field.

Despite the loss of a role model and friend in high school, Amber Burgess persevered, determined not to let her two violent classmates instill fear into her life. She maintained good grades and was the starting catcher for one of the top softball programs in the country, a feat sure to make Coach Sanders smile.

CHAPTER 4

TRANSCENDING SPORT TO HELP SOCIETY

This section brings together a group of athletes and coaches who were dominant in their sport. All are hall of fame players or coaches who were not only spectacular in their game but also went on to use that game to create a platform to make a better world.

Dot Richardson, while arguably the greatest softball player of her generation, simultaneously became a doctor. Her Olympic gold medals are perched next to her medical degree, catapulting Dot Richardson to be a role model for a generation of young girls to believe in what many had previously thought impossible.

Kareem Abdul-Jabbar is arguably the greatest big man ever to play basketball. Jabbar's teams were unrivaled in high school, college and in the pros. Jabbar took his intellect and applied it off the court as the writer of four books, an actor and a coach who took his game to a Native American reservation to coach a high school team.

"Tiny" Archibald, whose stature gave him his nickname, was anything but tiny in becoming an NBA superstar and a community activist in the New York Metropolitan area helping at-risk young people.

Dave Bing, an NBA superstar after a brilliant collegiate career at Syracuse, went on to show African-Americans that they can become entrepreneurs and leaders in industry.

Alan Page was one of the greatest players in Minnesota Vikings history. Like Dot Richardson, he earned his law degree while playing in the NFL. As a public servant, he was elected to the Minnesota Supreme Court as its first African-American member.

Bill Bradley took his academic and athletic talents from Missouri to become a college great at Princeton, a Rhodes Scholar, an NBA great, a United States Senator and a presidential candidate.

"Dr. J," a.k.a Julius Erving, made basketball into an art form in the NBA. Transforming the game, Erving became its ambassador and a major sports executive for the Orlando Magic.

Jackie Joyner-Kersee, believed by many to be the greatest athlete of her generation, never forgot her roots in St. Louis where she built programs to assist impoverished youth.

Lawrence Burton, a legendary NFL player as well as an Olympic athlete in track and field, became even better known at Boys Town in Nebraska where he devoted his life to helping young people.

Then there were the coaches who transcended the game.

Dean Smith became the winningest coach in college basketball history at the University of North Carolina. Smith also became the leading activist against alcohol abuse and took important stands on racial issues in sport and in society.

Joe Paterno, the coaching giant at Penn State who put together an astonishing career record of more than 340 victories led his team at the age of 79 to a 10 and 1 record and Big Ten championship in 2005. Paterno is among Penn State's most generous philanthropists as well as a man who has helped young people in his charge to become leaders among men.

Pat Summitt, the winningest coach in the history of women's college basketball, spent her years at Tennessee helping young girls become women and leaders, not only in sport but also in society.

Tom Osborne was an outstanding football coach at the University of Nebraska for more than two decades when he retired with three National Championships and 65 Academic All-Americans. He went on to become a United States Congressman and then ran for Governor in the State of Nebraska where his popularity was enormous.

Geno Auriemma led the University of Connecticut women's basketball team to one of the most extraordinary records in college sport with five National Championships. He is also known for his philanthropy and service to the community.

All these individuals, so great in their athletic careers, were even greater as leaders!

Dr. Dot Richardson
by Brian Wright

Ben Carson, the Head of Neurosurgery at Johns Hopkins University chronicled his life in the book "Gifted Hands." If there was another person who could write a book with that title it would be Dot Richardson. She is this title personified. As a child, Richardson was a major fan of baseball. Determined to become a member of a local team, she found an all boys baseball team and questioned the coach about joining the team. When she received no encouragement, Richardson was discovered by a fast-pitch softball coach who asked Richardson to join her team. Richardson soon found herself amongst a team of girls older and more experienced than herself. Seemingly unconcerned, she remained on the team and used the time to develop her skills. Richardson ultimately developed into an All-American softball player in college, establishing and breaking numerous softball records. She was named the NCAA Player of the Decade for the 1980's and still is one of the driving forces in the advancement of softball.

In 1979, Richardson had the honor of representing her country in the Pan American Games. This team won the gold medal. Richardson went on to win four other gold medals in the Pan American Games over her career. Richardson also helped lead the United States women's softball teams to four world championships. Richardson is a monumental figure in the sport of softball. In 1993, Richardson decided that she would take a break from softball and embark on a different dream and a totally new way to use her "gifted hands." Richardson enrolled in medical school.

The amazing athletic awards and accomplishments that Richardson had received thus far in life did not diminish her desire to help others. During her residency in 1996 at the University of Southern

California Medical Center, the Olympic Committee decided to include softball as an Olympic Sport. Richardson, with her experience and love for the game, pondered a return to the sport to represent her country. She knew that scheduling conflicts between softball and her residency would occur. Richardson decided an opportunity to compete for her country on the highest level of competition was too great of an honor to miss and began training for the Olympic team. Following strenuous and rigorous hours of work at the medical center, Richardson attended workouts at the UCLA campus softball field. Knowing her time at the field was limited by her responsibilities at the hospital, Richardson decided that she would bring the game closer to her. She built a batting cage in her apartment and used it on the days she couldn't make it to the field. Richardson spoke with the heads of the Medical Program at USC and they granted her a one year leave of absence from her five-year residency to pursue her athletic goals in the Olympics.

As the Olympic Games began, the United States team was considered by many to be the favorite, which was largely because Richardson joined the team. Fittingly, Richardson was the first person to hit a home run in Olympic history. This initial success continued throughout the tournament and Richardson hit the game-winning home run to win the gold medal in the 1996 Olympic Games.

In 1999, Richardson started the Dot Richardson Softball Association (DRSA). DRSA is an instructional, non-profit organization offering educational opportunities to softball coaches and athletes. The Coaches Educational Series is a six-part program that offers instruction on basic and advanced skills, coaching principles, health and safety issues, communication skills, and conditioning and nutrition issues.

Richardson returned to the Olympics in 2000 where, with her help, the United States, again, won the gold medal. With two gold medals on her long list of achievements, Richardson returned to medicine to pursue her life-long passion. In 2001, Richardson discovered a way to balance her career as a doctor with her passion for athletics. She became the medical director at the National Training Center in Clermont, Florida. The 300-acre sports, health, fitness and education campus is unique in that it unites athletic facilities with a hospital, medical office buildings, a community college and a four-year university. Physicians, medical specialists, nurses, athletic trainers, physical therapists, exercise physiologists, exercise specialists, personal trainers, coaches and instructors are all on staff to create this world-class training facility. The National Training Center currently boasts an aquatic center, track & field complex, cross-country course, multi-purpose athletic fields, softball and baseball fields and the plans for expansion are extensive. While Richardson no longer trains for the Olympics, she is able to help others on their road to Olympic glory.

Richardson's courage, competitiveness and determination to achieve excellence defined her Olympic appearances. While success in the Olympics usually leads to endorsements on Wheaties boxes and other lucrative opportunities, Richardson chose another route. She decided it was time for her to fulfill her life's goal to provide medical help to those in need. This selfless act reiterates Richardson's love and passion for helping and inspiring others. Dot Richardson's life shatters all stereotypes of today's selfish athletes and inspires us all to live our lives in service to those in need.

Kareem Abdul-Jabbar

by Jennifer Brenden

When Kareem Abdul-Jabbar was born as Ferdinand Lewis Alcindor Jr., there was no doubt that he was going to be a big man and accomplish big things. At birth, he was a 12 pound, 11 ounce baby boy who was 22 ½ inches long. Lewis grew up as an only child in a Catholic home in a middle-class section of Harlem. He was a quiet child but because of his size he hardly went unnoticed.

At age nine, Abdul-Jabbar stood 5 foot 8 and was bigger than all but one boy at the Catholic school he attended in Pennsylvania. Even though he was one of the biggest guys in the crowd, he was not one of the toughest. Abdul-Jabbar also stuck out at school because he received all A's in his classes and he was well spoken which contributed to his being harassed by the other kids at school. Abdul-Jabbar took his first shot at a basketball hoop when he was nine years old. The sport felt very natural to him. Basketball was the outlet Abdul-Jabbar used to get away from everyone and everything that was going on in his life. Basketball was his comfort zone.

Abdul-Jabbar continued to grow and develop both physically and as a basketball player throughout his pre-teen and early teen years. As an 8th grader he stood 6 foot 8 and was able to dunk a basketball. He pushed himself to get better and he constantly challenged himself.

By age 14, Abdul-Jabbar was standing at 6 foot 11 and he was the star of his varsity high school team at Power Memorial High School in New York City. His basketball domination began at the high school level and would continue throughout his career. The overall record of Abdul-Jabbar's high school team was 95-6, which included a 71-game winning streak. He was also a four-year letter winner (1962-65), three-time All-City selection (1963-65) and three-time All-American selection (1963-65) at Power Memorial High School. These were only stepping stones for accomplishments to come.

His stellar high school play earned him the opportunity to play at UCLA for one of the greatest coaches in basketball history, the incomparable John Wooden. The team Abdul-Jabbar played on would also go down in history as one of the greatest. Unfortunately, in those days, freshmen were ineligible to play on the varsity team. The freshmen had their own team called the Brubabes, and that year, they beat the two-time defending national champions and preseason No.1 varsity team 75-60. The Brubabes went 21-0 that season and Abdul-Jabbar averaged 33 points and 21 rebounds. The next year, in his first varsity appearance, Abdul-Jabbar set a UCLA record by scoring 56 points. He broke his own record later in the season by scoring 61 points.

The three years that Abdul-Jabbar spent at UCLA can only be described as complete domination. There was no championship title or individual accomplishment that he didn't achieve. He led the Bruins to a three-year record of 88-2 and to three straight national championships (67-69). He also accrued several accolades for himself. With those three national championships, he became the first player to be a three-time NCAA Tournament Most Valuable Player (67-69). Abdul-Jabbar was also *The Sporting College News'* and national Player of the Year in 1967 and 1969, the Naismith Award Winner in 1969, and a three-time All-American selection (67-69). He left the school as the leading scorer in UCLA history and the sixth highest scorer in major college history (2,325 points, 26.4 ppg).

While attending classes and playing basketball at UCLA, Abdul-Jabbar began studying the Muslim movement and the teachings of the Koran. A few years after he graduated from college, Abdul-Jabbar changed his name from Ferdinand Lewis Alcindor, Jr. The Muslim leader who served as his mentor renamed him Kareem Abdul-Jabbar, which means "noble, powerful servant."

In 1969, Abdul-Jabbar was drafted by the Milwaukee Bucks who had the worst record in the league in their conference. Abdul-Jabbar established himself instantly as a force to be reckoned with. He was a different kind of big man than the league was used to seeing. Typically, the center position tried to exploit force and strength but Abdul-Jabbar was a long, lanky, finesse player, who used his agility down low. His patented skyhook shot was virtually unstoppable and it has yet to be replicated by another player. He earned Rookie of the Year honors in his first season with the Bucks. He also led the team to 56 wins, a 29-game improvement from the previous season. During his second year with the team, the Bucks won 66 regular season games and continued on to win the world championship. Abdul-Jabbar won the first of his six MVP titles this same year.

Abdul-Jabbar was traded to the Los Angeles Lakers, prior to the 1975-76 season. He continued to succeed with the Lakers. Abdul-Jabbar helped lead the Lakers to five world championships (1980-82, 1985, 1987 & 1988). Abdul-Jabbar retired from professional basketball in 1989 at the age of 42. He was the first player to play 20 years in the NBA. The impressive list of highlights that Abdul-Jabbar accrued over his 20-year career has yet to be surpassed by any NBA player. At the end of his career, Abdul-Jabbar was at the top of nine NBA statistical categories, including points scored (38,387), seasons played (20), playoff scoring (5,762), MVP awards (6), minutes played (57,446), games played (1,560), field goals made and attempted (15,837 of 28,307) and blocked shots (3,189). Furthermore, he played in 18 NBA All-Star games (1970-1977, 1979-1989), was an NBA MVP (1971-72, 1974, 1976, 1977, 1980), an NBA Finals MVP (1971, 1985), and was selected to the NBA First Team (1971-1974, 1976-1977, 1980-1981, 1984, 1986), and to the NBA All-Defensive First Team (1974-1975, 1979-1981).

In 1993, Abdul-Jabbar was the first basketball player ever to receive the National Sports Award, presented by President Bill Clinton, and he was inducted into the "Presidential Hall of Fame" along with four other athletes. His induction into the Basketball Hall of Fame soon followed in 1995.

Since retiring from playing basketball, he has spent the majority of his time coaching and writing. His love and passion for the game will never end, so now he focuses on passing on his knowledge to the next generation. Abdul-Jabbar does many public speaking events retelling inspirational stories that led to his success or speaking of his inspirational writings and the messages that they convey. He worked on the Fort Apache Indian Reservation as an assistant coach, creating hope for and teaching basketball skills to Native-American basketball players. He believes that people in his position, with time and money to share, should do so. He has also helped to fight hunger and illiteracy. He has written several books *(Giant Steps, Kareem, A Season on the Reservation, Black Profiles in Courage* and *Brothers in Arms*) and appeared in movies as well.

He has also coached for the Los Angeles Clippers, worked as a consultant for the Indiana Pacers, and coached the USBL's Oklahoma

Storm. In 2004, he was hired by the New York Knicks, and most recently, he has been employed by the Lakers. Basketball is in his blood and he will continue giving back through the sport for as long as he can. Kareem Abdul-Jabbar was, and still is a very much admired basketball player, but he is much admired as a person as well.

Nate "Tiny" Archibald

by Jennifer Brenden

Professional athletes have been getting bigger, taller and stronger since the beginning of professional sports. Seven-footers in the NBA are now commonplace, and there are even 7 foot tall women playing in the WNBA. Size and strength are a big part of the game, but there are ways to play big without being big and to exploit strengths that aren't necessarily physical. NBA Hall of Famer, Nate Archibald, also known as "Tiny" Archibald, is a perfect example of the undersized player who had to work twice as hard to accomplish the same things that bigger, stronger competitors achieved.

Growing up in the Bronx, New York, Archibald was a very shy, reserved child. And his basketball skills did not become apparent until later in his teen years. He was actually cut from the basketball team in his sophomore year and he came very close to dropping out of DeWitt Clinton High School. Fortunately, for himself, and for all those who were "Tiny" Archibald fans during his career, he did not drop out of school and he did not give up on his aspirations to play basketball. He came back the next year and made the basketball team as a junior. From then on, he continued to improve and he earned All-City accolades in both his junior and senior years. In spite of being a quiet person, he was also the captain of the team his senior year, which says a lot about him as a player and his ability to lead. If this story sounds familiar, it's because Michael Jordan had a similar experience early in his basketball career, and he obviously went on to have a successful career.

The 6 foot 1, 160-pound point guard was very deceiving and he could do a lot more on the court than was apparent from his size. Spectators often doubted his ability. Despite his size, he was a dominating player at every level in which he played. It was always only a matter of time before he disproved those who had doubted him.

Archibald attended Arizona Western Junior College and maintained his aspirations to play in the NBA. After his first year, he transferred to the University of Texas at El Paso, where he averaged more than 20 points per game as a junior and as a senior. He was also an Honorable Mention All-American and was named Most Valuable Player of the Western Athletic Conference (WAC) his senior year in 1970. Years later he was selected to the WAC 20-year All-Star Team as well.

The Cincinnati Royals, coached by Hall of Famer Bob Cousy, took a chance on Archibald in 1970 when he was chosen in the second round of the NBA Draft. There were many skeptics, as there had been throughout Archibald's career, but just as he had done in the past, he would prove himself on the court. He far surpassed everyone's expectations that first year in the league.

Archibald was a quick and crafty penetrator who seemed to go to the basket at will. He was also a very impressive outside shooter with deep range and he possessed phenomenal passing skills as well. He was a triple threat player who was always ready to shoot, penetrate or pass. A defender couldn't play off of him and protect the drive because he could shoot the three. At the same time, if the defender played Archibald too tight, he would drive right around to the basket. And to really make things tough for defenses, nobody else's player could help because he would inevitably find the open man. Needless to say, his arsenal of offensive weapons made him a very difficult player to guard. When the Royals moved to Kansas City/Omaha in 1972, and became known as the Kings, Archibald received the nickname of "Nate the Skate" because of his smooth moves on the court. In the first season as the Kansas City Kings, "Nate the Skate" averaged 34 points per game, along with 11.4 assists. He became the only player in NBA history to lead the league in both of those categories in the same season.

Archibald's NBA career lasted 14 years. During those 14 years, he played for Cincinnati (1970-72), Kansas City/Omaha (1972-76), New York Nets (1976-77), Buffalo (1977-78, injured, did not play), Boston (1978-83), and Milwaukee (1983-84). He was a slasher and a penetrator, and when he went to the hoop, almost inevitably, he either scored or was fouled. Consequently, he led the league in free throws made three times and free throws attempted twice. Archibald was an All-NBA First Team selection three times in 1973, 1975 and 1976, an All-NBA Second Team selection in 1972 and 1981, a six-time All-Star Game selection and MVP of the 1981 All-Star Game. A high point of his career was when he helped lead the Boston Çeltics to an NBA Championship in 1981 along with three consecutive years of having the best NBA record from 1980 to 1982. Archibald was inducted in to the Naismith Memorial Basketball Hall of Fame in 1991 and named one of the 50 Greatest Players in NBA History in 1996.

Archibald retired from the NBA in 1984 and moved back to New York. He proceeded to run basketball schools for underprivileged kids and to work as the athletic director at the Harlem Amory homeless shelter until it closed in 1991. While he was working these jobs, Archibald earned a Masters Degree in Adult Education and Human Resources Development from Fordham University in 1990. He proceeded to earn his Professional Degree in Supervisions and Administration in 1994 and is currently working on his doctorate in education.

In more recent years, Archibald accepted a coaching position in the National Basketball Developmental League (NBDL). He became the head coach of the Fayetteville Patriots halfway through the NBDL's inaugural season in 2001. Archibald loves coaching and sharing his knowledge of the game with others. His passion for the game is obvious, which is why it was such a hard decision for him to step down from his coaching position less than a year after he was appointed.

In January of 2002, Archibald was offered a position with the NBA's Community Relations Team. It was a hard decision to make, but difficult as it would be to leave the sidelines as a coach, he could not turn down this unique opportunity with the NBA. He knew this position would allow him to combine his two loves of basketball and community service. The passion that Nate "Tiny" Archibald has in this area will surely drive him to be very successful in this new venture.

Dave Bing

by Jennifer Brenden

Dave Bing knew he wanted to own his own business at a very early age, even before he had thoughts of playing in the NBA. His interest in entrepreneurship started when he went to work with his dad who was a contractor. Helping his dad on construction sites helped Bing develop a strong work ethic that would guide him throughout his life, both as an athlete and as a businessman.

Bing had to overcome some obstacles early in his life to become a successful athlete. At the age of five he was playing with two sticks that were nailed together. As he was running around, he tripped and one of the nails struck Bing's left eye. Surgery saved his eye, but Bing was told by doctors that his vision would be permanently impaired. He was told by others that he was too small to play basketball. Pushed towards baseball when he was younger, it was his high school basketball coach who helped him realize his potential to earn a scholarship to play Division I college basketball.

Bing graduated from Syracuse University in 1966 as an All-American and educated for his future business ventures with degrees in economics and marketing. He was the second overall pick in the NBA draft, and he began his pro career with the Detroit Pistons. He averaged 20 points per game that first year and earned NBA Rookie of the Year honors for the 1966-67 season. The very next year he led the NBA in scoring with 27.1 points per game.

Tragedy struck prior to the 1971-72 season when Bing was poked in the eye during an exhibition game by a Los Angeles Laker. He had surgery for a detached retina and spent three months recuperating. Bing was back on the court in late December despite doctors telling him that returning to the court could continue to worsen his eyesight. Bing's peripheral vision which basketball players rely heavily upon was also impaired by the injury. One of Bing's many strengths on the court was driving to the basket, drawing defenders to him, and finding the open man and dishing off the ball. It was thus very impressive that Bing continued to be an assist leader after his injury.

After nine seasons with the Pistons, he got the opportunity to play for the Washington Bullets in front of his hometown crowd. He spent two seasons with the Bullets and one season with the Boston Celtics before retiring from the game in 1978.

Some athletes find the transition out of professional sports very difficult. This was absolutely not true in Bing's case. From the time he entered the NBA, he was preparing for his post-basketball career, when he would get his chance to fulfill his dream of starting his own business. During the off-season, when most professional athletes take the time to relax, rehab, and prepare for the next season, Bing chose to go out and get a job. He worked at a bank, for the Chrysler Corporation and for a small steel company over the course of his NBA career. When he retired, he was offered a job with Paragon Steel, but he chose to go into their management-trainee program and after only two years, he created Bing Steel.

It was a bit of a struggle at first, partially complicated by his image as an athlete. Overcoming the stereotype of being a black athlete made his transition harder. He had to create a new name and image for himself as a serious businessman with serious potential in the business world. Within two years, Bing Steel began to generate profits and by 1990 sales had grown to $61 million. Bing expanded his corporation and collectively, the different companies belonged to the Bing Group.

Bing's success in the steel industry shows that he became a successful businessman. But Bing has had other post-basketball successes as well that are manifest in his developing sense of social responsibility in metropolitan Detroit. The city has been plagued by serious unemployment for many years, and Bing took it upon himself to help the unemployed find and keep jobs. The problem was the people he wanted to hire weren't very qualified for the jobs that were available. Instead of simply passing over these candidates, Bing chose to help the candidates become more qualified. In 1999, the Bing Group teamed up with its biggest client, Ford, and built a $4 million dollar training facility in Detroit. Some of the trainees who came to the facility didn't work out as Bing had hoped, but the majority developed the skills they needed to work in Bing's manufacturing facility.

Sales totaled $344 million for the Bing Group in 2002. Today it is the 5th largest African-American owned business in America. His business plan intends to see sales of $1 billion by 2008. He wants to continue to break down the racial prejudices that still exist in corporate America and he will continue to be an advocate for social change in Detroit. Currently, Bing sits on several boards, such as the Michigan Minority Business Development Council and the National Association of Black Automotive Suppliers. In addition to those memberships, he also serves several different charitable organizations, many of which work to improve education for children in Detroit. Bing is truly a respected entrepreneur, philanthropist and leader in the community of Detroit, and many would like to see him hold political office one day.

Bing has been inducted in to the Naismith Basketball Hall of Fame, he's had his jersey officially retired by the Pistons, his company has been voted Company of the Year by *Black Enterprise* magazine, and he has improved the Detroit community through employment opportunities, giving to charities and education programs for children. With all that Dave Bing has achieved in his life and for all those people that he has helped, there will still never be a point when Bing will feel like he has done enough. He will continue to work for social change and economic improvement even as he continues to grow his own company and achieve increasingly great levels of professional success.

Alan Page

by Jennifer Brenden

Being a professional athlete is very intense and all-consuming and most athletes have little time for anything else but playing their sport. Alan Page managed to be a standout professional football player, while simultaneously earning his law degree. This was no easy task since attending law school demands a level of engagement that is probably the equal of participating in professional sports. Page graduated from the University of Minnesota Law School in 1978 and he didn't retire from professional football until 1981. Although Page accomplished some amazing feats in his football career, education has always been the most important aspect of his life. Valuing education is what Page emphasizes to the youth of his community.

Page began his professional football career with the Vikings in 1967 after being an All-American defensive end at Notre Dame. He was converted to a defensive tackle when he joined the Vikings and became a starter in the fourth game of the season. Those first three games were the only games in his 238 game career which he didn't start. Page was the first defensive player to be NFL MVP in 1971. He was Defensive Player of the Year in 1971 and 1973. He received All-Pro honors six times and he won four NFL/NFC title games. For his performance on the field, he was eventually inducted in to the NFL Hall of Fame in 1988.

Page concluded his NFL career with the Chicago Bears in 1981 but his legacy is even greater today. He practiced private law and later became Minnesota's assistant attorney general, a position he held until 1993 when he was elected to the State Supreme Court. Despite Page's legal responsibilities, he has always found the time to emphasize the importance of education to the community.

In a speech given at Kent State University, Page spoke of improving society through educating our youth, taking responsibility for our actions and ridding society of prejudice and bias. Page noted, "If we're going to solve society's problems, we're going to have to provide education opportunities and equal opportunities for all children and people."

Page's drive to get involved with the educational system came from a situation that occurred during his football career. He and a few teammates were asked to study their new playbook, and it became very apparent to him that several of them were struggling trying to read the text. It amazed him that his fellow professional teammates made it through high school and college without being able to read very well. Page was appalled not only at his teammate's inability to read but at the educational systems that failed students and he decided to make a commitment to improve those systems. This inspired Page and his wife to become co-founders of The Page Educational Foundation in 1988.

In his induction speech at the NFL Hall of Fame, he chose to focus on the establishment of the Page Education Foundation and promote the benefits of educating our youth. At that ceremony, Page focused as much on education as sports. "At the very best, athletic achievement might open a door that discrimination once held shut. But the doors slam quickly on the unprepared and the undereducated," Page said.

The basic purpose of The Page Education Foundation is to encourage Minnesota's youth of color to continue their educations beyond high school. The program offers a variety of resources ranging from mentoring and service-to-children projects to partial scholarships for college. After a scholarship applicant has been granted some kind of financial aid, the only requirement is the student volunteer in the community with elementary school students. The direct financial benefits that college students are receiving are a very important part of the program, but the goal of the program is more long-term. It is attempting to reach children at a very critical age and instill in them the importance of education. The children in the program are not simply trying to become more book-smart. The program also aims to develop the children's character and make them good people and good citizens as well.

In the Foundation's first year, there were ten scholarship recipients. By 2005, the Foundation had granted more than 3,000 scholarships. Most kids receiving these scholarships probably would not have gone to college without the help of the Foundation. Many recipients come from low-income families and are often first-generation college students.

Page says that he was very fortunate to have parents who taught him the importance of education at a very young age and he recognizes that many children today are not as fortunate. Several factors may cause parents not to stress education, such as poverty, discrimination, low literacy, or an inability to speak English at all. The Foundation wants to create a sense of hope within young children of color by providing opportunities for them.

In November of 2000, Page was recognized by the Minneapolis community where he currently resides by having a Twin Cities Landmark named after him to remind future generations of the impact he has had in the community. The Mixed Blood Theater celebrated its 25th year of existence by renaming the theater the Alan Page Auditorium. The Mayor of Minneapolis declared the day to be Alan Page Day.

Page has always taken his accomplishments in stride. He has achieved so much in his life, yet he still strives to do good deeds and help others everyday. Some may find this sort of ambition and drive wearing, but it is that drive that gets him out of bed everyday. He loves having that purpose to push him to be the best he can be all the time. He still hopes to teach one day but is unsure if he'll ever get the opportunity.

Page also occasionally attends local schools to hold hearings and then answer questions from students to give them some insight into the judicial system. He also helped establish the Kodak/Alan Page Challenge, a nationwide essay contest which encourages urban youth to recognize the value of education.

In May of 2003, Page joined a very elite group of people when he was honored by Scholarship America with one of its prestigious President's Awards. The President's Award is given to an individual who has demonstrated outstanding support to education primarily through the support of scholarship programs and programs designed to improve educational access and encourage educational achievement.

He received the award for establishing the Alan Page Foundation and the Page Scholars Program. Scholarship America is the nation's largest private sector scholarship and educational support organization. Page joined Tom Brokaw, NBC News; Roger Enrico, PepsiCo; and former Senate Majority leader, Robert Dole, just to name a few fellow award recipients.

The work that Page has done throughout the years in providing educational opportunities for children of color has made him a well-respected, well-known leader in the Twin Cities community. His strong educational beliefs, along with his athletic prowess, have made Alan Page a true hero in sports and education.

Bill Bradley

by Brian Wright

Growing up in the small town of Crystal City, Missouri, Bill Bradley had large dreams. Bradley developed a love of learning and the skills to participate in competitive sports while very young. At the age of nine, he picked up a basketball and became passionate about learning how to play the sport. As the years progressed, Bradley's basketball skills did as well. As a varsity high school basketball player, Bradley was a local star averaging over 27 points per game, and finished high school with over 3,000 points. Bradley was honored as a two-time Parade All-American selection during his high school career. As a student, Bradley was very diligent in balancing athletic and educational requirements. He maintained a very high grade point average and was considered by his teachers to be a superior student. At 6 foot 5, Bradley had swiftly become one of the most sought-after high school players in the country. He received more than 70 scholarship offers to very prestigious and well-known basketball institutions such as the University of Kentucky. So Bradley surprised many people when he chose to attend Princeton University where he paid for his own education since the school did not award athletic scholarships.

Bradley was able to adjust to collegiate life very quickly. He became a leader on the court and among the general Princeton student body. On the basketball court Bradley led the men's varsity basketball team in scoring each of his three years. He compiled over 2,500 total points, averaging over 30 points per game. Bradley led the Princeton Tigers to three consecutive Ivy League basketball championships as well as an unexpected trip to the NCAA Final Four in 1965. Bradley was named the 1965 Collegiate Basketball Player of the Year, an honor not typically awarded to members of basketball programs at Ivy League institutions. Bradley was awarded the James E. Sullivan Award which honors the United States' top amateur athlete. Bradley also had the honor to captain the 1964 gold-medal winning United States Men's Olympic team.

With such time and effort spent in developing and polishing his basketball skills, some assumed Bradley would have less time and energy for anything else. But Bradley was an exceptional student, which was recognized by the Rhodes Selection Committee when they awarded him a Rhodes scholarship to continue his studies at Oxford. Bradley was one of only 32 Rhodes scholarship winners from the United States. After graduating from Oxford, Bradley chose to pursue his childhood desire to play basketball professionally.

Bradley soon found himself in Italy, playing professional basketball with the Olimpia Milano team and competing for the European Cup. Bradley made a large impact on the success of the team which won the European Cup and in the process he caught the eye of NBA scouts. The New York Knicks, intrigued the most by Bradley, signed him to a contract. Bradley played the game with such intelligence and thought he was considered by many to be a model for playing with the proper fundamentals. While playing for the Knicks, Bradley was a key contributor, averaging 12.1 points per game and was a great compliment to other Knicks players. Bradley contributed to two different NBA Championship teams with the Knicks in 1970 and 1973. He played ten full seasons in the NBA before he retired and pursued new and different goals.

Bradley wanted to positively affect social change and believed the easiest way to do so was through politics. In 1978, Bradley ran and won his first post as the Senator from New Jersey, replacing four-term incumbent Senator Clifford P. Case. Though entering as a new member, Bradley took a strong stance on issues of education, child poverty, gun control and health care reform. Bradley also supported a campaign to stop racial profiling by federal and state police officials. Bradley's commitment to public service and social justice earned him the respect of the voters in New Jersey.

Bradley established an annual event where he would walk along the streets of Jersey City and meet people within the community which he coined the "Labor-Day talk-to-citizens stroll." Aware of the ever-growing problems within society, Bradley felt that he could better change the state of this country by becoming President. Bradley made his run at office in the 2000 presidential primaries when he challenged front-runner and Vice President Al Gore for the party's nomination. Bradley's campaign was based on his commitment to solve social problems that had motivated him to run for public office. He campaigned to end poverty, particularly among children. He also remained committed to ending the gun violence that had killed so many children. Education for all was also a major point of interest for Bradley. This was due in a large part to his experience as a student and how important a role it played on shaping and developing his life. Though he was unsuccessful in winning the democratic nomination, he pointed out some glaring social problems that needed attention and change.

Bill Bradley is truly one of a kind; he is the only professional athlete in American history who combined a superb record as a sportsman with a career as a political reader who aspired and nearly achieved his party's endorsement as a presidential candidate. He introduced the Student-Athlete Right-To-Know Act that, for the first time, allowed high school recruits to know the graduation rates of the colleges recruiting them. The Bradley Bill, an important piece of legislation which he sponsored and which carries his name did more to help integrate the peoples of the former Soviet Union and the Warsaw Pact countries into the world community of nations than any other initiative undertaken by the American government. But whether dealing with education or social justice or poverty in Kiev and Minsk or in Jersey City and Patterson, Bill Bradley's commitment to helping underserved populations are legend. He is a man among men; a hero among heroes.

Julius Erving

by Jessica Bartter

Legend has it the game of basketball started with peach baskets nailed to the gym wall, a soccer ball and a court half the size of current National Basketball Association (NBA) regulations. It took only 13 rules to explain the new game in 1891 when Dr. James Naismith, a Canadian-born American minister, invented "basket ball" to give young men more activity during the brutal winter months in New England. Obviously, the game has evolved year after year, with new generations of players and coaches inventing new moves and strategies hoping to outshine their predecessors. It may be hard for younger generations, particularly athletes, to imagine, but basketball did not always receive the interest and acclaim it is accustomed to now. The history of the NBA in the 1950's and 60's involved a few diehard fans, minimal television coverage and mediocre salaries for players. That is until Julius Erving emerged on the hardwood floor with his commanding hands that handled the ball like no one before him.

There would be others to follow, Michael Jordan, Larry Bird, Magic Johnson among them, but Julius Erving set a new standard for excellence on the basketball court. Fans, white and black alike, respected Erving for his humanity and celebrated him for his game. Erving put up the numbers in high school, college and his early career in the American Basketball Association (ABA), but went somewhat unnoticed until his time in the NBA. Erving first picked up a basketball when he was eight and quickly appreciated the challenge it presented. Erving started his career at Roosevelt High School in New York in 1964 at just 5 foot 9. A friend and teammate nicknamed him the "Doctor." When he became a professional athlete, teammates shortened it to "Dr. J," which is what he is affectionately known as now. In his junior and senior high school years, Erving made All-Conference, was named Outstanding Player and caught the interest of the University of Massachusetts as he grew to be 6 foot 3. In his very first collegiate game, Erving scored 27 points and had 28 rebounds, a school record at the time. Although he only stayed at UMass for two years, Erving left a huge mark. He started in all 52 games and finished with 1,370 points, the best in school history, even compared to the totals posted by many four year players. He broke or tied 14 school records ranging from rebounds to minutes per game. His talent certainly was worthy of an invitation to the first Olympic development basketball camp, but still Erving was overlooked after his sophomore year. When an invitee was injured, Erving arrived as the replacement. Although it was a last-minute decision, Erving proved he was the right choice. The team toured Eastern Europe and the Soviet Union and Erving emerged as the best player despite almost missing the opportunity entirely.

After the successful stint with the Olympic development team, Erving turned pro with the Virginia Squires of the American Basketball Association in 1971. His first professional game with the Squires remains his most exciting in what became a 16 year long career. He had 20 points and 19 rebounds that night. Erving knew the fast pace of his team coupled with their creative style was sure to change the game of basketball and please fans of all ages. Erving is credited with adding style to what was once a running game with physical giants who could dominate the basket. Erving continued to grow until he was 25, but at 6 foot 7, he did not play his size. Erving proved athleticism was a prerequisite for basketball. The graceful way he flew through the air like an agile six footer doing skills only previously performed by the giant seven footer amazed fans and filled arenas with spectators intent on seeing this basketball genius.

Erving played two seasons for the Squires before spending three with the New York Nets, also of the ABA. During those three seasons he was named to the ABA All-Star First Team each year, earned ABA MVP honors and two ABA Championships in 1974 and 1976. Erving led the ABA in scoring in 1973 with an average of 31.9 points per game and in 1974 with 27.4. In spite of stars like Erving, the ABA had been struggling for years and reached an agreement at the conclusion of the 1976 season to dissolve and merge with the NBA. While many players from disbanded teams were picked up individually by NBA teams, the Denver Nuggets, Indiana Pacers, San Antonio Spurs and Erving's New York Nets were absorbed into the league as teams. Shortly after the merger, Erving was traded the Philadelphia 76ers. Erving stayed with the 76ers from 1976 until 1987, leading his team with his play and his off-the-court presence. In 1981, at the age of 31, he was named MVP of the NBA. Erving appeared in the NBA All-Star game every year from 1977-1987. He was the game's MVP twice. He was named to the All-NBA First Team in 1978 and 1980-1983 and the All-NBA Second Team in 1977 and 1984. In 1983, Erving led the 76ers to an NBA Championship. While these are all great accomplishments for an athlete, it was more important for Erving that he be respected as a person by his teammates and the fans. The character and persona that Erving presented made it difficult for anyone to think otherwise. As Erving redefined the forward position, he defined the role of the professional athlete as well. He showed that he was a leader on and off the court, committed to his community with a dedicated attitude and strong work ethic. While his athleticism was unmatched, he served as a valuable role model for aspiring and current professional athletes.

Erving retired as a professional athlete in 1987 at the age of 37. He was ready for new challenges in life and was determined to never fully devote his life to just one thing again, other than his family. Erving has been involved in many business endeavors, both in and unrelated to sports. He has been one of the owners of the Coca-Cola Bottling Company in Philadelphia, Garden State Cable in New Jersey and Queen City Broadcasting in New York. He has served several companies including Spaulding Sporting Goods, Converse Shoes, Dr. Scholl's, Shearing Plow and Jiffy Lube as a spokesman, consultant or member of the advisory staff. Erving served NBC as a commentator, the Orlando Magic as executive vice president, NBA International as director, and the marketing and management firm JDREGI as president. Erving also enjoys giving motivational speeches sharing the countless lessons he learned as a professional athlete.

In life, Erving has a knack for seeing the whole picture. It was evident on the court that he could see more than his defenders. The values instilled in him as a boy from his mother were everlasting and helped him to think big. She stressed the importance of education and being a good person, something she thought was really not a difficult thing to do with the right mindset. Erving grasped her love and advice and developed into an intelligent and confident man ready to conquer anything. Erving's attitude helped him see the world and open his life to academics, family and other important aspects that helped him grow emotionally and spiritually. Even when basketball became the center of Erving's life, he wondered what other areas in his life he could expand. Erving emerged from the NBA as more than a great athlete, but also as a fine human being helping others succeed in and out of the world of sports.

Jackie Joyner-Kersee

by Stacy Martin

Jackie Joyner-Kersee has always had "a kind of grace"[1] as an athlete because while she is a tough competitor she has always demonstrated poise and charm on and off the track. Her race in life has been filled with obstacle after obstacle, but she breezed past each one with her head held high as if each was just another hurdle on the track. Her maternal grandmother, Evelyn Joyner, named her Jacqueline after former first lady of the United States, Jacqueline Kennedy Onassis, a woman known for her elegance. Evelyn knew that Joyner-Kersee would also be a first lady.

Joyner-Kersee quickly secured the title of "Greatest Woman Athlete of the Twentieth Century" [2] assuring her place as the first lady of track and field for quite some time. She competed in the heptathlon, a two-day event comprised of the 100m hurdles, high jump, shot put, and 200 meters on the first day, and the long jump, javelin, and 800 meters on the second. It's not simply that she was the first female to become so decorated in track and field, for as time passes her records will be passed on to future generations of runners. Rather, Joyner-Kersee will remain in our memories because of the way she conducted herself with such class.

Joyner-Kersee grew up in East St. Louis, Illinois and spent most of her time at the Mary Brown Community Center that offered sports to young people as well as story time and painting. Joyner-Kersee's neighborhood was plagued with violence and drug abuse, so the community center was as much a safe haven as it was an opportunity for personal growth. Al and Mary, Joyner-Kersee's parents, had married young and were barely out of childhood themselves when they gave birth to Jackie. Mary Joyner was extremely conscientious about her daughter's future and so she pushed her in the classroom and on the athletic fields, to break the cycle of babies having babies that seems so compelling in a poor community. Her daughter was to know greatness, not poverty. Joyner-Kersee's trek to the top would start when she joined the track club at age nine without any financial resources. She sold candles to her elementary classmates to raise money for track meet travel expenses. She ran in a pair of shoes until the rubber wore out or they fell off. She didn't need shoes to race past her competition. She was a good student as well. Joyner-Kersee had it all from a young age.

Evelyn Joyner doted on Joyner-Kersee by playing dress up with her and painting her tiny fingernails so they would match her own. Joyner-Kersee felt like the first lady when her grandmother was around. She was the adult who always made her feel special as a child. Evelyn planned a trip from Chicago to visit her darling granddaughter, and Joyner-Kersee could rarely contain her excitement anytime her grandmother planned a visit. The trip was only a few days away, when the family received a call that Evelyn would be visiting the angels instead. Joyner-Kersee's step-grandfather was a destructive alcoholic. He had come home drunk from the bar and shot her grandmother while she was sleeping with a 12-gauge shotgun. Joyner-Kersee had it all, except her loving grandmother. She never drank or used any recreational drugs because she saw how their use often leads to violence. She is proud of the fact that her family never became victims of violence because they continued to expect great things from one another and encouraged one another's hopes and dreams, just as Evelyn encouraged Joyner-Kersee to be the first lady of whatever her heart desired.

Joyner-Kersee became a talented high school athlete in track and field as well as basketball. She was so successful that she was offered a scholarship to the University of California at Los Angeles (UCLA), consistently one of the top track and field programs in the country. She was so talented that she is one of the few athletes who could handle the demands of two sports and her coursework. Her mother asked her to come home for Christmas her freshman year, but she declined and promised to come home in the spring. Unfortunately, she would return home sooner than that. Joyner-Kersee's mother died suddenly from meningitis just a short time after the Christmas invitation she declined. Joyner-Kersee went home to attend her mother's funeral. Her three siblings were terribly grief stricken. As the eldest child Joyner-Kersee had to remain strong. She held her head high above the abyss of emotion drowning everyone else. Returning to school, she remained strong for nearly a year but the wave of grief found her in Los Angeles the next Christmas when Joyner-Kersee realized that she wouldn't be getting a call to come home that year. The tears flowed and she momentarily lost the resilience that she so elegantly displayed on the athletic fields. Her indestructible façade may have cracked, but it would not crumble. She endured the almost insurmountable pain, and continued on the path her mother had set her on all those years ago. She continued her education to set an example for her family, showing them life will go on and they will not become victims of tragedy.

It is often said that when a door closes, there is an open window. However, one can get seriously scraped climbing through. Joyner-Kersee saw her open window as an open lane on the track, but in 1982 she developed a condition known as exercise induced asthma. As a woman who characterized herself as invincible she was shaken to the core when told that she has limitations. Jackie Joyner-Kersee denied that she had a disease, but today she admits that she was scared to acknowledge it. She went so far as to hide her inhaler from people, even when her breath escaped her and she needed to use it. Eventually, she couldn't deny its existence any longer; she didn't take her inhaler with her to practice one day and ended up in an emergency room feeling suffocated and losing control. When she woke up, she awakened with an awareness of her disease and realized that her medication was life-sustaining. However, her athlete persona had to realize that a new routine and workouts were part of that medication, and that she was not weak and vulnerable because of it.

Once again, doors seemed to be closing on her and her escape to the field or track from life's anxiety seemed to be slipping away. Someone special stepped in and helped her manage her disease as well as her track and field career. Bob Kersee was the assistant coach at UCLA and had experienced the loss of his mother as well. He offered his support to Joyner-Kersee and then helped her gain control of her asthma. He encouraged her to continue in track and field as the same fierce competitor that she had always been, and helped her realize that the asthma was not a limitation, just something to contend with and be treated for. His compassion and reinforcement were invaluable to Joyner-Kersee and they became good friends. Four years later, they became husband and wife. Bob has the same fire in him that Joyner-Kersee does when it comes to competition. He is her biggest critic and her biggest fan on the track. He will scream at her on the track and cook her dinner the same evening. They truly complement each other and their relationship has proven successful in life and in sport.

Joyner-Kersee became a household name because of her remarkable athletic achievements. Her willpower to compete with asthma enhanced her prestige. Her collegiate athletic career started her on the path to success when she set the NCAA record for the heptathlon twice. She continued to play basketball for UCLA during this time as well and was recognized as the UCLA All-University Athlete for three years. In 1984, Joyner-Kersee won the silver medal at the Olympics and finished 5th in the long jump. She won numerous heptathlon titles after that at the World Championships and Goodwill Games. She graduated from college, married Bob, and then in 1988, she struck gold. She set the world record in the heptathlon at the U.S. Olympic Trials and won the long jump. She traveled to the Olympics and won a gold medal for both the heptathlon and the long jump events. She beat her own world record in the heptathlon and set an Olympic record in the long jump. In 1992, she won gold once more in the Olympic heptathlon and stole silver in the long jump. Four years later, Joyner-Kersee won a bronze medal in the long jump after she had pulled a muscle and had to withdraw from the heptathlon. In fact, she did not lose a heptathlon for over 12 years from 1984 until the 1996 Olympic Trials.

Her success in track and field built the pedestal on which she so gracefully speaks from today. She was a star female athlete during a time when girls who competed in sports were commonly referred to as tomboys. She challenged that perception by exuding what she calls "a kind of grace." She describes her definition of grace in her autobiography which appropriately is titled *A Kind of Grace*. She continues to promote women in athletics and encourages young girls to follow in her footsteps.

Her career came full circle around the track and finished at her starting line in East St. Louis. The community center that she enjoyed so much as a child had closed while she was traveling the world for track meets and publicity appearances. She took a percentage of all of her endorsements and raised $40,000 to reopen the center for the children of East St. Louis and give them some of the same opportunities that had placed her in such an advantageous position. It wasn't enough, but Joyner-Kersee would not be deterred. She explored other ways to finance a brand new 37-acre facility that would boast both indoor and outdoor tracks, basketball courts and state-of-the-art computer rooms. She is determined to create opportunities for children who are facing the same tough decisions and turbulent lifestyles that she did when she was their age. One such experience that she provided was a trip to New York City for the Macy's Thanksgiving Day Parade for 100 children through her Jackie Joyner-Kersee Community Foundation. The inspiration that she received at the Mary Brown Center when she was nine was so profound that all of her efforts are focused on her foundation today.

She also speaks out about asthma as her next great opponent. She says that she approaches fighting the disease as if it is one of her competitors and her treatment is the training she needs to be competitive. According to Letterlough of the *Philadelphia Tribune*, African-Americans "only represent 12 percent of our population, [but] they comprise 26 percent of the deaths related to asthma."[3] Joyner-Kersee was fortunate enough to have the proper medical treatment for her disease, but she realizes that so many do not have the availability of sound medical care that is needed to manage the disease properly. She knows that African-Americans are more likely to simply attempt to live with asthma, and she wants to use her status to draw attention to how tragedy can happen without treatment and how one can live a full and complete life with it.

She also speaks about the importance of goal setting and violence prevention. She challenges her audience to think about what could happen at their school even though they have not experienced a violent act as of yet, and how they could prevent it. The loss of her grandmother had a profound influence on her life. She now wants to provide a positive influence for today's youth. She had goals and dreams that carried her out of an impoverished neighborhood and that brought her back to that same town with a renewed purpose. She emphasizes that having goals is a real antidote to violence. Her audience may have come to hear Jackie Joyner-Kersee, the world's greatest female athlete, but they left hearing a message that challenged them to be serious about their future.

Joyner-Kersee has experienced the power that sport can have, and she has done everything she can to utilize that power. She has even entered the business of sports, first and foremost through her endorsement money that she has funneled into the Jackie Joyner-Kersee Community Foundation. She ventured outside her sport to become certified as a sports agent with the National Football League Players Association from 1998 to 2001, a role that only five females had filled at the time. Her company Elite International Sports Marketing Inc. is designed to help athletes prepare for a career in athletics as well as what they can do after their career is complete. She has been extraordinarily successful in the heptathlon in track and field, and she is becoming an exceptional leader in the heptathlon of life.

[1] Joyner-Kersee, Jackie with Steptoe, Sonja. A Kind of Grace. New York: Time Warner, 1997.

[2] Duckett Cain, Joy. "The Jackie nobody knows" *Essence*, August 1, 1989.

[3] Letterlough, Michael. "Breathing Easy; Olympic gold-medalist Jackie Joyner-Kersee talks about her battle with asthma" *Philadelphia Tribune*, April 3, 2005.

Lawrence Burton

by Jennifer Brenden

Lawrence Burton was a football player, and a pretty good one at that. He was probably the fastest guy in the sport when he played at Purdue University in the early 1970's. Though his speed was very impressive, it was still unbelievable when he started running track at Purdue, and eight months later he qualified for the 1972 Olympic Games. It was an amazing accomplishment. Even when he continued on in the NFL, there was no one who could match his speed.

One would think that the fastest guy in college football would have been a track athlete but he wasn't until he went to college. He used his lightning speed on the football field of Mary N. Smith High School, in Eastern Shore, Virginia. That speed earned the 6 foot 1, 175-pound flanker back a scholarship to Purdue. There were other top programs knocking on Burton's door, but he chose to attend Purdue because the players who chaperoned him on his official visit told him that they had to study on Saturday night instead of bringing him to a bunch of crazy college parties. Typically, the fun and craziness of an official visit is what attracts football recruits. The recruits want a feel of the college atmosphere and a chance to hang out with potential teammates. Burton was not a typical recruit and he continued to be atypical, in a good way, throughout his college career. He was something bigger, something better. He also had something bigger to be preparing for, with the birth of his son and marriage that both took place in 1970, before he went off to college. Burton continued to prove his special qualities as he grew up and moved on with his life.

When Burton arrived at Purdue, academics and football were his top priorities (besides his wife and child), but he wanted to run for the track team as well. When he asked the track coach his freshman year if he could join, he was told it was too late. Burton was persistent, he came back the next year and the coach agreed to let him join the team. Burton was a natural, and people started turning their heads when this new guy started beating guys he should not have been beating. He set the world record for the 60-yard dash that year and went on to qualify for the 200-meter dash in the 1972 Olympic Games, in Munich, Germany. He came in fourth at the Olympics.

After his stint at the Olympics, it was right back to football training camp at Purdue. He proceeded to have successful junior and senior seasons. Burton graduated with his bachelor's degree in sociology and earned the NCAA Postgraduate Scholarship in 1975. Burton caught the eyes of the New Orleans Saints and he was their number one pick in the 1975 NFL Draft. Burton played three seasons with the New Orleans Saints and two full seasons with the San Diego Chargers. In 1980, during his third season with the Chargers, and his sixth season overall, Burton was performing well in training camp, but he made a personal decision that it was time to retire. His decision had nothing to do with football. He simply felt it was time to pursue some of his other goals. Although this was a sudden decision to outsiders, and many people were shocked, it was something Burton and his wife, Ida, had been discussing. She was very supportive and she knew of her husband's dreams and aspirations.

During the off-seasons of his years in the NFL, Burton worked with kids in a program through the New Orleans Police Department. He really enjoyed the work of helping children that were in need. As his football career wore on, he found himself thinking about the children more and more, and wondering who was helping them during his season when he couldn't be there. He found himself realizing that there was more out there than football and started to feel the strong desire to do more to help at-risk kids.

He didn't have any plans set in stone when he officially retired. His idea was for Ida and himself to start a foundation or home to help socially troubled youth get counseled back into their mainstream environment. One of his friends informed him of Boys Town, the well-known program in Omaha, Nebraska. This was a program that had been started by Father Edward J. Flanagan in 1917, and had been helping young people ever since.

Very much intrigued, Burton and his wife traveled to Boys Town to learn about the program and then bring that knowledge back to New Orleans to start their own organization. At the end of their visit, the two were offered jobs as family teachers and they gladly accepted. The program was exactly what they wanted to be involved with, and it didn't matter that they didn't create their own foundation. All that mattered was that they would be helping children.

Burton moved his wife and family to Boys Town, but it was much different than how it had been portrayed in the movie with Spencer Tracy. The movie was set early in the program's existence when Father Flanagan, who died in 1948, was still heading up the program. Needless to say, the problems kids were facing in 1975 were very different than the problems kids faced in the 1920's and 1930's. Burton entered the program when it was still adjusting to youth of a new generation.

After 13 years of housing troubled kids in Boys Town, being a good role model and acting as a father figure, Burton got the opportunity to start his own version of Boys Town in Los Angeles, California, and he jumped at it. When he left Boys Town to start the new chapter, the kids gave him an engraved clock that said, "Lawrence Burton An Inspiration." To Burton, that was more meaningful to him than a Heisman Trophy or a Gold Medal would have been. It was tough leaving the program in Omaha, and it was hard for some of the kids to see him go. It was also very fulfilling for Burton to hear the kids telling him what a difference he had made and how much he would be missed. He moved his wife and his youngest daughter out to California to start anew.

Along with his new Boys Town program, Burton also became the program director for the Price Family Campus and Coordinator of the Emergency Residential Care Center, in Long Beach, which houses homeless, runaway and abused or neglected kids ages 11 to 17 providing them with basic living and survival skills. The average stay is only 30 days.

He was the recipient of the Sports Illustrated Civic Leader Award for his work at Boys Town in 1993. Burton earned his master's degree in human development and family living from the University of Kansas. Burton has sat on several boards and committees in his local area of Long Beach, each one serving for the betterment of youth and the betterment of our society. He is a member of the Long Beach Area Chamber of Commerce, the NAACP and the Western States Youth Services Network; a board member of the California Child, Youth, and Family Coalition; on the Los Angeles Coordinating Council; a mentor for Long Beach Polytechnic High School; on the men's society of the First AME Church in Los Angeles and is a spokesperson and ambassador for the NFL.

Lawrence Burton was very lucky to find his passion to help others and have the opportunity to be driven by that passion. The people who have truly benefited from his passion are all of the children he has helped over the years. Burton was an amazing athlete but proved himself to be an amazing person with his decision to leave professional football and devote his life to helping at-risk children.

Dean Smith

by Drew Tyler

Dean Smith is one of the greatest basketball coaches of all time. Guiding the University of North Carolina men's basketball program, Smith developed a reputation as being one of the greatest minds to ever coach the game of basketball. Smith built a quality program by developing a host of new and innovative basketball strategies and by recruiting high quality student-athletes who proved successful on the court and in the classroom.

During his childhood, Smith quickly developed his teaching skills as the son of two school teachers. After graduating from high school in 1949, Smith took his academic and athletic skills to the University of Kansas where he played freshman football, varsity basketball and baseball. Early on, Smith's unique teaching qualities and athletic ability made it evident that he would one day go on to become a basketball coach.

Smith's legendary coaching career can be traced back to his own playing days at the University of Kansas. At Kansas, Smith was a three-time basketball letter winner and was a member of the 1952 National Championship team and 1953 NCAA finalist team. Under the guidance of fellow Hall of Fame coach "Phog" Allen, Smith used his time at Kansas to learn the finer points of the game. Smith was observant, and he built upon what he learned from Allen to develop such techniques as the Four Corners offense, the Run-and-Jump defense and the Foul-Line huddle. Throughout his career, Smith became highly regarded as one of the greatest innovators in the game. Smith was admired by coaches, players and fans alike for his contributions to basketball.

Smith's first coaching experience came as an assistant to Allen at Kansas. Following a brief stint as the assistant coach, Smith served in the U.S. Air Force where he was a player-coach overseas. In 1957, Smith returned to the United States as an assistant coach to Frank McGuire at the University of North Carolina. Three years later, Smith was named the Tar Heels head coach when McGuire left to become the head coach of the Philadelphia Warriors in the NBA. Smith held that post for the rest of his career.

Smith spent 36 years on the UNC bench as head coach. He compiled a career record of 879-254 (.776) and guided the Tar Heels to 13 Atlantic Coast Conference Tournament Championships, 11 Final Fours and two national championships. His 879 victories ranked him as the winningest coach in the history of collegiate basketball from 1997 to 2005 when Pat Summitt at the University of Tennessee passed his record with her women's program's 882 victories. In his honor, the University of North Carolina named its basketball stadium the Dean E. Smith Center, more commonly referred to as the "Dean Dome."

In addition to his on court accomplishments, Smith is probably best known for the relationships he developed with his players. During his 36 years at UNC, Smith graduated over 96 percent of his lettermen and earned a reputation for developing players who perform on the court, in the classroom and in the community. "He was always very supportive and provided me with invaluable insight for most of the major decisions I've made since 1971," said Charles Waddell. "He is one of the best teachers I had. He taught us to work hard, to sacrifice for the good of the team, to maximize your strengths and minimize your weaknesses."[1] Smith was genuinely cherished by his players and often considered by many as their second father.

Giving the lengthy duration of his coaching career and the strong bonds he developed with many of his former players, it is not surprising that many of the former players have become successful coaches in their own right, chief among them Larry Brown and Roy Williams. Brown has served as the head coach of several collegiate and NBA teams. In 2004, while serving as Head Coach of the Detroit Pistons, Brown guided the Pistons to the NBA Finals. After a Game 2 loss to the Los Angeles Lakers, Brown received a phone call from his longtime mentor and friend, Smith. Smith is always there to offer words of encouragement and in the days that followed, Brown led the Pistons to the NBA title.

After spending ten years as a North Carolina assistant, Roy Williams became head coach at the tradition-rich University of Kansas. Using many of the coaching strategies he learned from Smith, Williams reshaped the Kansas basketball program and became recognized as one of the greatest coaches in the game. In 2003, Williams received an offer he could not refuse and made the gut-wrenching decision to leave Kansas for the head coaching post at the University of North Carolina. In just his second season following in Smith's footsteps, Williams guided the Tar Heels to the 2005 NCAA National Championship.

Even in retirement, Smith continues to be an advocate for the welfare of student-athletes. Smith recognizes that progress has been made in college athletic departments with alcohol abuse education and stricter alcohol policies but he remains concerned about the close relationship between alcohol and college athletics. Smith joined forces with Campaign for Alcohol-Free Sports TV, a coalition of the Center for Science in the Public Interest (CSPI). Smith, other coaches and health advocacy groups work to convince university presidents, athletic directors and NCAA faculty representatives to promote banning alcohol advertisements during televised college athletic events.

In honor of his dedication to the game, Smith has received numerous awards and recognition throughout his career. Among Smith's most prestigious honors are four national Coach of the Year awards and the Arthur Ashe Award for Courage at the annual ESPY Awards. After his retirement in 1997, Smith was honored by *Sports Illustrated* magazine as the Sportsman of the Year. Smith was chosen for this award not only for his success as a coach, but also because of his concern for his players and his commitment to them as people as well as athletes. Dean Smith was a great coach; he is a stellar humanitarian.

[1] "A Tribute to Dean Smith." The Official Site of Tar Heel Athletics. [2005; November 15, 2005] http://tarheelblue.collegesports.com/sports/m-baskbl/mtt/unc-m-baskbl-dean-smith.html

Joe Paterno

by Jennifer Brenden and Drew Tyler

Most coaches and athletes are passionate about what they do. You can see it in their eyes, hear it in their voices and see it in their work. That passion still consumes "Joe Pa," Joe Paterno, the legendary coach of the Penn State Nittany Lions. The 78-year-old Paterno loves the game today as much as he did 60 years ago when he was a youngster playing the game himself. Although times have changed and Paterno has aged, he hasn't really changed too much. He still runs onto the field on game days, leading his Nittany Lions through the tunnel and into the stadium. He still refuses to put names on the jerseys of his players because he believes in team, not individual recognition. He still brings in the top recruits in the country and he still wins football games.

Because Paterno has been at the school for so long, he has many adoring fans. "Penn Staters" bleed blue and white for life. Game day at Penn State is quite an experience. Beaver Stadium now seats over 109,000 people. People travel for hundreds of miles to be a part of the game day experience. In a recent article published in *Sports Illustrated* on Campus Edition, attending a Penn State football game was called one of the greatest shows in college sports. Joe Pa is the face of Penn State football, bringing people back weekend after weekend, and year after year. Some claim that he is also the face of Penn State as a whole. He does more than represent his football team; he is an embodiment of Penn State culture.

Paterno grew up in Brooklyn and his football success began early in his career. As a senior in high school, he played on the best Catholic school team in the city and his only loss of the year came to a powerful St. Cecelia squad that was coached by Vince Lombardi. He earned a scholarship to play football at Brown University and eventually became the quarterback under coach Rip Engle. He also played two years of basketball at Brown. After Paterno completed his eligibility, he continued to work with the football team as he finished his degree. His plans were to follow in his father's footsteps and go to law school when he finished at Brown. He had been accepted into the Boston University law school. His plans were put on hold when Rip Engle was named the new head coach at Penn State and asked Paterno if he would move with him to Happy Valley as his assistant.

Paterno took the job and moved to State College. Starting in 1950, he served as an assistant coach for 16 years and then was appointed head coach in 1966, the day after Engle announced his retirement. He became only the third person to serve as the head coach of the same institution for more than 40 years. The other coaches were Amos Alonzo Stagg, who actually was a head coach for 57 years, 41 of them were at the University of Chicago, and Eddie Robinson who coached Grambling State University for 56 years. In his 40 years of coaching, Paterno rewrote the record books of collegiate coaching. More importantly, Paterno's program garnered the respect of the sporting world. Penn State not only won football games, but they won with class and they graduated their players. Paterno taught his players to respect the game, their opponents and their education.

On the field, Penn State's accomplishments have set Paterno alone atop the coaching world. Paterno has led the Nittany Lions to over 340 victories, an all-time record 19 bowl wins, and National Championships in 1982 and 1986. In 1968, 1969, 1973 and 1994, the Nittany Lions recorded undefeated seasons, but were not crowned National Champions.

Over the years, Paterno has received many awards and recognitions for his accomplishments. Most notably, Paterno has been named Coach-of-the-Year four times by the American Football Coaches Association, received the "Distinguished American" Award from the National Football Foundation and College Football Hall of Fame, and was named by *Sports Illustrated* as the 1986 Sportsman-of-the-Year.

Paterno has also excelled as a coach off the field. By emphasizing the importance of going to class and studying, Paterno has seen his student-athletes have great success in the classroom. Overall, Paterno has coached 20 first-team Academic All-Americans, 14 Hall of Fame Scholar-Athletes, 16 NCAA postgraduate scholarship winners and helped to graduate more than 80 percent of his players. These numbers reflect Paterno's belief that his success is measured by the number of quality and productive citizens the Penn State football program contributes to society, rather than by wins and losses.

Adding to Paterno's legacy has been the significant contributions he and his family have made to further education at Penn State. Recently, Paterno, his wife, Sue (also known as Sue Pa), and their five children donated $3.5 million to help endow faculty positions and scholarships, as well as support for the university libraries, and for the construction of two new buildings. The new interfaith spiritual center and the Penn State All-Sports Museum have both opened in the past three years. The recent contributions brought Paterno's lifetime giving total to more than $4 million. The Paterno Family donation is among the largest donations ever made by a college coach to a university.

Joe Paterno is much more than a football coach. The success of the Nittany Lions has made Paterno famous, but it has been the dedication of the Paterno family to Penn State that has made the Paterno name legendary. Recently, Penn State's Board of Trustees' made the decision to name the newest wing of the University Library after the Paterno family. For years, the Paternos have expressed the importance of family, learning, loyalty and commitment to the Penn State community. The Paterno Library will serve as a tribute to the Paterno family and a reminder of the values of the Paterno family.

Joe Paterno's legacy will live on for many years to come. But Penn Staters can't help but wonder what the institution and the football program will be like without Joe Pa on the sidelines. At the present time, Paterno isn't thinking of retirement. He says that as long as he is healthy and he remains passionate about his work, he will continue. Given the success of the 2005 Nittany Lions, Joe Pa might remain in Happy Valley for a long time to come.

Pat Summitt

by Drew Tyler

Pat Summitt was born in Henrietta, Tennessee, the daughter of Richard and Hazel Albright Head. Growing up, Summitt was forced to learn hard work because of her strong disciplinarian father, her constant competition with three older brothers and the demands of living on a family farm. In Summitt's family, hard work was not appreciated, it was expected. More so, laziness and excuses were not tolerated. As a child, Summitt's routine included attending school and church, and performing her daily chores working in the fields. After finishing her chores, Summitt played basketball with her brothers.

Summitt graduated from Cheatham County High School in Ashland, Tennessee and went on to play basketball at the University of Tennessee at Martin. Over her four years she helped to guide the Lady Pacers to a 64-29 record and in 1974 received her B.S. in physical education. In 1976, Summitt was named to the U.S. Olympic women's basketball team as a co-captain and earned a silver medal. Summitt returned to the Olympics in 1984 and become the first coach to guide the USA women's basketball team to the gold medal.

As head coach of the University of Tennessee women's basketball program, Pat Summitt's name has become legendary amongst the greatest collegiate coaches of all-time. Coach Summitt has achieved a tremendous level of success on the court, while also maintaining a top notch program in the classroom. Summitt has served as a mentor, educator, and role model to her players and constantly challenges her Lady Vols to reach their potential both as students and athletes.

Heading into the 2005 season, Summitt had notched 882 career wins and become the all-time winningest collegiate basketball coach for any NCAA men's or women's program. Along with the 882 victories, Summitt guided Tennessee to six national championships, 24 Southeastern Conference titles and 24 consecutive NCAA tournament appearances. She holds the record for most NCAA tournament wins. Her 1997 team is considered by many as the best collegiate women's basketball team of all. The team finished a perfect 39-0 and won by an average of more than 30 points per game. In the history of basketball, Summitt's six national championships trail only the legendary John Wooden who guided UCLA to ten NCAA titles.

Summitt's basketball program has produced an incredible amount of individual talent including 11 U.S. Olympians, 18 Kodak All-Americans, over 40 international performers, and 20 professional players in the ABL and WNBA. In honor of her accomplishments, the University of Tennessee officially nicknamed their basketball arena, "The Summitt."

After 31 seasons at Tennessee, Summitt is much more than a coach to her Lady Vols. She is a leader, master motivator, champion, educator, role model and friend. Summitt acts as a mentor to her players, teaching them to believe in themselves and reach their full potential as student-athletes at Tennessee and in life. In the classroom, Summitt's motivation has helped her players maintain a remarkable graduation rate. In fact, every one of Summitt's players who has completed her eligibility has also successfully completed her degree.

A great deal of the academic success of Summitt's athletes may be directly attributed to her tough demeanor. All of her players are required to sit in the first three rows of class, pay attention, complete all assignments on-time and show respect to everyone. Any player who chooses not to go to class has also made the decision not to play in the next game. The honor of being a Lady Vol comes at a price. Players must be dedicated to their team and academics, and be responsible for their actions at all times.

Summitt has become one of the most celebrated figures in women's sports for her accomplishments off the court as well. In addition to her work as a coach, Summitt has served as the Associate Director of Athletics at Tennessee, as Vice-President of USA Basketball, on the Board of Trustees of the Basketball Hall of Fame, and on the Board of Directors for the Women's Basketball Hall of Fame. She has authored two successful books, "Reach for the Summitt" and "Raise the Roof." She is highly recognized for her abilities as a motivational speaker, commencement speaker, color commentator and author.

In the community, Summitt is an active philanthropist and was once honored by former First Lady Hillary Clinton at a White House luncheon for the "25 Most Influential Working Mothers" chosen by *Working Mother* magazine. She has acted as a spokesperson for the Verizon Wireless HopeLine program, the United Way, the Juvenile Diabetes Foundation and the Race for the Cure. Additionally, Summitt is an active member of Big Brothers/Big Sisters and served as the Tennessee chair of the American Heart Association. Along the way, Summitt has accumulated many awards and recognitions for her contributions. In 1996, Summitt was awarded "Distinguished Citizen of the Year" by the Boy Scouts of America and in 1998 she was named the "Woman of the Year" by both *Glamour* magazine and the City of Knoxville. Most notably, in 2000, Summitt became just the fourth women's basketball coach elected into the Basketball Hall of Fame.

Pat Summitt is a truly unique individual in the coaching arena. Her success alone places her atop the coaching pedestal, but it is her unique ability to serve as a mentor and friend to her players that makes her a hero. While demanding, Coach Summitt has changed the lives of more than 100 young women and will always be remembered as one of the greatest role models in the history of women's sports.

Tom Osborne

by Jessica Bartter and Richard Lapchick

Tom Osborne may have had it easy at the University of Nebraska with the luxury of a fully-funded program that provided excellent compensation for his staff, wonderful facilities and a recruiting budget that would make most coaches envious. But don't be fooled. Osborne worked every bit as hard as any coach anywhere during his 36 years in Nebraska athletics, including his 25 year reign as head coach. He wanted to ensure that Lincoln, Nebraska served as a wholesome and safe environment for young boys who wanted to become men amidst the cornfields of America's heartland.

In Osborne's case, he saw firsthand how easy it was for a Division I-A program to build broad bodies with little concern for developing inquiring minds. In the 1960's, Osborne, then a graduate assistant coach, became Nebraska's first academic counselor and began his work to balance academics and athletics. Thirty years later, 82 percent of his student-athletes who completed their eligibility graduated. This is especially significant considering only 49 percent of football players graduated at that time nationwide. Today, Nebraska graduates 91 percent of all student-athletes who complete their eligibility, a figure that leads the Big 12 Conference. As of July 2005 the University of Nebraska leads the nation with Academic All-Americans in all sports with 222 since 1962. Of those, 65 were football players.

Osborne did not forget his athletes who left for the NFL before they finished their degrees either. Instead, he made every effort possible to convince them to come back to complete what they started. Six former Cornhuskers returned to graduate in 1994 alone. And Osborne's legacy lives on as seven former football players returned in 2004-2005 despite the fact that Osborne resigned his coaching position seven years ago.

Osborne enjoyed success for decades and Nebraska won its third national championship in four years in 1997 but he decided to move on and focus his efforts elsewhere. He was the first defending national champion coach not to return the following season. In his 25 years as head coach, the Nebraska football team never won less than nine games in a single season. The Huskers went to a bowl game every year and won 13 conference titles. Osborne posted a 255-49-3 record equivalent to a .836 winning percentage, the best for active Division I-A coaches at the time of his retirement and sixth best all time. Osborne's teams outscored their opponents 11,317 to 4,345. Since he first started with the team as an offensive coordinator in 1962, the Huskers have sold out every game, an NCAA record as of November 9, 2005.

But Osborne wanted to do more than just build great athletes in Lincoln. Osborne admitted that most of his time spent coaching was actually off the field assisting players with personal, family, cultural, academic and spiritual issues that in turn affected their performance on the gridiron. Osborne recognized that to be a good coach meant more than instruction on the field or in the weight room. He was committed to coaching his players in life as well.

In addition, Osborne was committed to coaching youth in life before they even considered becoming a Husker. Osborne and his wife, Nancy, established an endowment in 1991 that provides scholarships to students who have gone through his Husker TeamMates Program, which matches Huskers football players as mentors with at-risk junior high school students. Sensitizing and educating his student-athletes, Osborne is helping save lives in the community long after his retirement. The TeamMates Program has since become a state-wide mentoring program that pairs adult volunteers with middle school students for one-on-one mentoring. Nebraska athletics has the nation's most expansive school outreach program, reaching almost 112,000 young people in 2004-2005 with messages about making responsible choices about school and drugs.

Osborne is a fourth-generation Nebraskan and developed TeamMates to invest in the future of his home state. He and his wife noted the lack of adult interaction children were receiving and decided to step in to help children reach their full potential.

Born and raised in Nebraska, Osborne had been a standout athlete in football, basketball and track and field at Hastings High School, about 100 miles west of Lincoln. Osborne attended Hastings College before being drafted in the 18th round by the San Francisco 49ers. He was later traded to the Washington Redskins where he spent two seasons. Osborne didn't see his professional career going much farther in the NFL, so he returned home and enrolled at the University of Nebraska to pursue a master's degree and Ph.D. in educational psychology. Thus, began a relationship with the Huskers that spanned four decades.

Although Osborne was 60 years old when he left Nebraska football, retirement did not suit him for long. Just three years later, Osborne found a new job, one just as demanding and, just as rewarding. In January 2000 Osborne announced his plans to run as Republican Congressman for the 3rd District of Nebraska. At that time, four of the six Republicans who had announced their candidacy the previous fall dropped out. Despite his lack of political experience, Osborne's reputation in a state where Saturdays are dedicated to football helped to defeat his opponents before the campaign even began. Osborne's reputation enabled him to transcend traditional party politics and he won a landslide victory with 82 percent of the votes.

Osborne had never shied away from speaking out politically when it involved the NCAA, the College Football Association or the Big 12 or Big Eight Conferences. So, when at the age of 63, Osborne discovered a new venue to work on behalf of the American people and continue to improve the state of Nebraska, it seemed quite fitting that he use his new platform for that purpose. Osborne's success in the political realm has led to his third term representing Nebraska's 3rd Congressional District. The Nebraskan native is most concerned with keeping Nebraska's talented young people in the state and boosting economic development. Osborne pays particular attention to the abuse of methamphetamine by Nebraskan young people and he has developed a media presentation entitled "Methamphetamine: One of Rural America's Greatest Challenges." While in office, Osborne has also prepared a Rural Economic Development Handbook, an Entrepreneurship Handbook and a Youth Entrepreneurship Brochure.

An athlete at heart, Congressman Osborne led the fight for two measures regarding sports that were signed into legislation. The Anabolic Steroid Control Act lists anabolic steroids or steroid precursors as controlled substances, thereby prohibiting their over-the-counter sale. The Sports Agent Responsibility and Trust Act (SPARTA) protects student-athletes from deceptive and exploitative sports agents.

As part of the award ceremony that honored Coaches Tom Osborne and Willie Stewart in 1994 at the Center for the Study of Sport and Society's 10th anniversary celebration, the Center launched its Sport and Society Hall of Fame to honor people from the world of sport who make a truly distinctive contribution to society, one that extends far beyond the game itself. Muhammad Ali was rightly the sole initial inductee.

Ali watched, awaiting his turn to be inducted. Moved by the entire evening, Ali reflected on Osborne and Stewart: "That's what coaching should be all about." Coming from "The Greatest," this was perhaps the highest accolade of all.

Geno Auriemma

by Drew Tyler

In the mind of Hall of Fame basketball coach Geno Auriemma, coaching is just a small part of what he does. Auriemma told the *Journal Inquirer*, "As coaches, we're constantly trying to find things that allow us to feel like we're more involved than just coaching our teams. We feel an obligation to do things above and beyond coaching. We wish we could do more."[1] This determination has shaped Auriemma's career and helped him become one of the most successful coaches in NCAA history both on and off the court.

As a coach, Auriemma has established career marks that have never been equaled. Since being named head coach of the University of Connecticut's women's basketball program in 1985, Auriemma won his first 500 games more quickly than all but one of his coaching predecessors and recorded an astounding winning percentage at .834. Auriemma's other records include five consecutive appearances in the Final Four of the NCAA Championships, five national championships, and five national coach-of-the-year awards. Auriemma was named Coach of the Year four times by the Associated Press, three times by the Women's Basketball Coaches Association and six times by the Big East.

Auriemma has been successful beyond the collegiate level with his involvement in USA Basketball. At the 2000 Summer Olympic Games held in Sydney, Australia, Auriemma served as an assistant coach for the USA gold medal winning team. The 2000 Olympic team included two former players from the University of Connecticut in Nykesha Sales and Kara Wolters. Overall, 15 former University of Connecticut standouts who played under Auriemma have participated in USA Basketball.

Known for his development of national caliber student-athletes, Auriemma's success extends beyond winning basketball games. During his tenure at UConn, every freshman who has completed her eligibility under Auriemma has received her undergraduate degree. Remarkably, since the 1991-1992 season, 31 of UConn's starting players have been named to the Dean's List. Among these players are four of the most celebrated women's basketball players: Rebecca Lobo, Jennifer Rizzotti, Kara Wolters and Sue Bird.

As a sign of his commitment to academic excellence, Auriemma donated $125,000 to the University of Connecticut Library. In 1993, Auriemma was recognized for his contributions to UConn academics and elected into the National Mortar Board academic honor society. The following year, Auriemma was awarded the prestigious UConn Club Outstanding Contribution Award for his service and commitment to UConn athletics.

Adding to Auriemma's legacy at UConn has been his commitment to the community. Currently, Auriemma serves as chair of Why-Me of New England, a fundraising organization benefiting breast cancer research. Auriemma has also acted as the State of Connecticut honorary chair for the American Heart Association and co-chair of the Connecticut Arthritis Foundation. For all his accomplishments, the Basketball Hall of Fame honored him with "Geno Auriemma Day" on August 9, 1995.

Geno Auriemma is still at the reigns of the University of Connecticut women's basketball program. His devotion to both academics and athletics has helped build one of the best programs in the country and secure his place in coaching history.

[1] Adamec, Carl. "Auriemma lends a helping hand" *Journal Inquirer*, September 24, 2004.

CHAPTER 5

HURDLERS OVERCOMING OBSTACLES

In the introduction to *100 Heroes*, I wrote about how Taylor Ellis brought me a book that he read as a young man that inspired him to expand his horizons. It told the stories of seven athletes who overcame great obstacles in their lives. This section, *Hurdlers Overcoming Obstacles*, captures the lives of ten individuals who showed the world that they were able to smash whatever obstacles were before them.

Bob Love was an all-NBA player and superstar with the Chicago Bulls before anyone knew Michael Jordan. A life-long stuttering problem, hidden from the public during his NBA career, made his post-NBA career almost impossible until someone reached out to offer him help. Love has become the spokesperson for the Bulls in the Chicago community.

Someone read the life story of Mark Brodie and said this is the only story in the book that may be hard for a child to read. Mark Brodie was targeted for stardom as a high school basketball player. Because of his lack of attention to academics, he bounced around from college to college, became a drug addict and a male prostitute. After hitting rock bottom, Mark went back to school under the auspices of the National Consortium for Academics and Sports degree completion program. He not only finished his undergraduate degree but got two masters degrees and is now completing his Ph.D. at Auburn University.

President Clinton greeted Dwight Collins in the White House because this extraordinary young man who could not hear saw so much about life. By his example as a deaf athlete, he inspired his teammates at the University of Central Florida on the football team about what the human spirit could enable one to achieve.

Samantha Eyman became an outstanding softball player in spite of having only one fully- developed arm and hand. She did not allow what she lacked to inhibit what she could accomplish.

Dave Clark, in spite of two bouts with polio as a young man and as an adult, accomplished great things as a baseball player and coach in professional baseball.

Eddie Lee Ivery used his great skills as a football player to become a superstar at Georgia Tech and later to play in the National Football League. Then he succumbed to the temptations of drug abuse. Hearing about the opportunity to return to finish his degree through the Consortium at Georgia Tech, he did so and reclaimed his life and took control of his destiny.

Loretta Claiborne did not allow challenges to get in the way of becoming a great athlete. Her life became an inspiration for hundreds of young people and a movie was eventually made about her saga.

The amputation of a limb did not hold back Sam Paneno, a football player at the University of California, Davis, from pursuing his life's dreams.

Kathryn Waldo did not let cystic fibrosis stop her ice hockey career as a star player at Northeastern University where she kept getting back on the ice.

Born without hands and with malformed feet, Shane Wood refused to use prosthetics. Regardless, he played sports to build his character and confidence.

Looking at the lives of these ten individuals makes it more than understandable why Taylor Ellis found heart and inspiration from the stories of the seven athletes he read about more than 40 years ago. The ten athletes portrayed here in *Hurdlers Overcoming Obstacles* will give hope to anyone who reads about these extraordinary people.

Bob Love

by Jennifer Brenden

Bob "Butterbean" Love is widely known as one of the greatest players ever to sport the Chicago Bulls jersey. Love is currently employed as the Community Relations Director for the Chicago Bulls and is a well-known public speaker. While he has become an inspiration to everyone who hears him speak, it was not so long ago that he was in desperate need of some inspiration of his own.

Being one of 14 brothers and sisters growing up in a small town in Louisiana, Love's family didn't have much, so he didn't have a real basketball hoop to shoot at when he was younger. He used to shoot at a coat hanger hoop nailed to his grandmother's door. His love for the game became apparent at a very young age and he dreamt of becoming a professional basketball player. In addition to the economic obstacles that he faced, Love developed a severe stuttering problem when he was young that he struggled with for most of his life.

His insecurities about his speaking ability kept him very quiet in school. Love's alternative to excelling in school was to excel in athletics. Love was an amazing high school athlete. He was the quarterback of the football team and he found his words much easier on the football field than he did in the classroom or in a social setting. Love grew to be 6 foot 8 by the time he was 18. He was recruited to play college football at Southern University in Louisiana where he had a very successful career. Love found success on the basketball court as well, receiving All-American honors his sophomore, junior and senior seasons. He was also the first black athlete to make the All-South team, and he became the first player from Southern University to make the pros. In 1965, Love was drafted to the NBA, which at that time consisted of only nine teams, as opposed to the 30 NBA teams that currently exist. He was drafted by the Cincinnati Royals in the fourth round, and was first traded to the Milwaukee Bucks and then to the Chicago Bulls.

Love played for the Bulls from 1969-1976, during which time he became a three-time NBA all-star, led the Bulls in scoring for seven straight seasons, and scored enough points to be the second-leading scorer in Bulls history, accumulating 12,623 points. He ranks only behind Michael Jordan on the all-time Bull's scoring list. Even as an NBA star, Love was hindered by his speech impediment. Although he grew up, he did not outgrow his stuttering problem. No one had really taken the time to sit down and help Love with his speech. The media would pass him up for interviews because they said they didn't have the time, so he never got as much recognition as he deserved. Also, he was overlooked for endorsement opportunities because many of them involved speaking. Love was obviously a very dominant player in the league, but he never got to take full advantage of his superstar status. Even as an adult and an acknowledged basketball star, his speech impediment held him back.

Love's career was cut short by a back injury that forced him to retire in 1977. He was told by doctors that he might never walk properly again. Love had always depended on his physical skill and ability as an athlete. It was hard for him to accept that his body was letting him down. His physical health wouldn't be the only thing that would let him down. It was at this point that Love's life took a turn for the worst. To add insult to injury, one night he came home to find that his wife had left him, and she had taken the furniture from their home, his rings, and almost everything else of any value. She told him she didn't want to be married to a stutterer and cripple. Love hit rock bottom and stayed there for quite some time.

It took Love almost seven years to find a permanent job after his departure from the NBA. He found it hard to sell himself to any personnel director. He didn't have any work experience other than playing basketball, and his stuttering problem made employers believe he lacked confidence and competence. Communication is a key to success in the workforce, no matter where one works and the people Love was interviewing with felt his stutter would hinder him from communicating effectively.

Finally, in December of 1984, an old NBA friend of Love's hired him to work as a bus boy at Nordstrom's cafe in Seattle for $4.45 an hour. Each day he had to endure the embarrassment of someone recognizing him as a former NBA star and questioning what he was doing working at a café. Eventually, he moved up to washing dishes and then to preparing sandwiches. One of the store's owners, John Nordstrom, told Love that the company was willing to pay for a speech therapist if he was interested so that they could promote him.

In 1986, Love began working with a speech therapist, named Hamilton. Love could tell Hamilton genuinely cared about him and in improving his speech. Love worked with Hamilton two hours a day, three days a week, for a year. Essentially, he had to learn to speak all over again. He showed the same dedication to learning how to speak that he had demonstrated as a basketball player, and in June 1987, he gave a public speech at a high school awards banquet. It was a very emotional experience that brought tears to his eyes when he was finished. Armed with newfound confidence, he continued improving his speaking abilities. Love's boss kept his promise and promoted him to manager in charge of health and sanitation for 150 store restaurants nationwide. He held this position for about two years, until he was promoted to corporate spokesperson at Nordstrom's.

In 1991, Bulls Owner Jerry Reinsdorf expressed interest in having Love return to the Bulls organization as the team's goodwill ambassador to the Chicago community. Love's goal had been to somehow get back into the sports industry, so he was ecstatic about this opportunity. Love gladly took the position with the Bulls and he was so proud to be able to represent his former team. Love has been the Director of Community Relations ever since. In the years since Love took this position, he became only the second Chicago Bull in history to have his jersey retired at Chicago Stadium. The number 10 jersey hangs proudly from the rafters of the stadium. Also, he found a new love of his life and remarried. He is the subject of a book that was written about him, and he has become an effective motivational speaker.

Love makes over 400 appearances every year and speaks to thousands of teenagers and adults on behalf of the Bulls organization. He visits schools and other non-profit organizations telling the story of his life. He shares how he got to the position he is in today by overcoming many obstacles, working hard and never giving up. His presentations also focus on the importance of dreams and how to hold on to them. Love's story of perseverance can serve as inspiration not only to athletes, but to all people who are facing adversity.

Because of Love's popularity within the Chicago community, he was approached and encouraged by community leaders to run for the office of city alderman. This just shows that Love's arm reaches far beyond the basketball court. It is not his basketball skills and accomplishments that are making him successful, but the person he has become and the relationships he has created within his community. Bob Love's genuine love for the people of Chicago has made him very effective and tremendously admired in his home town and with whom everyone he touches.

Mark Brodie

by Richard Lapchick

Mark Brodie is a child of the 1960's and a teenager and young adult of the 1970's and 80's. His story should not have been anything special. Mark was raised in Queens Village, New York in a large Catholic family with a hard working father, a devoted mother and six very energetic siblings.

The reason's Brodie's story goes from what should have been "the boy next door" to the "disaster that waited beside the road," lies in the problems that always accompany a family where alcoholism and dysfunction are present. Brodie's family was strong but his father fought a losing battle with alcoholism and died when Brodie was only 17. His mother, who was Brodie's hero, tried to keep her family afloat with a mentally retarded daughter and a host of other problems. Brodie was a middle child and his prowess in sports enabled him to escape the turbulence at home. When he reached high school he had grown to 6 foot 4 and became one of the city's best basketball players by his junior and senior years at Bishop Reilly High School. After making Street and Smith's All-American team and other All-City and All-Queens teams, Brodie was heavily recruited nationally.

He chose Florida State over Hawaii and USC. Brodie later said that "I wanted to go away because I felt that being away from all the problems at home would make life easier on my Mom. I also was under the illusion that I would go pro within two years and that college was only a stepping ground for me. I was dazzled by recruiters of the 1970's with their flashy cars, flashy rhetoric and promises of gold and never paid attention to the wonderful offers that a free education would grant me." Brodie would learn that lesson later when he returned to school as a regular student.

Brodie enrolled at Florida State and played for legendary coach

Hugh Durham. Brodie was very thin and didn't play much as a freshman but was getting better when he flunked out of school. From there he enrolled in a junior college and, though he was ineligible for half the year, helped the team to a national #1 ranking at one time. After leaving junior college, he was recruited again and was settling on Jacksonville University when he decided to go back home and enroll at St. John's University. He attempted to be a walk-on with Lou Carnesecca. He was sure he would make the SJU Redmen but he arrived out of shape and out of focus. Sadly, he was cut by Carnesecca. Brodie said, "it was all timing…I wasn't used to being a walk-on and just figured I could show up and they would want me. The only problem was SJU wasn't going to wait for me to get in shape…It is too bad ….after a scrimmage at Madison Square Garden I started to feel my game coming back but Carnesecca let me go the next week. I always wonder if it would have been different had I succeeded at St. John's but this boy did not come back a conquering hero." After SJU, Brodie was lucky to get a scholarship to play in Canada for Steve Konchalski at St. Francis Xavier University where he blossomed into what he would have been in the States. With a 24 second clock, Brodie flourished. He was All-Canadian and broke or held seven school records in the two years he played there, but again he flunked out of school and was left without a team. His problems really started when he went to Europe and played professionally. This was where his small drug habit became an addiction and the tailspin that brought Brodie to the brink of disaster.

After developing a cocaine and valium addiction in Amsterdam, Brodie came home to the United States and returned to Queens Village. He worked during the day as a dispatcher for a cab company and at night as a prostitute to feed his drug habit. He was too ashamed to face his old friends and felt that he was a failure.

After a summer working in the Hamptons as a lifeguard, he had an epiphany of sorts. He was working as a prostitute when Len Bias died of a cocaine overdose. He said to his "'client' that he "used to be a ball player," and when the woman said "you are nothing but a whore," Brodie decided to change his life. He moved to Florida but after a few months was back into drugs and prostitution. When he overdosed and was waiting for medical attention, he came across an article about the National Consortium for Academics and Sports and how it helped former athletes go back to school. "I immediately straightened out, left the hospital and wrote a letter to the NCAS Director, Richard Lapchick. When Lapchick contacted me, my life changed to where I am today. It may seem unbelievable but I am a professor at Auburn University with two BA degrees, two MA degrees and am finishing my PhD. The NCAS program allowed me to enter school again at Virginia Commonwealth University where Dr. Richard Sander was my mentor and helped guide me back to reality and success. I kept talking to Dr. Lapchick who kept me afloat." School was terrifying at first for Brodie because he had never been a real student before. He was only an athlete. After finding his way as a scholar under the tutelage of Dr. George Longest, Brodie graduated with honor grades in history and English from VCU and went on to graduate school at Clemson University [MA], Bowling Green State University [MA] and presently to Auburn University where he is currently working on his dissertation under the tutelage of Dr. Jon Bolton.

Though he feels he has found his niche as a college professor, Brodie still remembers where he came from. "My biggest thrill at 40-something years old is when I have a student-athlete in one of my classes. I feel like I am looking in the mirror at myself 20 years ago and realize how much I want to tell them, how much I miss it, and how lucky they are. I want to make them realize what they have in their hands…success!"

Brodie noted "Many people, especially my mentor and friend Richard Lapchick, my mom and family, and many people who know my story, tell me I am a hero. I am no such thing. I am just extremely lucky to have friends and a mother who sacrificed everything for her children… especially the one (me) who really needed help. When I receive my doctorate, it will belong to her and my late brother Bill (the real scholar in my family), my family and to Richard Lapchick and the people at the National Consortium for Academics and Sports. I am eternally grateful."

"Sometimes when I feel life or academia is becoming too serious I always think to myself I may not be the only professor that is concerned with students and my chosen field of study. But I am one of the few who can dunk a basketball or sink a clutch basket in front of 10,000 people. I have had more than my 15 minutes of fame and that is why I love teaching and advising youngsters pursuing their dreams." Brodie says that, like Shakespeare's Falstaff, he "has heard the chimes at midnight…but has survived the darkest alleys and deepest demons to finally understand himself and the world he now inherits."

Mark Brodie wants to continue teaching and working with athletes. His dream is to advise athletes and work in compliance with a major university sports program. He is certainly more than qualified. Brodie said, "I have worked with many of Auburn's nationally ranked football players and in Carnell "Cadillac" Williams to Will Herring and Antarrious Williams, I have found youngsters who are not only gentlemen and super athletes but dedicated students and great young men who have benefited from the fine example set by Coach Tommy Tuberville and the Auburn athlete enrichment program." Mark Brodie has arrived after a very long and difficult journey.

Dwight Collins

by Jessica Bartter

If you can't hear the play from the coach, can't read the lips of your teammates and miss the cheers of the crowd, what kind of football player would you be? If your name is Dwight Collins, the answer would be exceptional.

Collins was not born deaf, but before he could learn to talk, he contracted meningitis at the age of 11 months; resulting in the loss of his hearing. A fighter from a young age, this did not deter Collins from success. Collins' parents encouraged his assimilation into the hearing world by putting him in public schools and forcing him to get summer jobs like most other teenagers. As a sixth grader, Collins found his love for football and began dreaming of stardom in the NFL.

Collins earned great attention on the field as a high school player for Barbe High School in Lake Charles, Louisiana. During his senior year, Collins amassed more than 2,000 yards rushing and scored 27 touchdowns. College scouts lined-up to watch Collins play in the hope that he would continue his stardom at their college or university. Upon learning he was deaf, most scouts ceased their efforts to recruit Collins.

A few universities saw past what others thought as a barrier, his deafness, and only saw the talent and spirit embodied in Collins' play. Collins considered athletic scholarship offers from Gallaudet University, McNeese State University and the University of Central Florida. Gallaudet is the only university in the world in which all programs and services accommodate deaf and hard of hearing students. McNeese State was located in his hometown of Lake Charles. But the University of Central Florida won Collins over by sharing his academic commitment in promising an interpreter on and off the field. Collins also believed Central Florida had the strongest football program, and he was ready for the challenge.

Note takers and interpreters assisted Collins in his classes, helping him to maintain a 3.8 grade point average. In an ultimate demonstration of support, running backs coach Alan Gooch enrolled in American Sign Language classes to better communicate with Collins, and signed plays to him from the sideline. Gooch took a crash course after Central Florida signed Collins so that on the first day the young athlete showed up to the field, he would have someone with whom to communicate. In 1997, Gooch was named the Assistant Coach of the Year by the American Football Coaches Association for his work with Collins, earning a $5,000 scholarship for the school.

Collins' inspiration is felt throughout the communities in which he has lived. In high school, a seven year old deaf boy's parents frequently made the two and a half hour drive to Lake Charles to inspire their son with Collins' attitude. Collins was able to challenge the boy's belief that he could not participate in sports and other activities with hearing people. By watching Collins, the young boy learned to believe in himself and follow his dreams of playing sports because Collins was proof that it is possible to beat the odds.

President Clinton welcomed Collins to the Oval Office during in his senior year at Central Florida. The President commented that Collins "gave hope to many people who had none before." Coming from the President of the United States, this is indeed lofty praise.

Samantha Eyman

by Jessica Bartter

Not many individuals would be glad to be born with only one hand, but that is the case with Samantha Eyman. Eyman's quick foot speed, great throwing arm and fierce competitiveness made her a standout outfielder for the Saint Xavier University's softball team. Her skill level alone was enough to get her noticed on the field, but her lack of a left hand made her abilities even more notable.

Eyman was born without a left hand, and remarkably would not wish it any other way. She looks at not having a left hand as a gift and believes with two hands she would not have accomplished the things she has with one, since it has pushed her to work that much harder. Eyman does have a left elbow and most of the forearm. When she was born, doctors made a thumb-like extremity out of her hip bone to make her arm more maneuverable. Because of it, she is able to tie her own shoes and much more.

Watching her two older brothers play in youth baseball leagues made Eyman an early fan. At their home in Palos Hills, Illinois, Eyman often joined her dad, a former Marine Corps baseball player, and brothers in their backyard practice sessions. At the age of five, she convinced her parents to take her to T-ball registration. She has never looked back since. Just a year later, Eyman debuted in the fastpitch softball world. Before Eyman began concentrating on softball, she also played volleyball, basketball, and ran track, but never soccer. Soccer, she said, never interested her because since hands are unnecessary; it was not challenging enough for her.

When Eyman was eight, she fulfilled a dream that many only fantasize about. She met her idol, Jim Abbott. Abbott, a former professional baseball player for 10 years, pitched for the California Angels, New York Yankees, Chicago White Sox and Milwaukee Brewers despite the fact that he was born without a right hand. Similarly to Abbott's style of play, Eyman would wear her glove on her right hand and, after catching the ball, would cradle the glove in her left arm, then pull out the ball with her right hand to throw it. Abbott taught her his quick ball exchange and now she teaches it to other kids.

In addition to her talent, Eyman's charismatic personality and spirit were a great attribute to her team. As a freshman, Eyman played in 44 games, posting a .943 fielding percentage in the outfield. Her sophomore season, Eyman started in 55 games, earned a .236 batting average and scored 30 runs, the second highest on the team. This effort earned Eyman the Most Improved Player honors in 2003, but she didn't stop there. As a junior and senior, Eyman continued to make strides, and in just her junior season at Saint Xavier University, she was named team captain.

Eyman utilized her time at Saint Xavier to volunteer her expertise each summer at the University's softball clinics where she offered valuable advice on working hard and never giving up. Eyman understands that parents of children with disabilities like hers may not know what to do. She wants to be there for them and show both the parent and the child the possibilities. Eyman is great with children, and this will come in handy after college for this elementary education major. Eyman leads with both inspiring words and actions and she has motivated a number of other athletes, some with similar disabilities, to achieve their goals. Eyman's inspirational attitude enables her to touch the heart of everyone she meets; athletes and non-athletes; young and old; male and female; regardless of whether they have one hand or two.

David Clark

by Jessica Bartter and Drew Tyler

His parents were told he would be lucky to live and if he did, he would have very little muscular movement. Experts said he would never walk and that he would be confined to a wheelchair for the rest of his life. Luckily, David Clark was too young to remember his life-threatening bout with polio when he was just 10 months old. His first memories, rather, are of physical activity encouraged by his parents despite doctor's predictions. When he was just three years old, Clark recalls that his daily routine consisted of sit-ups, push-ups, stretching exercises and chin-ups on a bar his father put up in the doorway. Clark did not know he should not have been able to do such physical activity, but he did know rather quickly that he could do whatever he set his mind to.

Clark's lifetime achievements make him a hero in the minds of many, but in his mind, there are no heroes greater than his own parents. Clark's mother and father never treated him differently and offered nothing but encouragement. In the 1950's, many kids who suffered from polio were forced to go to special schools, but Clark's parents placed him in Gregg School, a regular elementary school. For that, he is indebted to them.

Clark started school wearing leg braces and using crutches, far from the confines of a wheelchair. He faced ridicule from some of his classmates, but his physical education teacher, Bill Schnetzler, treated Clark like every other student in the class. In third grade, after Schnetzler explained the activities for the day, Clark turned and walked away, thinking he had to sit this one out. Schnetzler stopped him in his tracks and demanded he try before giving up. The students had to climb up a rope tied to the ceiling, and to his own surprise, Clark was the first student in the class to get to the top. When he got down, he was rewarded with an ice cream bar. Though delicious, the ice cream bar lasted only a few moments. But the lesson Schnetzler taught him about never doubting himself until he at least tried has lasted Clark a lifetime.

Throughout school Clark pushed himself athletically and found a love for baseball and ice hockey. In 1970, he graduated from East High School and enrolled in Corning Community College in New York. There he played goalie on the ice hockey team before transferring to Ithaca College. In 1971, Clark got his first big break and was signed with the Pittsburgh Pirates' farm team in Hunnewell, Missouri. Clark excelled as a pitcher but his hitting suffered. It took him 11 seconds to get to first base on crutches, compared to the average of four seconds it took most players. But in 1973, the designated hitter rule was instated and Clark's career was saved. Clark balanced his athletic career with his studies, and in 1974 he graduated with a bachelor's degree in physical education.

Clark played all over the country for teams in Florida, Indiana, Texas, New Jersey, Connecticut and Delaware before traveling overseas to play in Sweden. In the 1970's, American teams were paying Clark $40 a week, $5 a day for meals and covering some other expenses. Sweden offered Clark a four year $100,000 contract to play and manage that he couldn't pass up. Sweden was rewarding athletically and personally. Athletically, Clark coached and managed several Swedish Junior National Teams, including one that won three consecutive national titles. Personally, he met his wife whom he married in 1995. They now have a beautiful daughter.

The fullness with which Clark lives his life and the appreciation he shows for each day makes his journey look easy. But Clark had to push himself very hard for the success he enjoyed and he earned every bit of it. In the off-seasons, Clark would work out four hours a day during which he ran five miles on crutches. Despite the crutches, Clark typically ran a 13 minute mile for five consecutive miles. The physical strain eventually caught up with him and in 1988 when he was about 35 years old, Clark was diagnosed with post-polio syndrome. His muscles that had to work twice as hard to compensate for his polio damaged muscles were extremely fatigued from years and years of being overworked.

Though his playing days were over, Clark stayed close to baseball for many years. He has worked as a scout for the Florida Marlins, San Diego Padres, Baltimore Orioles, New York Yankees and Chicago White Sox, as coach and owner of an Indianapolis barnstorming baseball team, as head coach of the Corning Community College baseball team and in Atlanta was named the baseball supervisor of sports information at the 1996 Summer Olympic Games. Wherever Clark has worked, his determination and courage have made him an inspiration to everyone around him.

This same determination has been displayed at Clark's baseball camps. Clark owned and operated the Ocala (Florida) Baseball Camps and also opened the Southern Tier Physically-Challenged Baseball Camps in 1983. Each summer, hundreds of physically and mentally handicapped athletes travel to Clark's camp to compete, learn and enjoy the game of baseball.

Clark believes that people with limitations are not always given equal opportunities and are the recipients of prejudice and discrimination. Clark is a pioneer for the physically disabled in the baseball world. He was often ostracized, sometimes by his own teammates, but he kept his mouth shut and did his job on the field, eventually earning the respect of his teammates and his opponents.

Clark no longer has the physical agility he once had, but he is still very able. He travels extensively for speaking engagements telling his incredible story to men, women and children so that they too can realize what they can accomplish if they only try. Clark has spoken to the New York Islander National Hockey League team, at the Disabled Sportsmen Annual Dinner in Ontario, Canada, the St. Joseph's Hospital Foundation in Elmira, New York and to many more groups he has left speechless and inspired. In 2003, Clark experienced a huge thrill and honor to speak at the National Baseball Hall of Fame as part of their "Special Abilities Weekend." Clark's message when he speaks is that everyone can dream. He has nothing negative to say about his life, noting that he has been blessed with great opportunities and a wonderful family.

David Clark's entire life story has been one of overcoming the odds. Standing 5 foot 2 and weighing only 130 pounds, Clark hardly resembled your typical professional athlete, but he pushed himself to the limit everyday in order to prove that he belonged. Richard Lapchick acknowledged it is Clark's courage, valor and strength that "helped him overcome polio and post-polio to show people in the world of sports what actually can be done when one commits to something. His career as a player, coach and teacher has inspired thousands of other people who have fewer challenges to excel. More importantly, his achievements have encouraged others who have had physical challenges to realize that they can be overcome." Clark has taught so many about life, living and loving.

Eddie Lee Ivery

by Jessica Bartter

The National Consortium for Academics and Sports was created in 1985 in response to the need to "keep the student in the student-athlete." The mission to create a better society by focusing on educational attainment and using the power and appeal of sport to positively affect social change was first put to work with the Degree Completion Program (DCP). Innovative for its time, DCP allowed student-athletes to stay in school with tuition assistance beyond their athletic eligibility, as well as allowing former student-athletes to return to school to complete their degrees.

For many high school students, an athletic scholarship is their only means to earn a college education. Regardless of whether or not they make the grade, family incomes cannot always support the cost of college tuition. So when the next level, professional sports, comes calling and flashing dollar bills, many student-athletes take the bait and leave their college without completing their degrees.

One such former student-athlete is Eddie Lee Ivery. Ivery was raised by his mother and grandmother. Both were on public assistance and neither had even an elementary school education. But that didn't prevent Ivery's mother from putting pressure on him to get a college education. Even when the scholarship offers came pouring in, Ivery's mother sat him down and reinforced what a blessing it was for him to have the opportunity to get a college degree. In fact, Ivery received 90 scholarship offers from all over the country. Most likely, it was Ivery's record breaking 1,710 yards rushed his senior season that garnered such attention. While scholarships came in from coast to coast, Ivery decided to stay in his home state of Georgia. And Georgia Tech was happy to have him since he was dubbed the greatest football player ever to come from the state of Georgia.

At Georgia Tech, Ivery continued to accomplish great things on the football field. He scored 22 touchdowns for 158 points, set a NCAA single-game rushing record of 356 yards and a single-season rushing record of 1,562 yards. Though Ivery's single-game rushing record has since been broken, he set it in just 26 carries. Had the 20 mph winds and 20 degree temperatures been a little more accommodating, perhaps Ivery would have rushed for more than 356 yards in Tech's 42-21 win over Air Force. He went on to break seven Georgia Tech rushing records before he was drafted in the National Football League's first round by the Green Bay Packers.

Despite his success on the field, Ivery's professional career was filled with turmoil from injuries, drugs, alcohol and family problems off the field. After nine seasons, Ivery left the NFL but the fast-paced life didn't leave Ivery. For 15 years he was hooked on alcohol and cocaine and his life spiraled out of control. There were car accidents, the loss of jobs, arrests, bankruptcy, and eventually, divorce. He struggled with his addiction until his wife finally walked out and took their two children with her. Losing his family was a rude awakening for Ivery. In an attempt to get his life back on track, Ivery went back to Georgia Tech to complete his degree and was one of the early professional athletes to graduate through the National Consortium for Academics and Sports' Degree Completion Program. He earned his bachelor's degree in management in 1992.

Despite several stints in rehab, Ivery still struggled with an addiction until he checked-in for the last time in 1998. This time his rehabilitation program was successful, and Ivery was able to revive his relationship with his two children. He often flew to Florida to visit his daughter Tauvia at Florida A&M University. He watched his son, Eddie Jr., receive acclaim playing football and he crossed his fingers that he would follow him to Georgia Tech. Eddie Jr., who rushed for 1,430 yards and 14 touchdowns as a senior at Chamberlain High School in Tampa was a member of the National Honor Society with a 4.16 GPA, and he did commit to Georgia Tech in 2002. Perhaps making up for lost time, father and son are together at last because Ivery is also back at his alma mater and assists Georgia Tech Athletics as an assistant strength and conditioning coach. Ivery also serves as an assistant player development coach and uses his own experiences to help guide current Yellow Jackets to success, personally and professionally, academically and athletically. Although Eddie Lee Ivery is ashamed of some of the decisions he made in his life, he uses them to teach and thus help the athletes with whom he now works.

Loretta Claiborne

by Brian Wright

The power of sport is evident in the fact that 40 million American youth play organized sports. Sports can help kids make friends, build self-esteem, stay active and feel a part of something. They can also be a fun and engaging way for kids to learn the important lessons of working together, leadership, character development, sportsmanship and responsibility. Despite the positives associated with youth participation in sports, studies have found that 75 percent of those who play organized sports will quit by the time they are 14 years old. It has also been proven that if a female is not active in sports by the age of 10, there is only a 10 percent chance she will be participating at age 25. Loretta Claiborne is one of the few who broke the mold as her athletic involvement did not begin until she was 17, only to be followed by stardom as an athlete and as an individual.

Claiborne, born legally blind and mildly mentally disabled, was raised in a single-parent home in the projects of York, Pennsylvania with her six brothers and sisters. Unable to walk or talk until she was four, Claiborne was behind in what society declares as natural child development. After receiving corrective laser eye surgery and beginning school, Claiborne could not escape the teasing and torment she faced from her fellow classmates. She was constantly on the receiving end of ridicule from her peers at school and in her neighborhood. The relentless teasing isolated Claiborne, causing her to feel lonely, sad and angry. To compound her obstacles, school officials recommended she be removed and institutionalized. Luckily, her mother refused. Though down, Claiborne never counted herself out, and in 1970 she found her passion in running and in the Special Olympics.

The little girl who could not walk until she was four developed into a world class runner and Special Olympics Medalist. She was introduced to the Special Olympics by social worker and friend Janet McFarland. Claiborne has competed in more than 25 marathons across the U.S., and she has won numerous medals and awards in the Special Olympics. After years of feeling out of place and angry about being treated differently than others, Claiborne felt she "found a place to belong," thanks to sports. Claiborne was the first Special Olympic athlete to compete in the Boston Marathon and she placed in the top 100 female runners both times she ran. She also ranked in the top 25 runners in the Pittsburgh marathon. Claiborne found an outlet for her pain through running and in the process discovered several other sports. Claiborne won ten medals in seven different Special Olympic events and continues to train in figure skating, soccer, alpine skiing, basketball, golf, softball, aquatics and bowling. She even has a black belt in karate and she broke the women's record for her age group in the 5,000 meter event.

Vice President George Bush honored Claiborne with the Spirit of Special Olympics Award in 1981 and Special Olympics, Inc. honored her as Athlete of the Year in 1990. A year later, she was named Special Olympics Athlete of the Quarter Century by Runner's World magazine. She has been inducted into numerous halls of fame including the National Girls and Women in Sports Hall of Fame. In 1996, Claiborne was honored at ESPN's ESPY Awards Show with the Arthur Ashe Courage Award. Each year, the Arthur Ashe Courage Award is presented to the person or persons whose courage and conviction transcend sport. Fellow honorees of past years include Howard Cosell (1995), Muhammad Ali (1997), Dean Smith (1998) and Billie Jean King (1999). A movie was produced by Walt Disney Productions and aired on ABC-TV depicting the story of Claiborne's inspiring journey, and portraying her witty and compassionate personality.

Claiborne's achievements continued off the athletic field as well. She speaks four languages, including American Sign Language and has received honorary doctorate degrees from Quinnipiac College and Villanova University. It is believed she was the first Special Olympic athlete to receive such honors. Claiborne has worked tirelessly challenging government policies regarding individuals with mental disabilities. She has appeared on ESPN, Lifetime Television, Nickelodeon, CBS This Morning, ABC's Wide World of Sports and The Oprah Winfrey Show. Claiborne's efforts have expanded beyond the borders of the United States as well. She accompanied Arnold Schwartzenegger to light the Flame of Hope in 2001 in Capetown, South Africa for a campaign to increase the number of South African athletes involved in the Special Olympics. The campaign was co-chaired by Nelson Mandela, former South African president and leader of the anti-apartheid movement, and Timothy Shriver, former President, Chairman and CEO of Special Olympics. Claiborne also attended the Global Athlete Congress planning session in Dublin, Ireland to assist in the strategizing for the 2003 World Games.

Claiborne's accomplishments have earned her world-wide acclaim and recognition but what separates her from other athletes is her incomparable humility. Claiborne even turned down an invitation from President Bill Clinton to go running because she had to fulfill a promise she made to a friend who was performing at an event. If you ask Claiborne, she will tell you that her biggest accomplishment is positively impacting the lives of youth around the world. Claiborne has spoken before the United States Congress as well as to hundreds of other organizations, reaching over 100,000 people. The message Claiborne relays to audiences is simple but powerful: focus on one's abilities, not disabilities.

Claiborne's life journey has taken her places she could never even imagined and taught us to focus on what one can accomplish in life, not what others try to predetermine. Friends Lynn and Sigmund Morawski described Claiborne best as "an undiscovered treasure until Special Olympics opened her world to possibility. She is an unexpected find of incredible talent, worth and inspiration."

Sam Paneno

by Brian Wright

Jesse Jackson noted in one of his most famous speeches that "It's not your aptitude but your attitude that will determine your altitude." Sam Paneno personifies this quote. As an incoming transfer to the University of California, Davis football team, Sam Paneno was deemed an immediate impact player on the team and on the season overall. As the starting running back, he showed glimpses of greatness in his first game. This had the UC Davis campus and football team buzzing about the upcoming season.

In his second game of the season against Western Oregon, Paneno displayed the athletic ability and skill that had coaches and media raving about him. The game with Western Oregon remained close and regulation ended in a tie. Behind Paneno's 100 yards rushing and two touchdowns the UC Davis Aggies went into the overtime period confident that they could win the game. The Aggie players and coaching staff knew the importance of winning this game and how it could propel the team into a very promising season. The score read 33-33 as the overtime opening whistle blew. The crowd was anxious and the two teams were ready. The Aggies won the coin toss and elected to receive the ball. Paneno stood ready on the sideline for his chance to continue the game and his success on the field which would eventually lead his team to victory.

In the first play from scrimmage in overtime Paneno got the ball and made a move to free himself from the defense and find a hole in the defensive line to run through. Paneno found a running lane which was eventually closed, and he was tackled on what the coaching staff and spectators considered to be a routine play. As the pile of defenders cleared, Paneno was left on the ground holding his leg in excruciating pain. Team officials came to his aid and found he had injured his knee on the play. The trainers saw that his knee was dislocated but it didn't seem like an atypical football injury.

What initially appeared to be a common knee injury would soon take a turn for the worst. Paneno discovered that his knee dislocation would be a life-threatening and a life-changing injury. He was rushed to the hospital and doctors proceeded to work on his dislocated knee. What doctors had not planned on, and what added an extreme level of uncertainty about surgery was the severely damaged artery behind Paneno's knee. This is very uncommon in most knee injuries and the other damage from the collision was very troubling. The damage done from the on-field collision interrupted the normal blood flow between Paneno's leg and foot. As doctors realized the severity of this injury, they knew that the damage done to the muscles and nerves of Paneno's lower leg were probably irreparable. The doctors' immediate thoughts were to amputate the leg. Knowing Paneno's commitment and passion for sports they explored alternative procedures to repair his leg but amputation began to look like the only option. After numerous failed surgery attempts to save Paneno's leg, there was no choice but to amputate.

For most athletes in their prime this diagnosis and the resulting surgery would have been permanently devastating and in some cases would have led to depression and lack of hope for the life they had ahead of them. Paneno, however, had the courage to put the surgery in perspective and remained positive about his future. "I have no bitter feelings. I got a chance to play football for a long time. A lot of people don't get that opportunity."[1]

This is not to say that Paneno wasn't saddened by the fact that his football playing career was over. He certainly was. But he had the courage and the desire to embrace the positives rather than dwell on the negatives. This courageous attitude Paneno displayed is what being a courageous athlete is all about, and many times what is missing among athletes today. Paneno spent much of his recovery time in the hospital after the surgery reminiscing about the positive experiences and relationships he had due to his involvement in sports. Paneno realized that he had an important message to deliver to each and every individual he would now meet. The message was of how sports impacted his life in a positive way, and how it could positively affect others who participate in sports. Upon being released from the hospital, Paneno rejoined his teammates on the football field without any feelings of sorrow or remorse. His teammates and the Aggies coaching staff could see his extreme gratitude for all the experiences he had while participating as a student-athlete.

While facing the toughest loss of his young life, Paneno realized that a greater good could come out of his situation. He knew that through his experiences he could be a pioneer in helping adults and children cope with a similar condition to his own. He also realized that even without playing collegiate or professional football that he could still have a positive impact on others. Paneno's ideas of service to others became a plan of action as he currently mentors recent amputees and their families on how to cope with the lifestyle changes and the attitudes it takes to overcome this adversity. Paneno's amazing spirit and courage has influenced his coaches, teammates and everyone else who hears his remarkable story. Paneno personifies what we define as strength, courage, determination and the will to succeed. Whether Paneno has ever heard Jesse Jackson speak about people's attitude determining their altitude is not known, but he lives it. Everyday of his life he doesn't just think about helping somebody in need, he does it. Paneno's positive attitude has led him to great success on and off the field and has allowed him to have a positive impact on society. Sam Paneno has used his life experiences in sports to make things better in the world. Hopefully as his life's story and message spreads, his impact on society will continue to grow.

[1] Lafontaine, Pat. Companions in Courage: Triumphant Tales of Heroic Athletes. New York: Warner Brothers Inc., 2001.

Kathryn Waldo

by Jessica Bartter

Forced to skate at top speeds, stop suddenly on ice and start quickly on thin blades, with large sticks in tow wearing up to a quarter of one's body weight in extra pounds of equipment makes ice hockey a difficult sport. Furthermore, it has a harsh reputation built by hard plays, rough conditions and tough players.

It may not be the sport of choice for most parents when looking for physical activity for their three year old child suffering from cystic fibrosis. But for Maureen and Joe Waldo, this very decision back in 1979 may have been the smartest they ever made. In fact, it quite possibly has saved their daughter much pain and themselves much heartache, and perhaps even their daughter's life.

At only two months old, Maureen and Joe Waldo brought their newborn to the doctor with concerns over lingering congestion in her chest. The diagnosis was devastating. Cystic fibrosis is a genetic disease in which a defective gene causes the body to produce an abnormally thick, sticky mucus that clogs the lungs and leads to life-threatening lung infections. These thick secretions also obstruct the pancreas, preventing digestive enzymes from reaching the intestines to help break down and absorb food. In addition, the prognosis was that their baby girl Kathryn, would only live to the age of 18, 20 if she was lucky. Refusing to be innocent bystanders, Kathryn Waldo's parents encouraged their daughter to exercise; they even forced her to do so at times. They believed, despite doctors recommendations to the contrary, that deep breaths of fresh air were the best medicine for their daughter's condition. Moreover, during coughing bouts as a child, Joe Waldo ordered his daughter to sprint around the block in hopes it would help open her lungs and ease her breathing. Her parents even encouraged her older brother David to include her when he played football, baseball and basketball. Then, at the young age of three, Waldo followed her brother onto the ice rink.

Waldo's hockey skills earned her a spot on a boy's team where she played for years until high school. In high school, Waldo's hockey opportunities were still limited to the boy's team where she became the first girl to make the team. She went on to become the first female captain of the team as well. In a fast paced sport like hockey, lung capacity is important for stamina. Though Waldo's lung capacity is only 60 percent of that of a healthy individual her age, Waldo insists the cold air in the rink opens her airways and eases her breathing. Waldo also stayed active year-round by playing softball. This physical activity seemed to help Waldo's health. Doctors had warned she would constantly be in and out of hospitals, yet by the age of 18, she had only been hospitalized twice. In addition to the sports, Waldo has a strict regimen that helps her maintain her health. A hot shower in the morning helps open her lungs, followed by a five to eight minute nebulizer treatment to break up the mucus in her lungs. Cystic fibrosis also affects Waldo's digestive system, causing her to eat four times as much food as a healthy person her size and forces her to take pills each time she eats and drinks so that her body can absorb the nutrients properly.

Waldo proved that not much could hold her back and that she was one of a kind by earning a hockey scholarship to Northeastern University. Waldo stood out in the rink, but for different reasons than you may think. In her freshman year, Waldo led her team in scoring and was named MVP. Following her freshman season, shoulder surgery was followed by a lung infection that landed Waldo in the hospital where she missed the beginning of her sophomore season. Yet, Waldo returned later in the season to help her team win the conference championship. Though she missed much of her junior season due to another illness, she returned her senior year for another successful season.

While it was avoided in the past, medical professionals now actually recommend exercise for individuals suffering from cystic fibrosis. In part as a result, the life expectancy for cystic fibrosis patients has increased to 30 years. The Waldos may have rewritten history for their daughter, and Kathryn Waldo has gone on to do so for many others by defying the odds and inspiring and leading through example.

Shane Wood

by Stacy Martin

Necessity is said to be the mother of invention. It was necessary for Shane Wood to be able to play baseball, so Jake Harrison invented a leather baseball glove that resembled a lacrosse stick for him. Wood was a typical teenager with an unusual adaptation. He was born without hands and with malformed feet. Wood demonstrated a resilient and determined attitude at an early age. His mother fought with him to wear the prosthetic hands that were created for him. Dana Perry lost that battle when, at just 13 months old, Wood decided that he wanted no part of artificial limbs. He simply used them to take the devices off his arms and that was the end of that problem. Dana resigned herself to allowing Wood to use his natural hands, "a type of tough, calloused hands."[1] Wood could do almost anything with his hands and just as a young child learns the finer points of dexterity, Wood learned to grasp his own unique version of it.

He never thought of himself as disabled, incapable, or defeated. He identifies himself as a normal person who as a child was capable of playing sports and interacting with others all on his own. Once Wood made his wish to be like everyone else known, his mom made sure that she treated him as such. If he truly did not want help, there would be none forthcoming. Some might look at this omission of assistance as cruel treatment to a child with adaptive challenges, but Dana knew that it would only strengthen her son's will and independent nature. She would have been the toughest little league coach around, because there were no excuses and the word "can't" was not a part of her or her son's vernacular. Wood has never even said that word to his mother, with one minor exception. He will regularly say it in reference to what he is able to do with his artificial hand. The commonly accepted treatment of disabled people is to coddle them and assist them with tasks they cannot perform on their own. Wood defied the thought of such treatment. Instead he pushed himself to new limits everyday and his mother demands that he overcome the challenges that are placed before him.

When Wood was six he began playing soccer just like the other kids his age in a youth soccer league. Soccer is a physically taxing sport even for someone who doesn't have misshapen feet. Wood was certainly not disadvantaged though as he actually seems to use his adaptation to a competitive advantage. He quickly excelled at soccer; in fact by the time he was 13 he had perfected his scoring abilities. His team won the city championship and he was the leading scorer. His ability to run fast for a sustained period suited another sport as he became one of the fastest sprinters at Brownwood Junior High and competed in the mile run as well.

Wood thrived in middle school, and he began to explore new challenges. He tried out for the football team which instills fear in the hearts of some mothers with completely healthy, young boys. Dana only encouraged her son's newest endeavor with love and support. Wood was so skilled at the sport, and demonstrated such endurance and enthusiasm that he was able to play both offensive and defensive tackle. He starred in the classroom as well with a B+ average, and was a talented musician, playing the trombone in the band. He was actively involved in the student council. In the little bit of spare time he found, he learned how to bowl, fish, ski, and roller skate. Wood was a child with a seemingly infinite source of energy. He also regularly participated in his church's youth group. The activities listed would rarely be associated with a child who has disabilities, but Wood refuses to think of himself as disabled.

The only activity that seemed beyond reach to him was playing baseball. He had accomplished countless ventures with what he had been given, but limitations were disconcerting to Wood. He attempted to play baseball but it seemed like an insurmountable task without a way to grasp a baseball while catching or throwing. Wood has inspired many people with his ability to smash barriers; Jake Harrison was one of those people. He is a saddle maker by trade, and motivated by Wood's determination, he constructed a glove that would enable Wood to play baseball. His final design made it possible for Wood to throw a baseball with remarkable accuracy and play center field like a pro. He could even field ground balls with the lacrosse like scoop design. The Texas Rangers learned of Wood's talents on the baseball field when he was 13 and were so inspired by him that they granted him the honor of throwing out the first pitch on opening day of the 1991 season.

Wood's popularity grew at school and his excitement mounted as the day approached. He was going to meet Nolan Ryan, one of the greatest players of all time. He played for the "Little League" Rangers, but on April 8, 1991 he was going to be one of the Texas Rangers, attending team practice and the team dinner. It was all a little overwhelming, even for Wood who could overcome anything. Then the stakes were raised. President George H.W. Bush was going to join Wood on the pitcher's mound for the honor. A young man with a very outgoing nature became shy and quiet when asked about the opportunity to share the spotlight with someone so important. He wouldn't have traded that opportunity for anything, but he says that meeting Nolan Ryan was the highlight of his life.

Sports fostered Wood's strength and his character, and a well-known sports figure served as the ultimate reward for the young man's valiant efforts. The cooperation with his teammates and the self-confidence he gained through his own skill has surely set him on a path destined for success in whatever field he chooses in life. Shane Wood demonstrated tenacity and vigor so gracefully that it inspired a community, a professional baseball team, as well as a president. His courageous efforts should instill a belief in us that playing sports can open up doors even if they seem to shut us out. It just might take a little ingenuity.

[1] Inzunza, Victor. "On Opening Day 1991… A boy, a president" *Fort Worth Star-Telegram*, April 8, 1991.

CHAPTER 6

CREATING A BETTER WORLD

There are individuals whose names may not resonate in a huge way in the world of sport but whose lives are filled with acts that help create a better world. This section includes 13 such people who dedicated a significant part of their lives to *Creating a Better World.*

Dirceu Hurtado inspired his fellow students when he returned from a life-threatening brain aneurysm to rejoin his teammates on the soccer team at Fairleigh Dickinson.

Destiny Woodbury had her family ripped apart as a six year old. Determined to keep them together, she virtually became the mother of her younger siblings. Confronted with high crime and drugs among her peers, she chose to enroll in after-school programs to stay safe. She developed into such a great athlete that she was representing the University of Rhode Island in track and field when she won her award. Despite a childhood marked by poverty, her mother's drug addiction and her father's absence, Destiny Woodbury grew up and became an outstanding athlete and woman.

Stacy Sines was a collegiate swimmer who had an aneurysm in the wall between the upper chambers of her heart. While waiting to get permission to return to the pool, she helped others who had medical problems and became their hero. Stacy has become known for her character and compassion as much as her swimming abilities.

Jennifer McClain followed so many athletes before her who defied the odds by refusing to let a birth defect define her life. Born with spina bifida, she endured seven intensive surgeries in her first 22 years. While at Quinnipiac College, she was on the volleyball team and was a dean's list student.

Rashad Williams, although he lived 1,300 miles from the Columbine shooting, decided that he was going to raise money to help the victims at Columbine. He used sport as his means to that end. By running in the San Francisco Bay for Breakers 7.5 Mile Race, this teenager raised $18,000 for Lance Kirklin, one of the surviving victims of the Columbine shooting.

In his teenage years Lawrence Wright did not know if he would end up in jail, dead, or on an NFL team. By the time he was 18, he decided to pay the price to move in the direction that would help him at the University of Florida to succeed academically and athletically. By the time he did succeed, he created the "Right Trak" program to help bring others along with him academically and socially.

Lonise Bias suffered the tragedy and the death of her two children, both outstanding basketball players, and has committed to spend the rest of her life crusading against drugs and violence. The death of Len Bias in 1986, the number one draft choice of the Boston Celtics, made America realize that cocaine was not a recreational but a lethal drug. Dr. Bias has driven that home to audiences for nearly two decades since her tragic loss.

Alfreda Harris, a legendary figure in Boston, has helped young girls become women through sport. Say her name in Boston and you see inspired faces react to the greatness that she has been able to achieve for other people.

After Maggie Maloy was a victim of a horrible assault followed by a terrible accident, her body seemed to crumble. Yet she was able to come back to school and compete in track. She enrolled at Defiance College, almost as a statement that she was defying all of the odds and would succeed. Her courage overcoming all of the physical problems has inspired many others around the nation to overcome their hardships.

Jodi Norton, a diver who proved her greatness as a high school All-American, had critical health issues and injuries that could have ended her career. But she persevered and became a champion diver at Columbia University. Diagnosed in 1994 with Lupus, Jodi hasn't let that stop her. She created the LIFE Foundation which supports other people who have Lupus to be able to continue their college education.

Bob Hurley, Sr. has had an extraordinary record as a high school basketball coach in New Jersey. Hurley has taken children from the inner-cities and insisted they become students while becoming fine athletes. Discipline and academics became part of the successful formula that helped so many people overcome the odds on his teams and go on to college and productive lives.

Tanya Hughes-Jones became the NCAA's Woman of the Year in 1994 after a great career as a high jumper. She became America's top high jumper in 1992 and 1993 and represented the United States in Barcelona Olympics when she was only 22. It is the role model status that she created for other athletes around her as an Academic All-American, as someone who became successful in the business world and as a mother. She is now going to join the ministry with her husband who is already a pastor.

Michele Leary used the persistence and endurance swimming taught her along with the support of her teammates and coaches to overcome a heart attack at the age of 21. She plans to do for others what her doctors were able to do for her when she graduates medical school in the Spring of 2006.

Dirceu Hurtado

by Jessica Bartter

Described by his coach as magical on the field for his soccer prowess, Dirceu Hurtado is more like a miracle off the field. A standout soccer player in high school, this Peruvian native set the state record in New Jersey with 73 goals scored in his three year varsity career, during which he also earned All-Conference, All-County and All-State honors every year. Highly recruited for obvious reasons, Hurtado committed to Fairleigh Dickinson University in Teaneck, New Jersey because they shared his commitment to academics and agreed to let him take his freshman soccer season off just to focus on his grades.

After a full year of making the adjustments most college freshman face and working hard in the classroom, Hurtado was looking forward to starting his soccer career as a Knight at Fairleigh Dickinson University. But his career almost ended before it began. While home alone, Hurtado suffered such a severe headache that he called 911. When the rescue crew arrived, they found Hurtado unconscious and rushed him to the hospital. There he underwent surgery to relieve the pressure on his brain that an aneurysm left when a blood vessel burst. For one long agonizing month, Hurtado's parents sat by his side in the hospital while his condition left him in a coma. His father left his job to care for their eldest son but was reassured by the support his team pledged. His coach guaranteed his scholarship regardless of whether or not he played and his teammates organized a fundraiser to assist with the medical bills. Though doctors tried to warn his parents that Hurtado may not survive, to no one's surprise, he persevered.

Upon waking up, he recognized those whom were there in support, his coach, teammates, roommates and family, but had trouble talking to them and couldn't move his right side. After undergoing another surgery to drain fluid from his lungs caused by pneumonia, Hurtado faced months of therapy learning how to walk, talk and write again. This former soccer star's coordination was problematic, to say the least. His father, a former member of the Peruvian National Soccer Team, thought soccer would be Hurtado's best therapy. But what had brought him so much joy for years, was painful and frustrating. The realization that what used to come naturally now needed so much work was crushing to Hurtado's spirit.

For a year, Hurtado steadily improved his daily functions and his coordination. Had it not been for his family and friends, soccer may have been a thing of the past. Fortunately for his teammates, Hurtado returned as strong as ever. In Fairleigh Dickinson University's season opener in 2000, Hurtado made his debut, scoring a goal on his team's way to a 3-1 victory. His magic continued as he scored two goals in each of the next two games. Early on, he led the Northeast Conference in goals and was tied for the lead in assists, proving his ability on the field. Hurtado is an offensive force to be reckoned with, and doesn't think twice when distributing the ball among his teammates. The metal plate in his head did make Hurtado hesitate when heading the ball. He had to learn how to head the ball correctly so as to not affect the protective plate, and he must be wary of jumping in the air and challenging opponents; a battle he never forfeited before.

Hurtado completed his first collegiate season with first team All-Conference and Mid-Atlantic Region accolades, was named Most Valuable Player of the Northeast Conference Championships and Rookie of the Year by the Northeast Conference. He led his team with 43 points, 17 goals, five of which were game winning, and nine assists. His scoring average of 2.05 per game was 15th in the nation in 2000. With no doubt about his resolve, Hurtado was named Comeback Player of the Year by the New Jersey Sports Writers Association and was awarded the Eastern College Athletic Conference's Award of Valor.

Hurtado's return from a life-threatening brain aneurysm inspired fellow student-athletes, particularly his little brother who is following in his big brother's footsteps. His teammates appreciated his presence as they felt they played their best with him on the field as he pushes everyone to the top of their game. His coach was continually amazed by his magic feet and spectacular moves and his parents couldn't be prouder. However, it is what Hurtado has accomplished off the field that has made him a true inspiration.

Destiny Woodbury

by Jessica Bartter

As she and her younger brother and sister were being taken from their mother by the Department of Children, Youth and Families, the bright six year old held on to the hope that they would once again be a happy family. The six year old, Destiny Woodbury, was a mother to her siblings even at that age and viewed her own mother more as a big sister figure who was fun to be with - when she was around. Forced into a lifestyle demanding maturity, Woodbury graciously accepted the responsibility without hesitation. Upon returning home from school each day, Woodbury fed her toddler brother with the only food in the house, baby cereal, and gave her infant sister a bottle of milk. She took it upon herself to ensure that her and her siblings were fed and cleansed; not a typical lifestyle for a six year old but certainly one that Woodbury was good at. Even at that age, Woodbury recognized that her mother was using the family's food money to buy drugs and other substances for herself, some days forcing her three young children to go without any food at all.

Remarkably, Woodbury recognized that her family was living in poverty because of the daily choices her mother was making. Woodbury decided she could make a better choice for her and her siblings and asked her grandmother if they could move in with her because of the lack of food and care they were receiving from their mother. Woodbury's grandmother, Ella Mae, was shocked to learn that her daughter was still addicted to drugs and knew the circumstances must be rough for a six year old to want to move out. Perhaps Woodbury derived her courage from her grandmother, because in exceptionally courageous fashion, Ella Mae called a social worker in on her own daughter. The social worker contacted the Department of

Children, Youth and Families and within two days of Woodbury's request, she and her siblings were removed from their mother's home.

Between Woodbury and her two siblings, there were three different fathers, none of whom offered support. Ella Mae, who was working nights, was faced with the decision to raise her grandchildren or continue working. In Ella Mae's mind, it was no decision and she quickly quit her job. In addition to the new challenge of raising three young children, Ella Mae was faced with supporting the family off her nominal savings and a monthly $820 check from the state. After two years of making ends meet, Ella Mae was awoken by fire fighters, and gas and electric company employees who informed her that the building she called home was being condemned. After a few days in a hotel, Ella Mae and her grandchildren moved to a shelter, where they stayed for two and a half months. After living with Ella Mae's sister and her five children for a brief period things began to look up as Ella Mae got an apartment, the same apartment where she and the Woodbury children have been ever since.

Woodbury and her brother and sister saw their mother occasionally throughout the years, usually around birthdays and holidays. At times she appeared to have cleaned up her act, looking healthy with a new place to live, and in turn rekindling Woodbury's dream to have her back in their lives. But Woodbury's dream was dashed as her mother lost her battle with drug addiction and overdosed in July 1998, the summer before she entered high school. Though she would never see her mother again, Woodbury was determined to fulfill the rest of her dreams.

Woodbury knew her future would be determined by the choices she made then, so she enrolled in several after school programs, choosing to stay off the streets and away from drugs. Woodbury was active in Unified Sistas, Youth Talking 2 Youth, Teen Institute, Children's Crusade and America's Promise and joined the cross country, and indoor and outdoor track and field teams. In high school, Woodbury discovered two of her passions; running and chemistry, both of which helped her achieve her dream of attending college. Woodbury's grandmother had not made it past the eighth grade and her mother never graduated from high school, so Woodbury wanted to be the first in her family to attend college and in the process show her brother and sister that they were capable of the same success. Woodbury worked hard for years, not only for herself but to inspire her siblings and even challenge them to do better. Both her brother and her sister learned from their fearless leader and earned such good grades that they received the opportunity to attend private schools.

Woodbury is currently a student-athlete at the University of Rhode

Island and works hard to represent URI as an athlete and to succeed as a student. As a sophomore she anchored URI's 4x400-meter relay squad to indoor and outdoor Atlantic-10 Conference Championships as well as an indoor New England Championship. Woodbury and her teammates set indoor and outdoor school and Atlantic-10 records. Woodbury also works hard to maintain her grades and is committed to the community. She even made a presentation to the school board in her former community when they threatened to cut funding for her high school's cross country team. By impressively telling her story and the impact sports had on her life, the cross country team was saved. As a member of URI's Student-Athlete Advisory Committee, Woodbury represented her fellow student-athletes at the NCAA Leadership Conference in 2004. Her leadership skills continued to flourish and over the holidays, Woodbury organized her team's sponsorship of three different families. She was instrumental in organizing the families' needs, and the food and gift drives with her teammates.

Woodbury is on schedule to graduate in four years with majors in Chemistry and Secondary Education. She was named to the Atlantic-10 Conference Commissioners Honor Roll twice in just two years. She won the Victor J. Baxt Scholarship and earned a summer internship at the chemistry lab of Teknor Apex. Woodbury is considering teaching chemistry, for which she earned the Edward D. Eddy Memorial Scholarship, given annually to a graduate of a Providence, Rhode Island public school who is majoring in education and plans to teach in an urban school.

Despite a childhood marked with poverty, scarred by drug abuse and the absence of a father, Destiny Woodbury faced life squarely and triumphed over the adversities she faced. Every time she accomplishes a goal or a dream, she wonders how it can help those around her, especially her little brother and sister. This courageous student-athlete has lived through fearful times and seen fearful sights, but in the end, has emerged fearless.

Stacy Sines
by Jessica Bartter

Stacy Sines, some would say, has a heart of gold. Medical professionals were forced to disagree when they found an aneurysm in the wall between the upper chambers of her heart. This was not the first time Stacy had faced physical adversity and it would not be the last. But it was the most serious and challenging thus far.

Sines began her collegiate swimming career in 1999 at Washington College in Chestertown, Maryland. In the midst of her freshman year, Sines was hospitalized for two weeks with a pulmonary embolism, a blood clot on her lung. It was revealed that Sines suffered from Factor V Lieden, a condition that causes blood clots to form quickly.

Sines was crushed when she was told by her doctor that she could no longer train, and that she would most likely miss the remainder of her freshman season. Determined to contribute to her team, Sines hunted for a second opinion in which she received permission to train in moderation. It was a matter of days before Sines was training at full capacity and amazingly, in just four weeks she competed in her first Centennial Conference Championship where she swam five personal bests, earning five medals.

Sines' renewed appreciation for life and swimming carried her to success as a sophomore. Though she was constantly monitoring her physical condition, her sophomore season would later prove to be her only healthy one. She returned to the Conference Championships and took the crown, earning her a spot at the NCAA Division III Championships, where she place 2nd and 14th, earning All-American honors.

A shoulder injury slowed Sines her junior year, but didn't stop her.

An ultrasound revealed an aneurysm in her heart. Her coach broke the news to her and ordered her out of the pool. Reluctantly, Sines sat on the bench, but soon earned medical clearance once again, getting back into the pool within just ten days. Not missing a beat, Sines returned to the Conference Championships for the third straight year and won two individual events and one relay, earning three gold medals. Sines again placed 14th at the NCAA Division III Championships in the 200 yard freestyle. Sines was now a two-time All-American.

All the accolades Sines enjoyed her junior season came amidst the mental agony of her health. Sines, her family and her trusted team of medical professionals were constantly performing tests to determine her best medical options. A transesophageal echocardiogram allowed doctors to view the internal structures of the heart and its major vessels. Cardiologists discovered Sines had abnormal holes in the wall between the heart's upper chambers, an atrial septal defect (ASD), which increases flow to the right ventricle and lungs, potentially causing significant stress on the blood vessels. ASD combined with Sines' Factor V Leiden, put her condition on high alert. After much debate, Sines was convinced open heart surgery was the best for her situation, a decision she noted as the most mentally taxing part of the ordeal. The procedure was performed in late July of 2002, followed by three weeks of cardiac rehabilitation.

Although Sines was eager to swim competitively, she knew she had to wait for medical clearance. But that didn't stop her from jumping in to help others as she went to work as a lifeguard within weeks of the surgery. She even found the time and energy to teach swimming to young children.

Michael, one of Sines' swimming students, particularly touched her heart. Michael was a young boy battling a brain tumor. Familiar with hospital visits and medical costs, Sines wanted to raise money for Michael's family to help with their medical expenses. Her idea, "Bike for Mike," showed her compassion and competitiveness. Sines moved a stationery bike from the fitness center to the dining hall on the Washington College campus. She sent an e-mail to the entire campus informing them of her great intentions. Her determination enabled Sines to bike for eight hours and one minute straight, helping her to raise almost $700 for Mike. Sines later choreographed another fundraiser for a fellow swimmer who was confined to a wheelchair after a diving accident.

Perhaps during surgery, the instruments used were made of gold, because her heart shone even brighter than before. Stacy Sines' character and compassion are rare to find but easy to admire.

Jennifer McClain

by Jessica Bartter

Jim Abbott didn't let his lack of a right hand stop him from becoming an exceptional pitcher who spent 10 years in the major leagues and was a member of the 1988 U.S. Olympic Team. Lance Armstrong recovered from potentially deadly testicular cancer that had spread to his lungs and brain leaving him with a small chance of survival. Not only did he make a complete recovery but he also returned to the professional cycling circuit stronger than ever and has since won seven Tour de France races.

Jennifer "Tex" McClain is another of so many athletes who defied the odds and refused to let a birth defect define her life. McClain was born with a spina bifida, the most common permanently disabling birth defect. Though the effects are different for different spina bifida patients, the results can be debilitating for all. Spina bifida is a neural tube defect that happens in the first month of pregnancy when the spinal column doesn't close completely which can cause fluid on the brain, partial paralysis, bladder and bowel control difficulties, learning disabilities, depression and other issues. McClain's condition required her to have extensive surgery to remove meningocele from her lower vertebrae and spinal cord area. McClain was just one day old when she underwent this life-saving surgery. During her first 22 years of life, McClain underwent seven more intensive surgeries to strengthen her spine.

At an early age, doctors warned McClain that she would have severe motor skill damage that would prevent her from being able to run or jump. McClain thought she would see for herself rather than accept their opinion and took up volleyball, a sport that requires both running and jumping. McClain found that not only did she thoroughly enjoy volleyball, she was also very good at it. After a successful and highlighted high school season, she earned an athletic scholarship to Quinnipiac College.

The Spring, Texas native, who bears the nickname of her home state, was named captain during her sophomore, junior and senior seasons and led the team from her position as setter. In volleyball, the setter is similar to the quarterback of a football team. It is the setter's responsibility to call and run the plays, dishing out assist after assist, for her teammates to attack. In control of her offense at all times, McClain set several school records at Quinnipiac College. She still ranks in the top ten in games played per season and career, hitting percentage, assists per game, career service aces, service aces per game, total digs, solo blocks, block assists and total blocks. McClain still tops the career and season assist lists. While she led the Braves on the court, McClain pushed herself hard in the classroom and earned 3.33 grade point average. The international business major also earned the Eastern College Athletic Conference's Award of Valor in 1999.

McClain also found time to give back to her community. She visited recreation centers and middle schools to introduce the sport of volleyball and to teach children the fundamentals. McClain also reaches out to the spina bifida community as a motivational speaker and guidance counselor. She particularly enjoys helping young children born with spina bifida realize that they can accomplish many things despite doctors warnings or recommendations. She is a living example that the illness will not define you if you don't let it, and that her abilities as an individual, an athlete, a student and an inspiration are what define Jennifer McClain.

Rashad Williams

by Jessica Bartter

Following the deadliest school shooting in U.S. history, Rashad Williams was desperate to help despite the fact that he was 1,300 miles away and did not know anyone involved in the incident. Two students opened fire on their classmates and teachers in 1999 in Littleton, Colorado. The results were devastating for Columbine High School and for our nation: 12 students and one teacher lost forever. They were sons, daughters, friends, cousins, brothers, sisters, one father and so much more to so many. Twenty four more students were injured by the shooters and everyone associated with the school was left scared emotionally. Blame for the incident was attributed to the music kids listen to, the movies they watch, the violence they see on television and use of teenage anti-depressants. The only thing on 15 year old Rashad Williams' mind was how he could help. Williams turned to what he loved most and knew best: sports.

Williams recognized that the tragedy at Columbine could happen anywhere, even at his school. It could leave him or his friends injured, paralyzed or worse. Williams particularly took to the story of one boy, Lance Kirklin. Kirklin, a 16 year old sophomore, was shot five times by his callous attackers. He was shot point blank in the face with a 12-gauge shotgun, shattering the left side of his jaw; twice in his right leg, breaking his femur into 20 pieces and hitting a blood vessel; once in his left leg and once in his chest, piercing his lung. Within days Kirklin had undergone 28 hours of surgery by more than 30 different surgeons attempting to reconstruct his jaw and legs. Kirklin's family did not have health insurance and his father quit working to care for his son. The medical bills piled up quickly and there was no end in sight to Kirklin's medical needs.

Kirklin had been an athlete and the loss of his ability to compete deeply affected Williams. Since Williams was in the midst of track season he thought it best to use his healthy legs to raise money for this stranger who no longer could run. Williams entered the San Francisco Bay for Breakers 7 ½ mile race and sought sponsors to back him in order to raise money for Kirklin. After collecting $300 in pledges, Williams was satisfied with his success. Word of Williams' compassion traveled around town eventually reaching the San Francisco Mayor, Willie Brown. Mayor Brown was moved by Williams' efforts and informed the media which began to help. Within days, the $300 turned into $14,000. Mayor Brown even declared May 24 as Rashad Williams Day in San Francisco. As the Mayor presented the proclamation to Williams, his continuing pleads for donations increased the total from $14,000 to $18,000.

The money was greatly needed and appreciated by the Kirklin family, whose bills exceeded $1 million within just months of the shooting. Mayor Brown's office took care of Williams' travel arrangements so that he could hand deliver the check.

During the race, Williams struggled with the 7 ½ miles but the thought of Kirklin kept him going. It took courage for the 15 year old to admit he was tired, but then again, there was no doubt he was courageous, especially in the mind of Lance Kirklin.

Lawrence Wright

by Jessica Bartter

Six feet under or in a six by six jail cell was where Lawrence Wright was headed. However, at the age of 18 he made a choice that many adolescents don't know they have. He charted a new path for himself, headed for higher education, college football stardom and a career in the National Football League.

After losing his spot on the University of Miami's football squad because he failed the NCAA's required entrance exam, Wright decided his life needed to change. He enrolled in the Valley Forge Military Academy, a boarding school in Wayne, Pennsylvania, where he spent months learning discipline and the value of education. Valley Forge stresses academic excellence, character development, personal motivation, physical development and leadership. Upon completion, Wright emerged with a new outlook and appreciation for all that was ahead of him in life and a new sense of individual responsibility that drove him to pursue a college degree. He signed with the University of Florida hoping to lead their football squad to their first national championship.

As Wright's life began moving in the right direction as a college student-athlete, he realized that a little mentoring in his hometown could go a long way and possibly save more lives like his. He began to focus on how he could best be a mentor, not something most self-described fatherless street thug teenagers with an "F" average in school are cut out to be, but Wright was determined, and he had help.

In 1994, Wright, along with friends Arthur King and Marlin Barnes, founded a program called "Right Trak" in their hometown of Miami, Florida. It was marketed as a summer football camp to get kids ages 8 to 15 interested. Once they showed up, Wright was determined to teach them much more than football fundamentals. Wright wanted to teach the children, many of whom were fatherless like him, self-discipline and self-esteem by helping them with their studies, going on field trips and just hanging out. Wright and the Right Trak mentors were hard on the kids as well, teaching them proper study habits and demanding to see their report cards. Wright worked hard too. He wrote out the business plan, developed a budget, raised the funds necessary and set-up non-profit status for Right Trak.

Wright preached what he understood having faced many hard times himself. Tragedy struck Wright's life that, today, has him living for much more than himself. One of his best friends, Arthur King, an Austin Peay University football player died in his sleep of a heart attack in 1994. Within the next two years, Wright also lost best friend Marlin Barnes, a University of Miami linebacker who was murdered in his dorm room and Jean Francois, the father of Wright's godson, who committed suicide. Right Trak may have saved Wright who felt lost after losing three friends when he turned to the children to absorb the life from their vibrant outlooks. On the football field, Wright performed in memory of his friends. At practice he donned a jersey with number 156, the combined numbers of King and Barnes and during the games, his undershirt shined with the pictures of King and Barnes and the message "4 Ever #1 Life Goes On." Wright excelled on the field, achieving his goal to bring home the first national championship to the University of Florida. As a junior, this strong safety led the team with 109 tackles and 25 "big plays." In 1996, as a senior, Wright utilized his newly developed leadership skills and led the team to its fourth straight Southeastern Conference Championship and the Gators' first national championship. That year, Wright won the Jim Thorpe Award, given to the best defensive back in college football. In April of 1997, the Cincinnati Bengals signed Lawrence Wright as a free safety, kicking off his rookie season as a professional football player.

The first-team All-SEC and third-team All-American selection was named to the Southeastern Conference's All-Decade team for the 1990's in 2001. While the list of honors and accolades goes on, Wright was most proud of his selection to the College Football Association's Scholar-Athlete Team. As a ten year old, who suffered with dyslexia, Wright was unable to read. Dyslexia is a learning disability that affects one's ability to acquire and process language which typically causes trouble in reading, spelling and writing. Wright overcame this obstacle and was a regular on the Southeastern Conference Honor Roll.

In 1996, Wright was named a "community hero" and was honored to help carry the Olympic torch to Atlanta for the Summer Olympics. By that time, Right Trak had already assisted more than 40 at-risk youth in his hometown. He had help from doctors, lawyers, artists, physically disabled and professional athletes who he called upon to lecture the kids. Wright, who was a building construction major, designed the architectural plans for an all-inclusive community center to serve the athletic and academic needs of Right Trak full-time.

After three years with the Bengals in the NFL, Wright spent one year with the XFL. Then Wright returned to his community work. He created the World of Production that he and his wife, Richelle, run. World of Production is an umbrella company that manages a variety of Wright's companies that all pertain to creating a difference.

Production Construction is one of the companies under World of Production. It has partnered with Cohesion, an architecture company, to build a luxury high-rise residential tower in the Tampa Bay area. Wright hopes that the facility complete with a spa, restaurant and banquet hall, will provide jobs for community members. Production Construction is also working with Jesus People Ministries to build a 200,000 square foot JPM Enrichment Center. The Center will provide a variety of facilities and programs for the community, including a program for runaway teens.

Tools 4 Life is also under the World of Production umbrella. It is a mentoring program that teaches young men and women athletes important lessons about character, image and principles. Wright uses the lessons he learned playing football to design the fundamental principles of the program.

Wright still thinks about playing football and may consider coaching in the future. For now, he is focused on his family and helping the community.

Lawrence Wright's life is a story of perseverance and fortitude that proves everyone deserves a second chance. Brought up in an environment that would have served as his excuse for failure, Wright persevered and ultimately triumphed.

Dr. Lonise Bias

by Brian Wright

According to data compiled by the National Household Survey on Drug Use and Health, 46 percent of Americans 12 or older report illicit drug use at least once in their lifetime. It is alarming numbers such as this one that have shaped and directed Dr. Lonise Bias' life. As a parent, Bias lost two children to drugs and violence. From these tragedies, Bias now works to save millions of lives by educating youth, as well as adults of the consequences of drugs and violence. Bias described her life's mission to Richard Lapchick as helping youth to "realize their self worth, their potential, as well as their ability to be warriors in the fight against substance abuse."

Bias' first tragedy occurred at what should have been a time of great celebration. Her son Lenny was an All-American standout basketball player at the University of Maryland at College Park. Lenny was considered by many to be one of the most talented players ever to play basketball at the University of Maryland, as well as in the Atlantic Coastal Conference. He was selected second overall by the Boston Celtics in the 1986 NBA draft. Two days following the draft, Lenny was found dead in his dormitory room on the campus of the University of Maryland. The cause of death was cardiac arrest due to a cocaine overdose. Her son's death was a wake-up call for Bias who suddenly realized that there is something terribly wrong in a society in which those who are the most successful face such intense pressures that they cannot handle and often fall victim to their own successes.

Bias' second tragedy came four years later when her younger son Jay Bias was murdered. A promising student-athlete, Jay exhibited similar athletic and academic talent displayed by his older brother Len. Jay and friends, taking a break for lunch at a local area shopping mall were approached by a man in a jewelry store who accused Jay of flirting with his girlfriend. As Jay denied the accusation and decided to leave the shopping mall and return to work, his car was approached by the perpetrator's car, and seconds later gunshots were fired killing Jay Bias.

These tragedies that hit the Bias family and friends are not isolated events. Tragedies like this happen everywhere and virtually everyday. A dynamic public speaker, Bias now lectures on the effects of drugs and violence in the community. Bias is known for passionately and powerfully expressing her beliefs, because she can sympathize with victims and explain the tragedies she has had to face in her life as a parent. While some social activists leave parents out of the discussion, Bias does not. She feels that educating parents is a key part in solving the problem that plagues our communities. Bias feels "It is the duty of every adult to look out for not only their children, but the children of their neighbors as well."[1] As a society, we must confront drugs and violence in the community. Courageous and inspirational people such as Dr. Lonise Bias prepare us for that confrontation.

[1] Bannerman Menson, Ayittey "Parents Must Act To Save Children, Lonise Bias Says Speaker: 1959 Principles Won't Work on '93 Kids" *St. Louis Dispatch*, August 2, 1993.

Alfreda J. Harris
by Brian Wright

Too often, the goal of completing one's education while transitioning from amateur to professional athletes is sadly neglected. Those who promote the image of a student-athlete often forget that the individual is in fact a student as well as an athlete. One person who is definitely not guilty of this is Alfreda J. Harris. Harris has been a long-time promoter of the importance of academics for youth, whether or not they are athletes. She has played an active role in the betterment of society by focusing on developing and mentoring young people across all socio-economic classes, races, ethnicities and varying beliefs about the importance of attaining higher education. Throughout her lifetime of service to youth and the community, Harris has instilled strong values and goals for the young people with whom she has worked. She has made a positive impact and contribution to their lives.

As head basketball coach at Roxbury Community College and the University of Massachusetts-Boston, Harris promoted her philosophy of performance in the classroom as well as on the court to all of her players. Known for her "no-nonsense" attitude with regards to performance in the classroom, Harris gained the respect and love of her student-athletes that continues to this day. While compiling an outstanding 136-20 career record with these two institutions, she was able to develop extremely successful and educated athletes and professionals. Harris' guidance propelled many to outstanding careers. Harris always explained to her players that while basketball was important to their success at the University, excelling only in sport meant winning only half of the game. When asked about the role of sports in the education by staff of the Center for the Study of Sport in Society, Harris responded, "Basketball is a tool to get an education, but athletics without academics is a losing proposition." This quote epitomizes Harris' beliefs and shows her conviction about the importance of academics.

Harris continued to make a difference in the lives of young people through her work as the Founder and Administrative Coordinator of the John A. Shelbourne Recreational Center. Here Harris found ways to inspire youth in the local inner-city community. Harris also helps to prepare them for successful athletic and academic collegiate careers. At the Recreational Center, Harris teaches young men and women what they need to attain a full athletic or academic scholarship and what they need to do to be successful at institutions of higher education.

Harris was also the founder of one of Boston's oldest and most respected youth basketball leagues, the Women's/Men's Boston Neighborhood Basketball League (BNBL) as well as the Boston Shoot-Out Basketball Tournament. This league was used to promote positive interaction among the youth of Boston and also to provide an arena for these youth to display their talents while remaining off of the streets and away from trouble.

Harris has held many positions serving the community of Boston while touching the lives of the youth. She served as the Project Director for Harvard School of Public Health's "Play Across Boston" campaign as well as a Project Director for Northeastern University's Center for the Study of Sport in Society. In 1993, Harris was appointed to the Boston Public School Committee charged with seeking innovative ways to improve the education process for all of Boston's youth. Harris has been an integral figure in the Boston educational system as well as in the development of youth through sports and still serves as the elected Vice Chair of the Boston School Committee.

The countless hours Harris spends working with youth teaching important life lessons has played a major role in her life's mission to improve the education levels of the youth in Boston. She has been a visionary in her outreach programs and has touched countless lives of youth growing up in the City of Boston. She genuinely cares about the development of young people regardless of their race, gender, religion or economic status and strives daily to improve upon their awareness of their potential on the playing field as well as in the classroom.

Harris is loved by all who know her in the Boston community for her devotion to her players and students. Those she touches never forget her and the impact she had on their lives. Many of the young men and women who were touched by Harris have also taken up the challenge of improving public education in the communities in which they live and work. Some members of the Boston community refer to Harris as the "Godmother of Hoops,"[1] but if you ask any of her players, or anyone who has come in contact with Alfreda Harris they will tell you she is not only the Godmother of Hoops, but also the Godmother of Hope.

[1] May, Mike. "First Annual SGMA Heroes State Winners Announced." Sporting Goods Manufacturers Association's (SGMA) [1995; December 5, 2005] http://www.sgma.com/press/1994/press990463577-29903.html

Maggie Maloy

by Brian Wright

Every two minutes a woman in the United States is raped. Few teenagers at the age of 15 can imagine the pain and mental anguish of being a victim of rape. Maggie Maloy can. While participating in her morning cross country high school practice on September 16, 1994, Maloy was abducted, brutally beaten, raped twice and shot five times. Her abductor shot her in the head, jaw, back and armpit. Leaving her for dead, he fled the scene. With a collapsed lung and a paralyzed right arm, Maloy remained on the ground until she was found by police. Despite all the distress and pain, Maggie found strength in the hope of returning to her sport and competing at the highest level.

Defying all odds and expectations set by her doctors, Maloy was back in school within six weeks of the incident. By the spring of 1995, she was running on the track. After graduating from Galion High School in Ohio in 1997, Maloy enrolled at Defiance College. As a collegiate student-athlete Maloy competed with three of the five bullets still permanently lodged in her body, two in her right lung and one in her head. This was not a deterrent for Maloy. She offered no excuses, and competed successfully for almost three years at Defiance.

Maloy had just finished her third indoor-track season when disaster struck again. On February 13, 2000, while driving her car, an icy road caused Maloy to lose control and collide with a van. The accident left her pelvic bone broken in three separate places. This left Maloy essentially immobile from the waist down and she had to learn to walk again. Lucky to be alive, Maloy did not lose the desire to compete at Defiance because of the accident and knew from her past experiences that she had the power to overcome this new adversity in her life.

For three grueling months Maloy spent countless hours in rehabilitation with doctors and therapists. The payoff was priceless. Maloy was back on the track for the fall of her senior year in which she was able to compete in cross country, and indoor and outdoor track. She was selected as the captain of the team and received All-Conference honors for her accomplishments on the track. Maloy also helped lead the Defiance College cross country team to its first conference title in the school's history.

Maloy still holds three top-10 records for Defiance's outdoor track team. Maloy is 6th in the 800 meter run with a time of 2:31.8; 2nd in the 1,500 meter run with a time of 5:02.2; and 2nd in the 3,000 meter run with a time of 11:58.6. Maloy set each one of these records in 2001 after learning to walk all over again.

In the spring of 2001, Maloy graduated with her bachelor's degree in communication. Maloy is now in law school. In January 2002, she and Sam Paneno were the first student-athletes to be honored by the NCAA as recipients of their Inspiration Award. Maloy spreads her inspiration through public speaking all over the country. Maloy's mission is to help others understand "that when adversities arise in life, they have a choice – to fall victim to those adversities or to survive." Like Maloy, she hopes they choose to survive.

The courage Maloy showed in overcoming her physical and emotional hardships has inspired many others around the world to work to overcome their own hardships. Maggie Maloy is a true inspiration for her courage and determination in achieving her life's goals despite her adversities.

Jodi Norton

by Brian Wright

Most student-athletes suffer a variety of minor aches, pains and muscle soreness as they compete in their various sports. Jodi Norton was no exception. She was an All-American high school athlete who stood out on her high school team as well as on Team Orlando, an elite diving team. Norton balanced training four hours a day with her studies so she disregarded her fatigue, soreness and occasional dizziness as ordinary side effects of strenuous physical exercise.

Norton's hard work earned her a scholarship to the University of Arizona to compete for their diving team. In her first year of participation as a student-athlete at the University, Norton found that the frequency and intensity of pain she experienced was a little different than most others on her team. She was often sick with skin rashes and severe joint pain that forced her to miss some of her diving practices. Norton decided to leave the team to focus on getting the medical attention she needed, but unfortunately her condition was misdiagnosed.

Norton had an interest in medicine and transferred to Columbia University to study premed. Yet, Norton's excruciating pain continued to cause her to miss classes and diving practice. When the pain did not cease, Norton was admitted to the emergency room three months after transferring to Columbia. In the E.R., she finally heard a definitive explanation for the pain she had suffered from for years.

Norton was diagnosed with lupus, a very serious, incurable, chronic autoimmune disorder characterized by periodic episodes of inflammation of and damage to the joints, tendons, other connective tissues, and organs, including the heart, lungs, blood vessels, brain, kidneys and skin. Norton's personality and courage did not let her just give in to her disease. She decided to research it to become as familiar with her condition as possible. Though she was experiencing the effects of lupus on her body, Norton continued to compete. Her school and participation in athletics were frequently interrupted by trips to the emergency room for meningitis, pericarditis, swelling of tissue around the brain, and battles with Lyme disease. Nonetheless, Norton remained a strong competitor on the diving team. Her courage and desire were always on display as she battled her disease and continued to practice and compete.

At the 1995-96 Eastern College Athletic Conference (ECAC) Diving Championship, Norton managed to compete despite having a broken hand. At the end of the first day she had to be rushed to the emergency room for intravenous medication for swollen tissue around her brain. Remarkably, Norton returned the following day and was able to compete and amazingly finished 10th overall. She attributed her success to the fact that she would visualize the competition when she could not compete for health reasons. "I would visualize everything, so when I got up on the board, I was confident."[1] This was Norton's final competition and to perform so well under all the adversity she faced was a testament to her courage and desire to succeed.

During her spare time, Norton sits with medical students to share her experiences and also visits young children who have recently undergone chemotherapy. Norton graduated from Columbia University with a 3.7 grade point average. After graduation, Norton enrolled in Bryn Mawr College's Post-Baccalaureate Premedical Program.

While pursuing her own career in medicine, Norton helped establish an organization called Lupus Inspiration Foundation for Excellence (L.I.F.E.). L.I.F.E. promotes awareness of lupus and seeks to help college students with lupus earn their degrees. L.I.F.E. recognizes the obstacles students with lupus face while in college and assists them by providing them with scholarships. Scholarships are awarded to students who have shown courage and perseverance to overcome lupus.

Jodi Norton is a courageous, inspirational and skilled leader. Norton realizes that we all face adversities and hers is a model of how to deal with and overcome even the most serious of obstacles.

[1] Callahan, Amy. "Jodi Norton: adversity doesn't keep diver from soaring." Columbia University. [October 10, 1997; December 4, 2005] http://www.columbia.edu/cu/record/archives/vol23/vol23_iss6/16.html

Robert Hurley, Sr.

by Stacy Martin

It is not how he says it but what he says that makes the difference to his players. He may yell and, yes, even curse to get their attention, but he drives the point home. Robert Hurley, Sr. is a man who has devoted his life to a small Catholic school in Jersey City that is home to a majority of underprivileged students of color mostly from single parent homes. Adversity is an understatement when describing the situation that the students and the school face. St. Anthony High School is a private school in the inner-city seen as a safe haven by parents who work extra jobs to pay the $3,250 tuition that might give their children a better life than that which they could provide alone. Hurley is a man who accepted that responsibility and challenge and strives daily to teach kids the fundamentals of life through basketball. Bob Hurley has coached basketball at St. Anthony for the last 33 years and has won 90 percent of his games and 22 state titles.

Hurley knows what the typical fate of a child growing up in the inner-city. He witnesses it first hand everyday. Hurley has been a probation officer for Hudson County in New Jersey for as long as he has been a basketball coach. He knows most of these kids will join a gang, end up in jail or even a grave, but he also knows that some of them have a chance to grow up and go beyond the streets of Jersey City. That's why he has devoted so much time and passion into St. Anthony and his basketball team.

Every student at St. Anthony's is in some way an underdog. Many have always been taught that they had no chance. So when Bob Hurley walks into the gym and takes a chance on them, they listen even if he shouts. The team borrows gyms to practice in and home games really have not been possible. The only practice facility frequented by the St. Anthony Friars has been a local establishment called the White Eagle Hall that gets used more by its bingo patrons than the team. The floor is 29 feet too short, but to compensate the basketball goal is propped up on radiators making it two inches too high. The remaining 65 feet of the floor are menacing. It defends the offensive players better than the defense sometimes due to its jutting nail heads and water logged spots from leaks that absorb the ball from a player's dribble instead of returning it to his hand. After their grueling practices, the boys pay for their practice time by setting up the 200 chairs and 63 tables for bingo. The Eagle, as it is affectionately called, builds mental toughness. The players come from broken homes and dangerous streets and have never been given a thing, not even a gym. Hurley exploits these factors to instill a winning attitude in his players. He coaches his basketball team by telling them before every game that their next opponent is the best team they have ever played. He conveys the message that the team is going to have to fight and play hard for a win. Thus, his players know how to fight and how to struggle, and Coach Hurley taught them to know how to win.

Hurley is an old school coach, the one that kicks an athlete out of practice for just looking at him wrong so that he can create and maintain a disciplined atmosphere. He can just look at his team and deliver a stare that melts their hardened exterior. As a coach, he challenges his athletes to practice every day with intensity and desire. If they don't, they go home. Hurley's eldest son, Bobby Hurley, Jr., knows the intensity and the look all too well. Bobby was often kicked out of his dad's practices and mostly for no reason at all. But, the coach knows that kicking someone out, especially his own flesh and blood, serves his purpose. He wants to demonstrate seriousness in practice and prove that no one is safe from his wrath. Bobby had come to terms with his father's intense methods long before and knew when he had become an example for the team. One reporter over the years captured Bobby's thoughts on his dad with this quote: "We don't have a lot of what other teams take for granted, but we have my dad, and he's the reason St. Anthony is where it is today. You have to come to every practice ready to play because he never loses his intensity."[1] Bobby's younger brother, Danny, grew up in the house of Hurley too. At times Dan grappled with the pressure to fill his brother's shoes and carry the family crest of basketball. Bobby was an All-American at Duke and Dan played at Seton Hall. Bobby began a career in the NBA, only to have it cut short by a horrific car accident. Their father's influence on them certainly molded them into the successful athletes and human beings that they are today. Besides, they say imitation is the highest form of flattery and both sons chose to follow the footsteps of their father into coaching. Both have thriving teams and are complemented, like their father has been, for being a good person that takes a genuine interest in helping young men succeed. What made Bob Hurley unique in today's sports world though was his expectation of perfection and his never give up attitude.

Hurley is the coach that yells when the team is leading at the half because they missed their foul shots. Winning isn't enough for him. That's why he will scream at the team for an hour after a game for not playing as hard as their opponent even when his team won. It's been recounted that after a game one night Hurley asked his team to name the coach for the opposing team. When he called on certain players for the answer, the only sound was silence. He asked about another school's coach who happened to be a New Jersey legend like Hurley. Again there was silence. He immediately launched into a tirade regarding their attitudes being bigger than their knowledge of the game, because knowing the game meant knowing who was in it and its history and it was about having respect for those that came before you.

He called them out for acting too cool and told them to go back to their miserable existence as part of the group. But then he followed it with a challenge to step away from the Jersey City streets and the group that resided on its corners. Hurley left the gym that night naming every coach in New Jersey since he played in 1965, all the while wondering if he got through the generational gap. His coaching style has always been in another era, but he realized the disconnect between not only him and his players but also his players and the way things should be. They care about having car keys now, not the SAT scores that can get them into college and he told them as much to prompt a value change. Failure isn't acceptable and there are no excuses. He expects his teams to end their season in the final game of New Jersey's state championship, the Tournament of Champions. Most of all he expects his players to go to college. Anything else is a disappointment.

Basketball may be his means, but providing opportunity for the students at St. Anthony is the end goal. In Hurley's 33 years of coaching, all of his players have graduated from St. Anthony and gone on to college. Hurley will scream and shout during practice, but if his players can tolerate it, then he is abidingly loyal to them off the court. He has taken an interest in each player and encourages them to improve their test scores. It is an underprivileged private Catholic school in the inner-city that is on the brink of disaster or closing almost every year, but he has the full support of the nuns that run the school to get his players academic help so they can go beyond the streets of Jersey City and onto a basketball court on a college campus.

His 2003-2004 team struggled academically and failed to qualify anyone for a Division I institution. It is a failure that the coach is greatly embarrassed by. Hurley has stayed at St. Anthony High for 33 years because he knows he is making a lasting impression on the youth of Jersey City. The attachment he forms with his players goes beyond the walls of the gymnasium and the lines on the court.

The Rivers family received quite a lot of Hurley's care and consideration. Willie and Mamie Rivers worked multiple jobs and raised 14 children. Their son, David, was a star athlete for Hurley and went on to play basketball for Notre Dame and then the Los Angeles Lakers. David's younger brother Jermaine had a bright future under Hurley's leadership until he was plagued by frequent headaches. The doctors discovered a massive and inoperable brain tumor. Time was slipping away for Jermaine. Hurley organized a fundraiser for the family and sent Jermaine to South Bend, Indiana to see his brother one last time. Jermaine passed away just a year and a half after his diagnosis at age seventeen. The Rivers made a connection with Hurley that outlasted any basketball game, so when David's nephew, Hank, started getting into trouble with a gang, Hurley stepped in. Hurley was aware of Hank's history with grand theft, guns, and drugs as he was in and out of the Hudson County Courts since age fourteen. Hank was on the verge of a lengthy sentence that would usher him into adulthood. Hurley stepped into the court room and testified that he would save this kid from the streets and turn Hank's life around. Hurley was publicly known for his ability to reach kids on the basketball court and professionally he is known for being tough as a probation officer. If anyone could turn him around, it was Hurley.

He allowed Hank to practice with the St. Anthony team during the spring semester of his sophomore year after his plea was granted by the judge, but he was not permitted to join the team until he proved that he would be serious about his studies and change his behavior in the community. Hurley kept Hank off the streets and from his usual routine and influences by spending one on one time with him after practice to work on the 6 foot 8 player's post moves. Hurley taught Hank fundamentals for the court and off the court. He often spoke to Hank about changing his values system and his choice of so-called friends. He explained that Hank didn't have to be confined to Jersey City or even New Jersey's borders. The observation of what life could be like for a semester was motivation enough for Hank Rivers to make a change. Hank exchanged his gang colors for St. Anthony's colors, traded his gang members for his teammates, and spent time on homework rather than street corners. Hank's choices led to success on the court as well and he was the starting center for the St. Anthony Friars that year. When he was a senior he became ineligible for high school basketball because he had already turned 19. Some coaches would have walked away because Hank couldn't help the team anymore. Hurley doesn't give up though. He sent Hank to New York to play AAU basketball until graduation so he could develop his skills. Hurley knew that Hank's ticket out of town was basketball. He followed through once more and got Hank a scholarship to Southeast Community College in Nebraska, where row houses were replaced by rows of corn. Hank is now playing for Stephen F. Austin University in Texas and misses Hurley screaming at him to push him past what he thought his breaking point was. Now Hank pushes himself.

Hurley dares his athletes to be the best and does so by setting expectations for them above and beyond what any of them thought possible. He provides a structure for them that won't allow them to fail. That's why Hurley is legendary. He has been inducted into the New Jersey Sports Hall of Fame and named as a Sporting Goods Manufacturers Association Hero. He was named Sportsman of the Year by the Mercier Club of Montclair in 1992. He is likened to a miracle worker in *The Miracle of St. Anthony*, a book chronicling the storybook history of the school and its basketball teams. Hurley's heroic deeds and miracles occur in the lives of Jersey City youth, whether it's his children or the community's children. Robert Hurley, Sr. has screamed at his kids over the city noise for the past 33 years, so that they would hear something more than gunshots and sirens in their futures.

[1] Crothers, Tim. "The Friars are kings of the road" *Sports Illustrated*, December 18, 1989.

Tanya Hughes-Jones

by Jessica Bartter

The epitome of a *student-athlete*, Tanya Hughes-Jones constantly challenged herself to do better in the classroom and on the track, and she shone brightly in both. At the University of Arizona, Hughes-Jones stood out as an athlete, as a student and as a fine young woman. While majoring in interdisciplinary studies, earning four NCAA outdoor track championships and training for the Olympics, Hughes-Jones earned a 3.44 grade point average. Her hard work did not go unrewarded as she was recognized as a GTE Academic All-American. But it was not her grades alone that helped her be an inspiration to so many. Hughes-Jones was chair of the University of Arizona's NCAA Student-Athlete Advisory Committee and served as a spokesman for the University's NCAA Choices Alcohol Awareness Program.

Hughes-Jones' responsibilities as a spokesperson for social change were greatly increased when she represented the United States in the 1992 Barcelona Olympics. She was only 22, the youngest on the U.S. women's track team that year. Though she didn't come home with a medal, Hughes-Jones was the only American athlete to make the high jump finals. Hughes-Jones was also a member of the 1993 World University Games Team.

In 1992 and 1993, the United States Track & Field News rated Hughes-Jones as the best high jumper. In 1992, she was named NCAA Female Track Athlete of the Year and in 1994, she earned the highest honors for a collegiate athlete by being named NCAA Woman of the Year. Hughes was selected from a pool of 389 nominees that year. The criteria for this award include academic achievement, athletic excellence and community leadership, three qualities embodied by Hughes-Jones.

At the 1994 U.S. Olympic Festival in St. Louis, Missouri, she won a gold medal with a jump of 6' 1 ½". Hughes-Jones graduated from the University of Arizona in 1994 and went on to pursue her master's degree. Hughes-Jones now works with the IBM Corporation. She is planning to join the ministry with her husband who is already a pastor.

Hughes-Jones' civic leadership continued after college as she served as keynote speaker for the 1995 Project TEAMWORK Human Rights Squad Forum. Project TEAMWORK trains young people with diversity and conflict resolution skills, providing them with alternative strategies to handle the conflicts they face and avoid the violence that often stems from conflicts between individuals from different cultures, religions, races and ethnicities. After each Project TEAMWORK presentation, Human Rights Squads are formed at the school to serve as an active vehicle for students to promote the value of diversity, learn conflict resolution skills and foster life-long community service participation. At the end of the school year, the Human Rights Squad Forum brings together all chapters of the various Human Rights Squads where they are provided with a venue to demonstrate their knowledge and understanding of the Project TEAMWORK principles. Tanya Hughes-Jones' insights about diversity and conflict resolution were valuable to the participating youth in 1995.

Tanya Hughes-Jones became a role model for other student-athletes by achieving Academic All-American status, and by becoming successful in the business world and as a mother.

Michele Leary

by Jessica Barttter

Some people choose to become doctors to help people; others do it for the money. Some follow the footsteps of a parent; others want to discover the cure for Alzheimer's. It was Michele Leary's own health scare that originally turned her off of the medical profession but eventually made her realize her life's purpose and moved her to pursue her own career path as a doctor. Today, Leary is assisting surgeries, diagnosing patients and reading x-rays. About 15 years ago, Leary was on the other end of the medical spectrum, as a patient in the emergency room.

Leary competed for the swim team at the University of Massachusetts, Amherst in the late 1980's. The peaceful early mornings and calm waters had attracted her to the pool in high school where Leary first started swimming. Swimming to her "is as natural as breathing." While she thought her chances were dim, her love for the sport led this weary freshman to UMass, Amherst swim tryouts. Leary was a self-described "slow swimmer" but her potential impressed Coach Bob Newcomb enough to earn her a spot as a walk-on.

Leary's love for swimming continued to grow at UMass, Amherst as she fervently trained in the pool and studied in the classroom. On October 31, 1989, Leary was in the midst of her senior year, after three successful seasons representing her school, when she began feeling dizzy and experienced pain and tingling in her arms. Her family had a history of coronary artery spasms. Even so, it was a surprise to everyone including Leary and the medical professionals that a 21 year old healthy college athlete could suffer a heart attack.

Doctors told Leary she needed eight weeks to recover and that she would have to stay out of the pool until January 2, 1990. Leary followed her doctors' orders but was back in the pool on January 3. Leary swam in her first meet on January 6. Coaches and teammates were shocked by Leary's speedy recovery and were even more impressed with the success she had in the pool after two months off and little time spent training. That season, Leary broke New England records in the 50, 100 and 200 meter free-style, records that had been standing for over seven years. Leary finished her senior season with 13 record breaking competitions, seven of which were individual records. Three of her records still stood at the beginning of the 2006 season.

Leary attributed her impressive performance to the fact that "When people tell you that you can't do something, it makes you want to do it even more." Leary carried that attitude into her professional life when she began pursuing medical school. Despite the fact that she was well past the average age of first year medical students and that she was a female in a predominately male profession, Leary enrolled in Touro University College of Osteopathic Medicine in 2001, eleven years after she graduated from UMass, Amherst.

The challenges she faced as a student-athlete, balancing strenuous competition with demanding academics, prepared her for the demands she faces today. Leary is currently in her fourth year of medical school, applying to residency programs while starting a family. Leary and her husband, Gary Searer, welcomed their first daughter, Arden, to the world on June 2, 2004. Leary believes it is her participation in sports that "enabled her to juggle the demands of a husband, a baby and medical school" because sports gave her strength and endurance and taught her persistence. Leary credits her speedy recovery to her persistence and tries to teach its value to those she meets. As an active contributor to her community, Leary comes in contact with many young boys and girls who doubt themselves much like she did in her early swimming career. By sharing her story of determination, patience and perseverance, Leary is able to motivate many children who say "I can't" to say "I'll try." Her tale of triumph often inspires the "I'll try" to become "I did it!" Leary has volunteered her time and offered her story to participants in the Oakland City At-risk Girls-only Science Day, and Oakland inner-city youth and Master's swimming programs. She instructs the swimmers on stroke and turn techniques, but they all learn more about life from the inspirational Leary. Leary also volunteers with an adult literacy program.

For the past four years Leary has been learning symptoms, diseases, drugs and treatments because she is one of the medical students who enrolled with the intention to one day help people as a doctor. Leary is planning to become board certified in Family Medicine and Osteopathic Manipulative Medicine (OMM) and is hoping to be able to stay in California while doing so.

Leary credits the support she received from her teammates and Coach Newcomb with her ability to survive a heart attack mentally and physically, at such a young age. While she certainly learned a great deal about herself and about life, Michele Leary doesn't think of herself as a hero. "All I did was go back and forth a few 100,000 times in a pool." But what she doesn't realize is that with every stroke and every flip turn she defied the odds and inspired so many to realize what life is really about and all that can be accomplished with persistence.

CHAPTER 7

FIGHTING RACISM

A significant part of the work of the National Consortium for Academics and Sports has been to create programs that help combat racism in our country. Perhaps the problem that plagued us more than any other, racism has been a blemish on our society as well as in sport. There have been individuals in sport, some noted in the *Barrier Breaker* section such as Jackie Robinson, who have taken on enormous roles in that struggle. In this section we present the lives of five individuals whose names most people do not know but whose lives surely represent *Fighting Racism.*

Dionte Hall was a 14 year old boy who was followed into a fast food restaurant one afternoon by a group of white teenagers who taunted him with racial epithets and then put a noose around his neck. Hall quietly let the courts take the case while helping to educate his community on the history of lynching and its meaning.

Michael Watson, a college basketball player, was attacked by two white men in suburban Maryland. The incident was recorded on video tape yet the all-white jury acquitted the two attackers.

Darryl Williams, who was an aspiring NFL player, was gunned down by three white teenagers during the half-time of his first varsity game during the busing controversy in the 1970's in Boston. A quadriplegic, Williams has become an inspirational speaker against racism.

Richard Green and David Lazerson, an African-American and a Hasidic Jew, created a basketball program in the Crown Heights section of Brooklyn to combat the growing fear that was rapidly developing between the African-American and Hasidic communities which lived side-by-side in Crown Heights.

The lives of these five men are testimony as to what the individual can do to take on issues as gigantic as racism in our country.

Dionte Hall

by Jennifer Brenden

Hate crimes, racist jokes and racial stereotyping prove that racism is still very much in evidence in today's society. Although segregation was eliminated on the law books, there are instances like what happened to Dionte Hall to prove how much work still needs to be done to alter attitudes towards race relations and to curb racist behavior.

Dionte Hall, a 14 year old junior varsity basketball player from Largo High School, in St. Petersburg, Florida was walking through the parking lot of a fast food restaurant with two of his friends on January 14, 2004. Suddenly, he heard shouts from across the parking lot, so he turned around to see what was happening. He turned to see someone waving a rope, tied in a noose, in the air. As the boy, who was 19 years old, was waving the noose in the air, he was also yelling racial slurs. Hall and his friends did not react to the racist gesture and they entered the Wendy's Restaurant.

As the group of friends sat innocently, eating their food, the same boy from outside came up behind Hall and actually slipped the noose around his neck. The boy had been bet $10 by one of his friends to walk over to Hall and put the noose around his neck. He continued to whisper derogatory comments in Hall's ear as well. In spite of the rage festering inside of him, Hall chose to remain calm in this horrible situation. He didn't retaliate in a violent way, which would be the instinctive reaction by most people being harassed. He did not try to get into a fight and remained very calm. Rather than sue the boy for his actions, Hall wanted to retaliate in the most positive way he could, and he succeeded in doing that. He demonstrated a maturity that was truly way beyond his years.

Hall handled the matter by returning to school and talking about the incident with his basketball coach, who immediately took him to the school resource officer. Charges were brought up against the 19 year old boy who committed the horrible prank along with a couple of his friends who were involved in the incident. The attacker was charged with a misdemeanor battery and not a hate crime.

Because Hall handled the situation in such an exemplary manner, the local police department presented him with a proclamation and a letter of commendation. The letter stated "Dionte restrained himself from physical and verbal retaliation. He practiced the teachings of Dr. Martin Luther King, Jr., through nonviolence."[1]

Whether or not he knew it at the time, his ability to resist retaliating was the best possible stand he could take against hate crimes and discrimination, and for that he has been commended. We can only hope that others follow in Hall's footsteps and fight racism and discrimination in a strong, yet peaceful way.

This incident has changed Hall's life forever. He has refused to simply move on with his life like nothing ever happened. The incident has motivated him to make a difference and he has been active in working to change laws pertaining to minors and hate crimes. Hall has written to President Bush and he and his parents have held news conferences on the issues urging people to support the new law.

Hall and his family want aggressive prosecution for individuals who commit hate crimes and additional legislation that might hold parents responsible for instilling beliefs in children that might result in violence against others because of their race, ethnicity, sexual orientation or religious beliefs. Hall's parents obviously instilled positive values in the mind of their son and today Dionte Hall and his family are continuing to fight for tolerance, understanding and social justice.

[1] Tan, Shannon. "Teen who faced noose, slur commended for courage" *St. Petersburg Times*, February 18, 2004.

Michael Watson

by Richard Lapchick

The story of college basketball player Michael Watson offers a telling example as to why many African-Americans have so little faith in the American judicial system. The story could easily have taken place in Mississippi in the 1960's, but actually took place in Maryland in 1995. On the Wednesday afternoon before Thanksgiving, Michael Watson sat in a state court in Frederick, Maryland, waiting for his share of American justice.

His former teammates at Mount St. Mary's were practicing for the opening game of the 1995-1996 season. Seven months earlier Watson, then a graduate student, had helped lead the small school to victory as Mount St. Mary's beat Rider College to win the Northeast Conference Championship and advance to the NCAA Tournament. Watson had scored 15 points, garnered 11 rebounds and hit six straight free throws in the last minute to slam the door on Rider's attempt to get to the Big Dance for the third year in a row.

Those spectacular basketball moments had helped Watson forget more painful ones. Around 1:00 a.m. on October 30, 1994, Watson and his date pulled up to a Thurmont, Maryland convenience store to get some food after a college party. Inside the store, three white men assaulted Watson. The back injuries Watson suffered kept him off the basketball court for several weeks while he underwent physical therapy. The back pain recurs occasionally, but far less often than the mental agony.

About twelve hours earlier, a busload of hooded and robed members of the Ku Klux Klan had marched at the State House in Annapolis. They shouted "white power" while one carried a poster of the face of assassinated civil rights leader Dr. Martin Luther King, Jr. circled by a target. The caption read "Our dream came true." Klan members were outnumbered more than ten to one by protesters who shouted them down and tensions built in the state capitol.

Did those tensions travel across the state into Thurmont, near the home of the leader of the Maryland Klan? According to Watson, one of the three men who attacked him shouted, "You don't belong here. This is Klan country. You're a nigger, boy." At the trial, the assailants denied the remarks, but they could not deny what the store's videotape had captured. It clearly showed the three men assaulting Watson, shoving and hitting him while he held up his hands only to ward off their blows.

A shocked Mount St. Mary's President, George R. Houston, Jr., wrote a letter to the college community. In it he said, "We have all available resources, and we expect a fair, thorough and prompt investigation."

In a less celebrated version of the earlier Rodney King case in Los Angeles, the investigation produced the videotape and witnesses who only testified for Watson. While no one could verify the racist remarks, witnesses corroborated Watson's version that seemed indisputable given the evidence on the videotape.

Through the help of various local friends, counselors and nationally prominent activists, Watson began to recover from the emotional scars of the attack. He did not seek publicity. There were no television cameras in the court, no Chris Dardens or Marcia Clarks for the prosecution, and no F. Lee Baileys or Johnny Cochrans for the defense. There were no Mark Fuhrmans or Stacey Koons on the Thurmont Police. The case was an easy one for him to win from all possible perspectives.

While waiting for the slow wheels of justice to turn, Watson focused on basketball as his source of emotional rehabilitation. "There was no sense of race on our team. We were all so focused on winning. We worked together with a special solidarity. Our team was a safe haven for me and while we were together, I was able to forget what had happened outside the walls of Mount St. Mary's. My white teammates gave me the perspective that those three attackers did not represent all white people. However, when I was away from my teammates, the pain always came back."

Watching his attackers go to prison was going to be his final step toward recovery. Watson was poised to celebrate a heartfelt Thanksgiving. Dino Flores, the prosecutor, was confident that the case would be a cut-and-dried victory for the prosecution. When jury selection began on Monday the first ominous portent appeared. An all white jury was chosen. Still confident, prosecutor Flores took his case to them.

The witnesses in the store verified what was seen on the videotape. A defense lawyer called Watson a racist and claimed that he provoked the attack against the three white men. Raised to respect everyone regardless of color, Watson cringed in disbelief at what he was hearing.

Nevertheless, when the jury went out on Wednesday, Watson and prosecutor Flores felt confident. Watson said, "I was 90 percent certain of a favorable outcome. The evidence was clear and the judge had ruled favorably on most of Flores' motions. The 10 percent of doubt came only from what I knew about the fate of blacks in the justice system. But I was sure." Two hours later the jury returned with "not guilty" verdicts on the charges of assault and on the charge of committing a hate crime.

The verdict, read to an incredulous Michael Watson, lent a hollow ring to the end of Mount St. Mary President Houston's letter to the community. "It is imperative that all government officials, community and church leaders join us in making it inescapably clear that this country has 'zero tolerance' for racist actions such as these."

Watson said, "I just sat there for several minutes. The accused were gone before I totally realized what happened. There is nothing I can do but carry the scars throughout my life while these guys went out, free to celebrate or do whatever they pleased."

Thurmont, Maryland is seven miles from Camp David where President Clinton prepared for Thanksgiving. Without any national publicity, the President, like most Americans, did not know who Michael Watson was or why he could not join in his fellow countrymen in their Thanksgiving celebrations.

I was sickened when I watched the videotape of the attack. Surely the verdict should have been just as clear as it should have been in the first Rodney King Trial. I wrote a column for *The Sporting News* to bring this case to national attention and begin the healing process for Michael Watson. Though the national media picked up the article, Watson never got another day in court. I was inundated with more hate mail than at any time since the end of the apartheid era, and even received two telephone death threats after the article was published. The one good thing we both got was the beginning of a rich friendship that I treasure. The case unfortunately demonstrated the depth of racism in America and how hard it is for blacks to obtain justice without status and public attention to force a second look. We indeed have a long road yet to travel.

Darryl Williams

by Brian Wright

A hero is often someone with exceptional courage, nobility and strength. Fictional heroes are generally indestructible, possessing incredible physical strength and using that strength to right the world's wrongs. In real life, however, they are very different. Darryl Williams is a real world hero.

As a 15 year old high school student in 1979, Williams was an exceptional student and athlete. As an athlete, Williams participated in basketball and football. Like most 15 year olds, Williams thought little about race relations, violence and how those issues pertained to his life. Thoughts of making the next big catch for his high school football team or coming up with a key defensive stop in the fourth quarter of his basketball game seemed much more relevant.

One split second of racist violence inspired by hate quickly changed his life forever. At the end of the first half of a high school football game Williams excited his teammates and the crowd by making a seemingly impossible pass. With his spirits high Williams would never have guessed that his feelings of triumph would soon turn to pain and agony. As the third quarter of the game began, Williams stood on the sidelines waiting to enter the game. He never did. As Williams waited, three young white males had taken position on a nearby building waiting to take their shot to kill Williams. Shots of gunfire rang throughout the football field as Williams was stuck by the sniper's bullets. His career was over; Williams would never be able to play football again. Doctors' examinations found Williams paralyzed from the neck down. Williams, a 15 year old high school student-athlete, was devastated.

Williams lay in the hospital wondering "why." Why had this

happened? What had he done to anybody to make them feel like they had to take his life and his livelihood? After years of contemplation as to "why" this had happened, Williams found that he did not understand why and never would. He did understand though that it was a racially motivated hate crime just as many crimes before that had plagued this country. This hatred in many instances would have sparked retaliation or an equivalent hatred in his heart for an entire race or group of people. But Williams chose to love and motivate rather than to hate. He made a conscious decision to dedicate his life to helping people denounce racism and to work to promote tolerance, respect and understanding.

After losing the use of his arms and legs, and after hearing countless broken promises of medical and financial support after the shooting, Williams told a reporter from the *Boston Globe,* "A lot of people perceive me as a white-person hater, because my injury was at the hands of a white person. I can't fault the whole race for that because there are bad people in the white race; there are bad people in the black race as well. You don't hate a whole race of people for one other person." Williams continues to fight racism and promote racial understanding through public speaking where he uses his own experiences to inspire others. His ability to forgive as well as his passion for improving society has led him down a path of service to his community and for the entire human race.

Richard Lapchick said, "What greater sign of hope, of the black community's forgiveness for all the wrongs done to them over the centuries, than the attitude of Darryl Williams." Williams' remarkable display of forgiveness, courage, strength, as well as self-empowerment is a model by which all humans can live.

Richard Green and Dr. David Lazerson

by Brian Wright

The racial tension occurring in the Crown Heights section of Brooklyn, New York in 1991 seemed to be insurmountable to overcome by local residents. This downward spiral of negative sentiment was directly correlated to a fatal car accident that had occurred in the neighborhood. While walking down the street on a warm summer afternoon, a seven year old African-American child, Gavin Cato, was struck and killed by a car that had lost control and jumped the curb. The driver of the vehicle was identified as Yosef Lifsh, a Hasidic Jewish resident of the Crown Heights community. Stemming from the accident, emotions and tempers flared between members of the African-American and Hasidic residents of Crown Heights. The hostile emotions led to a racial uproar and riots between the two communities. Many in the African-American community considered the death of young Cato a homicide rather than a car accident. In an apparent act of retaliation to young Cato's death, a 29 year old visiting Australian rabbinical student was stabbed to death. Hatred and anger now engulfed both communities which seemed ready to wage war. There were leaders from both communities preaching war against one another and an eventual chaos seemed unavoidable. How could the eventual violence be prevented? Many individuals in the community felt hopeless, believing there was nothing that could be done to prevent the ensuing violence. Contrary to this common feeling of despondency, two local social activists, Richard Green and Dr. David Lazerson (or Dr. "Laz" as he is endearingly known by members of the Crown Heights community) knew that violence and war would lead to the eventual demise of Crown Heights.

As many men and women gathered in the community to promote

violence, irrational behavior and hatred, Green constantly combated these discussions with words of wisdom and peace. As his peace message began to spread, Green became the target of many negative comments and racial slurs from members even within his own community. Green was undaunted in his commitment and his message began to resonate among many former proponents of violence. As Green worked to instill awareness about peace within the African-American community, Lazerson simultaneously worked on the minds of young Hasidics. Lazerson, a serious intellectual with a passion for community relations, understood the importance of spreading a message of peace and understanding rather than violence. Green and Lazerson knew that a peaceful resolution of the existing tensions required a sense of cooperation and shared purpose where opposing sides could express their thoughts, feelings and concerns without fear of violence. In order to accomplish this, the two men arranged meetings between young members of the Hasidic and African-American communities to discuss the differences they were having in a safe and peaceful environment. Through these meetings members of both communities where able to express their feelings, experiences and concerns through a non-violent, open discussion. Green and Lazerson also arranged meetings with Mayor David Dinkins to discuss methods to obtain peaceful solutions to other issues surrounding the youth in Crown Heights at the time.

It was Green's feeling that for the African-American community to be angry at the Jewish community for all of their misfortunes was unfair and a mistake. He felt that the African-American community should instead be angry with the lack of resources and services throughout the community as a whole.

Green and Lazerson sought creative new ideas to bring together the youth of the two feuding communities, so they created an environment that would prompt discussion and ease fears. They concluded that sports would be the best medium. It had the potential to have a very positive effect on improving race relations within the community. Green and Lazerson introduced the idea to members attending the meetings. The young members of the group agreed on the positive impact sports could have on improving the current situation of the neighborhood and believed that playing sports was a great way to learn about and interact with one another. Green and Lazerson had assessed how sports transcended all cultures, genders and races as well as tearing down all barriers of hatred and bigotry. They knew that participating together in sports would shed a new light on why and how things were done differently in each community, and open the doors for a new open-minded approach to communication.

The teams they created at random, with African-Americans and Hasidic Jews on each, started playing weekly football and basketball games together. Soon suspicious behavior was replaced by teamwork and trust. The two groups struggled together and they began to see similarities in their struggles off the court as well. Crown Heights was transformed into an atmosphere filled with compassion and hopefulness.

While Green and Lazerson saw sports as an important ingredient for positive social change within the community, their ideas for improving racial cohesiveness and creating awareness between the two ethnic groups were not limited to involvement in sports. Green established the Crown Heights Youth Collective which provided counseling, tutoring, job-training, as well as art, music and dance-groups for youth in the Crown Heights community. This Youth Collective would eventually merge with the Crown Heights Jewish Community Relations Council to become what is known today as Project C.U.R.E. (Communication Understanding Respect Education). Green and Lazerson would continue to launch creative and innovative social and racial awareness projects as they started their own bi-racial rap group which held "CURE" concerts to promote positive social interaction between the two communities. Project C.U.R.E.'s vision and message had grown so much within New York City that members of Project C.U.R.E. participated in an exhibition basketball game during the halftime of a New York Knicks game at Madison Square Garden. This provided Green and Lazerson with national exposure to promote their cause and their vision for race relations in this small city of Crown Heights. Through the work of these two great men, Project C.U.R.E. has improved the lives of countless young men and women growing up in the Crown Heights area and in other parts of New York, and even throughout the rest of the world.

Richard Green is a leader and a visionary who seized the opportunity to make a positive social change in the way people acted within the community of Crown Heights as well as around the world. Dr. David Lazerson is also a visionary, with the belief that sports and other forums for communication can help transcend any barrier that the youth of Crown Heights faced in social differences and community relations. The two men understood that in order to prevent the detrimental dynamics from forming within the Crown Heights region, individuals were going to have to be open to embracing diversity and social differences. As they realized the positive effects that sports and other social programs could have on the community they also realized that it is creative programs like these that will help eliminate bigotry, racism, stereotypes, and violence around the United States and the rest of the world. Richard Green and Dr. David

Lazerson are social heroes not only in their home of New York City but also social heroes and role models to all of society.

CHAPTER 8

CREATING A NEW GAME PLAN FOR COLLEGE SPORT

I have written two books on ethical issues in college sport, one published in 1986 and one in 2006. It struck me how many of the problems in college sport that existed in 1986 persist to this day. Here are a group of leaders, some directly involved in college sport, others in higher education, and others who work from the outside. All have worked hard over the years to bring improvements to the lives of our student-athletes and integrity to the games they play. Those are some of the people we showcase in *Creating a New Game Plan for College Sport*.

Joe Crowley was the president of the University of Nevada, Reno for more than two decades. During that time, he also served as president of the NCAA and was a major change agent in that role on the issue of race and sport in college.

Clarence Underwood and C.M. Newton were both prominent athletic directors at Michigan State and the University of Kentucky, respectively. Underwood was one of the small number of African-American athletics directors in Division IA and has worked throughout his career to make sport be more equitable for women and people of color.

C.M. Newton, a prominent coach, integrated college basketball at Transylvania University and the University of Alabama. As athletic director at Kentucky, he made courageous decisions such as eliminating the alcohol sponsorships of Kentucky athletics at a cost of nearly $400,000 a year to the University.

Sister Rose Ann Fleming led the academic advising program at Xavier University in Cincinnati. Dedicated to her student-athletes, Sister Fleming made sure that every Xavier student-athlete succeeded in the classroom.

Judy Sweet was a pioneer for women. Serving as athletics director of the University of California, San Diego, Judy was a vocal advocate for the implementation of Title IX. She became the first woman to first serve as president of the NCAA and later joined the NCAA as one of its top leaders while remaining a strong advocate for women and girls in sport.

Dick Schultz, a former athletic director, became the executive director of the NCAA and began to address some of the "old school policies" in college sport that had led to so many athletics departments breaking the rules and creating a student-athlete population where graduation rates were very low in the revenue sports.

There were two men who worked for reform from the outside including Creed Black, a giant in the publishing industry, who started the Knight Commission on Intercollegiate Athletics in the 1990's. The Knight Commission pushed the NCAA to get presidents more involved in the overseeing of college athletics on their campus. Richard Astro, then the Dean of Arts and Sciences at Northeastern University in Boston, financed the start of the Center of the Study of Sport in Society. The Center had many pioneering programs teaching conflict resolution, working on the issue of men's violence against women, and getting students to balance academics and athletics. Richard agreed to have the Center help launch a national movement with the National Consortium for Academics and Sports in 1985. After positions as Provost at the University of Central Florida and Drexel University, Richard Astro joined the Consortium as its Chief Academic Officer. The Consortium, of course, implemented the degree completion program and the community service program, both of which have had such an extraordinary impact on college sport in America.

These men and women have been there for decades insisting that sport at the intercollegiate level live up to its ideals.

Dr. Joseph Crowley

by Richard Lapchick and Stacy Martin

Joe Crowley is best known for his presidency at the University of Nevada at Reno, as he served the institution for a record setting 23 years from 1978 to 2001. When he stepped down, he had served his university longer than any other president among the nation's leading universities. He also outlasted every chief executive in the State of Nevada. Concurrent with his presidency at Nevada, Crowley completed a term as the president of the NCAA from 1993 to 1995, a feat only accomplished by one other man.

Joe Crowley played an historical role in the history of race and sport when a dramatic confrontation was unfolding between the Black Coaches Association and the NCAA. Crowley, as the NCAA president, stepped in to mediate the controversy between the university presidents and the Black Coaches Association, thereby avoiding congressional intervention. Both parties now credit Crowley with resolving a conflict that could have possibly led to a significantly bigger confrontation including a walk-out of coaches.

His fervor for the advancement of women's athletics and his unconditional support of Title IX set the University on pace to be one of the most progressive institutions for female athletes. Crowley treasures the expansion of women's athletics at Nevada where there are 12 varsity sports for women. His support of intercollegiate athletics at the University of Nevada secured him the Jake Lawlor Award after his presidency in 2005. Crowley created opportunity all across the campus during his tenure. He was a catalyst for the remarkable growth and development of the University and the quality of its student body. When he took on the role of President, he set out to integrate the university and the City of Reno. The disconnect between the two had widened greatly. He established the UNR Foundation in 1987 to recapture the University's heritage as a land-grant institution in accordance with the intent of the Morrill Land Grant Act of 1862. The isolation of academia and the city didn't melt over night, but slowly advisory boards were formed with a renewed focus on the school's founding charter.

Dr. Crowley began his educational career in his home state of Iowa and received his bachelor's degree from the University of Iowa. He went on to attain his master's from Fresno State University and his doctorate from the University of Washington. For his service to the University, his own University of Nevada bestowed an honorary doctorate degree upon him. Although his commitment to higher education has been demonstrated throughout his presidency, Crowley's first impression was made in the classroom. He started teaching political science at the University of Nevada in 1966 and steadily made his presence known. He was the chair of the Faculty Senate, and then later he served as department chair of political science before he was asked to serve as Interim President. A year later, it was clear that Crowley deserved the position permanently.

History intertwines nicely with one of Crowley's favorite subjects to teach: politics. After retiring as President, he began to teach a course entitled "American Constitutional and Cultural History" at UNR. He also found time to lobby for higher education during the 2001 legislative session. His expertise was requested at San Jose State University in 2003 as that University searched for a new president. Crowley graciously came out of retirement and helped the school determine what its needs were and what characteristics they desired in a president. While at San Jose he conducted sessions that educated the students and faculty about the academic presidency, a subject about which he has a wealth of knowledge and experience as is evidenced by the four books he has published on the subject. After San Jose, Crowley began a new book chronicling the history of the NCAA as it approaches its centennial celebration in 2006. "In the Arena: The NCAA's First Century" commemorates the 100th Anniversary. As of this writing, he accepted the position of Interim President at UNR. Everyone wants him because he leads so well.

Joe Crowley's commitment to education has extended far beyond a classroom, an athletic program, and a campus. During his career he has served on the board for the National Association of State Universities and Land Grant Colleges and he served for a decade on the board for Collegiate Woman Sports Awards. He is a member of the executive committee of the National Consortium for Academics and Sports. Both Fresno State and

Iowa conferred distinguished alumnus awards upon him for his exemplary service in education. His most prized accomplishment will probably accompany his name being ascribed to the newly constructed student union on the University of Nevada at Reno campus. The dedication suggestion came from the students there to honor Joe Crowley who has made lasting contributions to their school and its campus that will continue to make a difference well into the future.

After his interim presidency, Crowley is planning to head back to his roots in the classroom to teach college sophomores in a "Western Traditions" course outlining the "American Constitution and History." Crowley hopes to establish a capstone course for seniors in journalism that examines the interaction between media and politics. In our modern world, Joe Crowley is above all an educator. In that regard, he serves as a model of what a university president should be!

Dr. Clarence Underwood

by Stacy Martin

Clarence Underwood is very much like "the man who is actually in the arena"[1] as described by Theodore Roosevelt in his poem "In the Arena." Underwood has lived "himself in a worthy cause."[2] He dared to better the lives of children in any way he could. The arena that Underwood chose for his worthy cause was education, and more specifically the education and development of student-athletes, "who strives valiantly" as a group themselves. Underwood's endeavors on sports fields began at a young age, but he never gave up the fight because he knew that making a positive difference in a young person's life would shape that person's future for years to come.

Underwood grew up in Gadsden, Alabama on the baseball and football fields in town. As an exceptional student-athlete, he also found time to compete in track and field. After graduation, this honorable young man went on to represent his country in the 82nd Airborne Division of the United States Army at Fort Bragg, North Carolina. In his youth he also joined Dr. Martin Luther King's efforts to help African-American adults finish their education and register to vote. Underwood's commitment to education and heightening awareness for others prompted his own return to the educational arena. He enrolled at Michigan State University (MSU), and a long relationship between MSU and Underwood began.

He received his bachelor's degree in physical education in 1961 from MSU. Underwood finishes what he starts and has maintained that philosophy throughout his career, no matter what the arena. This pattern and his deep ties to Michigan State might have started when Underwood furthered his education at MSU and received a master's degree in physical education and counseling in 1965. After a brief stretch as an educator in the public school system of East Lansing, Michigan, Underwood felt a void from being away from Michigan State. He soon took a position as the University's Assistant Athletic Ticket Manager, and happily became a member of the MSU staff.

He quickly moved up the ranks to Assistant Director of Athletics in 1972, a duty he fulfilled for a decade. His attachment to student-athletes was just beginning to blossom as were the programs that he implemented during this time. The pivotal difference Underwood made was a commitment to a student-athlete's academic career. He was charged with implementing academic support services that would be tailored to a student-athlete's needs. This devotion to a student-athlete's education was groundbreaking for the time. Athletes were being abused by the system and exploited for their athletic talents by universities without regard to what their lives would be like after sports. His concern about this problem was recognized by the National Academic Athletic Association when he was elected president by his peers. Overhauling a system and the values of the athletic department was an enormous undertaking in itself, but Underwood also organized all issues pertaining to eligibility, financial aid, rules interpretations, managing the staff and athletic certification.

Underwood never wanted to be a part of eliminating opportunities for education, especially for underrepresented groups. A large part of his career has been allocated to improving Title IX compliance and increasing gender equality at MSU. The length of his career mirrors the fight for women's equality, but in the 1970's the fight was just beginning. Again, Underwood took those brave steps into unknown territory and he developed Michigan State's first Title IX proposal to demonstrate their compliance to the new federal law. In 1983, another opportunity in the athletic world presented itself. Underwood had a chance to enter a larger more powerful arena, the Big Ten Conference. He was appointed as the Deputy Commissioner of the Conference. During his tenure he created the Big Ten SCORE program for inner-city children to learn that Success Comes Out of Reading Everyday. He was a proponent of the Big Ten Advisory Commission designed to draw attention to minority/equity issues. His familiarity with establishing standards for student-athletes in the classroom as well as on the field of play at Michigan State proved beneficial as he helped establish superior standards in academic advising conference wide. His people skills, always shining brilliantly, assisted him as he worked with every athletic director from the member institutions and as the administrator for men's sports.

Underwood's intimate knowledge of the rules that he gained during his Big Ten interlude would prove invaluable to Michigan State as they attempted to create a compliance program. The University requested that he return home to become the Assistant Athletics Director for Compliance. He is credited with the execution of MSU's first official compliance program. Underwood was passed over in 1992 for the athletic director position. The school chose its first female athletic director, Merrily Dean Baker, instead. He was thought of as the man for the job since he was so accomplished and educated, as well as the fact that he had been a Michigan State guy for most of his professional life. Trustee support, the former AD and football coach, and students were not enough influence though. Baker soon realized his potential contributions herself and promoted him in 1994 to Senior Associate Athletics Director. He was the department's official responsible for student-athlete welfare, a cause dear to his heart. He challenged the system to do more for these student-athletes as he created cultural programs that dealt with controversial and ethical issues they might face.

After two athletics directors were terminated at MSU, Underwood was named as the Interim Athletic Director in 1999. By the end of the year, his appointment to Athletic Director was approved. Underwood set his own term at three years. That was all he believed he needed to put the program back in order and fulfill important expectations.

Underwood was well-known for his people skills and communication abilities, so unifying the people in the department was an obvious place to start. He set expectations for his coaches regarding their treatment of their athletes. It was to never be dehumanizing or abusive and every coach had to take an interest in each of their athletes on and off the field. They were now accountable, but it didn't take the form of a malicious threat. Underwood hosted family events like Christmas ice skating, a welcome back tailgate, even a backyard barbecue at his house so everyone in the department could start to mend the fences between sports. Underwood knows that he had to befriend and care for his coaches so that he could make the University's athletic programs successful once again.

Next he drastically overhauled the athletic facilities on campus: a new basketball complex, reinstallation of natural grass in Spartan Stadium, reconstruction of the track and field complex, renovations to Jenison Field House and Ralph Young Field, and new artificial turf for women's field hockey. His investment paid off in one of the most successful periods in Spartan history. Men's basketball won an NCAA Championship, football won the Citrus Bowl, hockey won a CCHA Tournament title, and at least

15 sports sent at least one athlete to an NCAA Championship.

Clarence Underwood describes the Women's Athletics Varsity Letter Celebration as the most enlightening and joyous event of his tenure at Michigan State. It was organized in celebration of the anniversary of Title IX and in response to the years of correspondence with former female student-athletes from Michigan State. The AIAW, which formerly governed women's athletics and institutions, lacked the authority to grant these student-athletes varsity letters like their male counterparts. It was fitting that a man who had struggled for so long to provide an equal playing field for women's athletics awarded women who represented over 50 years in Spartan athletic history for exceptional performances. Underwood is a man "who knows the great enthusiasms."[3]

Underwood certainly knows the truth behind the first few lines of the poem, "It is not the critic who counts; not the man who points out how the strong man stumbles, or where the doer of deeds could have done them better."[4] He has faced his own critics and challenges over his 27 year professional career. He was a man concerned with the job and accomplishing things for others; he never looked for credit for himself. Clarence Underwood demonstrated the essence of leadership in the arena of college athletics with dignity and class.

[1] Roosevelt, Theodore. "The Man in the Arena." Chapultepec, Inc. [June 2, 2004; November 11, 2005] http://www.theodore-roosevelt.com/trsorbonnespeech.html

[2] ibid, pp.

[3] ibid, pp.

[4] ibid, pp.

Charles Martin "C.M." Newton

by Stacy Martin

Charles Martin "C.M." Newton is credited with changing the game of basketball. His career truly came full circle upon his retirement as Director of Athletics at the University of Kentucky in 2000. The knowledge and experiences he has acquired through his career encompass all realms of athletics, basketball in particular. He gained an intimate knowledge of the game as a student-athlete at the University of Kentucky and further applied that knowledge during his tenure as the head coach at Transylvania University, the University of Alabama, and Vanderbilt University and as an athletics officer at Andrews Air Force Base. His commitment to the rules was fostered throughout the years as assistant commissioner of the Southeastern Conference and during the time he served as the chairman of the rules committee for the NCAA. Although Newton's commitment to the game of basketball is impressive, the truly remarkable aspect of his career is his propensity to act with integrity in any situation he faced.

Newton exemplified the characteristics of a genuine athlete from an early age. In high school he was a star on Ft. Lauderdale High School's football, basketball and baseball teams, achieving all-state honors in each sport. His versatility as an athlete was attractive to a number of schools with prestigious athletic programs, but he ultimately chose the University of Kentucky to launch his collegiate career in athletics. While attending school, Newton pitched for the Wildcats' NCAA tournament baseball teams and was a letterman on Adolph Rupp's storied National Championship basketball team in 1951. He even found time to win a couple of campus intramural football championships as quarterback. After the championship, Newton signed a contract with the New York Yankees and pitched in the minor leagues for two years.

Newton participated in the Air Force ROTC program while he was at Kentucky. When he graduated with a degree in physical education in 1953, he was commissioned as an athletics officer at Andrews Air Force Base in Washington, D.C. In 1956, he briefly returned to professional baseball, until another offer arose that seemed like the right thing to do. Newton had been offered the Chair of the Physical Education Department and the head basketball coaching job at Transylvania University in Lexington. After careful consideration for the well-being of his young family, he decided that it was the best move he could make. His professional athletic career came to a close.

Newton has thought of his experience at "Transy," as he affectionately calls it, as one of his happiest.[1] He integrated the Transylvania basketball team with an African-American basketball player in 1965, an infrequent scene in those days, but he knew it was the right thing to do. After 12 years of coaching and teaching, he was recruited once again by a legendary coach for the head basketball coaching position at the University of Alabama.

Coach Paul "Bear" Bryant, who was the football coach at the University of Kentucky while Newton played for Coach Rupp, was now the football coach at Alabama and leading the search for someone to turn around the basketball program there. Having received Rupp's recommendation, Bryant hired Newton. Newton created a successful program after a couple of challenging years. His team's numerous accolades include three Southeastern Conference Championships, two NCAA Tournament appearances and four National Invitation Tournament appearances. The most lasting and heroic change that Newton made at Alabama was recruiting their first African-American scholarship player, Wendell Hudson from Birmingham, to integrate the basketball program. Thankfully, Bryant supported Newton and Hudson publicly, which eased some of the angst surrounding their bravery in a region seriously plagued by segregation. Newton recognized the weight his decision carried and it virtually opened doors for other African-Americans around the SEC to participate. Once again, Newton simply did what was right. Newton was awarded SEC Coach of the Year three times during his tenure at the University of Alabama.

He left Alabama and coaching in 1980 in search of new challenges. He saw an opportunity to gain experience in administration and accepted a position as assistant commissioner of the SEC. He had always demonstrated an affinity for the rules of the game as a coach and a player, and had begun to examine the game on a larger scale when he started serving on the NCAA Rules Committee in 1979. He continued to serve on the committee until 1985 and during that time implemented two rules that effectively brought basketball into the modern era, the shot clock and the three point shot. The game would never be the same. Once again, Newton left his mark.

He had hopes of becoming the commissioner of the SEC, but was lured back into coaching by Vanderbilt University. Vanderbilt was an institution determined to do things right, a philosophy close to Newton's heart, and so their offer was irresistible. He was challenged once more to rebuild a program, and succeeded again to the tune of two more NCAA tournament appearances and two more SEC Coach of the Year awards. A joyful time in his house was undermined by a troubling time down the road at his former home, the University of Kentucky. Kentucky's basketball program was beleaguered by NCAA violations with likely sanctions following close behind. After the 1988-89 season at Vanderbilt, Newton accepted his greatest challenge yet.

Newton was hired at the University of Kentucky as the Director of Athletics with the challenge to reform an entire athletics program weighed down by NCAA sanctions. The basketball program was under fire and desperately needed to be rescued. This longtime coach knew what to do: find someone to do things right. He convinced Rick Pitino to turn the program around. Pitino soon confirmed that Newton's decision was right. He had an overall record at Kentucky of 219-50 and three NCAA Final Four appearances along with an NCAA Championship in his eight year tenure. Newton credits Pitino as the catalyst for the rest of his success at Kentucky, because basketball was just the beginning.

Newton set out to make changes in every realm within his reach. He crossed lines of social reform yet again by hiring Bernadette Mattox to rebuild the women's basketball program too. Mattox was the University's first African-American women's basketball coach. She had a positive effect on the program and took the team to their first NCAA appearance in eight years. When he was again faced with an opening for the men's basketball coach when Pitino went to the Celtics, Newton broke new ground once more at Kentucky. He hired Orlando "Tubby" Smith to be the school's first African-American head coach. When questioned about his courageous choice, he simply responded that Tubby was the best man for the job, giving no weight to any inquisition regarding race. Tubby proved Newton's decision as his predecessor did by winning two NCAA championships for the Wildcats in 1996 and 1998. A unique opportunity presented Newton at the 1998 NCAA Championship as he was also the Chairman of the NCAA Men's Basketball Tournament Committee, so he was fortunate enough to present the championship trophy to Tubby Smith and his Wildcats. Newton also revived Kentucky's football program and made it competitive once again by hiring Hal Mumme as head coach.

That choice proved controversial after the fact and after Newton's retirement because unfortunately Kentucky returned to the NCAA sanction list, this time for football violations. One blemish can sometimes taint a previously untarnished record. But, Newton takes it in stride and accepts responsibility for the violations despite the fact that it was actually men he had hired in football operations whose misguided actions warranted sanctions.

Newton has obviously displayed a commitment to providing opportunities for those who are sometimes overlooked. Non-revenue sports are another group that fight for anything they can get. They are typically the programs cut due to the pressing need to comply with Title IX, so opportunities are limited for non-revenue sports. Newton added three sports to Kentucky's athletic program, women's and men's soccer and softball. It has proven difficult for universities to add programs due to the financial obligations that accompany them. Rarely does a department add a men's program due to Title IX compliance. But Newton knew it was right and that Kentucky should invest in their student-athletes. In fact, several of Kentucky's non-revenue sports have attained national distinction under Newton's watch.

The visible improvements to the University of Kentucky's campus are an important part of Newton's legacy. He changed the face of the campus through expansions to the baseball and football stadium and construction of a new soccer and softball complex, tennis stadium and Nutter field house, a building as important to the community as the track and field and football teams. The building that Newton expresses the most pride about is a $3 million dollar facility to house the Center for Academic and Tutorial Services (CATS), an academic center for Kentucky's student-athletes. The center opened in 1981 as the first in the nation, but Newton demonstrated that academics are a priority through the construction of the new facility in 1998. He has also been devoted to former Kentucky student-athletes finishing their degrees and has created the Cawood Ledford Scholarship Fund, named for the longtime "Voice" of the Wildcats, to fund their education. He knew that funding education was the right thing to do with the money, and encouraged all former student-athletes to come back and earn their degrees. Since Newton made this decision, Kentucky has always provided funding for finishing degrees and leads the country with one of the most extensive degree completion programs.

In a time when athletic department budgets are overstretched and some are folding completely requiring financial support from academia, the University of Kentucky Alumni Association under Newton's leadership has accepted fiscal responsibility for the University's William T. Young Library. They have pledged $3.2 million annually to retire the construction bonds for the library. Newton is undeniably a leader in the sports world, but he has demonstratively reminded people that he was an educator too through his loyalty to CATS, scholarships for student-athlete degree completion and funding a facility on campus where no sports will be played. Commercialism has crept into athletics funding for some time now and the illusive dollars are hard to resist.

After a drunk-driving incident involving a Kentucky student-athlete ended in a horrific accident and the student-athlete's death, Newton made an unheard of stand against the alcohol sponsors for athletics and refused to renew Anheuser-Busch, Miller Brewing, and Maker's Mark advertising contracts that provided more than $400,000 yearly. He placed a higher importance on every student's life, not just student-athletes' lives, than funding traced to a possibly destructive influence on college students. He has made moral and ethical choices as an athlete, a coach and as an administrator.

Newton served in numerous associations and on several boards and committees while he was a coach and an administrator. While he was serving as Kentucky's Director of Athletics, he found the time to support the game of basketball on an international level. He was actively involved with USA basketball (formerly ABAUSA), the governing body for basketball internationally. He became their vice president in 1988, and four years later he took on the role of president until 1996. He was responsible for the change from amateur athletes representing the Olympic team to the selection of NBA players and the original "Dream Team." He continued a dramatic effort to expand women's basketball internationally. His powerful impact on the game of basketball has not gone unnoticed. In 1997, the Naismith Basketball Hall of Fame awarded Newton with its highest distinction, the John Bunn Award. In 1999, the Atlanta Tip-off Club recognized his contributions with the Naismith Award.

Newton has distinguished himself in both the world of sport and education as a leader and proponent of change. His actions speak to the character that he embodies, a kind, determined, committed to being respectful and ingenuous character. His contributions to the game of basketball have ushered the game into the modern era and his contributions to society have crossed racial boundaries that have separated the human race for too long. He has set a precedent for academic excellence and commitment at all of the universities he served, and he has made dramatic and lasting changes at the University of Kentucky. C.M. Newton has truly come full circle in his career and has taken the time to teach everyone else what he has learned along the way.

[1] Neely, Tony. "Recognizable Class." *Kentucky Alumnus*. Summer 2000, Volume 71, Number 2.

Sister Rose Ann Fleming

by Stacy Martin

When athletes arrive on campus, they soon find out who is actually calling the plays, and it is not their coach. Sister Rose Ann Fleming wields tremendous power on Xavier University's campus. While teaching English and fiction at the University in 1985, she was approached about becoming a full-time academic advisor for Xavier's student-athletes. She had been working with several of the basketball players and had been quite successful. Xavier was a small institution of 6,600 students at that time and had no one in place to handle the special needs of student-athletes. She was not a stranger to academia, as she was currently pursuing a degree in business when the school asked her to take on this new role. Over the years Sister Fleming has earned several degrees. She has a Bachelor of Arts in English from the College of Mount Saint Joseph and a Master of Arts in English from the University of Detroit. While she was teaching English at Xavier she was pursuing a Master of Arts in Education. Later, she obtained a Master of Business Administration from Xavier as well. She has also earned a doctorate in Educational Administration and a law degree from Northern Kentucky University. Before she arrived at Xavier she served as President of the Summit Country Day School in Cincinnati and President of Trinity College in Washington, D.C. for eight years each. Xavier placed great importance on academics and wanted to convey that in her position with student-athletes, so Sister Fleming worked from academic affairs, not in the athletic department.

Some might say that it would be hard to establish relationships and networks with the coaches and athletes from such a position, but it wasn't an obstacle to her. She knew that her task of getting athletes degrees was of great importance and so it carried with it tremendous power. New coaches may be surprised to find her walking in and stopping practice, but it became a familiar scene. Former athletes would tell stories about a nun pulling them out of practice or chasing them down after a game to find out why they had slipped up in the classroom. At least once she has shown up to an NCAA tournament game with books in hand to discuss a basketball player's class work. She demonstrated that athletic success doesn't waive a student-athlete's academic responsibilities. It definitely is not a common sight and it definitely is not common practice on most college campuses. Sister Fleming set a standard of excellence and required accountability from her athletes early on. So, now if she calls, they answer. Speaking of calling, missing class is definitely not an option for student-athletes at Xavier. Professors at other institutions may let the occasional absence or tardy slide for athletes after they had a late night at the game or an early practice. However, there are no excuses for missing class according to Sister Fleming. Even though her frame is small, her presence is as strong as her tallest athlete. She has also been known to call an athlete missing class and patiently allow the phone to ring 100 or more times to wake them up. She has even shown up at their door ready to escort them to class when they get lost in their covers on the way to school.

Sister Fleming embodies another characteristic commonly attributed to nuns: discipline. Her athletes know her rules: don't miss a class, do your own assignments, study hard, maintain a 2.0 GPA, take a minimum of 12 credit hours, find a career and pursue it. Sister Fleming knows that she is preparing these student-athletes to be successful in life, not just in sports. She has plenty of time to emphasize these rules and even make them habits during her study hall sessions. She mandates that every freshman attend study hall for two hours Sunday through Thursday at the library.

After such strict expectations and rules imposed upon them, one might think the student-athletes would find it hard to work with Sister Fleming or at least be a little resentful, but that is hardly the case. A visit to Sister Fleming's office would quickly dispel that notion. Her walls are lined with photos capturing the friendships that she has formed with her student-athletes over the years. She is loved, admired and most definitely respected by all of her students. Some have likened her to a concerned and loving grandmother figure who conveys her eagerness for her students to do their best. She has built relationships with them, which is why they comply with her requests so willingly.

Working closely with the coaches over the years has helped her reach student-athletes. She knows that it doesn't work to punish someone who is doing her or his best. It is imperative that the student finds value in accomplishing the task. She has taken a motivational approach to encourage the behavior she desires from her student-athletes instead of an approach based on punishment. Although she is not opposed to the concept, most coaches give her the ability to bench a player for not meeting their academic obligations if she feels it is necessary. She is always fair and firm in her approach, treating all players equally no matter what their status on the team. Motivation and punishment are strategies that can be found in some coach's playbooks as well.

Now that she has established the system and the expectations, the student-athletes actually do some of the enforcing. When recruits visit the campus the emphasis on academics quickly becomes apparent. Sister Fleming credits the coaches for not just recruiting the best athlete, but an athlete who is also serious about academics. The Xavier athletes even start to screen the new recruits by stressing the significance of keeping the streak alive. Someone on the street would probably assume they were talking about winning basketball games, but it's more important than that. They are referring to the fact that since 1985 Sister Fleming has ensured that every basketball player who exhausts his or her athletic eligibility at Xavier earns a degree. Talented athletes have succumbed to their teammate's pressure of finishing their degrees instead of entering the draft and a chance at millions. Xavier University's graduation rate has consistently ranked among the best of NCAA Division I institutions. One might even credit Sister Fleming with a national championship in academics. In 1998, Xavier's 100 percent graduation rate was the best in the country. Xavier's athletes regularly achieve a higher graduation rate than the rest of the student population. Sister Fleming has instilled academic values in these student-athletes and knows that she is helping them to become better people.

She has been a pioneer in integrating the worlds of academics and athletics. When she started there wasn't a game plan in place. There was only the knowledge that someone needed to be responsible for helping athletes become student-athletes. The time demands and energy required by student-athletes can be extremely overwhelming, especially for freshmen. She knows that the life of a student-athlete is more difficult than the typical student so she guides them through the system. There were very few NCAA guidelines 20 years ago when she started in this field. She is now a powerful force behind them. As an exemplary leader in academics and sport, Sister Rose Ann Fleming has received numerous awards for her tireless efforts. Her alma mater recognized her life long service to education through the Alumni Career Achievement Award in 2004. Xavier's Head Basketball Coach, Skip Prosser, didn't believe in MVP awards for his team and has never awarded one. But he wanted to distinguish Sister Fleming's efforts to help student-athletes graduate. She wasn't the player with the most points, but she was definitely credited with numerous assists for student-athletes and the highest grade point average, so she earned the MVP award. In 2000, she was honored by Xavier University for her abundant accomplishments and contributions to the school when she was inducted into the Xavier University Athletic Hall of Fame. Sister Fleming is a testament to the fact that one need not be an athlete to make an important mark on the world of collegiate athletics.

Judy Sweet

by Stacy Martin

Judy Sweet is not a stranger to change. In fact, for most of her life she has been a proponent of change in sports. She pioneered the landscape of college athletics and helped transform it from a barren scene to one full of opportunity and promise. The idea of diversity is commonplace today, but when Judy Sweet was growing up in Milwaukee, Wisconsin in the 1960's it was radical. Her first groundbreaking move in sports was walking on to the sandlot to play a game with her brothers and cousins. She quickly proved herself and enjoyed plenty of opportunities to play sports, as long as she didn't stray outside the confines of the neighborhood. The sandlot was only the first of many changes she would make throughout her career and it was a valuable lesson to push the barriers of what was allowed. Judy Sweet has broken many barriers in her quest to cultivate women's participation onto the sporting landscape.

Sweet's journey has not been without struggle and opposition. Change is hard to accept for most and many take a great deal of comfort in doing things the way they have always been done. She left the sandlot and went on to high school and college only to be stifled once more by intramural programs instituted for educational and recreational purposes. Organization and competition elements familiar to boy's sports were absent from the girl's activities. Sweet missed the proverbial boat for women's sports when Title IX passed in 1972 banning the unequal opportunity that Sweet had experienced in her playing career. She had graduated with honors from the University of Wisconsin three years before. Sweet had majored in physical education and mathematics, which led her to take a position at Tulane University as a physical education teacher. Her humble and quiet start soon flourished and she moved across the country to Arizona. The Painted Desert's majestic scene surely inspired her to paint her own landscape.

Sweet began teaching at the University of Arizona and simultaneously pursued a master's degree in education. As usual she graduated with honors. Sweet stayed on at the University for one more year and began her career in athletic administration. A taste for change persuaded her to move closer to the ocean. She arrived in San Diego and taught at a local high school for one year before she began her long career at the University of California, San Diego. She joined the faculty as both a teacher and a coach. Her attachment to student-athletes and her mission to safeguard their welfare began. After only a year she became an associate athletic director. As previously demonstrated, Sweet is a woman who quickly excels at any task she undertakes, so just over a year later she was promoted to the director of athletics at UC San Diego. Sweet had made her first sweeping stroke of change to the inhospitable sporting landscape on a grand scale.

Control of both men's and women's athletic programs is atypical for a woman in the new millennium but it was non-existent in 1975, until Judy Sweet took a brave step into a constantly changing yet rigidly resistant environment for women. She became the first female athletic director of a combined intercollegiate athletic program in the nation. Athletic directors predictably were promoted from coaching a major male sport such as football, basketball or baseball at that time. In fact, some even served dual roles as the head football coach and athletic director. Sweet broke the mold. She faced opposition from her peers. Some were hesitant to accept her at all. The coaches whom she had befriended to shape student-athlete talents just two years before became antagonistic when she cut their budgets so she could create a more equitable environment between the men's and women's athletic programs. Every landscape has its own unique color scheme and the sports realm is no different. Color was added to Sweet's landscape by letters with "the most colorful" negative language that expressed resentment and biases for her newly acquired position. Sweet soon realized "the hurdles that had to be overcome."[1]

Pioneers have climbed mountains to pursue their dreams, and Sweet learned on the sandlot how to overcome such barriers. During her 24 years of service at UC San Diego she experienced unrivaled success, and started establishing new landmarks in the expanding environment for women's athletics. Her athletic department supported 23 varsity sports and brought 25 NCAA Championships home to San Diego. UC San Diego teams were National Runners-up 32 times in her 24 years. In 1997-1998, UC San Diego won the Division III Sears Director's Cup for program excellence; this marked the first time that an athletic department directed by a woman had been awarded the Cup. Additionally, it was the first time an athletic department without a football program had won the award. Sweet did not only keep her department in the forefront of success, she continued to foster her education and earned a master's of business administration with distinction from National University in San Diego.

Sweet committed herself to improving student-athlete welfare throughout her career without regard to gender, although she had a distinctive viewpoint as a female to guard opportunity for future female athletes. Her perspective has been sought out by 20 different NCAA committees over the years and her contribution has broadened her impact on college sports. She started out as the NCAA Division III Vice President in 1986 and then served as the first female Secretary-Treasurer of the NCAA from 1989-1991. During that time she also served as the Chair of the Budget Committee. She made history yet another time when she took on the role of NCAA President from 1991 to 1993. She was the first female president of the Association during a time when the position was voluntary and not contracted. She blazed a new trail across the sports landscape and created more opportunity for her female counterparts. Sweet's commitment to student-athletes has never been contingent on contracts of service. She truly cares about providing the best experience possible for student-athletes in any way she can. She has also served on the NCAA Council and Executive Committee as well as the Review and Planning Committee. For seven years she served as Chair of the Special Advisory Committee to Review Recommendations Regarding Distribution of Revenues, a committee formed in response to the $1 billion television contract with CBS.

Exhibiting leadership is second nature to Sweet. She has made ethical choices and implemented policy that benefited student-athletes. More importantly, she motivates others to join her cause. Sweet excels quickly at any endeavor she pursues. She has been recognized for her exemplary leadership with a variety of awards throughout her career. Sweet was National President of the Athletic and Recreation Federation of College Women from 1968 to 1969. Later in 1984 she was named Outstanding Young Woman of America. Just a few years later in 1990 she was the Los Angeles Times' selection for Top Southern California College Sports Executive of the 1980's. Southern California is an arena historically filled with fierce sports competitors in the administration as well as on the playing fields. The Times' selection speaks volumes about her extraordinary leadership at UC San Diego.

Her commitment to excellence transcended decades and the 1990's were no exception. Just like wines have very good years, 1992 was Judy Sweet's year. She was named the Administrator of the Year by the National Association of Collegiate Athletic Administrators. The W.S. Bailey Award was conferred on Sweet by the Touchdown Club of Auburn-Opelika to distinguish her from the nation's athletic administrators. Women's Sports Advocates of Wisconsin, Sweet's native state, inducted her into their Lifetime Achievement Hall of Fame. She has convincingly demonstrated her abilities.

One year later she was named Woman of the Year in District 38 by the California State Senate. Twelve calendar pages after that honor she forged through new country once more by offering her service and experience to the United States Olympic Committee Task Force on Minorities. Sweet dedicated her time to that committee for the following two years. Her wealth of knowledge and first hand experience on the front lines of the gender equity fight was invaluable to the minority task force. In 1998, Judy Sweet was the recipient of The Honda Award for Outstanding Achievement in Women's Collegiate Athletics. Sweet served on the Board of Directors for the National Association of College Directors of Athletics (NACDA). Sweet stepped down from her longtime position of Director of Athletics at UC San Diego in 1999 to return to a faculty position there.

Sweet's expertise was requested by the NCAA once more in 2001 to hold one of their premier positions as Vice President for Championships. Sweet would oversee planning and organization for all of the 88 NCAA Championships except Division I men's and women's basketball, football and baseball. Cedric Dempsey, the NCAA President at that time, was quoted by Wallace Renfroe in a *NCAA News* release as saying "Her depth of knowledge of college sports and administrative experience in running a broad range of events will ensure that NCAA Championships continue to be great experiences for student-athletes."[2] Sweet understands how valuable the experience of a championship is for student-athletes and wants to ensure that it is unforgettable as well.

Sweet joined the NCAA national office team and quickly took on additional responsibilities as the Senior Women's Administrator, a role designed to reflect a position typical to member institutions' athletic departments. The position has its roots in a role that was established in 1981 to look out for women's issues in athletic departments of universities, and the role had expanded in responsibilities by 1990 at those institutions but lacked reflection in the national office. Sweet was once again the first woman to take the job and has left a lasting impression on sports that will benefit her successors. The position may have originated with the idea of guaranteed female involvement at the top of the NCAA governance, but it has evolved into a position with appropriate responsibility and accountability in all facets of the organization that has the added benefit of a female perspective. She never made the fact that she was a woman an issue but instead used it as a competitive advantage. She has been described as "a quiet, effective fighter for opportunities" by Dale Neuberger, the former president of the Indiana Sports Corp[3]. Her focus on gender equity encompasses suggestions that come from both men and women.

Judy Sweet constantly seeks out new challenges and so she accepted the promotion to Senior Vice President for Championships and Education Services in 2003 in addition to maintaining her role as the Senior Women's Administrator. Her new role in education is to implement leadership programs. Leadership is a concept that Sweet knows inside and out. Myles Brand, the current NCAA president, has described Sweet as the "conscience of college sports" and regularly consults with Sweet for her indispensable knowledge.[4] She is one of the four senior vice presidents who reports directly to Brand, and the only woman. Sweet has gained so much status and prestige with the NCAA that she is the only living and active college sports icon to have her name grace the title of a meeting room at the NCAA Headquarters.

Judy Sweet's leadership is impressive and resilient, and she works everyday to instill the same drive and values in student-athletes. Her final alteration to the sporting landscape is the most irreversible and ongoing in affecting student-athletes lives by creating an equitable environment that provides a positive experience for both young men and women. Her hope is for them to become the leaders of tomorrow, when the sun sets on her majestic landscape.

[1] Montieth, Mark. "Clearing the path" *The Indianapolis Star*, October 30, 2005.

[2] Renfroe, Wallace, I. "Judy Sweet, Long-time Athletics Leader and Administrator, Joins NCAA Staff as Vice-President for Championships." *The NCAA News*, November 1, 2000.

[3] Montieth, op. cit.

[4] Montieth, op. cit.

Dick Schultz

by Jenny Brenden and Stacy Martin

Dick Schultz has managed to excel in athletics at so many different levels from high school, college, professional, and finally to the Olympic level. He has also worked in many different capacities as an athlete, an educator, a coach, and an administrator. Schultz started out as an athlete. He attended Central Iowa College where he received All-Conference honors in baseball, football and basketball. Schultz performed well enough in his college career to move on to the professional level where he managed a baseball team in an era in when pro athletes were not making the kind of money that they do today. Off-season jobs were common. Schultz found himself working at the high school level as a teacher, coach and athletic director. Schultz also honed his entrepreneurial skills and started his own construction business.

Schultz pursued his master's degree at the University of Iowa. He also coached freshmen teams in both baseball and basketball at Iowa. After Schultz finished the degree, he was promoted to the head baseball coaching position and the assistant basketball coach. He also became the head basketball coach in 1970, a position which he held until 1974. Schultz became the special assistant to the president at Iowa. Two years later he became athletics director at Cornell University which was followed by six years as AD at the University of Virginia before being appointed as the executive director of the NCAA in 1987.

When Schultz assumed the leadership position of the NCAA, the staff warmed to him quickly. It is rare that a leader is so forthcoming and generous with responsibility. He was accommodating as a manager and he attempted to flatten out the organizational structure so that his staff could take on more tasks. Schultz empowered his staff long before it became a trend in organizational dynamics. He valued their creative and analytical skills. He only wanted to help them do their jobs better and knew that it would reflect positively on him. Schultz changed the relationship between the National Collegiate Athletic Association and its member institutions. Formerly, the two were separated and the governance structure of the association seemed bureaucratic and dictatorial. But Dick changed all of that with "The State of the Association Address" from the Executive Director at the annual NCAA convention. Providing information and sharing responsibility became the theme for Schultz's tenure at the NCAA. His leadership translated into a change in hiring practices as well. The Association provided such a wealth of experience so that NCAA staff members moved to positions at universities or conference offices after a few years to expand the understanding of the NCAA by those offices.

Strengthening the role of the membership was an integral piece of Schultz's tenure at the NCAA. The reform movement that he was so well-known for encapsulated legislation that targeted the academic part of a student-athlete's collegiate experience as well as a distribution of revenues from the NCAA's mammoth television contract. He made the NCAA more accessible to its member institutions. In turn, he encouraged the university presidents and chancellors to take a more active role in the Association as well.

Schultz was a strong proponent of gender equity and initiated a study to look into its affects. The tide of college athletics was beginning to turn and the athletics directors at institutions were no longer the only ones responsible for the student-athlete's welfare. Schultz put responsibility back in the hands of capable people. Another part of his reform movement was to place sanctions on those institutions that violated the NCAA principles and bylaws. While NCAA chief, an internal investigation alleged that he might have been aware of a scandal while he was AD at Virginia. The specific violation was that booster club members had allegedly provided money to athletes as no-interest loans, along with graduate assistants receiving unwarranted compensation. The university received minor penalties. Schultz resigned from the NCAA because he didn't want to embarrass the Association and the work it was doing to restore the integrity of intercollegiate athletics.

During Schultz's last four years with the NCAA he also served on the executive committee of the USOC. The experience prepared him for the position of executive director of the USOC, which he assumed in 1995. His knowledge and experience in athletics was sought out by the USOC search committee and he was persuaded to accept the position of Executive Director after several phone calls. The NCAA supplied letters stating that Schultz was not guilty of collusion in the Virginia incident. Schultz employed many of the same management techniques that he utilized at the NCAA, like a flatter organizational structure and giving responsibility back to the employees. He also set out to provide the organization with a strategic vision that encompassed a global focus, an imperative factor for an effective Olympic Committee.

Schultz has certainly faced some difficult challenges throughout his career and he has faced each one with strength, integrity and determination. The Salt Lake Olympic Organizing committee, which was separate from the USOC, had its own alleged scandal of giving bribes to IOC members to secure the Salt Lake bid. Schultz cooperated with the investigation committee fully and condemned the conflict of interest. Members of the Salt Lake Organizing Committee were removed from their positions and an USOC member charged with accepting bribes was also dismissed. Schultz acted with integrity and attempted to restore the dignity of the Olympic Games. Dick Schultz crossed the finish line with his head held high.

Creed Black

by Stacy Martin

Creed Black was the quintessential newspaper man, always in search of the truth in the story. He started working at the *Sun-Democrat* in his hometown of Paducah, Kentucky at age seventeen and literally, a storied career was born. During the post World War II occupation period in Europe, he worked on the *Stars & Stripes* newspaper. He then decided to pursue formal training in journalism at the Medill School of Journalism at Northwestern University in Chicago. He enhanced his experience during his college years by editing the *Daily Northwestern*, and working the copy desk at both *The Chicago Herald-American* and *The Chicago Sun-Times*. Black graduated with highest honors from Medill with a distinction in political science, a subject that no doubt interested him enough to engage in a political science master's program at the University of Chicago.

Black was clearly a highly educated man with vast experience in journalism, an asset to any newspaper. He served as an editorial writer and executive editor of the *Nashville Tennessean* and as vice president and executive editor of *The Savannah Morning News and Evening Press*. He quickly climbed the ranks among editors and traveled across the country still holding steadfast to truthful stories. He also served as vice president and executive editor of *The Wilmington Morning News and Evening Journal*, and he fulfilled his duties as managing editor and executive editor at *The Chicago Daily News*. His success was notable and he was called upon to act as Assistant Secretary for Legislation of the Department of Health, Education and Welfare for eighteen months in Washington, D.C. *The Philadelphia Inquirer* quickly appealed to Black following his period of public service to accept their offer of vice president and editor. He not only accepted the offer, he went on to win Pennsylvania's most prestigious awards for both column and editorial writing. Black returned to his home state of Kentucky in 1977 when he was named chairman and publisher of The Lexington Herald-Leader Co.

Creed Black has been known for promoting integrity in journalism throughout his career. But it is in moments of great adversity when our values and ideals are challenged, and it is through that adversity that the character of great men is revealed. Creed Black was still the publisher of The Lexington-Herald Leader Co. in the early 1980's when the University of Kentucky's student-athletes were suspected of being bought by alumni. They really were hardly inconspicuous about how well they were living compared to the rest of the state, one of the poorest in the Union at the time. Driving expensive sports cars to the race track and parading to the twenty dollar window, it was just a matter of time before it could be proven. The question was: would someone actually publish the truth if it came out? The Commonwealth of Kentucky lived and died with the successes and failures of the University of Kentucky's athletic programs, the attachment ran so deep that any laceration to the Wildcats' reputation would clearly bleed deep blue. In 1985, two reporters finally exposed convincing proof that implicated both the basketball players and coaches of the University of Kentucky in a scandal that shook the entire state. The players had been on the take for years and the coaches were facilitating it.

Black was faced with the most poignant question of his journalism career. To publish or not to publish? The story was verified and true to his nature, he published the truth and stood by his reporters and editor who broke the story. Black's newspaper faced tremendous pressure as it was subjected to circulation and advertising boycotts publicly denouncing the paper printing the story. Marketing and circulation revenues are important to a paper for its very survival. But this was only the beginning of Black's adversity. The public had already convicted and condemned him and his staff, so the executioners came out of medieval times to deliver their sentences. A bomb threat evacuated the building, rifle shots cleared the pressroom and delivery men were chased down the streets by angry subscribers with axes. The public was outraged at such an attempt to malign the athletic department at the University of Kentucky. When no one else believed in him or the veracity of the *Herald's* story and his world was caving in around him, Creed Black held steadfast to his morals, values and integrity. He never waivered in his battle against corruption. In fact he wrote a piece saying that he could understand the uproar as he was a native of Kentucky as well, but he did not condone the tumultuous actions of the public.

Creed was a man who understood the value of education, and so as turbulent as the situation had been, he still knew it was an experience that carried with it a tremendous opportunity. He demonstrated so eloquently that subscribers of a newspaper do not read the stories because the paper pampers them with what they want to hear, but they subscribe for the facts and the truth delivered in a strong, objective manner that allows them to decide what they want to believe. In 1985, especially after all the paper encountered, one would typically assume that the newspaper's relationship with the public was beyond repair. In actuality, the newspaper became a case study for publishers everywhere. Their Sunday circulation went up 60 percent, and their daily circulation had increased by 30 percent without an evening paper. It is quite obvious why the Kentucky Journalism Hall of Fame inducted Creed Black in 1986.

The incident in Lexington and the unlikely, positive economic impact that resulted from it provoked study by executives of Knight-Ridder, Inc., a newspaper empire partly created by the Knight brothers, James and John. The Knights also created one of the largest private foundations in the country, the Knight Foundation, an organization dedicated to supporting the arts, journalism and higher education. Undoubtedly impressed by Black's dedication to journalism and fidelity, the two brothers requested Black to be president of the Knight Foundation in February of 1988. Black's uncompromising nature and sincere devotion to the integrity of education made him the man for the job.

The Knight Foundation soon established an independent commission to examine and to offer reformatory advice to collegiate athletics. Black wasn't a stranger to confronting corruption in athletics and knew that the problem had to be confronted with solutions not just exposed on page one of the country's newspapers.

The commission was formed to investigate the extent to which corruption and scandalous behavior of collegiate athletics has tainted institutions of higher learning and threatened their academic integrity. It recognized that intercollegiate athletics are suitably placed at universities when they are implemented in an appropriate manner and operated properly. The commission felt strongly that the downward spiral of intercollegiate athletics was in large part due to the heavy influence of commercialism involved in the game today. Black saw first hand what kind of impact a story about intercollegiate athletics corruption can have on a community. He realized that because of the high visibility associated with intercollegiate athletics, the scandals and violations attributed to an athletic team would most likely be attributed to the nature of the academic groups at the institution as well. Essentially, what someone knew about an institution's sports teams would be what they knew about the institution. Black and the Knight Commission set out to strengthen the focus on academics at Division I-A schools by placing some perspective on the role that intercollegiate athletics should play at a university. Black was careful to consider the hostility such an investigation would elicit, and so he cautioned the public that the commission's goal was to attack the flagrant problems by returning authority to the presidents and faculties of institutions because they are the individuals who can earnestly guard the intellectual and academic integrity of universities. So, the Knight Commission convened a panel of the presidents of universities from the major athletic conferences who could speak to the problems that they themselves know all too well.

Black resigned from his presidency of the Knight Foundation in 1998, although he still serves on the Board of Trustees. His work with the foundation helped it grow from a small organization to one of the largest private foundations in the country. The foundation grants approximately $23 million dollars annually to fund higher education journalism and arts programs as well as teachers and students. His leadership on the Knight Foundation's commission on intercollegiate athletics provoked "A Call to Action" by American universities and the NCAA when the report was published. Presidents were becoming more involved in the operations of athletics departments and the welfare of the student-athlete. Many new forms of legislation have been proposed and passed to change the face of intercollegiate athletics. Although, there are still scandals and violations, it is not the only print on page one of the country's newspapers today. Creed Black tackled corruption through discussion and publication of difficult issues in academics and sports that others were either too fearful of or too complacent in accepting the status quo.

He has received numerous awards throughout his career that have recognized him for his enduring commitment to integrity in education and journalism. He was welcomed into the National Conference of Editorial Writers as a life member in 1989. He received an honorary Doctor of Laws Degree from Davidson College in 1991 and an honorary Doctor of Humane Letters from Centre College in Kentucky in 1996. His alma mater of Northwestern thought that his illustrious service deserved a place in the Medill School's Hall of Achievement in 1997, where he became a charter inductee. He has always been a leader for each of his employers, and he has also led associations when he served as president of the National Conference of Editorial Writers, the American Society of Newspaper

Editors and the Southern Newspaper Publishers Association. One of the most prominent awards an author can receive is the Pulitzer Prize. One of the most notable honors an editor can receive is the request to serve as a Pulitzer juror. Creed Black's knowledge and breadth of experience certainly qualifies him for such an honor, his character and commitment to truth and justice certainly secured him the honor six times. Black still receives requests to speak at numerous institutions, especially journalism schools. Each time he conveys the importance of writing a story with objectivity and veracity, and not succumbing to pressures and prejudices.

Richard Astro

by Richard Lapchick

When you read the biography of Richard Astro, it conveys a tapestry of a distinguished academic career, a scholar of American literature with book and article credits on the likes of Steinbeck, Hemingway and Malamud, a successful 30 years in higher education administration as the Provost of Drexel University, M.C.P. Hahnemann Medical University and the University of Central Florida, a Dean at Northeastern University and a department chair at Oregon State.

The reflection in the mirror would seem to be of a scholar absorbed in scholarly work; a man whose academic life was the dominant theme in everything he did. There is no doubt that his many years in higher education have led to distinction and great achievement academically.

But Richard Astro says that when everything is said and done, his greatest achievement has been helping to found Northeastern University's Center for the Study of Sport in Society. Astro knew that there were problems in sport. Being an academic, he may have been thinking of studying those problems with possible proposals for solutions when he started to bring me and Bob Lipsyte of the *New York Times* to brainstorm about what Northeastern might do. The name that had been talked about was the "Center for the Study of Sport and Society." After a rich series of discussions between people from the world of sport and some of the academicians in Boston, particularly at Northeastern, I was approached to become the first director of the Center.

Astro knew there was something there and the combination of my life as an activist and his life as an academic resulted in the creation of the Center that became a combination think-tank but much more, an active agent for social change. Astro had the courage in tight budgetary times to have Northeastern put up the initial funding. That $200,000 initial investment would grow 20 years later to a Center that has a budget 15 times that size as well as the creation of the National Consortium for Academics and Sports (NCAS). Tom Sanders and I brought forth the NCAS as an idea to Astro to expand the work of the Center with degree completion and community service across the country. At the time, I might have expected Richard Astro to say, "No, this is ours. This is Northeastern's," in the way I have seen happen so many times in higher education. But Astro, a man with a vision, said, "Let's spread the programs around." The National Consortium was conceived and grew exponentially over the next 20 years. It now comprises 221 universities and colleges which agree to bring back any athlete who went to their school on a scholarship in a revenue sport with tuition paid in exchange for the students performing service in the communities where the schools are located. This organization has grown into one that is so important to college sport in America. More than 28,000 athletes who had not finished their degrees have returned. They have worked with over 14 million young people in the community service program on issues like conflict resolution, men's violence against women and academic balance with sports. Astro's willingness to start organizations, even if he wasn't so directly involved in the implementation, was critical to the success of Northeastern's Center and the National Consortium for Academics and Sports.

But it was in the first few month's of the Center's existence when we started our initial program with the New England Patriots that Astro's genius pushed us into the birthing canal. If the course that we taught with New England was successful, the Center might live past its first year. If the players weren't interested, then the Center would be forever small or would fail in a short period of time. So the "Bridge Course" was conceived to get those first 13 New England Patriots back into school to begin finishing their degrees. Richard Astro and Pete Eastman teamed up to be the front and back ends of the course. Astro assigned Eastman, the Chairman of the Speech and Communications Department, to engage the players in ways to improve their communication with the outside world, thus increasing their popularity and potential with commercial endorsements. I was more skeptical once we left the hands-on approach to hear Astro talk about Steinbeck and Hemingway and to tell pro athletes that there was some comparison between "The Old Man and the Sea" and themselves. The Patriots ate it up, as did the Bruins and the Red Sox after them.

The rest, as they say, is history. The Center's early successes, fueled by his vision and his application, launched the Center and the Consortium into what they are today. Among the 13 New England Patriots in the original class were Keith Lee, Robert Weathers and Lin Dawson. Robert is the Associate Director of the Consortium 20 years later, leading our community service programs. Keith, as the Chief Operating Officer of the Consortium, is responsible for all the day-to-day operations. I am still the President of the Consortium. Three people together after all these years; how happy we were when Richard Astro joined us as the Chief Academic Officer of the Consortium in 2002, coming full circle and no longer being the theoretician but an active, day-to-day implementer of the vision he helped create.

CHAPTER 9

CREATING THE ENVIRONMENT

Problems existed not only in college sport but at the high school, Olympic and professional sport levels. In the section *Creating the Environment*, the work of six men stood out.

Gene Upshaw and Paul Tagliabue led efforts in the National Football League and the Players Association to have the league serve its communities more effectively.

David Stern not only spirited the growth and development of the NBA but helped spread the NBA's message of service in communities where teams play and players live.

Billy Payne helped bring the Olympic Games to Atlanta in 1996 and used the Olympics as a platform to showcase not only the talents of individuals but what a community like Atlanta could do to serve the Olympic movement while benefiting its citizens.

H. Ross Perot, one of America's wealthiest men and later a presidential candidate, helped the State of Texas to create "No Pass, No Play" legislation. It was the first of its kind in the country and demanded that students had to maintain a "C" average in order to participate in sport in Texas.

Clinton Albury, a coach at Killian High School in Dade County, Florida, demanded that his football players succeed academically even without state mandates. Albury assumed the leadership of a football team whose players' academic performance met the state's standards, but not Albury's. He challenged them to perform in the classroom and converted his already winning team into a group of scholar-athletes.

Rich DeVos, the co-founder of the Amway Corporation and one

of America's wealthiest individuals, became owner of the Orlando Magic in the 1990's. His team served as a model for all sport in terms of sports organization that constantly gave back to the community. Rich DeVos also made the donation that made the DeVos Sport Business Management Program at the University of Central Florida a reality, helped create the Institute for Diversity and Ethics in Sport at UCF and then endowed the National Consortium for Academics and Sports with gifts to these organizations totaling $9 million.

Lewis Katz and Raymond Chambers invested in the New Jersey Nets and together donated their portion of the profits to the inner-city schools and children in the surrounding communities, the same communities where they started in humble beginnings.

Mike Ilitch dreamt of playing professional baseball as a young boy but grew up to own professional baseball and hockey teams instead. Ilitch utilized his business acumen to build his sports teams as both winners and contributors to the community.

Thomas "Satch" Sanders first led by example as a player and later, as an executive for the NBA. His appreciation for and understanding of the sport of basketball and the NBA allowed him to positively shape hundreds of citizens who were also professional athletes.

These men used their influence to make sport at the high school, Olympic and professional levels be all it could be.

Paul Tagliabue and Gene Upshaw

by Jennifer Brenden

"There is no 'I' in team," is a common saying used by anyone trying to motivate a group of people, or a team to work together in harmony to achieve a common goal. As a mock response to that saying, some may reply, "But there is a 'me' in team" implying that the individual performance overrides team accomplishments. For some reason, the team and the individual seem to be on opposite ends of the spectrum when it comes to professional sports, and it is extremely difficult to find that happy medium that satisfies the individual athlete, yet it is in the best interest of the team.

This is exactly the task that Paul Tagliabue, the NFL Commissioner since 1989, and Gene Upshaw, the Executive Director of the NFL Players Association since 1987, have undertaken. Over the past 16 years, the two have worked together to create the incredibly successful entity that the NFL is today.

Although Tagliabue works with all of the NFL teams and treats them all fairly, he will admit he was partial to a couple of teams as a kid. He was a fan of the New York Giants because they were so close to home. He also rooted for the Cleveland Browns because they had Italian-Americans on the team and Tagliabue was of Italian heritage. Of course these interests remain as part of his past and have no bearing on decisions he makes today for the teams in the league. Tagliabue was an athlete himself growing up in Jersey City, New Jersey. While he was not a standout football player, he was a stellar hoops star. His basketball skills and impressive grades earned him a scholarship to Georgetown University where he majored in government. He graduated from Georgetown in 1962 as senior class president, basketball team captain, Rhodes Scholar finalist and Dean's List honoree. He immediately received a public service scholarship to attend the New York University School of Law.

Tagliabue's first job was with a big-time firm in Washington D.C. that just happened to serve as the primary outside counsel for the NFL. Tagliabue has been working with and learning about the NFL since he started practicing law in 1965. That made him a logical candidate to follow Pete Rozelle as the commissioner of the League. There were some big shoes to fill as the head of the NFL when Rozelle decided to step down from his position after 29 years. Rozelle was in charge from 1960 to 1989. Obviously, a lot of change occurred during those three decades. Economically, socially and athletically, there was a lot to deal with not only in the world of sport, but in the world in general. It only made sense for Tagliabue to step in since he had served as Rozelle's chief legal counsel for over 20 years and he knew what was going on with the teams. Because of this connection, the transition from the 3rd commissioner to the 4th was very smooth.

Gene Upshaw had been serving as Executive Director to the NFLPA for two years by the time Tagliabue became Commissioner. Just as Tagliabue had been involved with the NFL prior to being appointed as Commissioner, Upshaw had been involved with the dealings of the NFLPA long before he took the head position as well. He was no newcomer to the workings of the Players Association.

Upshaw had been a part of the first AFL/NFL combined draft in 1967, after being named as a NAIA All-American at Texas A&I University (now known as Texas A&M-Kingsville). He was drafted in the first round by the Oakland Raiders and played in the NFL for 16 years until 1981. During his playing time he also served as an NFLPA player representative and officer for 13 years. He was an All-Pro offensive guard and was elected in to the Professional Football Hall of Fame in 1987, the first year he was eligible. Upshaw was voted as the Lineman of the Year in the AFC in 1973 and 1974 and received the honors of Lineman of the Year in the NFL in 1977. Upshaw is the only NFL player in history to play in three Super Bowls in three different decades.

Upshaw was the captain of the offensive team for eight of his years. During his 15 year tenure with the Raiders, they made 11 playoff appearances, won eight division titles, one AFL Championship, two AFC titles and two Super Bowl Championships. He is still revered as one of the greats, being named to the AFL-NFL 25 year All-Star Team and to the NFL 75th Anniversary All-Time Team. Upshaw was a leader which accounts for his success as head of the NFLPA for so many years. Upshaw has become known as a strong labor leader in America and has molded the NFLPA to be at the top of its class as a players association.

The relationship between the league and the players was not in good shape when Tagliabue took office in 1989. There was no collective bargaining agreement because the strike in 1987 had resulted in no contracts and the players union was filing a suit against the league.

At the top of Tagliabue's priority list when he was appointed as Commissioner was to develop a good relationship with Upshaw and the players union. Tagliabue realized that the league should not be competing and fighting with the players but rather should be working and communicating with them as much as management and labor can in order to make the NFL successful. Upshaw understood these sentiments and agreed with the philosophy. Eventually Tagliabue and Upshaw became known more as business partners as opposed to enemies working with conflicting interests. Upshaw did receive some criticism for this since the players union and the league had tended not to agree on things in the past, but Upshaw did what he believed was right and in the best interest of both the players and the league.

Since Tagliabue and Upshaw have come together as partners and created a stronger relationship, there have not been any strikes or work stoppages in the NFL. Every other professional league has had a stoppage of play in that time period. This is a big improvement after two strikes took place in the NFL in 1982 and 1987 prior to Tagliabue's arrival. A major issue that Tagliabue and Upshaw worked out a compromise for was having the owners agree to free agency, and in turn, the players agreeing to a salary cap. The Collective Bargaining Agreement (CBA) has been extended four times since Tagliabue's initial negotiations with Upshaw.

Tagliabue has plans to bring the NFL back to the Los Angeles market in the near future, and to increase the league's international popularity by possibly playing a couple of games outside of the United States and by continuing to improve NFL television packages. Upshaw is looking forward to working on the next extension of the CBA, which will be difficult to negotiate, but judging from the past that Tagliabue and Upshaw share, somehow they will get the job done.

Because of their unique relationship, Tagliabue and Upshaw have been able to get the players and the league heavily involved in service activities in the communities where they play. They have been generous with time and money as was epitomized by their combined efforts in the fall of 2005 in response to the tragedy of Hurricane Katrina. Through their combined efforts, more than $15 million was donated to the relief efforts demonstrating the power of sport to help society. Upshaw and Tagliabue have shown that management and labor can work together for the larger good. They are what real leadership in professional sport is all about!

David Stern

by Jennifer Brenden

Individual athletes have to take care of themselves and are responsible for their own actions, but there is a hierarchy of power and responsibility that lingers high above the position of the athletes. There are coaches that have some say over their individual players and above them is the team organization that has many structural layers. At the top of the organizational structure are the President, CEO, Owner and, sometimes, the General Manager. Even going further up the ladder, there are the league officials of all professional leagues, who are responsible for the teams, the coaches and the players. At the head of the league offices is the commissioner of the league, who has the responsibility of managing the entire league, which includes making decisions that are the best interest of the players, the teams and the coaches. Pleasing everyone all the time is an art form that is yet to be invented, so obviously the league commissioner has to deal with many tough situations with contracts, salary caps, league rules and punishments for breaking rules.

In the NBA, the Commissioner is David Stern, a role he has held since February 1, 1984. This is not what Stern dreamed of doing when he was boy, especially since he was seven years old when the NBA was officially started. His interest in basketball when he was young was limited to being a Knicks fan and playing basketball on the local courts in Chelsea, New York, where he grew up.

Wanting to stay close to home so he could continue to work at Stern's Deli, the family business that he had jumpstarted, Stern chose to attend Rutgers University. He graduated from Rutgers as a Dean's list student and as a Henry Rutgers Scholar in 1963. He immediately went to law school at Columbia University where he graduated from with his law degree in 1966. His first connection with the NBA was joining the firm Proksauer and Rose, which represented the NBA, as he served as outside counsel. Stern left the firm in 1978 and joined the NBA family by becoming general counsel. He was soon appointed the executive Vice President of the league in 1980. Four years later he was elected as the fourth commissioner of the NBA.

Prior to Stern's selection as commissioner, the NBA was not doing very well. The league was close to bankruptcy, fans were drifting away, drug abuse was a major issue among the players, and management-labor wars were occurring throughout the league.

Since Stern became commissioner, league revenues have increased over 500 percent. The increased popularity led to the addition of seven expansion teams. Stern has even crossed the gender barrier with the founding of the Women's National Basketball Association (WNBA). The National Basketball Developmental League (NBDL) has been created, and lastly, television exposure has shot through the roof.

Stern has worked hard to make the NBA more global. In addition to the expansion teams, Stern also opened international offices in Barcelona, Hong Kong, London, Melbourne, Mexico City, Singapore, Taiwan, Tokyo, and Toronto. The NBA now broadcasts games in over 200 countries in over 40 different languages.

Player rosters have become more and more diversified in recent years, so Stern and the NBA are trying to keep up with that trend. In 2005, there were a total of 82 international players in the NBA, coming from 36 different countries. These numbers keep growing every year, along with the NBA's global market. Stern wanted to reach people around the world so basketball fans from China could watch Yao Ming, fans from Germany could watch Dirk Nowitzki, the French could cheer on Tony Parker and Canadians could cheer for Steve Nash. There are also exhibition games that are being played internationally that helps the NBA reach out to youth around the world.

The league gives so much to children in America. Stern thought it would be a good idea and great connection to extend their good deeds to children around the world. Basketball Without Borders summer camps was created to give kids the opportunity to play basketball. This program is about more than simply providing courts, equipment and the opportunity to play. Basketball Without Borders aims to teach children more than just basketball skills. NBA players and other counselors teach the children the rules of the game and some X's and O's of offense and defense. More importantly the kids also learn about leadership, teamwork, cultural differences, the importance of education and living a drug-free lifestyle. Thus far, this program has reached out to kids in Turkey, Greece and over 20 African countries.

With the leadership of David Stern, the NBA and its players and organizations are involved in numerous community service programs, which Stern is a big proponent of. He knows what an impact the players can have in the community. A few of the other programs that the NBA is involved with are the Read to Achieve Program, child abuse prevention, alcohol abuse prevention, volunteerism, hunger relief and the Special Olympics.

The NBA and the WNBA have also had the best record for hiring women and people of color in all of sport. Both have had the top grades throughout the 18 year history of the Racial and Gender Report Card. The NBA, under David Stern's leadership was also the first pro sport to have Diversity Management Training implemented throughout the league.

Over Stern's 20 years as the commissioner he has had to deal with a lot of changes. He had to learn to evolve with the game. He's dealt with ballooning player salaries and the evolution of the professional athlete, shifting target markets and the change in a basketball game from being purely a sporting event to more of an entertainment event.

Stern's job is never dull. There will always be issues that need to be addressed. The latest issue to catch fire with the media was the NBA dress code, in which most people would agree that Stern is making a smart business decision, in terms of the league. As was stated before, there is never a way to please everyone, but Stern's job is to do what he believes is best for the league. David Stern has been making good decisions for over 20 years, and NBA fans around the world can thank him for that.

Billy Payne

by Jessica Bartter

Kids often have lofty dreams of representing their country in the sport they love and standing on the Olympic platform, beaming with pride and a gold medal while singing their national anthem and holding back the tears. On the contrary, Billy Payne's Olympic dreams did not start until he was almost 40 years old. Payne's dream was different. He did not want to run the 4 x 100 meter relay or swim the 200 meter freestyle or even play basketball with the American Dream Team. Although all three would have been an honor for this former football star, Payne's dream was to bring the Summer Olympics to Atlanta, Georgia.

Payne was born and raised in Georgia and felt a need to give back to the communities that had brought him so many good memories. The good football memories started in high school at Dykes High where he led his team as quarterback to the 1964 North Georgia Championship. Payne knew his destiny would take him to the University of Georgia where his father had been a star and later officiated Southeastern Conference games. Payne followed his father's footsteps and played lineman for the offense and defense at Georgia. While playing for Coach Vince Dooley, the Bulldogs lost only four games and played in three major bowl games during his three years on the team. Payne was team captain and earned All Southeastern Conference honors as a defensive end. Since football is not an Olympic sport, Payne's only chance of playing beyond college was in the National Football League. Payne decided his skills would be better utilized as a lawyer. After graduating from law school in the top 20 percent of his class in 1973, Payne was employed at a law firm in Atlanta. He specialized in real estate law but after two years, when the real estate market began to do poorly, Payne and a friend started their own law firm.

In 1987, Payne dedicated a new sanctuary for a church in Dunwoody, Georgia after a three year, $2.5 million fundraising project that he had chaired. The sense of collective joy that emerged from the crowd inspired Payne to do something else for the community so that he could experience that joy once again. Up before the sun the next day, Payne explored idea after idea until he was still left with nothing. Payne looked through the ideas he had already rejected and realized the common denominator among all of them involved sports and community. Like a light bulb, the word Olympics flashed in his brain. This was the beginning of a nine year project that Payne brought to fruition. The journey was met with doubt, criticism and personal debt but Payne fought back with sheer competitiveness, determination and personal sacrifice.

Payne thought the Olympics would bring a similar sense of collective joy to the City of Atlanta, but on a larger scale. Payne believed the international event could reshape the Atlanta community by crossing color barriers, improving economic status and fixing neighborhood disparities. Payne planned to leverage change in the city by sharing economic benefits with disadvantaged neighborhoods and building a sense of community. With such goals, it is hard to imagine the city did not support Payne's dream right away, but in fact, many laughed at or ignored him. He first approached the Chamber of Commerce to ask them to bankroll his plans but they did not even think his request was worthy of a response. Payne received similar reactions from the local community, business establishments and government.

Unfamiliar with failure, Payne refused to give up. He turned to wealthy friends who could easily write six figure checks to create a pool of seed money for the games. Despite the fact that he had two children at home, nearing the age of college which meant large bills for tuition, Payne quit his law practice and mortgaged some of his real estate properties, putting himself in $1.5 million in debt, an amount he added to the seed money. Payne's friends, now known as the Atlanta Nine, were the only ones who believed his plan could work. Payne volunteered himself for three years traveling and soliciting to have the 1996 Summer Olympics in Atlanta. Eventually Payne garnered support and positive recognition for his efforts. One key supporter was Mayor Andrew Young who was a civil rights leader, three-term congressman and former United Nations Ambassador. Payne recognized the symbolism a white organizer and a black mayor working together to bring a shared dream to life. Initially, Mayor Young's international credibility helped Payne's efforts with the

International Olympic Committee; then Payne's southern charm kicked in. After three years of living off savings and loans, Payne began earning a salary as the Chief Executive Officer of the Atlanta Committee for the Olympic Games (ACOG). With the official support of his city behind him, Payne persevered. Now that Atlanta was in the race, many believed the odds were stacked against the city or any other city in the United States for that matter because the 1996 Summer Olympics marked the 100th Anniversary of the modern Olympics. Athens, Greece was thought to be a shoe-in for the Centennial Games. Known as a fierce competitor, this did not deter Payne. On September 19, 1990 Payne's hard work and sacrifice was rewarded. It was announced in Tokyo that Atlanta had been selected over Athens by a vote of 51-35.

Though both Payne and the city were ecstatic, the work done to bring the Olympic Games to Atlanta had really just begun. Many thought Payne, the lawyer, would walk away as if just getting them to come to Atlanta was enough. But Payne planned to see his dream through and had no intention of stepping down as CEO of the Atlanta Committee for the Olympic Games. Instead, Payne made room for the experts and worked alongside them to establish a $1.7 billion budget and then oversaw the spending of it as well as 90,000 employees, volunteers and concessionaires. The Games were played in 31 different athletic venues around the Atlanta area, ten of which were built specifically for the Olympics. Some of the construction caused controversy, particularly in the poor, predominately black neighborhood of Summerhill where the new Olympic Stadium was constructed. Thirty years before, the city of Atlanta built a baseball stadium in the same neighborhood and now residents feared that once again, they would be excluded from the economic benefits of the stadium. However, Payne envisioned the Olympics in Atlanta to do just the opposite. He and the ACOG consulted a neighborhood committee regarding jobs, traffic patterns and parking to ensure that the stadium could reap compensation for the community. The stadium was a $209 million gift from the ACOG to the community after it was used for the Olympics.

In another effort to better race relations in the Atlanta area, Payne suggested golf be added as an Olympic Sport and that the Augusta National Golf Club would serve as host. An avid golfer himself, Payne was quite aware of Augusta's history of discrimination and hoped that raising the issue would help eliminate the lack of racial equality there. Though this idea was not passed, he knows it would have been the right thing to do for the exact reasons that it received opposition.

After years of seven day work weeks and 14 hour days that started in the office at 5 a.m., Payne finally saw his dream come to life when on July 19, 1996, the Summer Olympics opened in Atlanta. Atlanta welcomed over 2.5 million spectators to watch more than 10,000 athletes from 179 nations compete in 271 events in 26 different sports. The 1996 Games were successful for American athletes who took home 36 more medals than any visiting country including 44 gold, 32 silver and 25 bronze medals. The Games were also a success for the city of Atlanta that is now more internationally recognized and has experienced a higher tourism rate since 1996. Atlanta was only the third American city to host the Summer Games and the first to win the bid on its first try.

After a short recovery period, Payne had to return to work to pay off the numerous debts his passion for the Olympics had built for him. Though he toyed with the idea of a new career in sports with the Atlanta Falcons, the University of Georgia or numerous other sport company positions he was offered, Payne took a position in the corporate world. After several corporate jobs, Payne became a partner at an investment banking firm in 2000. Since 1996, he estimates he has made about 3,000 speeches describing his experiences in spearheading the Olympic effort. He is still called upon for advice by representatives from other Olympic hopeful cities, but the best advice Billy Payne could offer is how to believe in yourself when no one else does and how to stick by your dreams. You never know just how much you can accomplish until you try.

Dr. Clinton Albury and H. Ross Perot

by Jessica Bartter and Jennifer Brenden

Balancing academics and athletics is more often than not a difficult task for high school student-athletes. While athletics are the fun part of a being a student-athlete, emphasis on education needs to be reinforced from parents, coaches, teachers and even teammates to help teenagers juggle the demands of both. Texas governor Bill Clements was concerned the education system was not doing its part to emphasize academics in their athletic departments and decided to take a stand. He called on Ross Perot in 1982 for assistance to evaluate the state of Texas' public education and offer recommendations on how to make improvements. Ross Perot was a billionaire, born and raised in Texas, who often spoke out against the U.S. Government when he believed it had failed its people. Clements had seen success with Perot three years prior when he asked for his assistance in developing policies that reduced illegal drug use in Texas. Perot's early political involvements led him to run for President of the United States in 1992 and 1996.

College athletic programs work overtime to help their student-athletes succeed academically. The NCAA works to ensure that collegiate student-athletes abide by all the rules governing athletic eligibility. As college athletics have grown over the years, a mindset of putting sports ahead of academics had been created and was starting to trickle down to the high school level. "No Pass, No Play" was aiming to put a stop to that belief and put the emphasis back on education. If students start getting away with unacceptable academic performances in high school, the theme seemed to continue in college. Perot chose to take a stand with this program.

He put a lot of effort into this study, spending an additional $2 million of his own money so that he and his committee could travel to cities all over the state and hold public hearings and news conferences, and to gather as much information as possible. Some of the generalized recommendations were equalizing spending among rich and poor districts, tying teacher salaries to their job performance and putting more of an emphasis on academics rather than athletics in high school. In accordance with this last recommendation, Governor Clements and Perot instituted a major legislative change with the No Pass, No Play rule. No Pass, No Play required student-athletes to have passing grades in order to be eligible for competition with their school's sports teams. The specifics of the rule required competency testing and certification for teachers and barred student-athletes from participating in sports for six weeks if they failed a class. The rule impacted student-athletes by threatening a consequence that none of them wanted to face. It also prevented high schools from placing too much emphasis on sports.

Surprisingly, public opinion began to roll in support of No Pass, No Play. A poll conducted by the Public Policy Laboratory at Texas A&M University showed that 76 percent of Texas residents favored the new law. Nationally, a Gallup poll indicated that 90 percent of adults favored restricting those with less than a "C" average. In Dallas, Spruce basketball coach Val Rhodes reported a change in players' attitudes toward grades. More than half of his team began appearing in his office at 7:30 in the morning to study. Teachers knew they could contact Rhodes about potential problems and arranged conferences with parents, Rhodes and the student. The link between academics and athletics was being reforged.

Perhaps the group that got the biggest surprise was Texas coaches. Educators said No Pass, No Play worked *because* of the academic efforts of the coaches. Goree Johnson, the Roosevelt basketball coach in Dallas, emphasized the coach's influence. He held up the start of practice until 4:00 p.m. so his players could work with teachers after school. His staff also made weekly grade checks and assigned mandatory early-morning tutoring for athletes found to be behind academically. Johnson did not lose a single player.

In Dallas, the rate of ineligibility for varsity football players dropped from 16 percent in 1985 to 7.2 percent in 1986. Basketball saw a similar drop from 17.8 percent to 11.8 percent. An analysis by Theodore L. Goudge and Byron D. Augustin in *Texas Coach*, March 1987, showed how the percentage of ineligible athletes was directly related to the size of the school: the larger the school, the higher the percentage of athletes with academic problems.

The Texas landmark legislation was a stimulus to coaches across the country, one of the best examples of whom is Clinton Albury who took over as football coach of Dade County, Florida's Killian High School in 1984. He discovered that his team's grade point average was 1.3. Horrified, he instituted a mandatory study hall. There was only a "D" average eligibility standard, but Albury brought in honor students to tutor his athletes. In specialized study halls, they taught math and English three days a week, science and history the other two. By the 1986 season, the team's GPA had been raised to 2.45. No one failed a course. At the end of the season, 23 players signed with colleges and universities for athletic scholarships. That was believed to be the highest number of signed players in Dade County history. Dade is football country. All were Prop 48 eligible.

Were Killian's teachers merely marking them at an easier standard? Apparently not, since all 23 did well enough as college freshman to stay eligible. It was a testament to Albury, who later moved into a full-time academic position at Killian so he could offer the program to all student-athletes.

But the most startling case was that of Paul Moore. He was the type of player that many would say could never be eligible under a 2.0 (C average) system. He would, according to the argument, be victimized by society's good intentions. In fact, Moore was reading on a first or second grade level in 1984. Then Coach Albury got him into a program for learning-disabled students. He graduated in June 1987 with an 11th grade reading level and a 2.3 GPA in core courses. He exceeded 700 on his SATs. He was eligible under Prop 48 at Florida State in 1987-88 but was redshirted. He was a running back for the 1989 Sugar Bowl team.

In 1994, Albury left Killian High School when asked by the new principal at South Miami High School to join his staff. The principal invited Albury because of the success his athletic academic program had at Killian for 17 years. Nine years later, when Killian High School got a new principal, Albury was asked to return as Dean of Academic Discipline and Student Development. The new principal was well aware of Albury's academic impact on athletes and gave him full reign to resurrect the athletic academic program. Albury created an Athletic Academic Advisor position and together they ran the Basic Athletic Learning Links (B.A.L.L.) Program. B.A.L.L. was mandatory for all athletes whether or not they were in season. B.A.L.L. was divided into two programs. If the student-athlete was earning a C- or D in a core class he/she was assigned to Program I to receive tutoring from honor students. If a student-athlete was getting a D or F in a class, he/she was assigned to Program II and placed with a teacher for an hour after school each day. Within the first semester that Albury implemented his new program, 21 percent of the athletes assigned to mandatory study halls improved their grades to a C or higher. By the second semester, this figure reached 47 percent.

After his program lost support, Albury moved to Miami Springs Middle School where he is now the 8th grade administrator. While his new position deals mainly with discipline, Albury utilizes his time with students to provide the academic advisement he is known for.

H. Ross Perot and Clinton Albury worked hard to put the emphasis back on the student in the student-athlete. Independently, they each proved that with proper guidelines, encouragement and support, high school students can excel in both athletics and academics.

Richard DeVos

by Stacy Martin

Richard DeVos has dedicated his life to encouraging other people to give from their hearts to the fullest extent. His heart has always been overflowing with generosity and encouragement. The years of pouring affection took its toll on DeVos' heart and it began to fail physically when he was 70 years old. DeVos approached this challenge with the same ferocious faith and irrepressible determination that he did his business and philanthropic efforts. Even when faced with death, the ultimate finish line, he continued in his race to make the world a better place. The only hope the doctors gave him was a heart transplant. His donations to society have come back to him a billion times over throughout the years, and a new heart came his way too, just in time.

DeVos is among the strong and resilient people of the world. So the struggle and recovery from such an operation was not an insurmountable feat for him, although he will caution others to be prepared for the tough road to recovery. His caution is not meant to discourage others but instead is meant to help them strengthen their souls. DeVos had a history of heart problems over a 10 year period before the transplant, so finding a heart for him when the supply is so limited was a daunting task. A 70 year old man in failing health with additional complicating factors would be written off by doctors as a tragic tale, but DeVos has an air of magic about him. The doctors worked overtime to find him a heart that would match his generous soul. When they were stifled in the U.S., they crossed the ocean to find DeVos a heart. They located a doctor in London who believed in DeVos' will to live. So, DeVos moved to London. His spirit was undaunted and he relied on his faith to carry him through.

Time seemed to be passing much too quickly for DeVos, his heart was failing. One day a young woman waiting for a heart and lung transplant received the greatest gift she would ever know from a stranger. A car accident in the Czech Republic claimed a victim's life, but he donated his heart and lungs to the seriously ill young woman. Her disease necessitated a concurrent heart and lung transplant, which left her healthy heart available for someone else. Richard DeVos was that someone. One life was lost, but two hearts were found. It is very fitting that DeVos' donor remained alive and healthy. Only a vibrant, vivacious soul could donate a heart magnanimous enough to beat in his chest. Since his miraculous and marvelous recovery, DeVos has devoted his new life to persuading others to donate their hearts to others, both figuratively and literally, as organ donations seem to have flattened out.

DeVos is a compassionate and brilliant man who has been able to combine both qualities into a sound business. He graduated from Grand Rapids Christian High School with a diploma in one hand and a business plan in the other. He developed his plan further at Calvin College in Grand Rapids with his longtime business partner and high school classmate, Jay Van Andel. They embarked on several direct sales ventures and even formed their own corporation in 1949 called the Ja-Ri Corporation. They found that they enjoyed the entrepreneurial lifestyle, especially the countless hours and sleepless nights that afforded them their own business path.

Ten years after the Ja-Ri Corporation formed, DeVos and Van Andel had tailored their business acumen and polished the principles of their business to form the Amway Corporation. Amway set out to fulfill the American dream the American way. The two men set out to form a multilevel marketing company that recruited people to do direct sales and then rewarded them in accordance with their efforts. The company was founded on sound ethical and moral principles like helping people help themselves and helping neighbors, businesses and families surrounding the business. These two men felt so strongly about their employees conducting business with hope, freedom, family and reward in mind, that they carved this code into stone outside Amway headquarters. It has developed into a successful, multibillion-dollar international business with operations in over 80 countries around the world. In 2000, Amway became a subsidiary of Alticor, Inc, a $6.2 billion business with sister companies, Quixtar Inc. and Access Business Groups, LLC. The DeVos and Van Andel families still serve on that board and Dick DeVos and Steve Van Andel assumed their respective father's responsibilities in the company.

DeVos built his business on sales, but he would reference his heart instead. He has always believed in an individual's ability to accomplish noteworthy achievements, so he encouraged his employees to do just that. The word "encourage" has its roots in the French word for heart, "cour."[1] DeVos has built an empire on encouraging and enriching people's lives whether they are his consumers or his employees. He would say that he is in the business of hope. It is hope that keeps the heart striving for more, and it is hope that warms the heart when it is cast out into the cold. DeVos knows how tough rejection is, both as a salesman and a heart transplant patient. Facing rejection after the transplant is usually a daunting task for the patient because they have been sick for so long and their hope for survival is wrapped up in one organ. DeVos characterizes the post transplant rejection fears he faced as mild in comparison to someone's first sales pitch rejection, because he just has to maintain his anti-rejection medication regimen with a few pills. If science could encapsulate DeVos' hope for the world and genuine encouragement, then people could overcome life's rejections. Unfortunately, the pill doesn't exist, but DeVos' book titled *Hope from My Heart* does. He illustrates how positive reinforcement and patience are the medicine to overcome rejections in life. The first time a salesman knocks on a door, he is filled with fear of rejection. But, one day soon a knock will turn into a sale and faith will be restored.

DeVos has always lifted others' spirits, especially in tough situations. There have been countless stories through the years of his one-on-one pep talks and full-scale speeches about the importance of encouragement and the power of perseverance. He gave a commencement address to a class containing an extraordinary number of high achievers, but he spoke to the hearts of the young adults without honor cords and tassels assuring them that they too were still destined for greatness. Another unique aspect of DeVos is his personal involvement in other people's lives when they are discouraged. He has even gone for a ride with an Amway pilot the day after the pilot crashed one of the company's helicopters into Lake Michigan, to exhibit his faith in the young man's abilities. DeVos' heart is full of compassion, integrity and passion. One of those passions is the game of basketball.

In 1991, the DeVos family capitalized on another business opportunity and purchased the NBA's Orlando Magic. DeVos' four children have been very involved in his business endeavors and the Magic were no different. He wanted to establish a family atmosphere in the competitive and adversarial environment of sports, so he assigned the responsibility of the team to his daughter Cheri's husband, Bob Vander Weide. His presence is very much a part of the organization though, as he frequently visits the locker room to cheer on the players and encourage them in life outside the arena. His attachment to the organization runs deep and it reflects the principles that he holds so close to his heart. The team has been a model citizen of the NBA with its extensive philanthropic activities and respectful behavior. The Orlando Magic Youth Foundation, the giving arm of the team, has impacted an estimated one million children's lives. DeVos is a brilliant businessman with the foresight to realize that the model and message that the team conveyed would carry extraordinary weight in society. He envisioned a team that, by example, would create a special environment in the world of professional sports.

The sports business is still a business though, and a business must be profitable and successful to support the community service values that DeVos embraced. Success came relatively quickly for the DeVos family's newest endeavor. In the Magic's sixth season after their inception, they advanced to the NBA finals. DeVos initiated the team's campaign slogan himself for the Finals that year by simply asking, "Why not us, why not now?"[2] Many quickly recognized that DeVos' investment could be profitable for the long term. They were on their way to greatness. Unfortunately the team lost the championship series that season, but DeVos only saw it as another opportunity for encouragement. The team came back strong the next year and was considered a title contender once more if they could win against the Chicago Bulls and a Michael Jordan comeback. Denied once more, DeVos continued to preach the virtue of perseverance. Over the course of DeVos' ownership the team has won an Eastern Conference Title and two Atlantic Division Championships. They have had winning seasons 11 of DeVos' 13 years and have advanced to the playoffs eight times. DeVos incorporated the sound business principles that had catapulted him into one of the most successful businessmen in America when he purchased the Orlando Magic, putting his heart into a young basketball franchise.

The Magic play their games in the TD Waterhouse Arena, which is a relic of the former design style for basketball arenas. Early in the new millennium the team started advertising their need for a new arena to compete with the rest of the league and the latest trend of luxury corporate boxes. The Magic needed to turn a profit and they needed a facility where their fans would be comfortable. TD Waterhouse was not it. DeVos is truly the nobleman of owners because the Magic is a class organization and he has personally donated enormous amounts of money to causes in and around Central Florida. However, all the public heard was a billionaire asking for money. His battle was strictly a business decision. He needed to do what was right for the team as well as the town and began shopping the team around for buyers. All of them wanted to move the team out of Orlando. DeVos remained the owner and reaffirmed that this was Central Florida's team. Most owners would have sold, but DeVos knew what the team means to the town.

You can learn an immense amount about how to conduct business from Richard DeVos, and especially how to conduct it ethically in the sports business where the culture values winning above all else. DeVos and his wife Helen have established the Richard and Helen DeVos Foundation to support organizations that share their beliefs. One of the beliefs they value most is education. They have given to many educational institutions throughout the years. In Richard DeVos fashion, he found a beautiful way to blend philanthropy and business by creating a graduate sport business management program at the University of Central Florida that would encompass his values of diversity, ethical decision-making and commitment to community. The program was created from funding received by the DeVos Foundation and the gift was matched by the State of Florida. It provides a unique learning environment that is unparalleled across the nation due to its relationship with the Orlando Magic that provides first hand practical application. Richard DeVos has given these students hope and has encouraged the dreams in their hearts. He is always striving to make a difference in this world. What better way than to educate future leaders in the sports industry? Richard DeVos may have started out just leading by example in the sports industry, but has now created the standard for excellence, simply by donating his heart to others.

[1] Williams, Pat. How to be Like Rich DeVos. Deerfield Beach, Florida: Health Communications, Inc., 2004.

[2] Powell, Shaun. "Two owners who are the envy of the NBA (Leslie Alexander; Rich DeVos)" *The Sporting News*, June 19, 1995.

Lewis Katz and Raymond Chambers

by Jennifer Brenden

Buying a professional sports organization costs a great deal of money. But that cost can usually be turned in to a very lucrative profit, which is usually the driving force behind most investments. Most owners of professional sports teams try to make money, and lots of it. There is a significant amount of money floating around the NBA, not only amongst the players, but within management, ownership, and the league itself. Many people might argue that it is wrong for athletes, and sports in general, to be making so much money when there is so much need in our society and in the world. This wouldn't be as much of a problem if all sports team owners, or even better, everybody involved in sports, had the same mindset as Raymond Chambers and Lewis Katz. The majority of wealth belongs to only a few, but when those few choose to distribute the wealth to those less fortunate, good things happen.

Raymond Chambers and Lewis Katz have worked hard to be a part of that wealthy group of owners. They are great businessman. Chambers and Katz were actually the chief financial backers in the sale of the New Jersey Nets, but collectively, a group bought the team for $150 million in 1998. There is a group of 17 investors who have put money into the Nets organization and Katz tends to lead the group. Although the duo of Chambers and Katz work to make the organization profitable, just as they did in their prior business ventures, they don't want the money for themselves. Chambers and Katz have donated their 38 percent share of the profits to improving conditions in several New Jersey cities, including Newark, Trenton, Paterson, Camden and Jersey City.

Another aspect of this heartwarming story is that both Katz and

Chambers were born and raised in New Jersey. Katz grew up in Camden, New Jersey and graduated from Camden High School. Like many sports team owners, Katz began his career in the business world far away from the sports industry. He was raised by a single mother and attended Temple University on a scholarship. His summer job was selling dog food, which wasn't the most glamorous of jobs but it paid the bills. After Temple, he graduated first in his class from Dickinson Law School and established his own law firm of Katz, Ettin, Levine & Weber, P.A. He also has held the position of chairman and CEO of Kinney System Holding Corporation, which is a major parking company, prior to being a team owner. As Katz's hard work made him increasingly successful, he gave more and more back to those in need. Katz's success allowed him to dive into a totally different arena of business and to become the philanthropist that he truly was at heart.

Raymond Chambers, although he has the same big heart that Katz has, is quite a bit different from his philanthropic partner. He tries to stay out of the media as much as possible. Katz is more the spokesperson for the effort that he and Chambers take on in giving back through sports. Although this was the first venture in sports for both Chambers and Katz, they both have a good grasp of how to go about being effective in giving back to the community. They concluded that the very visible, public image of sports and athletes was a great pipeline to use for their cause. There needed to be role models showcasing the good that can be done, and that is exactly what Katz and Chambers are doing. Chambers, however, chooses to be more private about the issue and doesn't want public attention or acclaim for the good he is doing. He would rather the attention be focused on the people in need, perhaps prompting others to donate their time and resources.

Chambers, who also worked his way up from humble beginnings, was the son of a steel warehouse manager. He grew up in Newark and put himself through college at Rutgers University by playing keyboard in a band called the Ray-tones. He began his career as an accountant before he began investing on his own. The best business decision he made, prior to deciding to give his profits from the Nets to those in need, was creating a partnership with Wesray Capital Corporation. This was the corporation that established him financially, and allowed him to step down from his management position in the late 1980's. He then turned to philanthropy.

Both Chambers and Katz pledged their shares of the profits to the inner-city schools and the children living in New Jersey cities. The money actually goes to a trust called the Community Youth Organization, of which Katz is the co-chairman. Education is the main focal point of the Community Youth Organization. Specifically, the money goes towards minority education, scholarships and mentoring. The Boys and Girls Club of Camden and Newark, the two owner's hometowns, have been vastly improved as well. In addition to helping the kids of New Jersey, Katz is also very committed to the Jewish community. He has played a part in acquiring land and the construction of a new Jewish Community Campus both in Atlantic City and Cherry Hill, New Jersey. Chambers was also a vital contributor and fundraiser for the $190 million performing arts center project in Newark.

The new ownership took control of the New Jersey Nets in 1998. Their mission was not only to give back to the community through their financial donations, but also to get the Nets players more involved in community relations. Each player is expected to "adopt" a city in New Jersey and act as a mentor to the kids and members of that community. The owners realize that to many professional athletes this obligation may seem ludicrous and totally outside the scope of their responsibilities. The answer that Chambers and Katz have come up with to this opposition is simply not to bring those kinds of players to the Nets Organization. They are looking to hire athletes who share their view about the power athletics has to shape young lives and to accept that vision. There are many players in the NBA who don't fit that mold, but Chambers and Katz are committed to finding those who do. Thus far, the two have succeeded in discovering several players who are committed to their organizational philosophy and very willing to help out.

What Chambers and Katz have chosen to do is indeed very admirable, and what is even more commendable is that they are always looking for new ventures to take on and different ways to help others. There are so many people in need in the world and there certainly should be more people like Raymond Chambers and Lewis Katz.

Mike Ilitch
by Brian Wright

In today's sports world mostly dominated by the glamour and fame of the professional athletes many people working behind the scenes for the betterment of the sport get overlooked. One such person is Mike Ilitch, owner of the National Hockey League's Detroit Red Wings and Major League Baseball's Detroit Tigers. Many critics and analysts spend their time assessing the success of the owner of a franchise by the team's wins and losses, or the amount of money spent to sign players, or even the cost of tickets and concessions. Ilitch's contribution to the world of sports has made much more of an impact than just that short list of quantifiable items. As a young child, Ilitch dreamed of playing in Major League Baseball. He knew the opportunity to become a professional baseball player was a long shot, but he had set his mind on it and was determined. Little did he know at the time that he would become a member of an even more exclusive sports group as an owner of a professional sports franchise.

The path to success was not always smooth for Ilitch as he pursued a professional career in baseball. As a young man Ilitch was selected to join the Tiger organization as a player on one of its minor league teams. Playing shortstop, Ilitch was considered to be a great athlete who had a good eye and a strong bat. Though he had a more than respectable minor league career, Ilitch was never called up the Tigers.

This setback, which seemed a major obstacle at the time, would have a positive impact on his life for years to come. As his dreams of playing in the majors ended, Ilitch began to explore other alternatives to make a good living for himself and his family. Ilitch spent time deciding what he could be good at and what there was a market for and determined that his niche was in the restaurant business. As time progressed, his desire to open a restaurant of his own did as well. Ilitch decided that his main product would be pizza. With the entrepreneurial desire of owning his own pizza parlor, Ilitch did not have the financing or the experience to immediately take on his own store. He decided to approach a local businessman, an owner of a Detroit area night club, to pitch his pizza parlor. Ilitch presented the idea well enough to convince the man and began selling pizza out of the back room of the nightclub. Much to the surprise of everyone except Ilitch, the business began to boom and the demand for his pizza was rising.

As Ilitch's customer base grew, he knew he had established a successful business and wanted to find a way to expand it. Thus, Ilitch began looking for financing to move the business into its own establishment. After selling pizza door-to-door and taking out a small $15,000 loan, Ilitch and his wife Marian had made enough money to purchase their first store. In 1959 the pizza that was sold out of the backroom of a local night club was renamed Little Caesar's which was Marian's pet name for Mike. Today Little Caesar's is one of the largest take-out pizza restaurants throughout the United States and Canada. Ilitch took a simple dream and grew it into one of the nation's largest take-out pizza chains. Considered by many to be one of the top businessmen in the world, Ilitch has never become complacent.

In 1982, his passion for sports led him to the doorstep of the Detroit Red Wings of the National Hockey League. The then owners, the Norris family, had placed the Red Wings on the market for $8 million. Though the Red Wings were then one of the worst teams in the NHL, Ilitch knew their potential given their long tenure and successful history in Detroit. As he reminisced on the drastic growth of Little Caesar's, Ilitch realized what was possible when the organization is committed to putting a quality product out there for the public. Ilitch's determination to turn the organization around led to a quick change in performance on the ice. The team rapidly developed into one of the best teams in the NHL. Under Ilitch's reign, the Red Wings won ten Division Championships, four Western Conference Championships, four President's Trophies and three Stanley Cup titles. The support from the city of Detroit also increased under Ilitch's direction, achieving 367 consecutive sellouts at Joe Louis Arena. In 2004, *Forbes Magazine* listed the Detroit Red Wings as the most valuable franchise in the NHL at $256 million. *ESPN Magazine* also ranked the Detroit Red Wings as the eighth rated sports franchise in all of professional sports, as well as honoring Ilitch as the number one professional sports franchise owner in all of professional sports. It is awards and accolades such as these that display Ilitch's passion for success and his commitment to the organizations he operates.

Ilitch genuinely cared about the welfare of his players more than the record of the team. Truly committed to the education of the players, the Red Wings offered to pay 100 percent of the tuition for those players who wanted to complete their education. In 1991, more than 25 percent of the players enrolled in college courses thanks to Ilitch's commitment.

Though owning one of the largest pizza chains as well as one of the most prominent professional hockey teams was a task in itself, Ilitch felt that he could also assist the community of Detroit by purchasing and improving the Detroit Tigers of Major League Baseball. Ten years after purchasing the Detroit Red Wings Ilitch purchased sole ownership of the Detroit Tigers from Tom Monoghan. Though the Tigers have not achieved as much "on-the-field" success as the Red Wings, they are still regarded by most to be a well-run and potentially successful organization.

Ilitch's success in the Detroit community was not just achieved at the restaurant and professional sports levels. As a competing member of amateur athletics in his youth, Ilitch knew the role it played in his life, as well as the role it could play in positively affecting the lives of others. He wanted to somehow incorporate amateur athletics into the organizations he owned and add positive social value to the communities within the Detroit area. He decided to implement an amateur AAA Hockey Program under the Little Caesar's company umbrella. In this amateur hockey program there is the Little Caesar's Amateur Hockey League as well as the Little Caesar's Amateur Hockey Club. Through this outreach program Ilitch has touched the lives of over 200,000 young people throughout metropolitan Detroit. Ilitch's amateur hockey program has also produced 240 hockey players who have played or currently play collegiate hockey or in other professional hockey leagues. For Ilitch, achieving positive social influence in the community through amateur athletics was another way to reach the lives of youth and influence them to become positive contributing members of society. Ilitch's ability to see the "big picture" concerning our communities and develop a plan to positively change these communities is evidence of his creative and innovative leadership ability.

Today, Ilitch finds himself among few others who have achieved a great deal of success in the world of sports franchise owners as he has been inducted into the Hockey Hall of Fame in Toronto, Canada, as well as the Michigan Sports Hall of Fame. He has received numerous awards and accolades as a businessman and pioneer for positive social change in the sports industry. Mike Ilitch believes in the power of sports to impact the lives of others as it had positively impacted his youth, and he has employed his belief to work for the betterment of society.

Thomas "Satch" Sanders

by Jessica Bartter

The life of a professional athlete is more than guts, glory and glamour. The transition from high school and college to the pros is never predictable and often uncontrollable. Rookies are pulled in several different directions by their agents, their families, their coaches, their teammates and their own personal beliefs which are often challenged by the pressures of a new life in the fast lane of groupies, alcohol, drugs and money. Professional athletes go from the practice gym to the airport to a hotel to an arena, only to be off on an airplane to another city for the same routine over and over again. In the National Basketball Association teams play about 90 preseason and regular season games with a potential 28 more in the playoffs. This is equivalent to three or four high school or college seasons. The subsequent wear and tear on the athlete's body coupled with the emotional pressures can end the career of a great athlete too soon.

Thomas "Satch" Sanders was one member of the NBA whose hard work and durability enabled him to perform at the highest level game after game for years. In fact, during Sanders' 13 year career as a professional basketball player he played in 450 consecutive games. After a great career at New York University, Sanders was a highly valued player in the 1960 NBA Draft where he was the Boston Celtics' first and the eighth pick overall. Sanders spent all 13 years of his professional career with the Celtics where he was acclaimed for his defensive skills. While he was a force for the offense too, averaging 9.6 points per game for his career, it was his smart and talented play on the defensive end of the court that earned him recognition. Sanders played in 916 games, the 6th highest in Celtics history, totaling 22,164 minutes. He had 5,798 rebounds, 1,026 assists and 8,766 points. The 6 foot 6 center helped lead the Celtics to eight championships before retiring in 1973.

Like all athletes at the end of their careers, Sanders was faced with a difficult transition into the working world. In 1973, Sanders took the head coaching position of Harvard University's men's basketball program. He inherited a team with great potential including four high school All-Americans. Yet, the program had failed to capitalize on its talent and hoped Sanders would turn them around. Sanders utilized the tried and proven coaching strategy of legendary Coach Red Auerbach who focused on defense. Auerbach believed that most players enter the league with sufficient offensive skills and that it is their defense that requires the most attention. Sanders was known for his dedication as a defender so the strategy seemed like the perfect fit. Sanders also relied heavily on scouting reports and opponent films to develop a powerful offense, tough defense and a winning game strategy for his team. Before even stepping on the court, Sanders accomplished great feats. He was the first African-American to be named head coach at Harvard and the first African-American to coach basketball in the entire Ivy League.

Sanders' time with the Harvard Crimson was the perfect stepping stone to a coaching career in the NBA. And why not go where he was loved the most? Why not go where his number 16 jersey hung from the rafters? The fan-favorite returned to the green and gold of the Celtics as their coach during the 1977-1978 season and for part of 1978-1979. But the fates doomed Sanders' coaching career as injuries and unfortunate trades hurt the team. Satch left the Celtics before the end of his second campaign.

Sanders joined Richard Lapchick shortly after the founding of Northeastern University's Center for the Study of Sport in Society in 1984 as Associate Director. He helped conceive the Degree Completion Program and Community Service Program which became the cornerstones of the National Consortium for Academics and Sports which he helped create with Lapchick and Richard Astro in 1985. Now the NCAS is made up of more than 220 member institutions which have helped bring back more than 28,000 former student-athletes to finish their degrees. These athletes have worked with more than 14 million young people on conflict resolution, staying in school, violence prevention, saying no to drugs and alcohol, reading and much more. Sanders helped lay the foundation for what has become a large and impressive enterprise.

As a Celtic player in the late 1960's, Sanders was paid about $8,000 a season; compared to today's average NBA salary of $5 million. Sanders spent his off-season interning at an actuarial firm, working as a copywriter and selling Amway products. Sanders even took an insurance course one off-season planning for his retirement. While Sanders' transition into the working world was eased by the fact that during his day in the NBA, players usually had summer jobs anyway, he understood the transition for other athletes is not as simple. Especially in today's league where players make millions of dollars with their playing contract, endorsements and sponsor deals, only to leave the league a few years later, most without a college degree. Sanders recognized that the transition into the league is equally difficult, particularly for the teenage draft picks and young college dropouts. Interested in working with NBA players, Sanders joined the league offices of the NBA in 1987. He took on the challenging role of Vice-President and Director of Player Programs. Sanders' job entailed designing programs for current and former professional basketball players, focusing on rookies and veterans. The programs taught players how to cope with the special pressures associated with that status. Sanders oversaw an off-season player program that offered internships, classes and educational advancement opportunities so players might avoid the financial troubles that often comes hand in hand with temporary seven figure salaries. Sanders' programs also involved post-career counseling, educational development, employment opportunities, anti-drug and alcohol education, media training and non-profit foundation development.

Sanders wanted players to think of the life skills they would need after life on the court before it was too late. Through the NBA Player Programs, Sanders presented players with all the proper opportunities. During his 18 years in this department Sanders was able to develop relevant and interesting programs because he brought a wealth of experience to the job.

As a player, Sanders was once confronted in a club in Boston by a belligerent man. Jealousy drove the man to threaten Sanders and flash a gun that was concealed in his pants. Sanders was faced with the options of fighting back, surrendering or walking away. To no one's surprise, except to the belligerent individual, Sanders sat down and turned his back to the man antagonizing him. In the process he made himself a bigger target for insults and verbal abuse but dodged the inevitable violent and potentially dangerous attack. The man drew attention to himself which allowed management to take heed and escort him out. Sanders learned that, to an extent, it was possible to control his environment and he later passed on this valuable lesson to countless players.

In contrast, Sanders learned the difficulties in controlling one's surrounding environment in the face of racism. After accepting the Harvard coaching position, he purchased a home in an upscale suburb of Boston. Some neighbors and community members made Sanders feel unwelcome by yelling obscenities outside his house late at night and dumping trash on his lawn. Though Sanders was scarred by the experience, he learned from it and was able to use it and other experiences to work effectively with today's NBA players. Many of the players with whom Sanders worked moved on from basketball to successful careers in a variety of different fields. And while some may have been successful without Sanders' guidance, the fact is that the increased number of players who have successful post-basketball careers since Sanders assumed his position in the League office is proof that his impact on NBA players has been very substantial. From the time when he first donned a Celtic uniform in 1960, he has utilized his searing intelligence and his personal warmth and charm to help his fellow players. The NBA is a much better organization because Satch Sanders was a part of it for so many decades.

CHAPTER 10

COMING TO AMERICA

America has long been viewed as a haven and a refuge for oppressed peoples. Whether America is viewed in a favorable or unfavorable light at any given moment in its history, we always find individuals oppressed in their own country who come to America for freedom.

Coming to America is about four boys who escaped the horrors of their own countries and who came to the United States where they became successful athletes.

Gilbert Tuhabonye came here after most of his family and friends were murdered in Burundi. His own body was covered with burns.

Mohammad Rafiq's parents made a dangerous escape from Afghanistan to provide him and his siblings with an opportunity to achieve the American dream.

Sevin Sucurovic left Bosnia with his family to escape the ethnic cleansing that was ravaging the former Yugoslavia.

Macharia Yuot, one of the Sudanese Lost Boys, came to the United States to obtain freedom from the civil war which was claiming millions of lives in Sudan.

Tuhabonye graduated from Abilene Christian, where he was an All-American cross country runner and won an NCAA Division II title. Yuot became a soccer player at West Catholic High School in Philadelphia and later enrolled in Widener University where he ran cross country. Rafiq won a basketball scholarship at Idaho State University. Sucurovic was a football player at the University of Kentucky. All survived a personal horror to tell America the stories of the conflicts in their homelands.

Gilbert Tuhabonye

by Jessica Bartter

Many of us became aware of the Tutsi – Hutu conflict through our knowledge of global politics or interest in international news. Many have seen the movies "Hotel Rwanda" and "Sometimes in April." Gilbert Tuhabonye was there and witnessed the murder of his classmates, friends and teachers and narrowly escaped with his own life.

Tuhabonye was raised in Burundi, a hilly and mountainous, landlocked central African country that borders Rwanda. Tribal warfare has devastated the country for decades, leaving the fertile land mostly underdeveloped. Sparse resources and political turmoil have left Burundi as one of the poorest countries in Africa and in the world. The enormity of the conflict between the Tutsi minority with the Hutu majority contradicts the small size of the country.

As a seventh grader, Tuhabonye began developing his cross country skills by running five miles each way to and from school everyday. As a junior in high school, Tuhabonye's pastime began to put him in the spotlight. His athletic skills stood out in the 400 and 800 meter events. At age 18, while attending high school biology class, Tuhabonye was subjected to torture and death, memories he still sees in his nightmares. The incident was instigated on October 21, 1993 by the Tutsi-led assassination of Burundi's first democratically-elected president who also happened to be the first member of the Hutu tribe to hold office.

Tuhabonye's high school quickly became a target for retribution to the Hutu soldiers determined to kill Tutsi tribesmen. Without adequate warning, Tuhabonye, his classmates, teachers and other high school staff were surrounded. The Tutsi tribe members were stripped naked and beaten. Tuhabonye was struck in the chest with a heavy stick that caused him to cough up blood for two weeks. The tortured and beaten Tutsis were rounded up in the schoolroom, sprayed with gasoline and then locked inside a gasoline covered shed that was lit on fire by Hutu soldiers. As the students pounded on the door and screamed for mercy, Tuhabonye stumbled in the panic and found himself lying beneath the burning bodies of his classmates. Those bodies formed a human shield and saved his life.

After eight hours of enduring the stench of burning flesh, the sounds of agony and the sight of death, fear for his own life led Tuhabonye to a brave escape. After the fire died down, he grabbed the nearby skeleton of a dead friend and used it to break a window. After escaping the grim site of live cremation, Tuhabonye was forced to run from Hutus who spotted him fleeing. Since Tuhabonye was burning from his daring break out, the Hutus decided to leave him and let him die in the grass. But Tuhabonye survived the severe burns on his arms, legs and back and was finally found by Tutsis in the field two days later. At the hospital where he was taken for treatment, Tuhabonye was forced to sleep on the floor, because no beds were available.

Word spread quickly of Tuhabonye's survival, the only one to do so of the 250 individuals who perished that day at his school, and he was dubbed a spiritual being. The Tutsis hailed him as a god, while the Hutus feared him as the devil. Tuhabonye later came in contact with a Hutu soldier involved in the massacre. The soldier dropped to his knees in front of Tuhabonye and begged to be killed. Despite his traumatic experiences, Tuhabonye has forgiveness in his heart. He told the soldier to "get up, I forgive you"[1] and even offered to talk about it.

It took Tuhabonye a long time to fully recover, but the scars on his body will never let him forget. Tuhabonye began jogging again about a year after the incident and eventually returned to running competitively approximately a year later. In April of 1996, Tuhabonye was awarded a grant by the International Olympic Committee enabling him to move to the United States. Living in La Grange, Georgia, Tuhabonye trained for the 1996 Summer Olympic Games in Atlanta. Though he failed to make the Burundi team, he did carry the Olympic torch. An ironic celebration with fire, Tuhabonye wondered if it was in God's plan for him along.

Tuhabonye later enrolled at Abilene Christian University in Texas to continue his education and pursue his athletic dreams. In 1998, Tuhabonye was an All-American cross country runner and won the NCAA Division II indoor title at 800 meters.

Amazingly, Gilbert Tuhabonye continues to speak forgiveness, and like many other athletes he relies on sport to overcome his obstacles. Tuhabonye has successfully tried to use sport to show the world that there is more to Burundi than murder and mayhem. Visible individuals like Tuhabonye, the epitome of hope and humanity, open our eyes to an unfamiliar and horrifying world of genocide and help teach us the art of forgiveness.

[1] O'Connor, Ian. "Burundi's Tuhabonye works on his running a long way from war-torn home" *Knight Ridder Tribune*, July 25, 1996.

Mohammad Rafiq

by Jessica Bartter

As an Afghanistan-born Muslim, Mohammad Rafiq stood out as a minority student on the campus of the predominantly white Idaho State University in Pocatello, a small city in southeastern Idaho. Rather than shy away from talking about his culture and beliefs, he took it upon himself to educate non-Muslims about the religion that is so important to him and his family. Rafiq embraces his differences and celebrates the United States for the freedom it provides to individuals of all faiths.

Rafiq's home country is extremely different: 99 percent of Afghanis are either Sunni or Shi'a Muslims. But Rafiq calls the United States home now. In 1979, the Soviet Union invaded Afghanistan. Shortly thereafter, Rafiq's father was arrested for working with an American company in Kabul. When he was finally released, Rafiq's parents wasted no time in escaping their war-torn country. His parents, two older siblings and two uncles headed for the border between Afghanistan and Pakistan in the dark of the night. The border was patrolled by Soviet troops and his family was forced to hide in a cave while soldiers battled right outside the entrance. Rafiq was just a baby when they fled and his cries had to be muffled in a blanket to avoid capture. His family did not bring any food with them and were forced to sleep in the cave but successfully crossed the border into Pakistan.

Rafiq and his family lived in Pakistan as refugees for eight months until their applications for asylum and their church sponsorship were approved in the United States. Rafiq's first American experience was in Seattle, Washington. His family later joined other family members in Thorton, Colorado before settling in Yuba City, California. By this time,

Rafiq was in the fifth grade and began playing basketball with his older brother at the local recreation center.

Rafiq worked hard at the sport that he loved and in 2000 earned a full athletic scholarship to play basketball at Idaho State University, an NCAA Division I program. Rafiq felt a sense of accomplishment as his parents gleamed with pride in the realization that their American dream for him had been fulfilled. Rafiq's parents did not have the opportunity for higher education in Afghanistan and though they could not help their three children with their homework in the United States, they taught them the importance of becoming educated. Rafiq, the youngest of three, had just ensured his right to a college degree, becoming their third and last child to do so.

At Idaho State, Rafiq made the athletic honor roll in 2001 and 2002. Life at Idaho State was exciting and successful until tragedy struck our nation, hitting Rafiq too close to home. It was the fall of his sophomore year when 19 Islamic terrorists simultaneously hijacked four U.S. domestic commercial airliners crashing two into the World Trade Center, one into the Pentagon and the fourth into a rural field in Pennsylvania, commonly known now as 9-11. The attacks of 9-11 caused 2,986 deaths and changed the lives of millions. Americans were rightfully angry but many misdirected their anger toward Middle Easterners living in this country. Incidents of harassment and hate crimes against Middle Easterners became increasingly common. Nine people were murdered as a result of this backlash. Many were Sikh, mistaken for Muslim. Many American Muslims say they have experienced increased discrimination and suspicion since 9-11. Many are also frustrated that their religion is often viewed as extremist, even violent.

As a proud Muslim and a proud American, Rafiq felt a strong sense of responsibility to teach his team at Idaho State that being Muslim is not about suicide missions and hatred. After discussing the incident with his teammates and coaches, one coach decided to contact the National Collegiate Athletic Association (NCAA) where they determined that Mohammad Rafiq was the only Afghani Division I men's basketball player in the United States. Rafiq agreed to do an interview with ESPN's SportsCenter because he wanted to be a positive role-model for the Muslim and NCAA student-athlete communities. Later in 2002, he was selected to represent all of Idaho State's student-athletes at the NCAA Foundation Leadership Conference.

Unfortunately, Rafiq was needed elsewhere and was unable to attend the Conference. Following the events of September 11, 2001,

Rafiq's father was hired by the United States Department of Defense to work as an interpreter in Afghanistan which requires him to be out of the country 11 months of the year. Simultaneously, Rafiq's mother developed health issues that required tender care and attention.

Devoted to his family, Rafiq withdrew from Idaho State University and forfeited his scholarship to move back to California and provide his mother with the necessary assistance. Rafiq's mother only speaks and writes in Farsi, the most widely spoken Persian Language, so he escorted her to psychotherapy appointments where he translated for her. Rafiq also served as her translator through her diagnosis, treatment and surgery for breast cancer. Rafiq did not let the circumstances prevent him from finishing his education. While he was living with and caring for his mother in Yuba City, he enrolled in the University of California, Davis, approximately 55 miles away. Rafiq also joined the UC Davis basketball team though he did not receive a scholarship. Rafiq commuted over 100 miles a day to practice and class and then back home to attend medical appointments with his mother.

Rafiq juggled his responsibilities well but after one year as a student-athlete at UC Davis, Rafiq was forced to quit because of medical issues of his own. He experienced hip and back pain that was so excruciating it kept him up at night and made walking very difficult. His condition perplexed the athletic trainers and eight different specialists until finally he was diagnosed with a genetic deformity in his hip bones. Normal activity and years of basketball had resulted in bone-on-bone contact, tearing most of the cartilage in his hips. The specialist warned Rafiq that without special surgery, he would most likely need two hip replacements by the age of 35.

In what should have been his final semester in March of 2004, Rafiq went in for the recommended surgery on just one of the hips. Doctors surgically dislocated his right hip and inserted metal screws. Because he was in a wheelchair for six weeks, on crutches for the following six weeks and then had difficulty walking for a month, Rafiq was forced to withdraw from UC Davis. Rafiq scheduled surgery on his left hip in December 2004 but was better prepared for the necessary recovery time. He planned to attend UC Davis in the winter part-time and return full-time in the spring to avoid the mobility issues he faced with the first surgery. Rafiq's careful planning enabled him to juggle five different jobs and maintain a grade point average above 3.0. Rafiq's family responsibilities also grew as he got married and right before his second surgery, welcomed their first born, a son, into the world.

Because he cherished his time spent at Idaho State, Rafiq returned there to earn his master's degree in physical education with an athletic administration emphasis. Rafiq feels a strong sense of commitment to Idaho State because of the opportunity it provided him, not only with the athletic scholarship and the chance to earn a college degree, but also the support they offered during the many difficult and trying times he faced in his college basketball career and his personal life. Rafiq plans to return the favor by helping other young student-athletes realize their opportunities to receive a college education when financially, their options may be limited. Rafiq hoped to serve the Idaho State men's basketball team as an assistant coach, earning valuable experience to one day be a head coach of a Division I men's basketball program. Rafiq hopes his master's degree and his experience as a coach will later lead him to an athletics director position.

Rafiq is a basketball player, Afghani, husband, father, Muslim, coach and American. It is his diverse background and experiences that have enabled him to respond to challenges with a sense of humor and determination while recognizing the importance of things and prioritizing his many responsibilities. His devotion and appreciation for his culture and family have enabled him to embrace those who show a similar passion to the people and things they value most, despite the fact that they may differ from him. Mohammad Rafiq has faced the personal adversities in his life with maturity, motivation and an optimistic attitude in hopes that he will make a positive lasting impact on future generations. He already has.

Sevin Sucurovic

by Jessica Barttter

Just nine years old, a day in the life of Sevin "Sevy" Sucurovic consisted of constant ringing from surrounding gunfire, fear that his father might not return home from the front lines of war, and a five-mile walk each way to and from school in the poverty stricken, economically disadvantaged country of Bosnia.

Yet, like many children, Sucurovic dreamed of a professional career in sports, as either an athlete or an executive and even hoped to go to college one day and be the first in his family to earn a college degree. Though his dreams have been met by challenge after challenge and hurdle after hurdle, it would take much more to stop this courageous student-athlete.

The breakout of the Bloody War created havoc in the life of the young. In addition to the unrelenting concern for his father, Sucurovic said the "best years of my childhood were spent just struggling to survive instead of learning about life and pursuing my dreams." Sucurovic recalls "sleeping dressed in four pairs of pants and three or four jackets during the war all in order to have some clothes to change into later if we needed to leave our house quickly because of danger." While most would, Sucurovic didn't let his dreams die, and even turned to sports as an outlet. Kicking around the soccer ball served as an escape from the reality of a war-torn home. Even the "path to school was unsafe and I was constantly wondering if a grenade would strike at any moment killing me and everyone around me." Sucurovic found a calling in sport as he learned early on its impact on society and individuals like himself.

Five long years later, in 1995, the Dayton Peace Agreement was signed and there was a cease fire on both sides. The Bloody War left Bosnia, Sucurovic's home, in a desultory state. No jobs were available and even today, the country's unemployment rate exceeds 44 percent. The death toll from the war was estimated at 200,000 by the Bosnian government, and the United Nations agencies recorded approximately 1,325,000 refugees and exiles. Sucurovic's father decided it was time to pursue a better life outside Bosnia and believed the best opportunities for his wife and two boys would be in the United States. However, in order to come, they had to have a family member already living in the U.S. who would sponsor them. Fortunately, for the Sucurovics, they had relatives in Boston, Massachusetts. Unfortunately, the necessary paperwork took nearly two years to complete.

Finally, on February 17, 1998, the Sucurovic family left what had been their only home with nothing but three suitcases, $2,000 and high hopes. Two days later, Sucurovic first set his eyes and feet on American culture and soil at the age of 16. Success didn't come overnight, but the Sucurovic family was accustomed to working hard. Sucurovic's father was forced to work two and sometimes three jobs while his mother worked two of her own as well. Even Sucurovic worked at a nearby grocery store while going to high school.

Sucurovic's love for soccer quickly came into play. During a P.E. class at his new school, he was spotted kicking a ball by Coach Simpson, the football coach. Simpson was greatly impressed. Though Sucurovic did not know what football was and had never seen a game played, he greeted the football coach's interest with curiosity for a new learning experience. Sucurovic made the junior varsity team with little training and, after guidance from Coach Simpson, he was quickly competing for a varsity kicking spot.

Then Sucurovic's luck abruptly ran out when leaving football practice one day, he was struck from behind by a car whose driver was blinded by the sun. X-rays revealed fractures in the C1 and C2 bones, the top two vertebrae in his neck. The accident and injuries that could have left him paralyzed and that should have required surgery didn't break his spirit. Since the surgery would have stopped him from playing football, the new sport he had just discovered, he opted not to have the surgery and to let time heal his neck. Ironically, the driver of the vehicle happened to be the varsity kicker.

All this happened within the first year of Sucurovic being in this country, yet, he continued to pursue his dreams. He returned for his senior year during the 1999-2000 season and earned the recognition he deserved. Sucurovic made the All-City Team and earned Academic All-State Honorable Mention despite the fact that he was still learning to read and write fluently in English. Sucurovic enrolled at the University of Kentucky and even secured a walk-on spot on the Wildcats football squad. After two years as a "forgotten walk-on," Sucurovic earned playing time in his third year and went on to earn a scholarship in his fourth and fifth years. Sucurovic graduated as the fourth all-time leader for a single season punting average in Kentucky's history and even led the SEC in punting average his senior season.

Sucurovic's life experiences have brought many questions to his mind like, "How did I survive the whole long Bloody War without any injuries just to come to the United States in pursuit of a better life and be hit by a car? Why did I have to come to the United States to achieve equal opportunity? Why couldn't I, nor generations before me, have a childhood that American kids have enjoyed for years?" Though Sucurovic has not learned the answers to all these questions and may never do so, his most important lesson has come from sports. He believes sport has changed his life and he has witnessed first hand the positive impact it can have on a society. He has seen it can bring individuals from so many walks of life together to act as one, with common goals and common dreams.

Macharia Yuot

by Jessica Bartter

Fighting starvation, exhaustion, dehydration, the sub-Sahara sun, wild animals and militia gunfire describes just one day of Macharia Yuot's three year journey to freedom. A native of the Dinka tribe of Southern Sudan, Yuot was forced to flee his homeland and his family because of civil war that has raged on since 1983. At the innocent age of nine, Yuot left his parents, brother and three sisters because government troops were reportedly killing adults, enslaving girls and kidnapping boys. The boys who were kidnapped were used as cannon fodder or were forced to walk through minefields risking their lives to lead their violent captors to safety. In attempting to avoid their impending capture, Yuot and more than 26,000 young boys fled their village. Finding safety in numbers, Yuot began his journey with dozens of other boys. Together they walked about 1,000 miles without a steady supply of food or water, a lack of shelter and no adult guidance or supervision. Thousands lost their lives along the way, succumbing to fatigue, animal predators, gunfire, disease or malnutrition. Yuot persevered and 1,000 miles and two months later was one of the lucky ones who survived the arduous journey. From the story of Peter Pan, international aid workers named the survivors the "Lost Boys of Sudan" when they crossed Sudan's eastern border into Ethiopia.

After about three years in Ethiopia, the country's government changed leaving the Lost Boys unwelcome and on foot once again. The orphans were forced away in 1991 by more gunfire. The journey proved to be a deadly one again. As they were chased by government tanks and armed militia from Ethiopia, the boys frantically tried to cross the River Gilo and many were consumed by the river, either by drowning or by the crocodiles. They traveled another 400 miles along the Sudanese and Ethiopian border eventually crossing into Kenya about a year later. They were received into a refugee camp called Kakuma where survivors finally settled, and where Yuot received much of his schooling and even played soccer. It is estimated that only about 10,000 boys, less than half, survived this four year and still incomplete journey.

The story of the Lost Boys could not be ignored and in 1999, the United States committed to provide asylum to about 3,600 of the orphans. With the help of the Office of the United Nations High Commissioner for Refugees, the U.S. Department of State began transferring these youth to the U.S. for resettlement processing. Yuot was sponsored by the Lutheran Church and resettled in Philadelphia. As he arrived in the winter in the northeastern United States, the weather did not help Yuot's plight. Yet, he was welcomed into a home with several other Lost Boys and enrolled in the West Catholic High School as a junior. Yuot joined the soccer team. The athletic skills he brought with him from Africa helped him adjust to life in America.

In his senior year in 2002, Yuot began running competitively at the encouragement of friends who recognized his talent. He was not a stranger to long distance running and instantly excelled on the cross country team. Despite it being his first year on the team, Yuot finished third in the 3,200 meters at the Catholic League Championships which were held at Widener University in Chester, Pennsylvania. That was the first encounter Widener's track and field coach, Vince Touey, had with Yuot but he quickly recognized his potential as a collegiate athlete. Yuot was excited with the prospect that he could attend college and continue his new love for running.

While in Kenya, Yuot had studied Swahili, Arabic and English in addition to his native Dinka language. Yet, at the time of his high school graduation, Yuot was not fluent enough in English to enter college. Yuot studied English intensely at the Language Company's Pennsylvania Language Institute for several months. The Institute is located on the campus of Widener University so Yuot practiced with the student-athletes after each day's class. Yuot's intense studying paid off and after acing the English Test, Yuot enrolled in Widener in the spring semester of 2003. That semester, despite missing the fall cross country competitions, Yuot finished second in the Middle Atlantic Conference (MAC) Championships in the 5,000 meters in outdoor track and field. He ran it in 15 minutes and .12 seconds, missing the win and the national qualifying time by a mere five seconds. In his first cross country season the next fall, Yuot finished third in his first race, and then won every race thereafter, including the MAC cross country title when he ran five miles in 26 minutes and 19 seconds, beating the next closest opponent by 23 seconds. His domination in the sport and leadership on the team have been pleasant surprises to Coach Touey. By winning the MAC title, Yuot secured his spot at the NCAA Division III Cross Country Championships where he was the runner up in 2003. He also won the MAC cross country title in 2004. Later that academic year, Yuot took home the MAC Championships in the 1,500 meter run for indoor track, as well as the 5,000 meter run and the steeplechase events in outdoor track. These accomplishments earned Yuot the right to call himself the first Widener University student-athlete to receive All-American honors in cross country, indoor track and field and outdoor track and field.

Yuot received the 2004 NCAA Inspiration Award, which is part of the NCAA Honors Program. The Inspiration Award is presented to a coach or administrator currently associated with intercollegiate athletics or to a current or former varsity letter-winner at an NCAA member institution who when faced with a life-altering situation overcame the event through perseverance, dedication and determination and now serves as a role model, giving hope and inspiration to others.

Regardless of Yuot's personal struggles, it is evident that he is an accomplished athlete and dedicated student. Yuot knows his mother is now living in Kenya and that his father has died. The violence and death that has devastated the Sudanese has amounted to what is arguably one of the most brutal wars of the past century. Civilians have been targeted over and over, either by deadly raids or forced famine. According to estimates by the U.S. State Department, the combination of war, famine and disease in southern Sudan have killed over 2 million people and displaced another 4 million such as Yuot and his family. Though relief workers from the United Nations and Red Cross scrambled in the 1990's to provide the Lost Boys shelter, food and medical attention, their sheer number made it overwhelming. So did their needs resulting from the long-term effects of hunger, disease and dehydration. Many refugees remain at Kakuma surviving on food rations and a gallon of water a day for cleaning, cooking and drinking provided by aid organizations.

Yuot majored in psychology and social work and hopes to continue running beyond college and to one day work with people. Having lost everything, Yuot appreciates that he has a good place to stay, good friends and a good school. Yuot believes "I have everything."[1]

[1] McKindra, Leilana. "Early trials indicate Widener runner can go the distance" *The NCAA News*, April 26, 2004.

CHAPTER 11

LEGENDS LIVE ON

We are often asked what we want to be remembered for. Many of us, no matter how many good things we do and what life path we choose, would live on in the memory of our families and friends. But then there are some whose life contributions are so great that the memory of what they did while they graced the planet will continue to live on and bring inspiration to future generations. Such are the stories of the seven lives portrayed in *Legends Live On.*

Jerry Richardson, an African-American man, led a group of Native American girls who happened to play basketball to great success on the court on their Native American reservation. What Richardson and the girls did for others on their reservation helped many youngsters overcome the high rate of alcoholism and the high dropout rate from school. Still a young man, Richardson was killed in a car crash.

Coach Perry Reese, Jr., also an African-American, went to an Amish community where he was the only person of color. Initially resisted, he eventually won the hearts of everyone in the community who all came together to mourn his loss.

Derrick Thomas and Reggie White, two of football's greatest players were both taken from us early in their lives. But it was not until after they made extraordinary contributions in their communities where they devoted so much of their time to helping others.

Ewing Kauffman was the owner of the Kansas City Royals. His philanthropy enabled thousands of people and dozens of organizations to do work to better our society.

Coach Dave Sanders led student-athletes at Columbine High

School to success on the playing field. The beloved coach gave his life on the tragic day of the shootings at Columbine trying to save more students until he was finally stopped by the two shooters.

Finally, Ralph Wiley, one of America's most thoughtful writers who mentored most of today's successful African-American sports journalists, died of heart failure when he was just 52 years old.

The legacies of all of these people will always be remembered by those they touched and those who have heard and read about them.

Jerry Richardson

by Drew Tyler

August 31, 1996 was supposed to be one of the greatest days in the history of the University of Central Florida's athletic department. UCF had just moved up to Division IA football and had celebrated an exciting come-from-behind victory over the College of William and Mary in their first ever Division IA game. Sadly, within a few hours of the game, a night of celebration for the UCF athletic department ended in tragedy. Around 3:00 a.m., head women's basketball coach, Jerry Richardson, was killed when a stolen car traveling nearly 100 mph ran a red light and broadsided Richardson's van. Richardson was just 40 years old.

Only four years into his coaching career at the University of Central Florida, Richardson had become a strong force on campus and in the surrounding Orlando community. At the time of his death, Richardson served on the Board of the Coalition for the Homeless. While balancing a hectic basketball schedule with his philanthropic activities, Richardson actively gave the Coalition his time and involvement. After inheriting a basketball program in significant need of rebuilding, Richardson guided the Golden Knights to a conference tournament championship and UCF's first NCAA tournament appearance in his final season. Richardson had captured the attention of fans with the program he was building, but more importantly, he was using his past experiences to guide the overall development of the young women whom he coached.

As a talented young athlete in Texas, Richardson's basketball playing career ended abruptly. Citing a bad attitude, Richardson's high school coach and athletic director refused to recommend him to colleges, essentially blackballing him from ever having the opportunity to play collegiate basketball. Using his admitted mistakes as motivation for future success, Richardson attended Northwestern on a track scholarship and went on to receive a master's degree at Louisiana Tech. The keys to Richardson's perseverance were maintaining a positive attitude and a belief that nothing was beyond his reach.

Following college, Richardson was in need of a job and decided to accept a mid-semester job opening to teach English on the Navajo Nation Reservation in Shiprock, New Mexico. It was a culture shock for both Richardson and his students at Three Nations High School. Most of them had never seen a black man before and now they were to respect him as their educator and mentor. Though it was a challenge, Richardson gained the admiration of his students. In time, Richardson and his students learned to appreciate one another's cultures.

After encouragement from other teachers and town residents, Richardson agreed to serve as the head coach of the women's basketball team. During his nine years in Shiprock from 1982 to 1993, Richardson guided a previously unknown Lady Chieftans basketball program to four State Championships. The skill the Lady Chieftans developed under Coach Richardson caught the attention of friends and family members who followed the team by car to every game no matter how far it was.

In one critical cultural clash incident, Coach Richardson and his team were forced to confront and discuss the stereotypes that society had placed of each of their cultures. The team met in a hotel room right before their first state championship game to hash out the issues they were facing. Richardson made his team expectations clear and the girls began to emerge from their shy shells. Once Richardson opened up and showed the girls that he believed in them, they were able build confidence and believe in themselves. The Three Nations High School went on to win their first state championship.

Jerry Richardson and the story of the Shiprock Lady Chieftans is a story that rivals that of the Milan Miracle that was captured so wonderfully in *Hoosiers*. When Richardson arrived in Shiprock, the city and the team was a shambles. It was a town bereft of hope, and too many Navajo's had fallen prey to the hopelessness of Native Americans on reservations which manifests itself in joblessness and alcoholism. Gradually, year by year, Richardson changed all that as he coached the freshman, junior varsity and varsity Lady Chieftans simultaneously. Fathers stopped drinking; mothers and fathers gained a new sense of pride in their daughters and through their daughters, in themselves. Unemployment rates and alcoholism decreased. An entire community was reborn. Funds were obtained to build a new basketball gymnasium which was the finest building in all of Shiprock.

Richard Astro was serving as the UCF Provost when he met Richardson at an NCAS banquet. They talked about Shiprock, and Astro, in charge of the search for a new UCF women's basketball coach, probed Richardson's interest in the position. When Richardson didn't object, Astro arranged a site visit with Richardson in Shiprock. On a frigid Friday night in February, Astro, who had traveled from Florida to New Mexico to see Richardson and his teams in action, drove onto the Navajo Nation to see for himself. Absolutely amazed, he later told friends "it was Hoosiers on the reservation." An entire town was there – rallied behind the coach and his players – and, in the varsity game, Astro watched the Lady Chieftans dismantle a Farmington team with players a head taller and generally more talented than Richardson's charges. The fans were in a veritable frenzy, and those sitting next to Astro told him that this was commonplace every time "Coach's girls take to the court." That night, after Richardson had coached (and won) his three games, he and Astro talked long into the night. Astro felt guilty about seducing Richardson to Orlando. He told him as much. But when Richardson said that after ten years he needed new challenges and that he was confident that his assistants could maintain the quality of the program he had created, Astro called Richardson the next morning and offered him the UCF job. Richardson accepted. Returning to Orlando, Astro told acting-UCF President Bob Bryan that he had never hired anyone with more enthusiasm. When Richardson came to Orlando and met Bryan and other members of the UCF community, they concurred.

Richardson changed the lives of his athletes by preaching the importance of education. In a community filled with poverty and alcoholism and at school with a 50 percent dropout rate, Richardson saw 80 percent of his student-athletes not only graduate high school, but with his help and under his guidance, many went on to college.

Jerry Richardson was a quiet and introspective man, and even those who knew him best admitted that he was a private person. His friends respected his privacy because they knew that the public Jerry Richardson was a great teacher, a great coach, and a man who had not just improved, but had literally saved scores of young Navajos and their parents in Shiprock and had measurably enhanced the academic and athletic success of the young women he coached at UCF. Billy Joel wrote that "the good die young." Jerry Richardson was very, very good, and he died much too young.

Perry Reese, Jr.

by Drew Tyler

In the heart of Berlin, Ohio lies the largest Amish settlement in the world. It is a town without a high school football team, a fast food restaurant, or even a traffic light. Not surprisingly, when Perry Reese, Jr. was asked to become the assistant basketball coach at Hiland High School in Berlin, the entire town was skeptical. After all, Reese was African-American, Catholic, single. How would he fit into an entirely Amish community? At first, Reese found life in Berlin to be very difficult. He received threatening phone calls and at one point was denied a place to live because of the color of his skin. Reese, however, refused to let his unfortunate welcome deter him from teaching the game of basketball to the young people of Berlin, and in time became a beloved member of the Amish community.

Reese stuck out like a sore thumb in Berlin. Not only was Reese the only African-American in all of eastern Holmes County, but he was also a Catholic in a community where children grow up learning about how their ancestors were at one time burned at the stake by Catholics during the Reformation. Furthermore, Reese was a former college dropout who was not even qualified to teach at the high school so he took a job at Berlin Wood Products. A year later Reese became the head basketball coach after the former head coach quit. In a community averse to change, Reese was suddenly in one of the most important positions in town.

Working all day at Berlin Wood Products, Reese had a difficult time getting to know members of the Amish community. Many of them honestly believed that he was a spy sent to keep an eye on the Amish. Dubbed the original Black Amishman, Reese shrugged off the constant ridicule and kept on smiling, laughing and most importantly, winning basketball games. Winning was probably the only reason that Reese was able to stay in Berlin. After guiding the Hawks to 49 wins in their first 53 games and to the 1986 state semifinals, it wasn't long before Reese was one of the most highly admired men in Berlin.

It wasn't just winning that helped Reese win over the Amish community. As time went by the people of Berlin began to realize that his values were virtually the exact same as theirs. Reese fit in as coach and teacher because he taught the virtues of the Amish: hard work, discipline and respect. Furthermore, Reese was humble, unselfish, reverent and family-oriented. He made sure not to let winning go to his head, required that his players pray before and after each game, and made sure that his young men respected their families. In many ways, his actions made Reese seem more dedicated to the Amish beliefs than many in the Amish community.

After finally earning a college degree, Reese became even more entrenched in the community when he began to teach history and current events at Hiland High School. As students and parents spent more and more time with Reese, his role became much more than just a coach and educator. Each morning Reese greeted every student who arrived at school. He had an open door policy for students to speak with him about race, religion, relationships and other troubles and on Sundays he would take his players to church. Amazingly, Reese's home even became a hangout for students and a place where parents trusted their kids to stay the night. Reese had become a teacher, coach, role model, friend and in every way a valued community member.

When it was discovered that Reese had been diagnosed with a malignant, inoperable, brain tumor, the entire community flocked to his bedside. Within days, hundreds of people crowded the hospital hallways waiting for one last opportunity to speak with "Coach." Former players flew in from Atlanta, Chicago, South Carolina and even Germany for a prayer vigil that drew more than 800 people quietly reflecting on the life of a man who had dedicated so much of his life to their children.

On the day he died, 17 years after his arrival to Berlin, the halls of Hiland High School became a celebration of Reese's life. Six ministers and three counselors walked through the halls to comfort students and teachers. Many students spent time in silent prayer well others gathered to tell stories in remembrance of Coach Reese. The outpouring of love and support would be unusual in any community, but in a town like Berlin it was unheard of. Most likely, all of the love and attention would have just made Reese feel uncomfortable in person, but the impact he had made on the children of Berlin was something that everyone wanted remembered.

Through the game of basketball, Reese brought magic to Berlin. Using the game as a tool to bridge the gap between the Amish and the modern world, Reese showed the Amish community that his values were the same as theirs. Reese brought the town together by building a winning basketball team. He taught his players hard work, discipline and respect and made sure they placed God, family and education before basketball. As a teacher, Reese became a father figure to every student in Hiland High School. He was a role model and a friend with whom students knew they could share their troubles. When asked, most people in Berlin are unable to even put into words the impact that Coach Reese had on their lives. Reese's journey was undoubtedly unique, amazing and really quite magical.

Derrick Thomas

by Stacy Martin

Derrick Thomas was a man capable of inciting fear and instilling hope in the hearts of men. It is hard to accept the idea of one heart embodying both compassion and brutality, but Thomas was the epitome of both. He was one of the greatest linebackers of all time on the football field, but Thomas was also a great humanitarian. Fans normally recognize football players by the number or name on the back of their jerseys. Kansas City fans knew Derrick Thomas, number 58, simply as Derrick. His contributions off the field far outweighed the significance of his record breaking performances on the field. The lives he brightened through the generosity of his kind spirit will remain as symbols of what goodness and concern for our fellow man can accomplish. Thomas truly demonstrated how sports can better this world and the value of helping someone who is less fortunate than oneself.

It would have been easy for Thomas to follow a different path in life. He never really knew his father. Captain Robert Thomas' B-52 Bomber was shot down during Operation Linebacker II in Vietnam when Thomas was only five years old. The loss that he felt was manifest in his juvenile delinquency. He was arrested for stealing a car and burglarizing a home, and his mother frequently prayed for his safe return from the Miami, Florida streets when she heard gunshots and sirens. Thomas was one of the lucky ones. It's almost as if someone was looking out for him.

A number of adults stepped in to provide him with some guidance or at least deter him from his youthful transgressions. Because these individuals took the time to care about him, he survived a difficult adolescence and safely arrived at the University of Alabama to play football. He was an All-American and broke the career record for the number of sacks with 52. Even his own teammates feared him on the field, but off the field they characterized him as the social worker. He sought out opportunities to do good things for others and always wore a smile wherever he went. He was selected in the first round of the 1989 NFL Draft by the Kansas City Chiefs.

Thomas found a home in Kansas City with the Chiefs. He would play out his entire 11 year NFL career there. Soon after he arrived in Kansas City he established the Derrick Thomas Third and Long Reading Club. He nurtured this organization's mission to fight illiteracy among inner-city youth through support from the Kansas City Public Library and the Storytellers Program. Thomas could be found reading to the children at the library on Saturday mornings and frequently brought teammates with him. His contribution was not enough to satisfy him. He expected more of his teammates and encouraged them to contribute as well. Thomas had an innovative and entrepreneurial spirit, and so when he was moved by someone's hardship, he made it his cause. One particular week he decided to feed close to 800 families in the Kansas City area, so he started collecting donations from his wealthy teammates. This is when Thomas' ability to incite fear in grown men became useful off the field. He wouldn't accept less than $100 from these millionaires and typically intimidated them to donate more. When he left the locker room, he entered the front office and continued to negotiate with the organization. His drive and determination, so powerfully displayed on the football field, transitioned smoothly to his causes off the field.

Thomas had an innate ability to disrupt an offense by sacking the quarterback; it was as if he had super-human vision. His commitment to certain individuals seemed to employ the same talent. He was actually considered small for his position on the football field, but the size of his heart was as impressive as the football stadium he played in. One young man's relationship with Thomas reveals his capacity to love and how attentive he was towards children. Thomas read the headlines about basketball tournaments being cancelled in Lone Wolf, Oklahoma because no one wanted to play with a young boy named Philip Tepe who had AIDS. The world was hysterical about the disease because they didn't understand it. Children struggle every day on the playground to get picked for a team, but it was as if Tepe wasn't even allowed on the playground. This courageous young man just wanted to play sports, so Thomas sent a limo to bring Tepe to a Chiefs game. He took Tepe golfing, bought him a video game system and gave him a football autographed by the legendary quarterback Joe

Montana. Tepe may not have been welcomed on the court in Lone Wolf, but he was certainly a part of a charity game that included Thomas and his friends Barry Sanders and Thurman Thomas. A professional athlete's life is demanding, but Thomas knew how important it was to make time for Tepe. The illness progressed, and Tepe was enduring more pain than Thomas could ever deliver on the football field. Thomas flew in once more to visit with his buddy and gave him his All-Pro jersey, the first one he ever gave away. It didn't ease the pain, but it brought a smile. Tepe died in March of 1994, just two days after the visit, taking a piece of Thomas with him forever. It is easy to see why Thomas was named NFL Man of the Year the season before and why he was the Kansas City Chief's MVP the following season although those committees probably knew nothing about Philip Tepe.

Tepe's story is just one of many stories about Thomas' devotion. Rahman McGill was a young student in Thomas' Third and Long Foundation. McGill describes their relationship as "a journey that was short in number of years but great in the knowledge and wisdom I gained."[1] During one of their first reading sessions, McGill told Thomas of his dream of becoming a Supreme Court Justice. Thomas admired his lofty goal and sought ways to encourage it; giving hope and confidence to a young mind will do wonders for his future. He began small by calling him "Justice" and then one day Thomas arranged a surprise visit from Supreme Court Justice Clarence Thomas.

Justice Thomas reinforced Thomas' goal setting for McGill, and promised this young man that he would secure a clerkship for him when he graduated from law school. Due to Thomas' encouragement to read, McGill speaks more eloquently today than many adults. Helping people like McGill was actually Thomas' goal in life. It was not necessarily to win football games, be MVP, go to nine consecutive Pro Bowls, or own the single game sack record in the NFL. Those were nice. To Dan LeBatard of the *Miami Herald* Thomas once said, "It's not important what I do in this game. What matters is 20 years from now, if I'm walking down the street and a doctor or lawyer or teacher says I made a difference in their life… I want to be remembered as someone who made a difference."[2] Thomas definitely made a difference in Tepe's life, in McGill's life, in those starving families' lives, and in the countless other lives he touched.

Although Thomas did not place great significance on his performances on the field, his career was remarkable and inspiring in a completely different way. His athletic ability was a marvel. On the field he was the kind of athlete who seemed to make time stop because his strength and quickness were unmatched by his opponents. Young boys' eyes would gleam as they got lost in their daydream of being number 58. Old men would revel in his seemingly effortless movements. He captured fans attention just as he did Rahman McGill's concentration when reading. Thomas' feats on the football field were staggering. He had a career total of 126.5 sacks, 728 tackles and 45 forced fumbles, no doubt related to his well-known sack and strip maneuver. He was named consensus Defensive Player of the Year in 1989. He also won the Mack Lee Hill Award during his rookie season. He recorded the most sacks (7) in a single game in the NFL, a performance he attributes to his father's inspiration. That game was played on Veteran's Day in 1990. When planes flew over the stadium Thomas dedicated that game to his father. The loss of his father had scarred Thomas for so long, but he was able to turn the terrible fate of Operation Linebacker II into the finest operation of a linebacker in NFL history.

His life was full. Some would say that he had lived three or four lifetimes in his mere 33 years. Thomas would only play 33 years in the game of life due to a car accident on an icy road in Kansas City on January 23, 2000. He was on his way to the airport to fly to St. Louis with two friends to watch the NFC Championship game when he lost control of his vehicle and it flipped several times throwing Thomas and one of his friends, Michael Tellis, from the car. Tellis was killed instantly. The other friend, the only one of the three to wear a seatbelt, escaped with minor injuries. Thomas was a resilient man and had taken poundings on the football field, but he had broken his neck and his spine and was paralyzed from the chest down. It is such a wicked twist of fate when a vivacious athlete becomes aware of his vulnerability. Thomas fought through the injuries and seemed indomitable even from this tragedy. He was thought to be recovering well, considering the circumstance, and his spirit was unconquerable as always. Thomas' game clock expired on February 8, 2000, when a pulmonary embolus caused cardio-respiratory arrest. Thousands poured into the Chiefs' Arrowhead Stadium to see their beloved Thomas one last time, to thank him for his kindness.

It would be easy to call Thomas' death a devastating tragedy, but it is much more appropriate to call his life illuminating. Successful football players are sometimes referred to as stars for their supreme talents. Thomas was a star that shined so brilliantly and brought hope to those in despair. Thomas truly believed in serving others and for living an exemplary life of service he was recognized by President George Bush in 1992 as his 832nd Point of Light. Thomas was the first and only NFL player to receive this honor. In 1994, he was awarded the Genuine Heroes Award by Trinity

College in Chicago for service to his community. In 1995, he was awarded the Byron "Whizzer" White Humanitarian Award. Thomas had remained involved with the Veterans of Foreign Wars throughout the years. He was the keynote speaker on Memorial Day in 1993 at the Vietnam Veterans Memorial in Washington, D.C. He had also been a supporter of Project Uplink, a group that collects prepaid phone cards for soldiers overseas. In 1999, Derrick Thomas was an obvious choice as a recipient of the VFW Hall of Fame Award, an honor that would surely make his dad proud. Thomas was also inducted into the Kansas City Chiefs Hall of Fame posthumously, and the MVP award for the Chiefs has now been named the Derrick Thomas Award.

Thomas might have left this world but the light that remains is as impressive as ever. Within days of Thomas' death, more than $25,000 had been raised to promote literacy for inner-city youth through his Third and Long Foundation. Thomas' commitment to education was always apparent during his life, so it is fitting that an Edison School now bears his name. The Derrick Thomas Academy of Kansas City is in its third year and has championed Thomas' commitment to community involvement. Thomas touched so many lives during his short time. Gunther Cunningham, the Chief's head coach, never wore his seatbelt, but thinks of Thomas every time he buckles up now. Derrick Thomas should serve as an inspiration for us all; a beacon to guide us as we work to live his dream of making this world a more equitable and caring place.

[1] Teicher, Adam. "KC's tribute in memory of Thomas" *The Kansas City Star*, February 15, 2000.

[2] Le Batard, Dan. "A bright light goes dark too soon." MacBrud Corporation of Miami Florida. [November 23, 2005] http://seatbeltsafety.com/derrickedwards.htm

Reggie White

by Jennifer Brenden and Richard Lapchick

The power of sport and the power of athletes who play sports have an immense impact in our society. People want to know what athletes are doing, where they are going, where they have been, who they are dating, what they are wearing, how much money they make, and what they had for dinner last night. Every intricate little detail associated with a professional athlete's life can somehow be spun in to an earth-shattering news story for consumption by a public obsessed with such trivia. But despite these excesses, the fact is that the power and appeal that sport commands among our populace can do a whole lot of good.

Reggie White was as admired as any professional player when Green Bay prepared to play Dallas for the 1996 NFC Championship. Five weeks before the game, White was scheduled to have surgery. However, on the day of the surgery, he announced that he would continue to play. He said that God gave him a miracle.

A religious man, White was co-pastor of the Inner-City Community Church in Knoxville. On Monday before the game, 18 incendiary devices were placed in his church and the walls were covered with graffiti. The original reports in Knoxville indicated the resulting fire was an accident. There was no acknowledgement of the incendiary devices or the graffiti.

The incident received national attention only when the co-pastor of the church was identified as Reggie White. The three other predominantly black churches in Tennessee that were firebombed in 1995 received no national attention, nor did the three black churches in Alabama and dozens of others around the nation that were also firebombed in the months before the destruction of the Inner-City Community Church. The eyes of the entire nation were forced open because a popular athlete's church was threatened and not just that of another black pastor.

White was born and raised in Chattanooga, Tennessee, and was an all-star basketball and football athlete at Howard High School. When White was 12, he told his mother and grandmother he was going to be a preacher. White was very serious about and very committed to his religious beliefs, and just five years later, at the age of 17, he became an ordained minister. His early ability to hold an audience's attention would prove helpful in his NFL career and in his lifelong commitment to helping young people. He would be quick to say that all that he had came from God and all that he did was in the name of God. White played football at the University of Tennessee. Coupling his religious status along with his stellar play on the field, he was nicknamed the "Minister of Defense" which would stick with him throughout his football career. White was a consensus All-American and SEC Player of the Year in his senior year. To this day, he still holds Tennessee records for sacks in a career, a single-season and a single game.

White began his professional career with the Memphis Showboats of the United States Football League (USFL) in 1983. After the USFL folded in 1985, he joined the Philadelphia Eagles in the NFL. That year he was named NFL Defensive Rookie of the Year. The 6 foot 5, 300 pound lineman became a force to be reckoned with on the field. He was quick and agile for a man of his size, so he was known throughout the league for his sacking ability. Offensive linemen and quarterbacks always had to be aware of where number 92 was on the field. Even though White was only one of 11 guys on the field playing defense, he could amazingly turn a game around all by himself. Although opponents were not very excited to see him on the other side of the line, they still appreciated having him on the field. White was greatly respected by his peers, not only for his playing ability, but also for his sportsmanlike conduct. Trash-talking was not his game. He let his actions speak for themselves. White always helped guys up, making sure they were alright. He was a genuine class act.

In his eight years with the Eagles, he recorded more sacks than games played, 124 and 121 respectively. He is the only player in NFL history to have done that. In 1993, White joined the defensive efforts of the Green Bay Packers, and vastly improved a struggling team defense. After taking a year off in 1999, White finished his career by playing a year with the Carolina Panthers and then retiring in 2000 at the age of 39.

But White's career went beyond the game as he worked tirelessly in the off-season with inner-city youth. Throughout his 15 year professional career in the NFL, White made it clear that it was a priority to be in a major city where he could minister to black youth.

When White concluded his career, he left the game with 198 sacks, an NFL record at the time. White was voted to 13 consecutive Pro Bowls, also a record. His focus and commitment to the inner-city remained. In 1991, he opened a home for unwed mothers on his property in Tennessee. The Reggie White Foundation was developed to help the underprivileged. It primarily focuses on the needs of underprivileged children, but also works with many other groups including unwed mothers, prison inmates and other at-risk individuals.

Sadly, Reggie White passed away on December 26, 2004 at the young age of 43. Initially, his death was said to have been caused by a heart attack, but an autopsy report showed that it had been caused by respiratory problems, including sarcoidosis and sleep apnea. The NFL may have lost one of the best defenders to ever step on the field, but society also lost a wonderful humanitarian as well. There will be others that try to emulate his intimidating play on the field, but it will be harder to find someone with the passion and love he had for God, for football and for helping people. Teammates, current players, fans and NFL executives all had the same resounding words of praise for White, both as a player and as a person. He will always be remembered as one of the greats. Though White's life was tragically short, his positive impact on everything and everyone he touched was anything but.

Ewing Marion Kauffman

by Jennifer Brenden

Ewing Marion Kauffman was involved in the world of sports for many years, but he is more well-known as a successful businessman and a caring philanthropist. Kauffman was a very powerful man, but all those who worked with him would consider him to be the ideal co-worker, or in sports terms, an ideal teammate. Kauffman was a true team player, and he treated his co-workers as teammates, whether he was working in the business community or the world of sports. He created an atmosphere where everyone on the "team" was working toward the same goal. Even though he was usually in positions of power and authority, he would consider himself as just another player on the team.

Kauffman was born in Garden City, Missouri in 1916, but moved to Kansas City with his family when he was a young boy. He lived in Kansas City for the remainder of his life, until he passed away in 1993. Living in the same place for so long allowed him to create a special bond with the people of the city, which motivated him to make his community a better place and really give back to the people of Kansas City.

His business skills developed at a young age with one of his first jobs selling fish and eggs door-to-door. Over the years, Kauffman honed his entrepreneurial skills to become a very successful businessman, but he never forgot where he came from or how he started. Kauffman was a strong believer and advocate of entrepreneurship and worked hard throughout his life to help others understand the very real virtues of dedication to one's goals and hard work to achieve them.

After serving in the Navy in World War II, Kauffman returned to start working in the pharmaceuticals industry, and by 1950 he created his own pharmaceuticals company in the basement of his home. This endeavor allowed him to put his "team player" philosophy into practice. Through his philosophy, he considered himself to be just one piece of the puzzle for success for his company. Falling in line with this philosophy is the name he chose for his company. He chose to use his middle name for the company, Marion Laboratories Inc., because he didn't want to take all the credit for the company. During the first year of his company's existence, sales reached $36,000 and the net profit was $1,000. By the time he sold his company to Merrell Dow in 1989, it had grown to $1 billion in sales and employed 3,400 associates.

In the midst of running a billion-dollar international pharmaceuticals company, Kauffman brought major league baseball to Kansas City when he bought the Royals in 1968. Kauffman used the same business strategies that he used with Marion Laboratories Inc. with the Royals, and not surprisingly came up with the same successful results. The team won six division titles, two American League pennants and a World Series Championship in 1985. The team's success was beneficial to the city as well. The Kansas City Royals brought economic growth to the city, thousands of job opportunities and a sense of pride that may be unique among baseball teams in small market cities. Professional sports teams have the amazing ability to bring a community together, and that is just what the Kansas City Royals organization did for Kansas City.

Bringing professional baseball to Kansas City is not the only thing Kauffman did to improve the community. Perhaps the legacy that will last the longest when people hear of Ewing Kauffman is the Ewing Marion Kauffman Foundation. He created this foundation in 1966 for the purpose of encouraging entrepreneurship and improving the education of children, particularly those from economically disadvantaged backgrounds. The goals of the Foundation remain the same even unto the present day.

Education is at the center of the Foundation's goals. The Ewing Marion Kauffman Foundation works with educators to create awareness of the importance of entrepreneurship and to give people the opportunity, through programs and classes, to develop those skills and abilities. The Foundation promotes entrepreneurial success at all levels. This range includes people of different ages, from young, school-age students to college students to professional business-people. The range also spans from working with individuals to families to entire companies or organizations.

During the 1980's, Kauffman made the Foundation more focused on development, education and entrepreneurship and it began launching more specific programs in these three areas. Project STAR (Students

Taught Awareness and Resistance) was the first operating program created in 1984. The goal of this program was to prevent the use and abuse of alcohol, tobacco and other drugs among young people. In 1988, Project Choice was developed. This program was created from a deal Kauffman made with a class from his former high school. He told the high school students that if they would stay in school, remain drug-free, avoid teenage parenthood, graduate from high school, and commit to being good citizens, he would pay for their secondary education. Project Early was developed to assist families in the early stages of development of a child through child care, health care and general family support. In 1990, Project Essential was created to develop self-esteem in children through storytelling, moral dilemma discussions, workbook lessons and experiential activities.

Kauffman believed that entrepreneurial skills are very important skills to obtain, but not enough people have the opportunity to do so. Kauffman chose to use his expertise to teach about the importance of entrepreneurship. The Foundation is located in Kansas City and it aims to help and educate those who live in the community, but it is not limited to Kansas City. One of Kauffman's underlying goals was to make Kansas City a beautiful and pleasurable city to live in by continually updating and improving the quality of its business, educational and cultural life.

Kauffman's name and legacy will not soon be forgotten, nor will the things he did for Kansas City. In the early 90's, Kauffman created a succession plan that was designed to keep the baseball team in Kansas City after the sale of the team and after his death. The plan also ensured that the proceeds of its sale went to local charities to benefit the city. Recently, the Ewing Marion Kauffman Foundation made a donation of $26 million to the Metropolitan Kansas City Performing Arts Center. This money came from a portion of the funds created from the sale of the team.

Currently, The Ewing Marion Kauffman Foundation has become one of the nation's 25 largest foundations in the U.S. The Kauffman Center for Entrepreneurial Leadership, which is a portion of the Foundation, is the largest organization in the United States focused solely on entrepreneurial success at all levels. Also, the Foundation announced in 2003 that it would spend over $70 million in the next 20 years to put 2,300 economically disadvantaged Kansas City area kids through college. The recipients will be chosen in middle school. Even after his death, the values and goals Ewing Kauffman instilled in his foundation are continuing to make a difference in the community of Kansas City, and it seems as though this trend will continue far into the future.

Dave Sanders

by Jessica Bartter

Dave Sanders spent his life trying to help his students and student-athletes. He gave his life trying to save them that fateful day at Columbine High School.

The teaching profession is one of the most demanding jobs but can also be one of the most rewarding. Teachers are often overworked and underpaid, disrespected by their students and overlooked by their administration. Parents across the country entrust teachers with their children, placing the responsibility on their shoulders to make our young people smart, responsible citizens. The best teachers gladly accept this charge and happily work to help the young people whom they work to educate.

One such teacher was William "Dave" Sanders. A favorite among his students and the staff, Sanders was always accessible, either in the classroom, on the softball field or on the basketball court. Sanders was raised in the small Indiana community of Newtown. He excelled in basketball, baseball, and track and field at Fountain Central High School and earned a basketball scholarship to Nebraska Western University. Upon graduation from college in 1973, Sanders chose education as his career and began teaching at Columbine High School in Littleton, Colorado. Sanders taught computers and business, and he coached girl's basketball and softball. He was the assistant softball coach since the sport was sanctioned by the Colorado High School Activities Association and helped the team become League Champions in 1990, 1993 and 1998; District Champions in 1988, 1994 and 1996; and State Runner-up in 1993 and 1995. Sanders was the head basketball coach and in his first season in 1997-1998, his team produced a winning record after finishing next-to-last the year before.

Sanders enjoyed teaching and was successful because he loved to help young people. Sanders touched the lives of countless high school students during his 24 years at Columbine High, particularly on the frightful day of April 20, 1999. This day ended in tragedy when two students turned on their classmates, murdering 13 and wounding 24 more in the most devastating shooting in U.S. school history. Sanders heard the shooters coming down the halls and ran anxiously from room to room warning students to lie on the ground, seek coverage or run and pointed them to the safe exits. Sanders searched the school securing safety for hundreds of students and faculty members without regard for his own life. Just steps ahead of the heavily armed shooters, Sanders entered the cafeteria which was full of almost 500 students on their lunch break. He led the students to a stairway leading to a safe exit but rather than following them, he turned back to the school to save more students. Until Sanders entered the cafeteria, the background sounds of shots being fired were assumed to be a senior prank as it was only weeks before graduation. By the time one of the shooters entered the cafeteria, only a handful of students remained. The killers had picked lunch time hoping to come across a large number of the student body at one time and even planted two bombs in the cafeteria that easily could have killed all 488 students. Sanders most likely prevented the Columbine High School shooting from being remembered as the Columbine High School massacre.

After escaping from the cafeteria, Sanders was on his way to the library to warn more students when one of the gunmen appeared in the hallway and opened fire. Sanders was shot twice. He stumbled into a classroom where about 30 students were hiding. Though scared, the students tended to Sanders wounds and ministered to him as much as was possible under the circumstances. Two students in particular, Aaron Hancey and Kevin Starkey, held pressure on Sanders wounds and talked to him about his family. He asked them to pull out his wallet so that he could look at a picture of his wife. He often spoke of his wife, his three daughters and his ten grandchildren. Students assured Sanders he would see them again but there was no sign of help. After a couple of hours of waiting for assistance, they held a sign up through the window trying to let authorities know that Sanders was bleeding to death. Students could see the authorities surrounding the building but they were taking necessary precautions before entering the school. Though police reports later indicated that the gunmen took their own lives shortly after wounding Sanders and killing ten students and wounding 12 more in the library, at the time, there was no way of knowing. The police department was trying to secure the building and ensure safety for themselves and anyone still trapped inside. Though Sanders fought for his life for almost four hours, by the time paramedics were able to reach him, he had lost his fight. Sanders tragically died in a classroom where he had spent over half his life, living it to the fullest by enriching the lives of thousands of students.

Investigations later discovered 99 explosives planted all over Columbine High School by the two gunmen. Thirty bombs blew up in the school, but thankfully no injuries or deaths resulted from any of the explosives. The two large propane devices in the school's cafeteria could have killed everyone but thankfully were not set off since the area had been emptied by Sanders. At his funeral, over 3,000 relatives, friends and community members mourned the loss of a hero. Both past and present students stood up to thank Sanders for changing their lives, and many thanked him for saving their lives that terrible day. Though grieving, two of his daughters agreed that had their dad lived and had Eric Harris and Dylan Klebold, the two student gunmen, lived, that he would have been the first to visit them in jail, and that he would have still believed they could be saved, a testament to this fallen hero's character.

The next fall, the Columbine softball team dedicated its field to Coach Dave Sanders before its home opener. In February of 2000, ESPN presented Sanders' wife and daughters with the Arthur Ashe Courage Award in his honor. It was awarded at the ESPY Awards held at the MGM grand in Las Vegas before a tear-filled crowd of professional athletes and executives who gave a standing ovation after watching the tribute video of Sanders. Coach Sanders joined the likes of past recipients of the Arthur Ashe Award for Courage including Billie Jean King, Dean Smith, Muhammad Ali, Loretta Claiborne and Howard Cosell.

Teachers and coaches are far too often forgotten heroes. Heroes of today's American youth are movie stars and professional athletes for their stardom, fame and wealth. They are stars they have never met and who have had no impact on their lives. Yet, they forget to thank the middle school teacher that taught them the valuable lesson on integrity when caught cheating; the coach that stayed in the gym to run drills one-on-one rather than go home to his family, the high school teacher who lent his ear when a student could not go to his or her parents with a teenage dilemma; or the algebra teacher who gave extra attention to a student until he or she finally understood some difficult mathematical equation. Dave Sanders, teacher, coach, father, husband, grandfather, friend, and hero fell, but he will never be forgotten.

Ralph Wiley

by Jessica Bartter

Far too often the world loses leaders in their prime before they are done doing great deeds and making this a better world. Ralph Wiley's impact on sports and society is everlasting. He was never afraid to stand-up against injustice and he left his mark despite the fact that his time on earth was much too short.

Wiley was born and raised in Memphis, Tennessee. His father died at a young age so his mother, Dorothy, worked as a humanities professor to support the family. Rooted in education, Dorothy often read to her son, planting an early seed for his love of literature. Wiley showcased his literary skill in several plays he wrote during high school. Wiley also developed a love for sports and displayed his athletic skill on the track and football teams at Melrose High School. Wiley's football and academic prowess carried over to Knoxville College, about 400 miles east of his home in Memphis. He played wide receiver until a knee injury convinced him to drop the athlete from the student-athlete and focus his collegiate career more on his studies in business and finance.

Wiley was quickly rewarded as he received his first journalism job writing for the sports section of the *Knoxville Keyana-Spectrum*, a weekly publication. Wiley's experience landed him a job in Oakland, California as a copy clerk for the *Oakland Tribune* after his graduation from college in 1975. Wiley worked diligently for a year as a copy clerk until the sports editor asked him to write an article about Julius Erving. The article also involved the dissolving of the American Basketball Association and its merger with the NBA. Wiley knew the opportunity this one article presented and he gladly accepted the challenge. His article was so well received that the *Oakland Tribune* promoted him to prep sports writer. Wiley's impressive writings helped him ascend the professional ladder. He was soon promoted again, first to city beat writer and then, a year later, to sports writer. He covered boxing for the sports section where he finished almost seven years with the *Tribune*. During that short span, Wiley became a highly regarded sports journalist in the Bay Area as a very young man. Most notably, Wiley is credited with the creation of the phrase "Billy Ball" referring to the Billy Martin managed Oakland A's. In 1982, Wiley took his skills as a columnist to New York City where he joined the staff of *Sports Illustrated*. In nine years with *Sports Illustrated*, Wiley wrote 139 articles, 20 of which graced the cover of the popular magazine. He left *Sports Illustrated* as a senior writer in 1991 which surprised many who thought he was at the top of his game.

Wiley had published his first book in 1989 and devoted the next decade and a half to writing several more books. Wiley's favorite uncle was a boxer so he found an early love for the sport. His experience with the *Oakland Tribune* and *Sports Illustrated* helped him learn about the lives of many fighters. He chronicled their struggles and triumphs in "Serenity: A Boxing Memoir." It was published in 1989 and was well received by critics and readers. In 1991, "Why Black People Tend to Shout: Cold Facts and Wry Views from a Black Man's World" was released after it had been turned down by an estimated 25 publishers. "Dark Witness: When Black People Should be Sacrificed (Again)" was Wiley's third book which most notably offers his not-so-kind insight on O.J. Simpson. Wiley's success as an author led him to co-author "Best Seat in the House: A Basketball Memoir" and "By Any Means Necessary: The Trials and Tribulations of the Making of Malcolm X," both written with producer, director, actor and writer Spike Lee. He also co-wrote "Born to Play: The Eric Davis Story" and "Growing Up King: An Intimate Memoir."

Wiley's commentaries were in high demand, and he made appearances on Sportscenter, The Jim Rome Show, The Oprah Show, Donahue, Larry King Live, Court TV's Cochran & Co., Nightline, The Charlie Rose Show, The Arsenio Hall Show, BET Talk, ESPNRadio, ESPN the Magazine show with Dan Le Batard and more. He was also an original member of NBC's NFL Insiders and ESPN's Sports Reporters. Most recently, Wiley joined ESPN.com Page 2 during its inception in November 2000 where he contributed over 240 articles. Wiley also wrote articles for the magazines *Premiere*, *GQ* and *National Geographic*, as well as several national newspapers.

Known for his unique and provocative perspective, Wiley often challenged his readers to think outside the box and from inside someone else's shoes, particularly those of an African-American. Wiley had the ability to dissect an athlete to the core, presenting all sides of the person, rather than just the jock. In doing so, he did not shy away from the truth. Wiley was willing to expose the facts no matter what he discovered, both good or bad, heroic or tragic, in an effort to deliver the best and most authentic stories to his readers. Wiley served an important role in the sports journalism world that is largely dominated by white males.

On June 13, 2004 Wiley had just settled in for Game 4 of the NBA Finals when he died of heart failure in his home. He was just 52 years old. Wiley used his voice to better each one of us as he truly understood the impact of sports on society. Wiley is remembered for his passion, his intelligence, his vibrancy, his honesty, his humor, his opinions and his friendship. Wiley wholeheartedly immersed himself in each piece he wrote commanding emotion out of his readers and colleagues. Some agreed and some disagreed, but he made each and every reader think.

Shortly after his death, Richard Lapchick wrote the following for ESPN.com. "Ralph Wiley was a dear friend of the National Consortium for Academics and Sports and is greatly missed. As someone who writes and thinks about race and sport and social issues and sport, Ralph Wiley is a never before, never again figure. He made me rethink all that I had thought and challenged all of us to make ethics and integrity the pillars of our lives. Wiley and I talked even more often since I became an ESPN.com Page 2 columnist. I always wanted to know what he thought about what I was writing and thinking. Now I will only be able to imagine it as I will miss this special gift to humanity known as Ralph Wiley."

CONCLUSION

As is evident in the stories of these 100 heroes, sport can change one's life for the better. It can open the door to opportunity and help young people avoid paths which are nothing but dead ends. It can encourage athletes to become civically engaged members of the communities in which they go to school, even as they work to succeed in their various sports. Sport teaches teamwork, commitment and accountability, all of which are crucial ingredients of a successful personal and professional life.

Sport reaches all kinds of people for all different reasons. Sport can be played competitively or recreationally or sport can be watched and enjoyed as entertainment. We watch sports we never play and we play sports we never watch. Sport can help build friendships, families, respect, confidence and character. Sport provides health benefits some medical professionals can only begin to understand.

Most importantly, sport is unique in the boundaries it crosses with both its participants and its audience. Differences in gender, race, physical and mental abilities, age, religion and cultures are irrelevant in the huddle, on the field, in the gym or in the water. Sport smashes these barriers like nothing else can.

Whether one is an athlete, coach, administrator or a fan, *100 Heroes* demonstrates by example how our heroes have defied the odds and overcome obstacles; how through sport they have offered hope and inspiration to others; how they as athletes have used sport to affect meaningful social change. The possibilities athletes possess are endless.

Sport has survived and even flourished in the United States through world wars, women's suffrage and the civil rights movement.

It has evolved as Americans have evolved, always offering a form of enjoyment, a respite from the challenges of daily life. But sport can also be an important vehicle for social change.

A great deal has been achieved over the last century through sports, particularly during the last 20 years during which the National Consortium for Academics and Sports has grown from a small program in Boston to a national organization of more than 220 colleges and universities. During the last half of the 20th Century, we have witnessed the integration of professional leagues, the development of women's leagues, the establishment of Title IX, the setting aside of international conflict for brief moments in sport competitions and the increased funding for athletic programs for disadvantaged youth. Sports have become an even more integral part of the fabric of our social and cultural life in big cities and small towns, from Maine to Montana, from Miami to Maui.

The 100 heroes described in this volume should serve as a light, indeed, as a beacon for us all. They followed their dreams and helped us dream as well. They served others even as they succeeded on the playing field. They found hope where others believed none existed. Let us cheer their accomplishments as we follow their example and emphasize that it is more than just wins and losses that will continue the evolution of sports' positive role on society.

ABOUT THE NATIONAL CONSORTIUM FOR ACADEMICS AND SPORTS (NCAS)

The National Consortium for Academics and Sports (NCAS) is an ever-growing organization of colleges, universities and individuals. The mission of the NCAS is to create a better society by focusing on educational attainment and using the power and appeal of sport to positively affect social change.

The National Consortium for Academics and Sports evolved in response to the need to "keep the student in the student-athlete." The NCAS was established by Dr. Richard E. Lapchick and since its inception in 1985, NCAS member institutions have proven to be effective advocates for balancing academics and athletics. By joining the NCAS, a college or university agrees to bring back, tuition free, their own former student-athletes who competed in revenue and non-revenue producing sports and were unable to complete their degree requirements. In exchange these former student-athletes agree to participate in school outreach and community service programs addressing social issues of America's youth.

There have been hundreds of people who have worked in NCAS programs over the past twenty years to help us fulfill our mission. Each has helped because of his or her passion for combining academics, sport and the way we use sport to bring about social change for our children.

The NCAS started with 11 universities in 1985 and now has more than 220 member institutions. Members of the NCAS have brought back 26,399 former student-athletes to complete their degrees through one of our biggest programs. The Degree Completion Program was just a dream in 1985, but more than 26,000 now say that dream has become a reality.

Returning student-athletes participate in outreach and community service programs in exchange for the tuition and fees they receive when they come back to school they. They have reached over 14 million young people in cities in America, rural America and suburban America. Wherever there are college campuses, our student-athletes are in the community helping young people face the crises of the last 20 years. Member institutions have donated more than $295 million in tuition assistance to these former student-athletes. With no athletic participation in return this time around, the biggest return possible is to the student who leaves with the degree he or she was told would be there for them when they first enrolled. The NCAS and its members have been able to work with children on issues like conflict resolution, improving race relations, reducing men's violence against women, stemming the spread of drug and alcohol abuse, and emphasizing the importance of education and the importance of balancing work in the classroom and on the playing field.

The NCAS has worked with organizations and schools to help them understand issues of diversity, not only as a moral imperative, but also as a business necessity. The NCAS utilizes the Teamwork Leadership Institute (TLI) to teach our colleges, professional sports and all of the people that sport touches the importance and value of diversity which then in turn reflects back on society as a whole. The mission of TLI is to help senior administrators, team front office and athletic department staff, through the provision of diversity training services, to apply the principles of teamwork to all areas of athletic departments and professional sports organizations. Challenges that stem from cultural prejudice, intolerance and poor communication can be aggressively addressed in intelligent, safe and structured ways. TLI works with staff members to help them anticipate, recognize and address the problems inherent to diverse teams and staff. Diversity training demonstrates that diverse people have a great deal in common. Rather than being divisive issues, racial, ethnic and gender differences can serve as building blocks. Just as in sports, these differences can strengthen the group. TLI has provided workshops for over 130 athletic organizations, including college athletic departments, the National Basketball Association, Major League Soccer, Maloof Sports & Entertainment (Sacramento Kings) and the Orlando Magic.

The NCAS also teaches the value of diversity to young people through Project TEAMWORK. Violent acts are often the result of conflict between individuals from different cultures, religions, races and ethnicities. Young men and women need the tools to deal with tension in innovative ways. Project TEAMWORK creates sensitivity among young people to racial, ethnic and gender issues impacting their lives and trains them with diversity and conflict resolution skills, providing them with alternative strategies to handle the conflicts they face. The TEAM, made up of multiracial athletes, demonstrates that these tasks can be best accomplished, just as in sports, by working together. The essence of the Project TEAMWORK mission is to promote respect, responsibility, pride, inclusion and cooperation. Project TEAMWORK won the Peter F. Drucker Award in 1994 as the nation's most innovative non-profit program leading to social change, after being evaluated as "America's most successful violence prevention program" by leading public opinion analyst Lou Harris. In 1995, President Clinton recognized Project TEAMWORK as a model violence prevention program. Project TEAMWORK was founded at Northeastern University's Center for the Study of Sport in Society.

The Mentors in Violence Prevention (MVP) Program is a leadership program that motivates student-athletes and student leaders to play a central role in solving problems that historically have been considered "women's issues:" rape, battering and sexual harassment. The mixed gender, racially-diverse former professional and college athletes that facilitate the MVP Program motivate men and women to work together in preventing gender violence. Utilizing a unique bystander approach to prevention, MVP views student-athletes and student leaders not as potential perpetrators or victims, but as empowered bystanders who can confront abusive peers. The MVP approach does not involve finger pointing, nor does it blame participants for the widespread problem of gender violence. Instead it sounds a positive call for proactive, preventative behavior and leadership. MVP has facilitated sessions with thousands of high school and college students and administrators at dozens of Massachusetts schools as well as with hundreds of student-athletes and administrators at over 100 colleges nationwide. MVP has also conducted sessions with professional sports leagues including players and staff from the National Basketball Association (NBA), National Football League (NFL) and International Basketball League (IBL) as well as with personnel from the U.S. Marine Corps. MVP has also trained the rookie and free agents of the New England Patriots and New York Jets, minor league players of the Boston Red Sox and Major League Lacrosse (MLL).

With the alarming rate of alcohol use and abuse among students, the NCAS, in collaboration with The BACCHUS and GAMMA Peer Education Network, sought a solution through education and developed the Alcohol Response-Ability: Foundations for Student Athletes™ course in 2004. It is a 90-minute, internet-based alcohol education and life skills program designed specifically for student-athletes and those who work with them in the college and university setting. In this first program of its kind, student-athletes receive a customized educational experience that is interactive, interesting and designed to help them reduce harm and recognize the consequences associated with alcohol abuse in their campus communities. In its first year on college campuses, results came back overwhelmingly positive. Ninety three percent of the students who took the course said they learned something new, and 95 percent of them said they would try at least one of the strategies they learned to lower their risk. An impressive 83 percent said they would likely make safe decisions as a direct result of the course. These figures prove that much more needs to be done with alcohol abuse education.

Each of the 100 heroes whose lives you will read about was honored in celebration of National STUDENT-Athlete Day (NSAD). NSAD is celebrated annually on April 6th providing an opportunity to recognize the outstanding accomplishments of student-athletes who have achieved excellence in academics and athletics, while making significant contributions to their communities. In addition to honoring student-athletes, the Annual National STUDENT-Athlete Day program selects recipients for *Giant Steps Awards*. These awards are given to individuals on a national level who exemplify the meaning of National STUDENT-Athlete Day. Each year nominations are received from across the country, and the Giant Steps Award winners are chosen by a national selection committee in categories ranging from civic leaders, coaches, parents, teachers, athletic administrators and courageous student-athletes. This book is a compilation of the inspiring life stories of the first 100 to be chosen in honor of the "giant steps" they have taken in sports, in society, and in life itself.

ABOUT THE AUTHORS

Richard Lapchick

Human rights activist, pioneer for racial equality, internationally recognized expert on sports issues, scholar and author Richard E. Lapchick is often described as "the racial conscience of sport." He brought his commitment to equality and his belief that sport can be an effective instrument of positive social change to the University of Central Florida where he accepted an endowed chair in August 2001. Lapchick became the only person named as "One of the 100 Most Powerful People in Sport" to head up a sport management program. He remains President and CEO of the National Consortium for Academics and Sport and helped bring the NCAS national office to UCF.

The DeVos Sport Business Management Program at UCF is a landmark program that focuses on the business skills necessary for graduates to conduct a successful career in the rapidly changing and dynamic sports industry. In following with Lapchick's tradition of human rights activism, the curriculum includes courses with an emphasis on diversity, community service and philanthropy, sport and social issues and ethics in addition to UCF's strong business curriculum.

Lapchick helped found the Center for the Study of Sport in Society in 1984 at Northeastern University. He served as Director for 17 years and is now the Director Emeritus. The Center has attracted national attention to its pioneering efforts to ensure the education of athletes from junior high school through the professional ranks. The Center's Project TEAMWORK was called "America's most successful violence prevention program" by public opinion analyst Lou Harris. It won the Peter F. Drucker Foundation Award as the nation's most innovative non-profit program and was named by the Clinton Administration as a model for violence prevention. The Center's MVP gender violence prevention program has been so successful with college and high school athletes that the United States Marine Corps adopted it in 1997. Athletes in Service to America, funded by AmeriCorps, combines the efforts of Project TEAMWORK and MVP in five cities across the nation.

The Center helped form the National Consortium for Academics and Sports (NCAS), a group of over 220 colleges and universities that have adopted the Center's programs. To date, more than 28,584 athletes have returned to NCAS member schools. Over 11,000 have graduated. Nationally, the NCAS athletes have worked with more than 14 million students in the school outreach program, which focuses on teaching youth how to improve race relations, develop conflict resolution skills, prevent gender violence and avoid drug and alcohol abuse. They have collectively donated more than 13.5 million hours of service.

Lapchick was the American leader of the international campaign to boycott South Africa in sport for more than 20 years. In 1993, the Center launched TEAMWORK-South Africa, a program designed to use sports to help improve race relations and help with sports development in post-apartheid South Africa. He was among 200 guests specially invited to Nelson Mandela's inauguration.

Lapchick is a prolific writer. 100 Heroes is his 11th book. His 12th book, New Game Plan for College Sport will be published in the spring of 2006. Lapchick is a regular columnist for ESPN.com, Page 2 and The Sports Business Journal. Lapchick is a regular contributor to the op ed page of the Orlando Sentinel. He has written more than 450 articles and has given more than 2,600 public speeches.

Considered among the nation's experts on sports issues, Lapchick has appeared numerous times on Nightline, Good Morning America, Face The Nation, The Today Show, ABC World News, NBC Nightly News, the CBS Evening News, CNN and ESPN.

Lapchick also consults with companies as an expert on both managing diversity and building community relations through service programs addressing the social needs of youth. He has a special expertise on Africa and South Africa. He has made 30 trips to Africa and African Studies was at the core of his Ph.D. work.

Before Northeastern, he was an Associate Professor of Political Science at Virginia Wesleyan College from 1970-1978 and a Senior Liaison Officer at the United Nations between 1978-1984.

Lapchick has been the recipient of numerous humanitarian awards. He was inducted into the Sports Hall of Fame of the Commonwealth Nations in 1999 in the category of Humanitarian along with Arthur Ashe and Nelson Mandela and received the Ralph Bunche International Peace Award. He joined the Muhammad Ali, Jackie Robinson, Arthur Ashe and Wilma Rudolph in the Sport in Society Hall of Fame in 2004. Lapchick won Diversity Leadership Award at the 2003 Literacy Classic and the Jean Mayer Global Citizenship Award from Tufts University in 2000. He won the Wendell Scott Pioneer Award in 2004 for leadership in advancing people of color in the motor sports industry. He received the "Hero Among Us Award" from the Boston Celtics in 1999 and was named as the Martin Luther King, Rosa Parks, Cesar Chavez Fellow by the State of Michigan in 1998. Lapchick was the winner of the 1997 "Arthur Ashe Voice of Conscience Award." He also won the 1997 Women's Sports Foundation President's Award for work toward the development of women's sports and was named as the 1997 Boston Celtics "Man of the Year." In 1995, the National Association of Elementary School Principals gave him their first award as a "Distinguished American in Service of Our Children." He was a guest of President Clinton at the White House for National Student-Athlete Day in 1996, 1997, 1998 and again in 1999.

He is listed in Who's Who in American Education, Who's Who in Finance and Industry, and Who's Who in American Business. Lapchick was named as "one of the 100 most powerful people in sport" for six consecutive years. He is widely known for bringing different racial groups together to create positive work force environments. In 2003-04 he served as the national spokesperson for VERB, the Center for Disease Control's program to combat preteen obesity.

Lapchick has received 8 honorary degrees. In 1993, he was named as the outstanding alumnus at the University of Denver where he got his Ph.D. in international race relations in 1973. Lapchick received a B.A. from St. John's University in 1967 and an honorary degree from St. John's in 2001.

Lapchick is a board member of Wings of America, the National Conference for Community and Justice, SchoolSports, the Team Harmony Foundation, and the Black Coaches Association and is on the advisory boards of the Women's Sports Foundation and the Giving Back Fund.

Under Lapchick's leadership, the DeVos Program launched the Institute for Diversity and Ethics in Sport in December 2002. The Institute focuses on two broad areas. In the area of Diversity, the Institute publishes the critically acclaimed Racial and Gender Report Card, long-authored by Lapchick in his former role as director of the Center for the Study of Sport in Society at Northeastern University. The Report Card, an annual study of the racial and gender hiring practices of major professional sports, Olympic sport and college sport in the United States, shows long-term trends over a decade and highlights organizations that are notable for diversity in coaching and management staffs.

In another diversity initiative, the Institute partners with the NCAS to provide diversity management training to sports organizations, including athletic departments and professional leagues and teams. The Consortium has already conducted such training for the NBA, Major League Soccer and more than 80 university athletic departments.

In the area of ethics, the Institute monitors some of the critical ethical issues in college and professional sport, including the potential for the exploitation of student-athletes, gambling, performance-enhancing drugs and violence in sport. The Institute publishes annual studies on graduation rates for all teams in college football bowl games, comparing graduation rates for football players to rates for overall student-athletes and including a breakdown by race.

The Institute also publishes the graduation rates of the women's and men's basketball teams in the NCAA Tournament as March Madness heats up.

Richard is the son of Joe Lapchick, the famous Original Celtic center who became a legendary coach for St. John's and the Knicks. He is married to Ann Pasnak and has three children and two grandchildren.

Jessica Bartter

Jessica Bartter is currently the Communications and Marketing Coordinator for the National Consortium for Academics and Sports (NCAS). At the University of California, San Diego Bartter was a member of the nationally ranked NCAA Division II volleyball team where she was elected team captain during her junior and senior years. The UC San Diego Tritons went to the playoffs every year, including a Final Four appearance her junior season. As an individual who values teamwork, Bartter considers her "Best Team Player" award one of her greatest accomplishments. Exercising her talent on the sidelines as well, Bartter coached sports camps and youth leagues in her spare time. Bartter attributes many valuable lessons she has learned to her experiences in sport and works to apply them outside of the sport arena and into her professional life. Prior to moving to Orlando, Florida to work for the NCAS, Bartter worked for the UC San Diego Recreation and Intercollegiate Athletic Departments while she earned her bachelors degree in management science, with a minor in psychology. Born and raised in Orange County, California, Bartter attended Valencia High School before becoming a Triton. Bartter is grateful to her father who first introduced her to sports and to her mother who taxied her to softball and volleyball practices and even dared to catch wild pitches in the backyard. Bartter is the eldest of four siblings including Jackie, Brian and Kyle, all of whom have proudly donned the jersey #13. Bartter currently resides in Los Angeles.

Jennifer Brenden

Jenny Brenden is a first-year student in the DeVos Sport Business Management program at the University of Central Florida. She is a graduate assistant for Dr. Richard Lapchick in the Institute for Diversity and Ethics in Sport. She also mentors UCF student-athletes through Academic Student Services for Athletes (ASSA.) Being a former student athlete herself, Jenny knows both the hardships and the glories of being a student-athlete. Jenny graduated from Penn State University in May of 2005 with B.A. degrees in Public Relations and Media Studies and minors in Business and Sociology, and a cumulative GPA of 3.89. She was on the Dean's List eight of her ten semesters in school, and she earned several academic awards, including Academic All-Big Ten Honors in 2002, 2003, 2004 and 2005. She also spent five years as a member of the Penn State Lady Lion Basketball team, two of those years serving as team captain. Jenny's team had much success during her tenure on the team. They were two-time Big Ten Champions in 2003 and 2004, and their play in March Madness brought them to the round of the Sweet-Sixteen twice and to the Elite-Eight once. Jenny worked with student-athletes at Penn State on the Student-Athlete Advisory Board, which she served as President her senior year. She was also very involved in the community at Penn State through Habitat for Humanity, Easter Seals, Lift for Life, and Lifelink. Currently, she works with an organization called Restore Orlando, working as a stable role model for at-risk youth. Though her days of being a student-athlete are over, Jenny wants to remain close to the world of the student-athlete, hoping to help them have the same great experience that she had. Basketball has been a part of her life since a very young age, and she wants basketball and athletics to remain an integral part of her life. She aspires to be an athletic director in the future and really work at connecting her school and her athletes with the community.

Jenny hails from the Land of 10,000 lakes. More specifically, Sauk Rapids, MN, is where she calls home. She is one of two children in her family and her older brother is currently in Law School at the University of MN. They are both looking forward to graduating from graduate school in the spring of 2007.

Stacy Martin

Stacy A. Martin grew up in Bloomington, Indiana where she had such a successful athletic career that she was named the Gatorade National Female Track & Field Athlete of 1999. Auburn University offered her a full athletic scholarship in track & field. She credits her success to her parents Maureen and Randy, both former coaches. As an Auburn athlete, Stacy set new school records in the shot put, discus, hammer and weight throw. A condition called compartment syndrome that had plagued her legs for eight years finally required surgery after her junior year and she had to learn to walk again as well as begin her training all over. In spite of this obstacle, her numerous accomplishments included an SEC Championship in the Shot Put, Academic as well as Athletic All-American honors, a Junior World Championships competitor, and she finished her Auburn career as a NCAA finalist in discus. She was named to the SEC Good Works Team, was a NCAA Leadership Conference Representative, President of the Student Athletic Advisory Committee, as well as being named to the SEC Academic Honor Roll and an Auburn Top Tiger Recipient all of her years at Auburn. She graduated with honors from Auburn University with a Bachelors of Science in Education, Health Promotion and a Bachelors of Science in Business Administration, Human Resource Management. The pinnacle of her athletic career was qualifying for the 2004 Olympic Trials in both shot put and discus. She has passed the torch on to her younger brother, Cory, who has already earned All American honors for Auburn University in the throwing events and has also been a Junior World Championships competitor for the United States.

She has now turned her focus to earning a Masters of Sports Business Management and a Masters of Business Administration at the University of Central Florida's DeVos Sport Business Management Program. She is currently a graduate assistant to Dr. Richard Lapchick and the Institute for Diversity and Ethics in Sport and a leader on the Orlando Magic Street Team. She participates in the Deliver the Dream weekends for families that suffer from terminal illnesses. She is looking forward to graduating in the spring of 2007 and becoming a leader in the sports industry.

Drew Tyler

A recent graduate of the DeVos Sport Business Management program, Drew has earned both a Masters in Sports Business Management and a Masters in Business Administration from the University of Central Florida. Additionally, Drew has earned a Communications degree from Clemson University. Drew has amassed a great deal of experience in athletics working for the Orlando Magic, Florida Collegiate Summer League, University of Central Florida Athletic Department, Seattle Storm and Tampa Bay Devil Rays. Outside of sports, Drew has spent a substantial amount of time working with the community. A former Eagle Scout, Drew has been actively involved with Young Life ministries and attended Clemson on a choral scholarship, where he performed with Tigeroar (men's acapella) and had the lead role in "South Pacific."

Brian Wright

Brian Leroy Antonio Wright was born in Takoma Park, MD on April 9, 1982. As the youngest member of a large family consisting of brother Rodger and sisters Nicole, Kahlarah, and Hillary, Wright quickly learned the concept of operating as team from his parents Wayne and Amybelle Humphrey. This team concept captured Wright's mind as he at a very early age became very passionate about sports, which would help shape the rest of his young life. After lobbying between two or three different sports Wright finally decided that basketball was his sport of choice. Wright attended Takoma Academy in Takoma Park, MD for high school and was a standout student-athlete there receiving various academic and athletic awards including a McDonald's High School Basketball All-American Team nomination in his senior year. Wright was also an active participant in the local metropolitan community volunteering with local community service organizations in feed the homeless projects as well as an outreach program for disabled children. Upon graduation from Takoma Academy Wright attended La Sierra University in Riverside, California. As a student-athlete, Wright excelled on the basketball court serving as team captain for three years as well as in the classroom academically as a student. In his junior and senior seasons, the city of Riverside Sports Hall of Fame honored Wright for his athletic accomplishments while at La Sierra University. In 2004, Wright graduated from La Sierra University with a bachelor's degree in Business Administration. Currently, Wright is a member of the DeVos Sports Business Management Program graduating class of 2007 at the University of Central Florida. In his spare time away from school, Wright enjoys spending time with friends and family, playing basketball, and reading. Upon graduation from the DeVos Program Wright would like to work in business development or marketing for the National Basketball Association and one day serve as the NBA's commissioner.

The following materials were used as references to write to stories of *100 Heroes.*

CHAPTER 1

Rachel Robinson

Chass, Murray. "Standing by Her Man, Always With Elegance." *The New York Times*, April 16, 1997.

Robinson, Rachel. Jackie Robinson: An Intimate Portrait. New York: Harry N. Abrams, Inc., 1996.

Robinson, Rachel. "Rachel Robinson Bio." The Jackie Robinson Foundation. 2004.

Schwartz, Larry. "Jackie changed the face of sports. ESPN.com." [October 21, 2000; December 9, 2005] http://sports.espn.go.com/espn/classic/news/story?page=moment001024robinsondies

"The Robinsons." The History Channel. [2005; December 9, 2005] http://www.historychannel.com/exhibits/valentine/index.jsp?page=robinsons

Jackie Robinson

Robinson, Rachel. Jackie Robinson: An Intimate Portrait. New York: Harry N. Abrams, Inc., 1996.

Herman Boone and William Yoast

Becker, Christine. "Remember the Titans' Coaches to address Congress of Cities." *Nation's Cities Weekly*, December 4, 2000.

Carlton, Jeff. "Boone still spreading King's beliefs" *The North Carolina Piedmont Triad*, January 18, 2001.

Stepp, Diane R. "Roswell takes nostalgic trip with former coach." *The Atlanta Journal and Constitution*, June 7, 2001.

Williams, Kam. "Reminiscences of the real-life coaches of 'Remember the Titans.'" *New Pittsburgh Courier*, December 13, 2000.

Ryneldi Becenti

Attner, Paul and Deenise Becenti. "A culture of responsibilities - athletes as role models." *The Sporting News*, March 28, 1994.

Draper, Electa. "Trying to turn the game into more than a dead end" *The Denver Post*, May 17, 2005.

Phillip Castillo

Bartlett, Shanna. "Wings' new program aimed at young runners." *Indian Country Today*, May 11, 1994.

Monastyrski, Jamie. "Acoma, N.M., Indian man competes in 2000 Olympic marathon trials." *Knight Ridder Tribune*, March 15, 2000.

"Wings of America." Wings of America. [March 3, 2004; September 6, 2005] http://world.std.com/~mkjg/Wings.html

Pam White-Hanson

Bartlett, Shanna. "Wings' new program aimed at young runners." *Indian Country Today*, May 11, 1994.

"Wings of America." Wings of America. [March 3, 2004; September 6, 2005] http://world.std.com/~mkjg/Wings.html

Anita DeFrantz

Collier, Aldore. "Olympic power." *Ebony*, July 1, 1992.

Dilbeck, Steve. "'Why not?' Most insiders say it's not her time to be IOC President. Anita DeFrantz begs to differ" *The Daily News*, July 15, 2001.

Moore, Kenny. "An advocate for athletes; Anita DeFrantz is an unlikely member of the powerful IOC." *Sports Illustrated*, August 29, 1988.

Ernestine Bayer

Anonymous. "Beyond Esther Williams…" *Lilith Magazine*, July 1, 2002.

Miller, Bill. "The Bayer Collection." Friends of Rowing History. [December 2002; June 29, 2005] http://www.rowinghistory.net/bayer.htm.

Nutt, Amy. "Going nowhere fast." *Sports Illustrated*, January 27, 1997.

Donna Lopiano

Mann, Fred. "Lopiano is still playing hardball against gender inequity." *Knight Ridder Tribune*, November 9, 1994.

Wolff, Alexander. "Prima Donna: women's athletic director Donna Lopiano has taken the bull by the horns at Texas." *Sports Illustrated*, December 17, 1990.

"Texas Women's Hall of Fame." Texas Woman's University. [August 18, 2004; July 27, 2004] http://www.twu.edu/twhf/tw-lopiano.htm

Nancy Lieberman

"Athlete Profile Nancy Lieberman-Cline." Women's Warriors. [2004; November 28, 2005] http://www.womenwarriors.ca/en/athletes/profile.asp?id=115

"Hall of fame taps Nancy Lieberman-Cline ODU basketball greats." *The Virginian Pilot*, February 12, 1996.

"Nancy Lieberman." Basketball Hall of Fame. [2002; November 28, 2005 http://www.hoophall.com/halloffamers/nancy_lieberman.htm

"Nancy Lieberman Biography." NancyLieberman.com. [2005; November 28, 2005] http://www.nancylieberman.com/biography.asp

Annie Boucher

Scheer, Stephanie. "Grandma's on the varsity." *Sports Illustrated*, December 16, 1991.

"Alfred University Athletics – Hall of Fame." Alfred University. [August 8, 2005] http://www.alfred.edu/athletics/hall_of_fame/

Lee Elder

Cash, Rana. "Lee Elder: 25 years ago a ground-breaking moment at Augusta." *Knight Ridder Tribune*, April 5, 2000.

Harber, Paul. "Lee Elder, now a Senior star, recalls when times weren't so good." *Knight Ridder Tribune*, August 1, 1994.

Latimer, Clay. "No forest, only woods Tiger's success hasn't yet brought increase of black professionals." *The Rocky Mountain News*, April 1, 2001.

Mell, Randall. "Lee Elder says it's time for Augusta to change policy on women." *Knight Ridder Tribune*, September 17, 2002.

O'Neill, Dan. "Trailblazer with his triumph, Tiger smashes a special barrier for minorities." *St. Louis Post-Dispatch*, April 14, 1997.

CHAPTER 2

Willie Davis

Albom, Mitch. "The best role models aren't on tv." *Jewish World Review*, April 3, 2001.

Lin, Cindy. "Custodian Coach." ChannelOne.com [2005; October 15, 2005] http://www.channelone.com/news/2003/03/05/custodian/

James Ellis

Doku, Sam. "Michael Norment on course to becoming 1st African American to represent U.S. Olympic swimming?" *Washington Informer*, March 1, 2000.

Lelyveld, Nita. "2 swimmers hope to be first African-Americans on Olympic swim team." *Knight Ridder Tribune*, March 1, 1996.

Slear, Tom. "Water Colors." USA Swimming. [2005, November 20, 2005] http://www.usaswimming.org/USASWeb/ViewMiscArticle.aspx?TabId=515&Alias=Rainbow&Lang=en&mid=850&ItemID=928

Jack Aker

Retherford, Bill. "Where are they now: Jack Aker." BaseballSavvy.com. [2005; July 11, 2005] http://www.baseballsavvy.com/archive/j_aker.html

"Baseball Camps, Clinics and Private Instruction." Jack Aker Baseball. [2005; July 11, 2005] http://www.jackakerbaseball.com

Dorothy Gaters

Garcia, Marlen. "Dorthy Gaters' marshall plan as she records her 700th victory, the legendary and controversial girl's basketball coach reflects on her career, missed opportunities and her critics." *The Chicago Tribune*, January 14, 2001.

Bert Jenkins

Kirkpatrick, Curry. "Can't hold this tiger." *Sports Illustrated*, February 20, 1989.

Marian Washington

"Marian Washington." KUathletics.com. [2005; July 18, 2005] http://www.kusports.com/w_bball/roster/washington.html

"Marian Washington Biography." Hit! Run! Score! Inc. [2005; July 18, 2005] http://www.hitrunscore.com/marian-washington-biography.html

C. Vivian Stringer

"C. Vivian Stinger: The Stringer File." Rutgers Athletics. [2005; August 12, 2005] http://www.scarletknights.com/basketball-women/coaches/stringer.htm

Carolyn Peck

Montville, Leigh. "Miracle worker: Carolyn Peck won an NCAA title in her second year at Purdue. Her next tick: building a brand-new WNBA team in Orlando." *Sports Illustrated*, June 14, 1999.

Schad, Joe. "Florida officially names Carolyn Peck as coach." *The Orlando Sentinel*, April 4, 2002.

"Carolyn Peck." GatorZone.com [2005; November 15, 2005] http://www.gatorzone.com carolynpeck/

Mike Sheppard

Schutta, Gregory. "Hall's Sheppard hits milestone." *The Record*, March 26, 1997.

Sullivan, Tara. "Seton Hall's Good Sheppard." *The Record*, May 10, 1998.

"Sheppard named Seton Hall baseball coach." PhillyBurbs.com. [June 30, 2004; November 20, 2005] http://www.phillyburbs.com/pb-dyn/news/104-06302004-324906.html

Bob Shannon

Mayes, Warren. "East St. Louis football coach believes in leading by example." *St. Louis Post-Dispatch*, May 5, 1993.

Halperin, Jennifer. "Bob Shannon wants leaders on his East St. Louis team." Illinois Periodicals Online. [October 1993; August 12, 2005] http://www.lib.niu.edu/ipo/1993/ii931012.html

Ken Carter

"About the coach." CoachCarter.com. [2005, October 16, 2005] http://www.coachcarter.com/about.htm

"Paramount to make Ken Carter bio." Killer Movies. [June 13, 2002; October 16, 2005] www.killermovies.com/o/oldschoolthekencarterstory/articles/1851.html

Beverly Kearney

Lee, Rozel A. "Kearney's feet have carried her on long journey." *The Tampa Tribune*, December 30, 2002

"Head Coach Beverly Kearney." The Official Site of the University of Texas Athletics. [June 2005; December 6, 2005] http://www.texassports.com/index.php?s=&change_well_id=2&url_article_id=167

"UT track coach Kearney injured in crash" *AP Online*, [December 27, 2002; December 6, 2005] http://www.highbeam.com/library/doc3.asp?DOCID=1P1:70617591&num=1&ctrlInfo=Round18%3AProd%3ASR%3AResult&ao=&FreePremium=BOTH

Jennifer Rizzotti

Easterbrook, Jonathan. "More than a summer job: how does Jen do it?" *The Hartford Observer*, Fall 2001.

"Jennifer Rizzotti bio." University of Hartford Athletics. [September 12, 2005] http://www.hartfordhawks.com/index.cfm?md=fc_roster&tmp=detail&rstID=113&rsiID=1088

Willie Stewart

Feit, Maria. "Anacostia Football Coach Joins 'Coaches Against Gun Violence'." Alliance for Justice. [October 10, 2003; August 30, 2005] http://www.afj.org/news_and_press/press_release_collection/collection/press_anacostiacoach.html

Jackson, Koyan. "The godfather of football." [August 12, 2004; November 21, 2005] http://www.sportscombine.com/scripts/p_tm_news.asp?t=221693

Lapchick, Richard. "These two coaches are linked by heroism" *The Sporting News*, December 12, 1994.

Reed, William F. "Another chance." *Sports Illustrated*, November 2, 1992.

"Updates on NFL steroid hearings." ESPN.com [April 28, 2005; November 21, 2005] http://sports.espn.go.com/nfl/news/story?id=2047293

CHAPTER 3

Derrick Brooks

Attner, Paul. "Lighting up young lives (athletes and social work)." *The Sporting News*, July 31, 2000.

"Derrick Brooks Player Bio." Tampa Bay Buccaneers Website. 2005; 11/15/2005. http://www.buccaneers.com/team/playerdetail.aspx?player=Brooks,Derrick,55

Justin Allen

Witz, Billy. "ASU's Allen has 'won big battle'." *Los Angeles Daily News*, February 14, 2002.

"Justin Allen's battle against cancer helps another student." Official site of Arizona State Sun Devils. [March 25, 2002; September 29, 2005] http://thesundevils.collegesports.com/sports/m-baskbl/spec-rel/032502aaa.html

Felipe Lopez

Crothers, Tim. "Felipe Lopez." *Sports Illustrated*, December 20, 1993.

Gonzalez, Ozzie. "What ever happened to NYC basketball star Felipe Lopez." Latino Legends in Sports. [April 8, 2000; November 21, 2005] http://www.latinosportslegends.com/whathappenedto_Felipe_Lopez.htm

Hermoso, Rafael. "Decision near for blue-chipper – one country's hero is another country's most coveted prize." *The Record*, March 21, 1994.

Mallozzi, Vincent M. "The City Game, New York's Greatest High School Hoops Stars." The Village Voice News. [March 14, 2001; November 21, 2005] http://www.villagevoice.com/news/0010,mallozzi,13110,3.html

"Living up to hype is hard: Lopez hoping for a fresh start, long career in the NBA." CNN/Sports Illustrated. [June 22, 1998; November 21, 2005] http://sportsillustrated.cnn.com/basketball/nba/1998/draft/news/1998/06/22/felipe_lopez/

"Students: Dominican Basketball Phenom." The Hispanic Outlook in Higher Education. [November 1, 1994, November 21, 2005] http://www.highbeam.com/library/doc3.asp?DOCID=1P1:28354453&print=yes

Warrick Dunn

"Warrick Dunn Biography." Atlanta Falcons.com. [2005; September 2, 2005] www.atlantafalcons.com

"Warrick Dunn Biography; Foundation Programs." Warrick Dunn Foundation. [2005; September 2, 2005] http://www.warrickdunnfoundation.org/

Priest Holmes

"Priest Anthony Holmes #31 Biography." Priest Holmes. [2002; November 15, 2005] http://www.priestholmes.com/biography.htm

"Priest Holmes #31- Interview on community involvement." NFLPlayers.com. [2005; December 12, 2005] http://www.nflplayers.com/players/player.aspx?id=25151§ion=media

"Project provides dental safety to KCMSD students." Kansas City, Missouri School District. [November 17, 2005] http://www.kcmsd.net/home.asp?l=1&b=10&d=&id=122&catid=

"The Glenn S. 'Pop' Warner Inspiration to Youth Award." Pop Warner Little Scholars. [2005; November 17, 2005] http://www.popwarner.com/articles/Priestholmes.asp

Amber Burgess

Schley, Stuart. "Fast women." *Colorado Biz Magazine*, May 1, 2004.

CHAPTER 4

Derek DeWitt, Dave Frantz and Jake Porter

Habib, Hal. "A good sport for a change." *The Palm Beach Post*, December 24, 2002.

Lee, Robert. "Magical moment: the goodness of America." *The New American*, December 30, 2002

Posnanski, Joe. "A job well done, Ohio teen with learning disability big inspiration to small school." *Kansas City Star*, September 21, 2005. Retrieved from http://apse.dallasnews.com/contest/2002/writing/over250/over250.columns.first1.html

Walker, James. "Human Touch: Jake Porter's emotional story has gripped the Southern Ohio region." *The Herald-Dispatch*, November 10, 2002. Retrieved from http://www.bridges4kids.org/articles/1-03/Herald11-10-02.html

Dot Richardson

"Dr. Dot Richardson." Saint Leo University. [2005; October 3, 2005] http://www.saintleo.edu/SaintLeo/Templates/Inner.aspx?durki=6393&pid=6393

"Healing hands." Dot Richardson-NBC Olympic Profile. [October 3, 2005] http://members.aol.com/sharkey1/731dot.htm

"Welcome to the National Training Center!" National Training Center. [October 3, 2005] http://www.usat-ntc.com/

Kareem Abdul-Jabbar

Hammer, Joshua. "In a blunt autobiography Kareem Abdul-Jabbar gets open off-court for the first time." *People Magazine*, January 16, 1984.

"Kareem Abdul-Jabbar Biography." Basketball Hall of Fame. [2002; October 20, 2005] http://www.hoophall.com/halloffamers/Abdul-Jabbar.htm

"Kareem Abdul-Jabbar Biography." NBA History. [2005; October 20, 2005] http://www.nba.com/history/players/abduljabbar_bio.html

Nate Archibald

"Hall of Famer, Nate "Tiny" Archibald." Sacramento Kings. [2005; November 10, 2005] http://www.nba.com/kings/history/nate_archibald_hall.html

"Nate "Tiny" Archibald." Basketball Hall of Fame. [2001; November 10, 2005] http://www.hoophall.com/halloffamers/Archibald.htm

"Nathaniel Archibald Complete Bio." NBA History. [2005; November 10, 2005] http://www.nba.com/history/players/archibald_bio.html

Dave Bing

Koch, Barbara. "Dave Bing 1943-." Directory of Business Biographies. [2005; November 23, 2005] http://www.referenceforbusiness.com/biography/A-E/Bing-Dave-1943.html

Shaw, Susan. "From Basketball to Billions." *The Black Perspective*, Fall 2001.

"David Bing Complete Bio." NBA History. [2005; November 23, 2005] http://www.nba.com/history/players/bing_bio.html

Alan Page

Graydon, Royce. "New Stage for Page." *Star Tribune*, November 5, 2000.

Inskip, Leonard. "Page Foundation lights a promising path for students." *Star Tribune*. May 16, 2000.

Lavrich, Brian. "Football hall of famer Alan Page emphasizes education in Kent State U. speech." *University Wire*. February 23, 2001.
"Alan Page Biography." Pro Football Hall of Fame. [2005; October 26, 2005] http://www.profootballhof.com/hof/member.jsp?player_id=171
"The Honorable Alan Page." The National Press Club. [2005; October 26, 2005] http://www.npr.org/programs/npc/2001/011115.apage.html

Bill Bradley
"Office of the American Secretary, The Rhodes Trust." The Rhodes Scholarships. [2005; November 1, 2005] http://www.rhodesscholar.org/
"Bill Bradley." Basketball Hall of Fame [2000; November 1, 2005] http://www.hoophall.com/halloffamers/Bradley.htm#top
"Bill Bradley." Wikipedia, the free encyclopedia. [December 11, 2005; December 15, 2005] http://en.wikipedia.org/wiki/Bill_Bradley

Julius Erving
Deford, Frank. "Last rounds for the Doctor; as Julius Erving says goodbye, seven writers remember." *Sports Illustrated*, May 4, 1987.
"Defying gravity." Academy of Achievement. [February 5, 2005; November 12, 2005] http://www.achievement.org/autodoc/page/erv0int-1
"Julius Erving Biography." The Basketball Hall of Fame. [2001; November 12, 2005] http://www.hoophall.com/halloffamers/Erving.htm

Jackie Joyner-Kersee
Baum, Bob. "Ending Painful for Joyner-Kersee." *AP Online*, July 16, 2000. Retrieved from http://www.highbeam.com/library/doc3.asp?DOCID=1P1:29953554&num=1&ctrlInfo=Round18%3AProd%3ASR%3AResult&ao=&FreePremium=BOTH
Baum, Bob. "Olympics Lure Joyner-Kersee Back." *AP Online*, July 13, 2000. Retrieved from http://www.highbeam.com/library/doc3.asp?DOCID=1P1:30588980&num=1&ctrlInfo=Round18%3AProd%3ASR%3AResult&ao=&FreePremium=BOTH
Duckett Cain, Joy. "The Jackie nobody knows (Jackie Joyner-Kersee)." *Essence*, August 1, 1989.
Hollinshed, Denise. "Joyner-Kersee brings her message home at center's opening, She says people must believe in themselves street is renamed for her." *St. Louis Post-Dispatch*, March 2, 2000.
Joyner-Kersee, Jackie with Sonja Steptoe. A Kind of Grace. New York: Time Warner, 1997.
Letterlough, Michael. "Breathing Easy; Olympic gold-medalist Jackie Joyner-Kersee talks about her battle with asthma." *The Philadelphia Tribune*. April 3, 2005.
Resnick, Rick. "For Jackie Joyner-Kersee, excitement is building (Olympian returns to hometown of East St. Louis, Illinois and builds a recreational and educational center on 37 acres in the town.)." *Time*, December 15, 1997.

Rosenthal, Bert. "A champion's tears: Joyner-Kersee says farewell." *AP Online*, July 26, 1998. Retrieved from http://www.highbeam.com/library/doc3.asp?DOCID=1P1:19563835&num=1&ctrlInfo=Round18%3AProd%3ASR%3AResult&ao=&FreePremium=BOTH

Rosenthal, Bert. "Joyner-Kersee's magnificent career ending near her roots." *AP Online*, July 16, 1998. Retrieved from http://www.highbeam.com/library/doc3.asp?DOCID=1P1:19560813&num=1&ctrlInfo=Round18%3AProd%3ASR%3AResult&ao=&FreePremium=BOTH

Runyon, Aaron E. "Jackie Joyner-Kersee stresses importance of goals to Marshall U." *The Parthenon via University Wire*, September 20, 1999.

"Jackie Joyner-Kersee says 'tomboys' are in." *Jet Magazine*, October 19, 1998.

"Olympian Jackie Joyner-Kersee becomes NFL agent." *Jet Magazine*, February 9, 1998.

Lawrence Burton

Montville, Leigh. "A man to lean on (former athlete Lawrence Burton working at Boys Town)." *Sports Illustrated*, December 21, 1992.

"Ex-Purdue All-American enjoys life as Boys Town counselor." *NCAA News*, Volume 27 Number 46, December 26, 1990.

"Lawrence Burton Honored at Purdue University." Purdue University Official Athletics Site. [April 27, 1998; August 30, 2005] http://purduesports.collegesports.com/genrel/bit/pur-bits-1998427.html

Dean Smith

Perry, Jason. "Dean Smith Coaching Tree." CHN College Basketball. [June 29, 2004; November 20, 2005] http://www.collegehoopsnet.com/acc/unc/062904.htm

"A Tribute to Dean Smith." The Official Site of Tar Heel Athletics. [2005; November 15, 2005] http://tarheelblue.collegesports.com/sports/m-baskbl/mtt/unc-m-baskbl-dean-smith.html

"Dean Smith." Tony's Tar Heel Page. [2005; November 20, 2005] http://users.adelphia.net/~tonyhutch/smith.html

Joe Paterno

"Greatest Show in College Sports" Survey. *Sports Illustrated on Campus*, October 27, 2005. Retrieved from http://198.64.150.35/rd/results/rdq_football/www.gopsusports.com/Football/home.cfm/search4it_official_site_featuring_statistics_schedules_and_results.html

"Joe Paterno Biography." Penn State Athletics. [November 27, 2005; November 27, 2005] http://www.gopsusports.com/Football/people/paterno/paternobiobody.cfm

"Joe Paterno's legacy is himself." Penn State Nittany Lions Football. [2005; June 29, 2005] http://www.psu.edu/sports/football/Paterno/paternobio.html

Pat Summitt

Malone, Janice. "It was "all about women." *Tennessee TRIBUNE*, September 8, 2004.

"Pat Summitt Profile." CSTV Online, Inc. [April 19, 2005; September 6, 2005]

Tom Osborne

Brand, Madeleine. "Profile: Former University of Nebraska football coach Tom Osborne and his quest for a seat in Congress." *National Public Radio*, April 28, 2000.

Lapchick, Richard. "These two coaches are linked by heroism." *The Sporting News*, December 12, 1994.

Marantz, Steve. "The silent plainsman." *The Sporting News*, December 19, 1994.

"Congressman Tom Osborne Biography." Nebraska's Third Congressional District. [November 21, 2005] http://www.house.gov/osborne/biography.htm

"Hall of Fame Coach Tom Osborne." The University of Nebraska Athletics. [July 25, 2005; November 21, 2005] http://www.huskers.com/ViewArticle.dbml?DB_OEM_ID=100&ATCLID=3306&SPID=22&SPSID=2

Geno Auriemma

Adamec, Carl. "Auriemma lends a helping hand." *Journal Inquirer*, September 24, 2004.

"Meet Coach Geno Auriemma." Red Rock Computing, LLC. [2005, July 11, 2005] http://www.genoauriemmacamp.com/coach.html

"Head Coach Geno Auriemma." University of Connecticut. [2005; October 15, 2005] http://uconnhuskies.com/sports/wbasketball/coaching/bkwcoachbio.html

CHAPTER 5

Bob Love

"Bob Love." Leading Authorities. [2005; November 05, 2005] http://www.leadingauthorities.com/3525/Bob_Love.htm

"Bob Love." Sports Stars USA. [2000; November 05, 2005] http://www.sportsstarsusa.com/basketball/love_bob.html

"Bob Love: Ole' Butterbean…On top of the world-again." Sterling Speakers. [2003; November 05, 2005] http://www.sterlingspeakers.com/love.htm

"From NBA all-star to busboy and back." American Dreams. [2002; November 05, 2005] http://www.usdreams.com/Love.html

Dwight Collins

Clemons, Veronica. "Deaf student beats odds and plays college football." *Jet Magazine*, September 8, 1997.

King, Kelley. "Setting the tone: deaf fullback Dwight Collins leads Central Florida backs to daylight." *Sports Illustrated*, October 16, 2000.

Samantha Eyman

Edwards, Mark. "1 hand, 0 gripes." *Decatur Daily*, May 5, 2000.

Henricks, Josh. "Overcoming all obstacles." Saint Xavier University. [December 9, 2005] http://www.sxu.edu/SharedMedia/CAM-UR/magazine/2003/summer/sports%20summer%2003.pdf#search='Samantha%20Eyman'

"Samantha Eyman Bio." Saint Xavier University. 2004.

Eddie Lee Ivery

Asher, Gene. "True Gridiron Grit." *Georgia Trend Magazine*, January 2003.

"Eddie Lee Ivery joins Tech athletics staff as strength coach." The Official Online Service of Georgia Tech Athletics. [2005; June 29, 2005] http://ramblinwreck.collegesports.com/genrel/071100aaa.html

Loretta Claiborne

Fleischman, Bill. "Mentally retarded athlete wins Arthur Ashe award at ESPY awards." *Knight Ridder Tribune*, February 13, 1996.

Russell, Heidi. "Claiborne rises to the top Special Olympics has offered special challenge." *Rocky Mountain News*, March 31, 1996.

"Global Athletes Congress-Loretta Claiborne." Special Olympics. [December 7, 2005] http://www.specialolympics.org/Special+Olympics+Public+Website/English/Initiatives/Athlete_Leadership/Global+Athlete+Congress/Delegates/Claiborne_Loretta.htm

"Loretta's Story." Loretta Claiborne. [December 7, 2005] http://www.lorettaclaiborne.com/bio.htm

"The Loretta Claiborne Story." *Columbus Times*, January 5, 2000.

"The Loretta Claiborne Story: A courageous spirit, a generous heart" *New Pittsburgh Courier*, January 12, 2000.

Sam Paneno

Lafontaine, Pat. Companions in Courage: Triumphant Tales of Heroic Athletes. New York: Warner Brothers Inc., 2001.

"Quotes on Attitude." Random Terrain. [December 15, 2005] http://www.randomterrain.com/quotes/attitude.html

"Sam Paneno Profile." The Official Site of UC Davis Athletics. [2005; December 15, 2005] http://ucdavisaggies.collegesports.com/sports/m-footbl/mtt/paneno_sam00.html

Kathryn Waldo

Roberts, Robin. "Extreme Athlete." ABC Good Morning America, ABCNews.com, March 9, 1999.

Russo, Karen. "Where's Waldo? She's playing hockey." *The NewStandard*, November 14, 1998.

Shane Wood

Inzunza, Victor. "On Opening Day 1991… A boy, a president." *Forth Worth Star-Telegram*, April 8, 1991.

CHAPTER 6

Dirceu Hurtado

Fox, Ron. "DBT star picks FDU." *The Record*, July 12, 1998.

Schutta, Gregory. "Heads up!" *The Record*, September 21, 2000.

Sullivan, Tara. "Friends organize tournament to benefit ailing soccer player" *The Record*, July 3, 1999.

"Dirceu Hurtado Profile." Fairleigh Dickinson University Athletics. [2002; October 25, 2005] http://fduknights.collegesports.com/sports/m-soccer/mtt/hurtado_dirceu00.html

Destiny Woodbury

Szostak, Mike. "URI's Destiny Woodbury overcomes mother's drug-use death." *The Providence Journal*, December 24, 2004.

"URI student's painful choice put her on track to success." The University of Rhode Island. [November 23, 2004; January 31, 2005] http://www.uri.edu/news/releases/index.php?id=2883

Stacy Sines

Free, Bill. "With resilience, Sines regains golden touch." *The Sun*, December 20, 2002.

"All-American swimmer returns to form after open-heart surgery." *The Sho'men Club Newsletter*, February 2003.

"Multidisciplinary team at Christiana Care puts an All-American back in the swim." *Physician Focus*, November 2002.

"Sines Shows Heart of a Champion" *Washington College Magazine*, Spring 2003.

Jennifer McClain

"Women's Volleyball, Quinnipiac Volleyball All-Time Records." Quinnipiac University – Official Athletic Site. [2002; December 9, 2005] http://quinnipiacbobcats.collegesports.com/sports/w-volley/spec-rel/qu-all-time-records.html

Rashad Williams

Bartels, Lynn. "A race to help another San Francisco teen's efforts raise $18,000 for Columbine victim." *The Rocky Mountain News*, June 19, 1999.

Batson, Amber. "Shooting victim gets special gift from special friend." *The Rocky Mountain News*, June 23, 1999.

Dahler, Don. "California teen raises money for shooting victim." ABC Good Morning America, abcNews.com, June 22, 1999. Retrieved from http://www.highbeam.com/library/doc3.asp?DOCID=1P1:29281556&num=1&ctrlInfo=Round18%3AProd%3ASR%3AResult&ao=&FreePremium=BOTH

"California student runs to aid Columbine shooting victim." CNN.com. [June 22, 1999; October 7, 2005] http://www.cnn.com/US/9906/22/columbine.gift/

Lawrence Wright

Bianchi, Mike. "Lean on Lawrence." *The Sporting News*, December 2, 1996.

Urriste, Sarah. "Wright's passion." *The Gainesville Sun*, July 22, 2005.

Lonise Bias

Brennan, Christine and Donald Huff. "Bias II: There'll be no more 'wait for Jay'." *Washington Post*, December 5, 1990.

Nakamura, David and Mark Asher. "10 years later Bias's death still resonates." *Washington Post*, June 19, 1996.

"Dr. Lonise Bias." AEI Speakers Bureau. [2004; November 15, 2005] http://www.aeispeakers.com/speakerbio.php?SpeakerID=96

"Drug Use." U.S. Department of Justice · Office of Justice Programs Bureau of Justice Statistics- Drugs and Crime Facts. [October 6, 2005; November 15, 2005] http://www.ojp.usdoj.gov/bjs/dcf/du.htm

Alfreda Harris

May, Mike. "First annual SGMA heroes state winners announced." Sporting Goods Manufacturers Association's (SGMA) [1995; December 5, 2005] http://www.sgma.com/press/1994/press990463577-29903.html

"Alfreda J. Harris." FOCUS On Children, Boston Public Schools [December 5, 2005] http://boston.k12.ma.us/schcom/profile_harris.asp

Maggie Maloy

"Rape Statistics – General, Youth, College, Situations." Women's Issues, About, Inc., part of the *New York Times* Company. [2005; November 3, 2005] http://womensissues.about.com/od/rapecrisis/a/rapestats.htm

Jodi Norton

Callahan, Amy. "Jodi Norton: adversity doesn't keep diver from soaring." Columbia University. [October 10, 1997; December 4, 2005] http://www.columbia.edu/cu/record/archives/vol23/vol23_iss6/16.html

Thorn Allan, Jenny. "A champion in so many ways." Community Health Charities. [2005; October 3, 2005] http://www.healthcharities-nca.org/pubs-stories3342/pubs-stories_show.htm?doc_id=169945

Bob Hurley, Sr.

Barker, Barbara. "Jersey city's coach." *The Record*, March 3, 1995.

Crothers, Tim. "The Friars are kings of the road." *Sports Illustrated*, December 18, 1989.

D'Alessandro, Dave. "King's Hurley answers to two coaches." *The Record*, November 10, 1995.

May, Mike. “SGMA Hero in New Jersey.” Sporting Goods Manufacturer’s Association International. [October 15, 1996; November 15, 2005] http://www.sgma.com/press/1996/press990530174-17256.html

Rosen, Dan. “Hurley’s quest: save St. Anthony.” *The Record*, October 9, 2002.

Sullivan, Tara. “Hurley enters New Jersey Hall with sons at his side.” *The Record*, May 10, 2000.

Wojinarowski, Adrian. “What about Bob?” *The Record*, March 27, 2001.

Wetzel, Dan. “All Aboard.” Yahoo! Sports. [March 7, 2005; November 15,2005] www.sports.yahoo.com/ncaab/expertsarchive?author=Dan+Wetzel

Wojinarowski, Adrian. “Saving Souls One life at a Time.” *The Record*, February 14, 2005.

Wojinarowski, Adrian. “Hurley teaches the game of life” *The Record*, February 13, 2005.

“Hurley Sr. to be honored.” *The Record*, February 16, 1992.

Tanya Hughes-Jones

Metcalfe, Jeff. “High goals: Olympian’s pursuits not limited to business on track.” *The Knight Ridder*, November 9, 1994.

CHAPTER 7

Dionte Hall

Samuels, Adrienne P. and Shannon Tan. “Noose, $10 bet lead to slurs, hate crime charges.” *St. Petersburg Times*, January 16, 2004.

Tan, Shannon. “Facing noose and slur, teen kept cool.” *St. Petersburg Times*, January 12, 2004.

Tan, Shannon. “Teen who faced noose, slur commended for courage.” *St. Petersburg Times*, February 18, 2004.

Michael Watson

Lapchick, Richard. Smashing Barriers: Race and Sport in the New Millennium. Maryland: Madison, 2001. pp. 284-287.

Darryl Williams

Feldscher, Karen. “Steady On.” *Northeastern University Magazine*, January 2005.

Fitzgerald, Joe. “Courageous man shows meaning of the overrated word ‘hero’.” *Boston Herald*, April 28, 2003.

David Lazerson and Richard Green

Horn, Miriam. “Side by side, apart: the difficult search for racial peace in Brooklyn (lacks and Jews in Brooklyn, N.Y.).” *U.S. News*, November 4, 1991.

Lipman, Steve. “Present at the creation; for Jewish Week reporter with insider’s view of black-Jewish dialogue, film is basically loyal to history.” *The Jewish Week*, February 13, 2004.

Mark, Jonathan. "Apocalypse then, healing now: things are calm on the surface of Crown Heights 10 years after the riot. Is anything lurking beneath?" *The Jewish Week*, August 10, 2001.

"Dr. Laz & the 'CURE'." Project CURE. [November 14, 2005] http://www.drlaz.com/html/project_cure.html

"Quietly, Blacks and Jews are rebuilding bridges friendship blossom in NY neighborhood." *St. Louis Post-Dispatch*, November 24, 1994.

CHAPTER 8

Joe Crowley

Pike, Deidre. "You go, Joe." Reno News and Review. [January 4, 2001, November 10, 2002] http://www.newsreview.com/issues/reno/2001-01-04/news.asp

"Nevada to honor Joe Crowley with Lawlor Award." Marketing and Communications. Nevada News. [July 6, 2005; November 10, 2002] http://www.unr.edu/nevadanews/detail.aspx?id=1175&terms=lawlor

"University seeks to name new student union after Joe Crowley." Stewart, Brandon. Nevada News. [November 4, 2005; November 10, 2002] http://www.unr.edu/nevadanews/detail.aspx?id=1334

Clarence Underwood

Henning, Lynn. "Underwood goes quietly, leaves legacy." *The Detroit News*, July 31, 2002.

Roosevelt, Theodore. "The Man in the Arena." Chapultepec, Inc. [June 2, 2004, November 11, 2005] http://www.theodore-roosevelt.com/trsorbonnespeech.html

"Underwood Named MSU Athletic Director." University Relations, Michigan State University. [December 10, 1999; November 11, 2005] http://newsroom.msu.edu/site/indexer/577/content.htm

"Retired MSU Athletic Director: Dr. Clarence Underwood." Ralph Young Fund, Michigan state University. [2005; November 11, 2005] http://www.ryf.msu.edu/spartan_profiles/underwood.html

"Undergoing changes at the top; Underwood ends long career at the 'U'." *The State News*. [August 24, 2002; November 11, 2005] http://www.statenews.com/article.phtml?pk=11539

"Q&A with Clarence Underwood." Athletic Management. [July 2002; November 11,2005] http://www.momentummedia.com/articles/am/am1404/qaunderwood.htm

Charles C.M. Newton

Neely, Tony. "Recognizable Class." *Kentucky Alumnus*, Summer 2000, Volume 71, Number 2.

"C.M. Newton - Presentation Announcement." Women's Christian Temperance Union. [December 18, 1999; October 31, 2005] http://www.wctu.org/cm.html

Sister Rose Ann Fleming

Kay, Joe. "Nun, not coach, has most clout at Xavier." *Associated Press Online*, February 28, 2005.

Sun, Victoria. "Studies are 1st at XU." *The Cincinnati Post*, October, 25, 2002.

Tate, Skip. "Standing tall." *Xavier Magazine*, Spring, 2005.

"Xavier Hall to induct three." *The Cincinnati Post*, September 8, 2000.

Judy Sweet

Hawes, Kay. "Sweet role, NCAA Senior Women's Administrator builds new position." *The NCAA News,* January 7, 2002.

Montieth, Mark. "Clearing the path." *The Indianapolis Star*, October 30, 2005.

Renfroe, Wallace, I. "Judy Sweet, long-time athletics leader and administrator, joins NCAA staff as vice-president for championships." *The NCAA News*, November 1, 2000.

"1992- Judith Sweet, San Diego." Women's Sports Advocates of Wisconsin, Inc. [2005, November 24, 2005] http://www.wsaw.org/lifetimeachievement/halloffame/index.asp#1992%20-%20Judith%20Sweet,%20San%20Diego

Dick Schultz

Brown, Gary T. "50 years = A staff-century of service." *The NCAA News*, June 10, 2002.

Hawes, Kay. "Voice for Change." *The NCAA News*, December 6, 1999.

Montre, Lorraine Kee. "NCAA's Due Process Failed Schultz." *The St. Louis Post-Dispatch*, May 15, 1993.

Spence, Mike. "Schultz looks for progress as he takes over Olympic Committee." *Colorado Springs Gazette Telegraph* via *Knight Ridder/Tribune News Service*, September 5, 1995.

"Richard D. Schultz Biography." Current Biography Excerpts: Sports Business. [1996; December 7, 2005] http://www.hwwilson.com/currentbio/sprtbus.html#schultz

"Senior U.S. Olympic Committee member resigns over Salt Lake scandal." CNN.com [January 15, 1999; December 7, 2005] http://www.cnn.com/US/9901/15/olympics.01/

"Salt Lake Olympics rocked by resignations, evidence of payments." CNN.com. [January 8, 1999; December 7, 2005] http://www.cnn.com/US/9901/08/olympic.bribes.03/

"Sports News You Can Use: Issue 20—Association and Organization Management." Sports News-OnlineSports.com. [1997; December 07, 2005] http://www.onlinesports.com/sportstrust/sports20.html

"USOC implicated in Salt Lake report." CNNSI.com. [February 10, 1999] http://sportsillustrated.cnn.com/olympics/news/1999/02/10/saltlake_usoc/

Creed Black

Carroll, John S. "Boycotts, bomb threats, and courage." American Society of Newspaper Editors. [June 12, 2002; November 10, 2002] http://www.asne.org/index.cfm?id=3604

Shultz, Scott. "New NCAA regulations called for by commission." *The Daily Bruin via University Wire*, July 3, 2001.

"Creed C. Black." Alumni Affairs, Northwestern University. [November 10, 2002] http://www.medill.northwestern.edu/alumni/honors/profiles/black.html

"John S. and James L. Knight Foundation Board of Trustees: Creed C. Black, Trustee." John S. and John L. Knight Foundation. [November 28, 2005, November 10, 2005] http://www.knightfdn.org/default.asp?story=about/trustees/creed_black.html

"Knight Foundation forms blue ribbon sports panel." John S. and John L. Knight Foundation. [July 29, 2005; November 10, 2002] http://www.knightfdn.org/default.asp?story=athletics/releases/1989_09_27_kcia.html

"NCAA and NAIA, Knight Commission Report." National Association of Collegiate Directors of Athletics. [2005; November 10, 2002] http://nacda.collegesports.com/convention/proceedings/1990/90knight.html

CHAPTER 9

Paul Tagliabue and Gene Upshaw

"Gene Upshaw Biography." Manheim Touchdown Club. [2005; November 28, 2005] http://www.manheimtouchdownclub.com/upshaw_bio.html

"Gene Upshaw Biography." Pro Football Hall of Fame. [2005; November 28, 2005] http://www.profootballhof.com/hof/member.jsp?player_id=220

"Gene Upshaw." Raiders Hall of Fame. [2005; November 28, 2005] http://www.raiders.com/history/hof_upshaw.jsp

"Paul Tagliabue 1989-Present." Tank Productions XXII. [August 26, 2002; November 25, 2005] http://www.sportsecyclopedia.com/nfl/comish/tagliabue.html

"Paul Tagliabue Biography." Current Biography Excerpts: Sports Business. [1996; November 25, 2005] http://www.hwwilson.com/currentbio/sprtbus.html#stern

Pedulla, Tom. "Tagliabue says NFL far from labor agreement." *USA Today*, February 6, 2005.

"Tagliabue's skills help NFL flourish." NFL.com [April 15, 2004; December 15, 2005] http://www.nfl.com/news/story/7259979

Richard, Dave. "Catching Up With…Paul Tagliabue." NFL.com. [April 22, 2005; December 15, 2005] http://www.nfl.com/news/story/8406928

David Stern

"David Stern 1984-Present." MMIV Tank Productions. [February 21, 2004; November 25, 2005] http://www.sportsecyclopedia.com/nba/comish/stern.html

"Hall of Distinguished Alumni – 1999." Rutgers College. [2005; November 25, 2005] http://www.alumni.rutgers.edu/hda/hda.php?show=86

"Basketball Without Borders Expands to Four Continents." NBA.com. [2005; November 25, 2005] http://www.nba.com/bwb/fourcontinents2005.html

Billy Payne

Cazeneuve, Brian. "Catching up with Billy Payne, Olympic Chief: January 8, 1996." *Sports Illustrated*, July 4, 2005.

Meyer, John. "Man with the plan after nine years, finish line in sight for Billy Payne's grand vision of Atlanta Olympics." *Rocky Mountain News*, May 5, 1996.

Smith, Vern E. "No Payne, no games." *Newsweek*, July 17, 1995.

Clinton Albury and H. Ross Perot

Lapchick, Richard E. and John B. Slaughter. The Rules of the Game; Ethics in College Sport. New York: McMillan Publishing Company, 1989. pp. 24-25.

The Reform Party-Ross Perot: Life and Career. All Politics. 1996; 11/30/2005 http://www.cnn.com/ALLPOLITICS/1996/conventions/long.beach/perot/life.career.shtml

"Press Conference by White, August 8, 1985." Texas State Library & Archives Commission. [August 8, 1985; November 30, 2005] http://www.tsl.state.tx.us/governors/modern/white-nopass-1.html

Richard DeVos

Williams, Pat. How to be Like Rich DeVos. Deerfield Beach, Florida: Health Communications, Inc., 2004.

Levin, Doron. "Fate, patience bring DeVos a new heart." *Detroit Free Press*, October 8, 1997.

Powell, Shaun. "Two owners who are the envy of the NBA (Leslie Alexander; Rich DeVos)." *The Sporting News*, June 19, 1995.

Whitley, David. "DeVos' nice guy routine puts Magic in city's court." *The Orlando Sentinel* via *Knight Ridder Tribune*, March 5, 2002.

Poytak, Tim. "DeVos may sell part of Magic; family intends to retain control and keep NBA team in Orlando." *The Orlando Sentinel* via *Knight Ridder Tribune*, January 10, 2002.

Grant, Linda. "How Amway's two founders cleaned up: strong overseas sales helped Richard DeVos and Jay Van Andel add billions to their fortunes." *U.S. News & World Report*, October 31, 1994.

"About the DeVos Foundation." DeVos Sport Business Management Program. [2005, November 30, 2005] http://www.bus.ucf.edu/sport/cgi-bin/site/sitew.cgi?page=/devos.htx

Perry, Patrick and Cory SerVaas. "The Inner Strength of Rich DeVos – author and heart transplant patient" *Saturday Evening Post*, January, 2001.

"Who We Are." Amway Corporation. [2005, November 30, 2005] http://www.amway.com/en/default.aspx

Lewis Katz and Raymond Chambers

"Lewis Katz Biography." Delaware Valley Rhythm and Blues Society, Inc. [December 11, 2005; December 11, 2005] http://www.dvrbs.com/CamdenPeople-LewisKatz.htm

Brennan, John. "Nets owners aimed high, fell short." *The Record*, May 28, 2004.

Brennan, John. "Nets Owners Unveil Grand Plans." *The Record*, December 1, 1998.

Canavan, Tom. "Nets' largest shareholder is trust aimed at helping communities." *AP Sports Online*, December 1, 1998. Retrieved from http://www.highbeam.com/library/doc3.asp?DOCID=1P1:19422266&num=1&ctrlInfo=Round18%3AProd%3ASR%3AResult&ao=&FreePremium=BOTH

Kirkpatrick, David. "Hoops spring eternal." *New York Magazine*, February 15, 1999.

Mike Ilitch

"Induction Showcase Mike Ilitch – Builder Category." Hockey Hall of Fame. [2005; October 26, 2005] http://www.legendsofhockey.net/html/ind03ilitch.htm

"News and Press Releases - Affiliated Companies." Detroit Red Wings. [2005; October 26, 2005] http://www.detroitredwings.com/wings/article.jsp?id=877

Thomas Sanders

Bock, Hal. "Satch and Bantom: Caring for the NBA's corps for kids." *AP Worldstream*, November 11, 2001.

Fitzgerald, Joe. "Ex-Celtic still feels pain of past prejudice." *The Boston Herald*, February 9, 2000.

Fitzgerald, Joe. "For some, celebs have bull's-eyes on their backs." *The Boston Herald*, September 25, 2002.

Landry, Peter A. "New basketball coach comes to Harvard." *The Harvard Crimson*, June 14, 1973.

"Where are they now? – Tom 'Satch' Sanders." The Boston Celtics. [January 2004; November 10, 2005] http://www.nba.com/celtics/history/WhereAreThey_Satch.html

CHAPTER 10

Gilbert Tuhbonye

O'Connor, Ian. "Burundi's Tuhabonye works on his running a long way from war-torn home." *Knight Ridder Tribune*, July 25, 1996.

Reid, Ron. "Runner from Burundi recalls perilous days in homeland." *Knight Ridder Tribune*, April 20, 1999.

Macharia Yuot

Josephs, Ira. "A refugee finds a home at Widener." *The Philadelphia Inquirer*, November 15, 2003.

McKindra, Leilana. “Early trials indicate Widener runner can go the distance” *The NCAA News*, April 26, 2004.

CHAPTER 11

Jerry Richardson

Crepeau, Richard C. “A Moral Coach.” Sport and Society Broadcast. [September 6, 1996; June 29, 2005] http://personal.ecu.edu/estesst/2323/readings/richardson.html

Perry Reese, Jr.

“Amish town embraces coach with brain tumor.” Slam! Sports. [2005; October 15, 2005] http://slam.canoe.ca/BasketballArchive/jul29_ami.html

Ferguson, Dana. “Born again…and again…and again.” The Fourth Presbyterian Church of Chicago. [April 29, 2001; October 15, 2005] http://www.fourthchurch.org/www.fourthchurch.org/www.fourthchurch.org/04.29.01print.html

Derrick Thomas

Le Batard, Dan. “A bright light goes dark too soon.” MacBrud Corporation of Miami Florida. [November 23, 2005] http://seatbeltsafety.com/derrickedwards.htm

Luder, Bob. “Friends, teammates pay tribute to Derrick Thomas.” *The Kansas City Star*, February 15, 2000.

Posnanski, Joe. “Derrick Thomas sure had a lot of friends.” *The Kansas City Star*, February 15, 2000.

Teicher, Adam. “KC’s tribute in memory of Thomas.” *The Kansas City Star*, February 15, 2000.

Tucker, Doug. “KC fans say farewell to Derrick Thomas at Arrowhead.” *The Kansas City Star*, February 14, 2000.

Whitlock, Jason. “Keeping Thomas’ memory alive by doing something for others.” *The Kansas City Star*, February 15, 2000.

Whitlock, Jason. “Thomas deserves to be remembered and celebrated by all of us.” *The Kansas City Star*, February 14, 2000.

“Chiefs’ Hall of Fame: Derrick Thomas – 2001.” Kansas City Chiefs. [2005; November 23, 2005] http://www.kcchiefs.com/hall_of_fame/derrick_thomas/

“Chiefs’ Thomas Dead at 33: apparent heart attack claims 9-time Pro Bowl star.” CNN/Sports Illustrated. [2003; November 23, 2005] http://sportsillustrated.cnn.com/football/nfl/news/2000/02/08/thomas_death_ap/

“Derrick Thomas.” Infoplease, 2000-2005 Pearson Education, Inc. [2000; November 23, 2005] www.infoplease.com/ipa/A0801298.html

“Derrick Thomas Academy.” Kansas City Chiefs. [2005; November 23, 2005] http://www.kcchiefs.com/community/derrick_thomas_academy/

“Derrick Thomas, a true hero.” James Alder. Football, About, Inc., part of the *New York Times* Company. [2005, 11/23/2005] http://football.about.com/od/legends/a/aa020800.htm

"Thomas' children will cling to memories." *The Kansas City Star*, February 15, 2000.

Reggie White

Huston, Margo. "To the Rescue: White flooded with offers to rebuild." *Journal Sentinel*, January 13, 1996.

Lapchick, Richard. Smashing Barriers: Race and Sport in the New Millennium. Maryland: Madison, 2001. pp.282-283.

"Minister of Defense." Reggie White's Unofficial Homepage. [2004; July 11, 2005] http://olympia.fortunecity.com/white/225/1regprofile.htm

"Reggie White (1961-2004)." RingSurf.com. [2004; November 25, 2005] http://www.ringsurf.com/info/People/Celebrities_in_the_ News/Reggie_White/

"White Dies Sunday Morning." ESPN.com. [January 6, 2005; July 11, 2005] http://espn.go.com/classic/obit/s/2004/1226/1953400.html

Ewing Marion Kauffman

"About Ewing Kauffman; About the Foundation; A History of the Ewing Marion Kauffman Foundation." The Ewing Marion Kauffman Foundation. [October 26, 2005; November 28, 2005] http://www.kauffman.org/

"Ewing Marion Kauffman: Entrepreneur, Leader, Philanthropist." Centerpoint for Leaders. [2004; June 29, 2005] http://www.centerpointforleaders.org/leadership/kauffman.html

Dave Sanders

Kelly, Guy. "Teacher died for students; Dave Sanders alerter lunchroom and then warned others before being fatally wounded." *The Rocky Mountain News*, April 22, 1999.

Kilzer, Lou, Gary Massaro. "New view of Sanders' heroics instructor who helped evacuate cafeteria was shot on way to library." *The Rocky Mountain News*, May 16, 2000.

Massaro, Gary. "Profile in courage ESPN pays tribute to heroism of slain Columbine Coach Dave Sanders." *The Rocky Mountain News*, February 15, 2000.

Ralph Wiley

Lapchick, Richard, et al. "Remembering Ralph Wiley." Page 2, ESPN.com. [June 2004; November 22, 2005] http://proxy.espn.go.com/espn/page2/story?page=memory/wiley

"Wiley, 52, was provocative, respected writer." ESPN.com [June 16, 2004; November 22, 2005] http://sports.espn.go.com/espn/news/story?id=1821759